D1393772

By Naomi M. Stokes from Tom Doherty Associates

The Tree People
The Listening Ones

The
Listening Ones

Naomi M. Stokes

TOR®

A TOM DOHERTY ASSOCIATES BOOK
NEW YORK

This is a work of fiction. All of the characters and events portrayed in this novel are either fictitious or are used fictitiously.

THE LISTENING ONES

A Tor Book
Published by Tom Doherty Associates, Inc.
175 Fifth Avenue
New York, NY 10010

Tor Books on the World Wide Web:
http://www.tor.com

Tor® is a registered trademark of Tom Doherty Associates, Inc.

ISBN: 0-812-54295-9
Library of Congress Card Catalog Number: 97-2146

First edition: July 1997
First mass market edition: February 1999

Printed in the United States of America

0 9 8 7 6 5 4 3 2 1

To Joe
and in Memory
of Our Friend
Paul Petit
of the
Quinault Nation

WE NEED ANOTHER AND A WISER AND PERHAPS A MORE MYSTICAL CONCEPT OF ANIMALS.

Remote from universal nature, and living by complicated artifice, man in civilization surveys the creature through the glass of his knowledge and sees thereby a feather magnified and the whole image in distortion.

We patronize them for their incompleteness, for their tragic fate of having taken form so far below ourselves. And therein we err, and greatly err. For the animal shall not be measured by man. In a world older and more complete than ours they move finished and complete, gifted with extensions of the senses we have lost or never attained, living by voices we shall never hear.

THEY ARE NOT BRETHREN, THEY ARE NOT UNDERLINGS; THEY ARE OTHER NATIONS, CAUGHT WITH OURSELVES IN THE NET OF LIFE AND TIME, FELLOW PRISONERS OF THE SPLENDOUR AND TRAVAIL OF THE EARTH.

—from *The Outermost House*
by Henry Beston

And God said, Let the earth bring forth the living creature after his kind, cattle, and creeping thing, and beast of the earth after his kind: and it was so. And God made the beast of the earth after his kind, and cattle after their kind, and everything that creepeth upon the earth after his kind: and God saw that it was good.

—THE FIRST BOOK OF MOSES CALLED GENESIS

In the beginning of all things, wisdom and knowledge were with the animals; for Tirawa, the One Above, did not speak directly to man. He sent certain animals to tell men that he showed himself through the beasts, and that from them, and from the stars and the sun and the moon, man should learn. Tirawa spoke to man through his works.

—CHIEF LETAKOTS-LESA OF THE PAWNEE TRIBE

If all the beasts were gone, men would die from a great loneliness of spirit, for what happens to the beasts also happens to man. All things are connected. Whatever befalls the earth befalls the sons of the earth.

—CHIEF SEALTTH

(Corrupted to Seattle; Chief of the Duwamish tribe, in the State of Washington, when confronted with the foreseeable and inevitable demise of his people.)

Author's Note

There are four major ceremonials portrayed in this book. The ones described in chapter one and chapter six are still going on today in several South American countries.

Part One

Chapter 1

1   Antonio Salinas was eight years old and very frightened. Everything was so different in this faraway place of trees and rain.

His home was in a small village on a vast plateau high in the Andes where all the strangeness had started on his eighth birthday.

He had always known that his grandfather of whom he was in proper awe, and his beloved uncle whom he adored without reservation, were businessmen down in the city of Santiago.

And as far back as he could remember, both men always returned to the village for his birthday parties.

On the day he turned eight, however, his parents explained gently that neither his grandfather nor his uncle would be present at his birthday party this year. Both men had left the country, his mother said, to travel far north to the United States.

When the boy began to cry, not about his grandfather especially, but about his uncle whom he longed to see, his mother dried his tears and promised that neither man would be gone forever. Soon they would return, she said, with a wonderful, although late, birthday gift for him.

One month later, both the boy's parents died suddenly from a strange fever that afflicted no one else in the village.

After the funeral, which in accordance with custom was a sky burial with the bodies first dismembered, then left in a special high place for the condors, Father Lavate, who taught English to the village children, told the boy that he had sent word to his grandfather and uncle of his loss.

"Do not grieve, my child. It is the will of God," the priest murmured. "Obviously, He needed them in heaven."

Will of God? the boy thought rebelliously. Who was God to take one lonely boy's parents when He had the people of the whole world to choose from?

"But I need them here!" he wailed, clenching his small fists while tears streamed down his face.

Two weeks later the priest came back to see the boy, who was staying with a kindly neighbor.

Father Lavate had just received instructions, he said, as to the child's future. Since there were no other relatives, the little boy was to go to his grandfather and uncle.

Hearing the words, Antonio's heart soared like those condors he watched riding the thermals, carrying his parents' hearts within them.

He was going to be with his uncle! His very own uncle who was so handsome, so kind, with eyes that always looked on the little boy with love.

Early the next morning, the priest took him to the chapel

where he hung a small broken medal suspended on a bright woven wool ribbon around the child's neck, warning him never to take it off.

"Antonio," the priest said solemnly, "this is from your family. From your ancestors. No matter where you go in the world, this will help you remember who you are. That the other half of you will always be here, high in the Andes."

Then priest and small boy went down the mountains in a rattling flatbed truck, a journey that lasted all day over winding, rutted roads and included several stops for the changing of flat tires.

When they arrived at the air terminal in the city, the priest purchased the little boy's ticket and placed him in the care of a smiling stewardess.

"Remember, Antonio," the priest said in parting. "The other part of your medal will always be in the village, waiting for you."

During the long air trip, involving several disembarkings and embarkings, he tried not to think of his parents because that kind of thinking was too painful.

Instead, he thought about seeing his uncle again and, even better, living with him. Then his mind went to the birthday present he would receive, the gift that was surely even now awaiting him.

He made up his mind not to sleep on the plane, not to miss one instant of this journey, but grief, excitement, and weariness combined to defeat the boy and he spent long hours in exhausted slumber.

The final landing was made during a rain and wind storm. He asked the stewardess if they were in the United States. She said yes, they were near one city called SEE-atl and another city called tak-OMA.

She accompanied him off the plane and, still holding his small damp hand, delivered him to his grandfather who was waiting in the terminal.

The little boy looked all around.

Where was his uncle?

His grandfather thanked the stewardess with grave courtesy; she leaned down and kissed Antonio good-bye, and then left, the old man's eyes following her every step.

As the little boy shook his grandfather's hand, he noticed that people were turning to stare at something.

When he peeked around his grandfather's trousered thigh, the blood plunged from his face.

For standing there was Machi Juana, the sorceress from his village and a woman he had always feared.

The boy hid his face in his grandfather's trouser leg, then peeked again. It was her, all right. She was very short and very square, with very broad shoulders and awfully long, crooked arms.

What was that terrible female doing here in this new country? The boy had seen her in their village just a few days before. In fact, she had been present at the funeral of his parents.

Machi Juana slanted her eyes down at him, then muttered two grudging words as if tossing out the garbage.

"Mari mari," she said, a traditional village greeting meaning "May you be ten times fortunate."

The boy remained silent. He wasn't fooled. He suspected that this old woman didn't want him or anyone else to be fortunate.

Seething with disapproval, she drew closer to him and growled, "I left an important appointment with my potatoes to fly up here and welcome you. I hope you appreciate that."

She reached out to examine the broken gold medal around his neck, and as her pockmarked face with its crude features descended, the little boy backed away, afraid she would bite him, inadvertently stepping on his grandfather's foot as he did so.

"Where's Uncle?" he asked hopefully, looking up at his grandfather's face.

"Not here," the old man replied. "As any blind person could plainly see. And please stay off my feet."

The boy blinked away tears, knowing that his grandfather's moods were like the winds of their homeland; hot one minute, cold the next, so changeable the unexpected became expected.

His grandfather took the little boy's hand and led him expertly through crowds of people. Turning his head as he ran to keep up, the boy saw that Machi Juana waddled swiftly along behind them.

Outside the terminal, still in his grandfather's grip, they ran through pouring rain to the public parking area. Held aloft in his grandfather's other hand was a ruffled lavender umbrella with one broken spine that shielded only the old man's head.

Their destination was an enormous black sedan where the boy sat up in front with his grandfather while Machi Juana crawled into the back.

Unused to cars and dwarfed by this one's size, Antonio was awed when he saw the old, but to him wondrous, interior fittings, crushed leather upholstery, soft carpeting underfoot, crystal flower holders at each window.

But when he turned to look in the back, his heart rose up in his throat.

Crouched in a corner opposite Machi Juana was a dark, thin man with glittering red eyes and the grin of a skull: Maximo Coa, Machi Juana's ceremonial partner and a fearsome thing.

Shivering, he moved closer to his grandfather, who drove for hours while sleety rain sounded on the car's roof like clattering tin cans. Now and then they passed a truck loaded with bark-covered logs.

Their damp clothes steamed up the car's interior, causing his grandfather to expel curses and lower a window, through which immediately swept another deluge of rain, wetting them down all over again and requiring the uttering of additional curses.

As they drove, the little boy listened to the rainwater streaming over the car, pouring onto land and into creeks and rivers, and roaring under bridges.

Finally, lulled by the sound of the car's engine and the rhythm of the falling rain, he fell asleep.

When his grandfather awakened Antonio, they were at an isolated house made of logs somewhere deep in a forest. Although the building was a falling-down ruin, the boy thought it looked good compared to the houses in the village he had come from.

"I fought the bear for this house!" his grandfather said proudly. "The bear lost!"

The boy got out of the car, peered all around, and then up, way up. He lay down on the moist ground and looked up again trying to see the tops of the trees, but they were too far distant, lost in the clouds.

When he gazed at the rain and the greenery, his eyes filled with tears and his heart felt as if it might break and he did not understand why he was so moved.

It was not like the sadness he felt about his parents' deaths. Rather, it was a glorious melancholy for which he had no words, not even in his own language.

Wherever he stepped there were soft, wet cushions of green underfoot; tangles of green, dripping rain in the air wherever he turned his eyes; clouds of green overhead bleeding cool rainwater down on his upturned face.

He found any shade of green spellbinding, for only two things grew on the mountaintop moors of the boy's home-land: parched, skeletal gray shrubs and tall cacti that stood around like thin, starving men.

He had never seen trees like these. Huge trees, huger than he could even have imagined, all different shades of green with black shadows in their crotches where branches grew from massive trunks.

Did the moving branches of the trees make the wind? he asked himself. Or did the wind move the branches and speak through them?

In spite of their overwhelming size, he found the trees friendly, like kindly uncles, and he thought he could hear them calling to him in their whispery voices.

Almost immediately he understood that this strange new world was held together by these trees, like the pattern in the weavings his mother used to make. Why, their great trunks must hold up the clouds. And even the sky!

Furling the lavender umbrella, one of its spines sticking out like a broken bone, his grandfather warned, "Do not grow infatuated with those trees. They are beguiling but treacherous."

Treacherous? How could anything so green and beautiful be treacherous? That was like saying God was treacherous, which was blasphemy.

Then the little boy comprehended a terrible thought. God *was* treacherous. He had taken the boy's own parents when He'd had the whole village to choose from. Even the whole world.

All right, then, it was like saying his beloved uncle was treacherous, which, of course, was an impossibility. But the boy remained silent for he had always known never to argue with his grandfather.

"Can I walk among them, Grandfather?" he asked.

"Why, of course." Then the old man held up a hand in warning. "But I must warn you. Walk at your own risk. These are burial trees. There are dead people lying in canoes far up in their branches. Some of the dead lurk in hollow tree trunks."

Having said that, the old man opened the door of the log house and walked inside.

The little boy's eyes widened. "Dead people!"

He saw Maximo Coa give a lipless smile. "Clever grandfather who knows how to keep a little one from wandering away," the terrible man whispered in his grating voice.

Machi Juana shrugged her massive shoulders. "To my way of thinking it's been a long time since the natives around here buried their dead in trees."

When they began to enter the log house, his grandfather ordered Machi Juana, "Sweep this place out!"

Machi Juana imperiously passed the command on to her assistant, then sat down on an ancient kitchen chair.

His grandfather showed the boy a small cot on which he would sleep. "This is your home now, Grandson," he said. "Your parents are dead so that makes you an orphan."

The word *orphan* struck fear into the boy's heart for he had heard rumors of what sometimes happened to orphans.

"Where's Uncle?" he asked.

"Not here. Taking care of business," his grandfather replied, his tone of voice clearly meaning *ask no more questions, foolish child!*

The boy saw Maximo Coa look up from the broom and eye him like a thoughtful snake. Machi Juana remained seated on the chair, chewing coca leaves.

"But we are here!" his grandfather said. "And soon we shall eat."

The old man busied himself taking down supplies from a rough, unpainted shelf, then mixing things in bowls on a battered wooden table.

He turned on the fire under two camp stoves. On one of the stoves sat a black pan full of oil.

When it became hot, he rolled out dough and, holding the resulting thin pancake on the end of a wire that tore a hole in its center, lowered it into the boiling oil.

His grandfather did this repeatedly. Soon there were many crisp, yellow pancakes with holes in their middles stacked on a cracked willowware plate.

The boy's mouth watered.

Next, his grandfather prepared *api*, a drink that consisted of two liquids; one, dark purple, made from blackberries, which simmered in the other saucepan.

The second liquid, made from maize, was cold, thick, and cream-colored, almost like a gruel. He filled four tall glasses half-full with the maize drink, then poured steaming purple syrup over the top.

It was a delicious drink, the hot sweetness diluted by the

cold nourishing gruel, each unmixed mouthful being hot and cold at the same time on the boy's tongue.

Together with the sugar-sprinkled crisp pancakes, it made a good meal. While the boy ate, his grandfather and the others chewed noisily.

During the days that the boy lived in his new home, he frequently asked about his uncle but was told nothing.

When he wondered aloud about his birthday gift, his grandfather smiled and said they were waiting for the arrival of his uncle.

He saw no one except his grandfather, Machi Juana, and Maximo Coa. His grandfather cooked the meals but was gone at night, leaving the boy alone and terrified with the other two.

When his grandfather arrived at dawn, he prepared breakfast, then played cards with the others or dozed until it was time for another meal.

One late afternoon after dinner and before the little boy's grandfather departed for the night, Machi Juana took a green frog out of a cage made of damp moss.

The frog, about the size of the palm of the boy's small hand, had an extraordinary electric-green back, a lightly spotted white underside, and deep black eyes.

"What's that for, Grandfather?" he asked, crawling off his cot.

"Quiet!" his grandfather ordered.

Chastened, the boy hung back and watched his grandfather help the *machi* tie the frog's legs to four small posts nailed into the tabletop where it hung suspended like some strange green trampoline.

After the frog was secure, Machi Juana sat on a kitchen chair and with great concentration began to milk the frog's elongated center toe between her fingers.

His grandfather looked at the woman's ceremonial partner and raised his eyebrows. Both men laughed quietly. Then Maximo Coa rubbed his crotch slowly and deliberately. Machi Juana ignored them both and continued with her stimulations.

When the secretions began, Machi Juana aimed the frog's long center toe like a cow's teat, collecting the milky liquid in a brown glass bottle with a wide mouth. She then carefully placed the frog, unhurt, back in its moss cage.

The little boy saw that Maximo Coa, with a dreamy look on his bladelike face, continued rubbing something long and hard that had grown inside his trousers.

When the man turned his back, the boy heard the sound of a zipper being lowered, and saw the man's right arm move pistonlike in an ever-escalating rhythm.

He watched Machi Juana kneel with difficulty in front of Maximo Coa and hold out the brown glass bottle.

Growing ever more puzzled, the little boy heard Maximo Coa start to pant and saw the man's right arm move even faster.

For a time there was no sound except the man's whistling breath and the measured rub of cloth of sleeve against cloth of shirt.

Then, as if forced to act by something greater than his own will, Maximo Coa's arm fell down, he stumbled sideways, raised his head, and his eyes opened shockingly wide as if in terror or extreme pain.

There was a moment of breathless silence and frozen movement. Then Maximo Coa shrieked and continued shrieking as wet, metallic-looking streams shot from his body in pulsing arcs.

Machi Juana cursed, fell over, crawled to Maximo Coa, grabbed his jetting body part, and aimed it into the wide-necked brown bottle as she had done with the frog's toe.

The little boy had seen enough to know that whatever had spurted from Maximo Coa came from somewhere on the bottom of the man's penis, not from the end, as did his own urine.

The boy shivered and buried his face in his pillow, too frightened to cry, images of Maximo Coa's swollen and exploding body part crowding all other thoughts from his mind.

He could not fathom what he had seen. Was this the beginning of Maximo Coa's death? Would the man's entire body explode, one limb at a time?

Determined to understand, he sat up and looked directly at his grandfather, hoping to hear an explanation or, at the very least, to find comfort in the old man's face.

He saw only that his grandfather had no time for silly children. The old man still stared transfixed at the ceremonial partners, his cheeks pale.

Maximo Coa now lay fully prostrate on the floor, so still that he may have been dead, tears evident on his slack cheeks.

Because they, too, glistened, the little boy wondered if it had been a great supply of tears that had so recently burst from the sorcerer's lower body.

Machi Juana got to her feet and stirred the two secretions in the brown bottle with a peeled green twig.

After plunging a cork in the bottle's opening, she walked over and handed the bottle to the boy's grandfather, prodding Maximo Coa with her foot before returning to her chair.

Maximo Coa grunted, then turned his head and stared at the little boy, who was still on his cot. Something gleamed from the man's slitted eyes that started a strange fire in the boy's belly.

Watching Maximo Coa watch him, the little boy grew chilled. Then his belly began to burn with a full, hungry heat he had never before experienced.

He thought about sobbing, but something, he wasn't sure what, started to feel so good that he decided not to. Instead, he would remain absolutely still and enjoy this new feeling.

Suddenly there was a strange stirring between his legs.

Feeling himself through his clothes, he realized that the body part he used for urination had grown hard as iron and swelled to three times its normal size.

He was going to explode like Maximo Coa had done!

In amazement and terror, he cried out to his grandfather for help.

As if coming out of a trance, his grandfather sighed, wiped his hands over his face, then turned and saw a distressed small grandson holding himself.

He moved the little boy's hand away and when he untied the boy's cotton pants, a small, angry-looking penis reared up.

His grandfather laughed and called out to Machi Juana. "A cold rag will take care of this problem."

She got up from her chair, grabbed a dishcloth hanging from a peg, walked outside, dipped the cloth in a moss-covered rain barrel, wrung it out, walked back in, and advanced upon the boy, whose young hard-on quickly wilted at her heavy-footed approach.

Shamefaced, the boy tied his pants while his grandfather smiled at the disposition of his grandson's small manhood.

"You are wondering about the frog," he said.

The boy nodded.

"From the green frog, a frog smuggled to me from the backwaters of the Peruvian Amazon, comes *sapo*. From the man, a man whose ejaculation causes extreme pain as well as pleasure and thus makes him different from other men, comes a certain substance. When mixed together, these substances show us where the animals are."

What animals? the little boy wondered. *Why do we need to know about the animals?* But he was wise enough not to speak.

That night after his grandfather had departed, the boy fell asleep, as usual, to the sound of great snores from Machi Juana in the other bed and thin, gasping whines from her assistant, who slept on the floor under the table.

The boy dreamed a strange dream.

In it, he awoke to hot breath in his face. When he opened his eyes, a huge creature on two legs leaned over him.

The little boy thought it must be an animal because of its

fur, but the expression in its eyes reminded him of his mother.

He felt no fear. There was a gentle touch on his hair and the thing was gone. Later he heard a shrill scream coming from the depths of the forest and an answering one even farther away.

In his sleep he wondered if those were the animals the *sapo* and something else from the man had brought.

On the fifth day after the little boy's arrival, a dark, lowering afternoon with strong winds and sweeping gusts of rain, his grandfather did not arrive until late.

The old man came in quietly, ordered the boy to stay in the house with Maximo Coa, then walked outside with Machi Juana, where the two talked together on the dilapidated porch.

With his grandfather behaving so strangely, the boy was too nervous to play any of the games he usually amused himself with. So he sat very still, ignoring the stares directed at him by the *machi*'s assistant.

Occasionally Maximo Coa's eyes slitted and he rubbed his crotch, then beckoned the boy to come to him. The little boy looked away and closed his eyes.

Later, as the four of them sat at the kitchen table eating an early supper, the boy's grandfather asked him, "Isn't it nice here? Lots of rain. A blessing from God."

The little boy did not reply because he did not know what to say.

His grandfather went on. "It is like our homeland, is it not? Mountains all around."

The old man waved his arm in a summoning sweep as if to call the mountains outside right into their small room.

Still the boy remained silent. He was beginning to feel frightened. There was something very different about his grandfather today. And about the others.

"Well, speak up, my boy. Has a lizard got your tongue?"

"We don't have rain," the boy said quietly, "and our mountains don't have trees."

"That is true. But don't you like it here? Wouldn't you like to stay forever?"

"I'm lonely, Grandfather," the boy said, staring down at his food and trying not to cry. "I want Uncle."

His grandfather looked at Machi Juana and smiled. After a moment or two, she smiled. Then Maximo Coa laughed, *chuckle, chuckle, chuckle,* in a grating voice.

Machi Juana got up and went outside. Maximo Coa followed, obsequious, moving like a snake.

The boy's grandfather arose, towering over the child, who was still seated. "How would you like to go see your uncle right now?"

The boy's solemn face broke into radiant, unbelieving smiles. Soon he would see Uncle! And receive his birthday gift! At last!

"What are you waiting for?" his grandfather asked. "Prepare yourself. Unless you don't want to see your uncle after all? Or receive your birthday gift?"

The boy ran to the basin, quickly washed his face and hands, then dipped one hand back into the water and smoothed it over his hair.

Before they left, his grandfather brought out a plastic bag of dried coca leaves that cracked as the old man ground several between finger and thumb.

"These are good for the journey," he said, placing a few brittle, aromatic pieces in the boy's mouth, then wiping his big thumb on the inside of the boy's lower lip. "Now chew. Hunger and thirst and tiredness will not appear."

A bitter taste like raw spinach flooded the boy's mouth. Soon his tongue and gums grew numb. For a minute or two everything turned peculiar. He stood absolutely still and held on to the table's edge so he wouldn't float off into space.

"*Vamos! Vamos!* Let us go, child!" his grandfather said.

"When?" the little boy asked, looking around at the walls that seemed strangely tilted.

"*Ahora! Ahora!* Now!"

* * *

Black clouds boiled out of the west when they set out in early twilight, his grandfather holding a flashlight in one hand and a broad-bladed knife in the other.

The boy had seen such knives before and momentarily he hung back in spite of his joy.

Noticing the boy's hesitation, his grandfather said kindly, "Do not be afraid. This is only a machete, absolutely necessary to hack our way through the underbrush."

"Where's Machi Juana and the other one?" the boy asked cautiously.

"Gone. Who knows? Who cares?" He laughed and ruffled his grandson's hair.

The boy's brief sense of disorientation from chewing the coca leaves soon passed and he felt light and free, almost like a butterfly skimming over the ground.

For a long time he had no trouble keeping up with his grandfather even though they climbed continually, hacking away at drenched underbrush, crawling over fallen timber.

Then suddenly, as if a plug had been pulled, the boy collapsed and could walk no farther.

When his grandfather picked him up and carried him, Antonio felt warm and safe and fell asleep thinking he might someday come to almost like his cold, distant grandfather.

Much later, the boy awakened as his grandfather lowered him to the ground. Opening his eyes, he saw that it was night and the rain had stopped.

He felt warmth. Turning, he saw flames leaping from a campfire. Nearby, visible in the firelight, was a huge granite boulder that had been partially hollowed out by the onslaughts of nature.

And wonderfully enough, there stood his uncle, a big, white smile on his loving face.

The little boy shouted, "Uncle! Uncle!" and threw himself into his uncle's outstretched arms.

They hugged and kissed. The boy cried and his uncle

cried, both from happiness, for they loved each other very much.

His uncle sat down on a nearby stump and, delirious with happiness, the little boy scrambled into his uncle's lap.

Boy and man, they talked and laughed together until his uncle reached behind the stump and handed him a large, colorfully wrapped package.

Eyes wide, the boy shouted, "My birthday present!" and eagerly tore off the wrappings.

When he saw what was inside, he was so happy he could actually feel his eyes growing so big they seemed to take over his whole face.

"A truck!" he breathed. "A real truck!"

His uncle laughed, then said, "It is a model of a logging truck like the people around here use to haul trees out of the forest."

"It's made of wood!" the boy breathed. "And it's carrying *real logs!*"

Patiently, his uncle pointed out all the careful details: the wooden wheels that turned, the mud flaps on the back wheels, the brass chains that held the small smooth logs on the trailer that was carefully linked to the cab.

"This is called a collector's item. It's not meant for rough play."

"Oh, I'll never be rough with this. I'll be very careful. I'll keep it forever. Just like I'll stay with you forever."

At his words, the little boy saw the expression on his uncle's face change, but he soon decided the momentary look of sadness was caused by shadows from the fire.

When his grandfather called out to them, they both turned and, to the boy's surprise and distress, saw that Machi Juana and Maximo Coa were present.

The little boy trembled with fear of the sorceress and her assistant, but soon he relaxed, comforted and calmed by his uncle's caresses and soothing words.

Lightning flashed, followed by thunder, and Antonio saw that Machi Juana now wore a black and green shawl over her shoulders. An elaborate silver ornament covered her chest. She held a drum whose round surface was divided by red paint into four quadrants.

There was a frown on the sorceress's face. "Something is watching us," she said. "I feel it."

"What?" his grandfather asked.

"I do not know."

"It is only the trees. They watch everything. Now let us begin."

The old woman sat down on a fallen log under the overhanging branches of a large Douglas fir and began to rhythmically beat her drum.

At first the sound of the drum was hardly faster or louder than a slow heartbeat. Maximo Coa kept exclaiming and interjecting, helping the sorceress enter the trance state, coaxing her into ecstasy.

As the rhythm picked up, the *machi*'s accompanying chant became intense. Her breathing was labored, and perspiration rolled down her face as she worked herself into a frenzy.

Finally the drumming and chanting grew so wild that Machi Juana began to hyperventilate.

At the last moment, her face white, her eyes protruding, when it seemed she must faint from her appalling exertions, the woman stopped dead, trembling all over.

The forest fell silent, except for the whisper of huge tree branches moving all about them. Shadows crept from the fire, stealthy as assassins.

The boy's grandfather, crucifix swinging from around his neck, held up a large clay bowl from which he drank, then handed it to the boy's uncle who, steadying the boy on one knee, also drank.

"Pacha Mama must drink, too," his uncle said as he poured what was left in the bowl onto the earth.

Now, his eyes bits of dark flame, his grandfather turned to the boy and began to speak, his voice unusually soft, his words slow and measured like those of a thoughtful judge.

"Antonio Salinas, we are all far from our homeland, in a strange land with strange people. Nevertheless, customs must be carried out. Our beliefs and our traditions, our religion, will go on as they have throughout the ages. It is our solemn duty to see that this is done." He fingered the crucifix around his neck.

The little boy listened, mouth open, totally fascinated. His grandfather had never paid this much attention to him nor had he ever spoken this seriously to him.

He realized that something very important was about to happen. Even Machi Juana and Maximo Coa were silent, waiting outside the ring of firelight like hungry village dogs.

Could it be his puberty rites? He was only eight years old. But maybe it was. Perhaps they did things differently in the United States. He must remain silent and discover what was to happen next.

"You may have feared, in your childishness and innocence, that I do not love you because I am not a demonstrative man," his grandfather continued.

"Quite the contrary is true. As my only daughter's only child, you are my only grandchild. Now my only daughter is dead. All I have left is my son, your uncle."

The old man sighed.

"As a consequence, my feeling for you is deeper than affection, deeper than love. The blood running through your veins calls to the blood running through mine. Do you understand what I speak of, child?"

"I think so, Grandfather. Sort of."

Uncle smiled, hugged him, and squeezed him close.

"I declare to you now in front of these witnesses that you are the most precious thing in the world to me. Your body and your blood are part of my body and my blood."

The boy brightened and sat up straighter on his uncle's lap.

He couldn't believe what he was hearing. His grandfather had just said he really, truly loved him.

Just then a cold wind began to shiver slyly through the

trees. His uncle wrapped the boy in his own jacket, the toy logging truck still held tightly in both the boy's hands.

His grandfather gazed into the fire for long minutes, watching the wind dance with the flames.

"Everything that has happened to you, Grandson, happened for a purpose. Your parents died of a fever because it was the will of the gods that you be without mother or father. It was the will of the gods that you become an orphan."

The little boy trembled.

He knew about God, of course, but who were these gods of whom his grandfather now spoke?

He remembered people in his village talking about the gods as if there were more than one but he hadn't paid much attention. At the time, it sounded like they were gossiping about their neighbors.

"I don't know the gods, Grandfather," he said in a small voice. "Who are they?"

"Our gods, of course. The gods who have ruled since before the beginning of time. White people's minds are too simplistic to understand these mysteries. They claim to have only one god who has only one son. Stupid idea, is it not? If I were a god I would have many sons. And hundreds of grandsons just like you, little one."

The boy thought that made sense, sort of.

"Now I will speak of gifts. I know you loved your gift because I saw the joy in your face when you received it. It was an important gift, a wondrous gift, was it not?"

"Oh, yes, Grandfather!" The boy nodded his head vigorously.

"We gave you that gift because we love you. In the same way, we give gifts to the gods to show our love for them."

His grandfather moved closer so that now he stood directly over the boy.

"The gods require gifts from man. When we give to the gods we give that which is most precious to us. What kind of a gift is something without value? That is not a gift; it is an insult."

When his grandfather leaned down and kissed him on the forehead, the boy felt once more that deathlike chill, but now it was even colder—so cold!—and seemed to come from within his own body.

"You must understand how you are being honored," his grandfather said.

Voice small, lips barely moving, the boy asked, "Honored?"

"Yes, my dear grandson. The gods make orphans so that we may present them as gifts."

Helplessly, the little boy looked up into his uncle's eyes, now strangely glowing.

And he knew the truth.

Never would he live with his uncle. Never again would he play with his logging truck, never again taste his grandfather's *api* or crisp sugar-sprinkled pancakes.

"Let it be as it was from the beginning!" his grandfather cried, using the age-old words and slashing his right arm downward in the age-old gesture.

With a terrible, pleading smile, his uncle kissed the boy, then lifted him from his lap, the little wooden logging truck falling to the ground, and handed him over to the grandfather.

In spite of the boy's shrieking cries and his struggling efforts to cling to his grandfather's body, he was given to Machi Juana, who shouted to her ceremonial partner for assistance.

"I'll be good, Grandfather! Please! Help me, Uncle! Please! I love you!" the little boy screamed, realizing that his most secret and hideous fears were about to come true.

And since the boy's own grandfather had already turned him over to the power of the *machi*, there was nothing that could be done, even had someone wished to, which they did not, to prevent what must follow.

Antonio saw again the knife, the machete, now in Machi Juana's hands, how sharp and shining it was, and he hoped it wouldn't hurt too much.

Machi Juana and her ceremonial partner stretched him on the ground.

Fearing he could not stand the pain, the boy's mouth opened wide and the screams flew out and out and out like bats from an endless cave . . .

The first cut sliced into his ankle and his right foot flew off and blood spurted and he expected it to hurt more than anything had ever hurt before.

But instead of pain, he felt a sudden overwhelming tranquillity, a releasing tiredness like that which always came at the end of a busy day of play.

Fully conscious, watching what was being done to him, he saw a hacking at his groin, chop after chop, foiled by the bone, but not for long, and soon his upper leg lay severed from his body . . .

The machete moved in a great swing, and when he dreamily tried to lift his right arm he saw that his hand was gone and blood was pouring from the small stump.

Then came another *Slash! Slash! Slash!* and what was left of his right arm fell useless onto his body . . .

Grunting, Machi Juana moved to his other side and the little boy heard the sound of machete on bone, like his father chopping wood, and the thump of hand and foot, arm and leg, as they fell away from his body.

Oddly without fear now, the little boy smelled the warm, flooding blood and felt a feather touch at his throat.

The feather touch turned to sudden ice. Everything whirled and turned over as his head jumped into the air, bounced on the ground, and landed at his uncle's feet.

Even as the last shred of consciousness faded, the boy felt himself being lifted—strangely without weight—to receive his uncle's final kiss and see the beloved face opposite his.

Somewhere nearby an owl was hooting.

Then the boy died, never knowing that his death had taken less than one minute.

When it was over, the grandfather and the uncle each took a small piece and ate, for the child's heart was pure.

Each man then lifted the crucifix he wore around his neck and kissed it reverently.

The little boy's grandfather left immediately with Machi Juana and Maximo Coa. The next day the sorceress and her assistant would be airbound back to South America, she extremely rich by the standards of their village.

His uncle remained in the forest the rest of the night making certain dispositions.

The man was happy, secure in the knowledge that the ancient ceremony they had paid to have performed, and in which they had participated, would guarantee success in their business endeavors, even in this strange country, just as it always had in their homeland.

The beloved little boy, of course, had been done an inestimable favor. By their actions they had bestowed upon him the gift of eternal life.

He was now a young saint, destined to live forever in the world of the great ancient gods, in a position to grant them favors.

When all movement had ceased around the fire, a female cougar with astonishing blue eyes moved gracefully down from her perch on a Douglas fir to examine what man had done.

She stepped cautiously, each footfall seeming as light as the touch of maribou feathers, sniffed, sprang back, and disappeared. Her kind did not care for the meat of humans.

The ocean was Father; he, who tended Mother, the land.
Today, Father Ocean still gives food, his breath still moistens the
forest, and he still counts time in each wave, each tide, and each
salmon run.
But the ocean is not always an absolute, not always predictable. It
shifts here and there, back and forth and, in its vagaries is neither.
—JACQUELINE M. STORM,
Land of the Quinault

Chapter 2

1   Head bent, hands clasped behind her back, eyes
searching the damp sand for gifts from the sea, a
solitary young woman walked the wide evening beach at
Taholah, her footprints following her like those of a dis-
carded yet relentless lover.

Heavy mist tightened the black curls that surrounded her
head like a cap, beaded on her long black eyelashes, then
fell like tears down cheeks the pale ecru of handspun linen.

She was tall, six feet at least, and slender. Her name was
Jordan Tidewater and she was more than just another handsome face.

She was tribal sheriff for the Quinault Indian Nation.

More even than an officer of the law, Jordan was a shaman of The People, a follower and teacher of the old ways, one who had recently and painfully returned to the beliefs of the ancients.

Occasionally she stopped to observe the inhabitants of various tidepools, scallops, green abalone, eyehole limpets, hairy tritons, mussels, buffalo sculpin, fish-eating sea anemone, some with milt oozing out to meet up with other cells and produce more of their kind.

The tide had been low for quite a while. Now she knew that it had turned and was beginning to rush back in, soon to cover the pools she had been exploring.

Piled along the beach in uneven drifts, some as deep as eighteen inches, were thousands of dried and drying *valella,* those little blue jellyfish that sometimes washed ashore during the Olympic Peninsula spring.

Jordan knew that when the *valella* appeared it was a good time to start watching for floats, glass balls, and Japanese sake bottles. It was also a sign that tuna would appear in the summer off the Washington coast.

She watched the April sun, optically misshapen by purple storm clouds boiling low on the horizon, collapse into the thunderous waters of the North Pacific sea.

As she stood quietly observing the sunset, she saw Raven circling overhead, carrying something in his beak. He landed not far away, on top of a clump of flotsam being pushed in by the tide.

When she approached, Raven squawked and flew away. As the incoming tide shoved the clump of flotsam ever farther onto the beach, Jordan saw that something glittered in a different way than the usual sparkling effervescense seen in a backlit wave.

Hoping for a Japanese glass float to add to her extensive collection, she grabbed the offering from the sea, then ran back up onto the dry sand where she knelt down to examine her find.

On top of the conglomeration of sea wrack, broken seashells, and sharp bits of small rock, Jordan found what looked like the broken half of a small medal attached to a bright woven ribbon. A vertical half of the ribbon was missing. Its colors were vivid: orange, purple, scarlet.

When she picked up the damaged medal and ribbon with her bare hands, she was assailed by a bone-deep chill that had nothing to do with the weather or her sea-soaked Nikes.

Studying her find, she suspected that the medal was made of gold. It showed part of a full-length figure that looked like a jaguar. The torn, stained ribbon was threaded through a gold clasp.

Lost in thought, she put the medal and ribbon in her jacket pocket and began walking along the tide line again. She wondered about the meaning of her finding the medal. She knew that Raven was many things, one of which was a trickster.

Now the storm clouds streamed landward, swiftly obliterating stars that were just beginning to come out, although the moon and Jupiter still formed a striking pair high in the western sky.

It's getting dark and cold, she thought. *Time to go home.*

As she turned to walk back up the beach, she saw a solitary figure furiously paddling a dugout canoe landward through the roiling breakers.

Thunder roared. Flashes of forked lightning from Thunderbird's eyes etched the scene in liquid silver. The canoe came to rest on the shore about fifty feet north of where Jordan stood.

A figure emerged, dragged the dugout canoe along behind it, and disappeared into smokelike fog rising from the cooling land.

Jordan walked back up the wet sand and saw that the figure had left footprints, along with hers, which the inrushing tide was swiftly devouring, forcing her off the sea-soaked part of the beach as it did so.

She hurried along, the dry sand uttering little whistling shrieks under her feet, until she reached the mouth of the Quinault River and climbed over the breakwater.

She got in her truck, which she had parked earlier near the fish cannery, and drove to the old house she and her young son, Tleyuk, shared with Old Man Ahcleet, her great-grandfather and one of the tribal elders of the Quinault Nation.

It was home, where she would find warmth and light and the love of a very old man and a little boy. Also, a hot dinner, for Old Man Ahcleet loved to cook.

Inside her great-grandfather's house, Jordan checked the mail and found an invitation to Hannah McTavish's book party to be held the next night at Lake Quinault Lodge. Fortunately, Jordan would be off duty so they could all go.

She washed her hands and face, combed her hair, then hid the broken medal with its torn woven ribbon deep in a desk drawer that she kept locked.

Somehow there was evil connected with that thing, and she would not mention its existence in the harbor of her home.

At the dinner table, Jordan told Old Man Ahcleet about seeing the dugout canoe.

"One of ours?" he asked.

"Must have been. It had that distinctive high-prowed Quinault design, Grandfather."

Old Man Ahcleet listened intently as he chewed freshly caught broiled salmon topped with chive butter, then swallowed a sip of coffee.

"What color was the canoe?" he asked.

"It was black."

"And the markings?"

"There were none."

Ahcleet took more salmon, then split and buttered a homemade biscuit.

"Could you see what the person in the canoe was wearing?" he asked.

"Something very odd. It looked like a long black robe that fell from humped shoulders."

Ahcleet dropped the biscuit. "The Klokwalle!" he whispered.

Maybe, maybe not, she thought.

"It left footprints, Grandfather."

"Don't you think the Klokwalle leaves footprints when it takes form?" Ahcleet asked.

"What's a Klokwalle?" Tleyuk asked.

At eight, Jordan's son was full to bursting with questions, especially when the ensuing reply provided an opportunity to avoid eating his broccoli, which he detested.

Ahcleet wiped his fingers and his mouth on a paper towel before he spoke.

"The Klokwalle is a spirit who lives in the west beyond the ocean. When he comes to our world he comes all alone in a black canoe."

The old man rubbed the deep white scar on the bridge of his nose. "He is black all over and wears a black robe."

"But what's he for, Grandfather?" Tleyuk persisted.

Ahcleet pointed to the boy's plate. "You will learn these things after your training starts. Now eat your broccoli."

Then he looked at Jordan. "The Klokwalle hasn't been around for a long, long time. I'll have to think on why he came tonight and why he allowed you to see him."

After dinner, Jordan went to bed and set her alarm for eleven P.M. She must be on patrol at midnight.

As Jordan slept, she experienced fitful, unsettling dreams about the mother she'd never known, the woman who had died at the births of herself and her twin brother, Paul Prefontaine.

When the alarm rang, she got up feeling restless and tired. She showered, dressed, and had coffee with her great-grandfather, who sipped hot chocolate in a well-worn easy chair in front of the fire. Tleyuk had long since been in bed.

"How did you sleep, La'qewamax?" Ahcleet asked courteously.

"Not well. I dreamed about my mother."

"Did she bring you any messages?"

She shook her head, not mentioning the broken medal with its torn woven ribbon her mother was holding out to Jordan in her dream. Nor her mother's bloodstained hands.

"She was just a presence I was trying to reach. I could never see her face. Grandfather, what was she like?"

Ahcleet stared into the flames. "Jocasta was small and plain. She gave you your *hoquat* name."

Hoquat was the old word for white man. La'qewamax, which means "the shaman," was Jordan's real name, the Native American name Ahcleet had given her at birth.

They both knew it was all right to speak the woman's name aloud for she had been dead more than ten years.

"Does the name Jordan mean anything special?" she asked. "It's certainly not a Quinault name."

Ahcleet drank more chocolate. "It's from the Christian mythology. Something about death and a river, I think."

"My mother became a Christian?" Jordan was surprised. She had not known.

Ahcleet nodded. "She got crazy with the *hoquat* religion."

"What did my father think about that?"

She could not speak Mika's name aloud for he had been dead for only a couple of years.

"He endured. Eventually he drank."

"I used to ask Dad about my mother. But all he'd say was that she was a fine woman. I could never get him to talk about her. Neither could Paul."

"It hurt him too much. Your father loved your mother until the day he died." Ahcleet sighed. "And his grief continues for he is without her now in the Land of the Dead."

Jordan was acquainted with the Land of the Dead. She had been there with Ahcleet; had brought her little boy's soul back from that mythical and terrifying place.

Knowing now about her mother, she realized that of course the dead woman would have gone to one of the two Christian places of death. She hoped for Jocasta's sake it was heaven.

When she rose to leave for work, Ahcleet stood up with her. "Are you looking for anybody special tonight?" he asked.

"Poachers," she said. "There's something new going on but I can't get a handle on it. All I've found so far are mutilated remains. I don't even have any suspects."

Ahcleet grunted. "It's those *hoquat* out there. They all look suspicious to me."

"Not necessarily, Grandfather."

"What else can I think about a people whose heroes are serial murderers?"

"Suppose it's not whites. What if it's some of us?"

"Impossible," he replied serenely. "All of us, The People, we're *human beings*. Those doing those bad things, they're *creatures*."

"Whatever or whoever they are, they're doing it on our land, as well as in the park."

The Olympic National Park, which covers some nine hundred thousand acres, partially abuts Lake Quinault, as does the Olympic National Forest. The park and the forest are two separate entities. The lake itself belongs to the Quinault Indian Nation.

As she left the house, Ahcleet followed her out on the porch. "Be careful—" he managed to say before a surge of wind and rain tore the rest of his words out of his mouth.

When lightning sizzled on the gravel road in front of the house, he pulled Jordan back inside.

"Be extra careful." He took hold of her arm. "Is your truck all right?"

She knew the question meant: Do you have a good spare tire? Plenty of gas in the auxiliary tanks? Has the oil been checked lately? Are your brakes all right? *Will you get back home safely?*

For she was going into deep, forested wilderness and deserted cutover lands; driving old fire roads and overgrown trails—hidden, dangerous places where, if she ran into trouble, her truck telephone could not function.

"The truck's in tiptop shape," she said.

"But who else is out there tonight?"

Jordan put her arms around the old man. "It's my job to find out, Grandfather. Why are you so worried now?"

"Because you saw the Klokwalle. I know now what that means. He is the spirit who inspires courage." He took both her hands in his. "Something is coming. Something for which you will need more than human courage."

"What is it, Grandfather?"

He shook his head. "I do not know."

2   Jordan's truck was a Dodge power wagon with balloon mud tires, spotlights on either side, a hundred-foot Rover winch in front, and a CB radio with a ten-foot whip mounted off the back bumper.

The seal of the Quinault Indian Nation appeared on the door as did the seal of the United States of America for Jordan was also a U.S. deputy marshal.

As such, she could serve federal warrants and subpoenas and pursue investigations across state lines. And she could carry a gun interstate and onto a plane.

Accustomed as she was to driving hard patrols in wilderness areas, Jordan reflected that she had seldom seen a stormier night.

Wind and rain thundered through the Quinault Valley and up through the mountain passes, their passage toward the Olympics attended by courts of lightning splendid enough for the gods.

Thunderbird is busy tonight, she thought.

Since she was near Anson's place, she decided to stop in and see that all was well with him.

Anson was a white man, one she had known since she'd

been a teenager. Her father, a former tribal policeman, had told her and Paul about Anson, that he was a good man, a highly intelligent man, with a lot of trouble not of his making out in the white world.

Years ago he had fled into the Quinault Nation as into sanctuary, built himself lodgings in a huge cedar stump, and lived off the land.

He must have had a last name but nobody knew what it was or cared to invade his privacy by asking.

There were several men like that, her father had told her and Paul. Men who lived deep in the reservation, bothering no one, seeing no one, refugees from the escalating horrors of civilization.

When Mika found them, he always checked them out, and if they met his standards, he allowed them to stay, mentioning their existence to no one. If he didn't like them he kicked them off the reservation.

"It's a hell of a note," Jordan remembered her father muttering one day, "when a damned social security number is supposed to follow a man to his grave. Like a number on a convict."

Anson appeared on the outside now and then, usually around logging operations, digging out cedar stumps for shake blocks, first making it clear he would accept only cash in payment. When he accumulated the money he needed to live on for another year or so, he disappeared again.

Jordan drove through underbrush to a huge stump, just another cedar blowdown, the main tree having toppled at least a hundred years ago and serving now as a nurse log for a healthy community of young trees.

She got out of her truck, ran through the pouring rain, and knocked on the tree.

"Anson, it's me, Jordan," she called loudly in the thunderous night.

Startlingly, an unseen door in the tree opened. A heavily bearded man appeared in the doorway holding a kerosene lamp.

"Come in and welcome," he said.

She wiped her feet on a pile of fresh young hemlock branches placed outside the door and stepped inside. The floor was carpeted with numerous treated bearskins.

When he saw Jordan glancing at the skins, Anson said, "I've been meaning to talk to you about bears next time you came around."

"What about them?"

"I've been finding them all over with only the paws and galls taken. When I do, I skin and treat the hide, because I can use it, and leave the meat for the critters. There're poachers out there, Jordan, and they're not the homegrown variety. They're professionals. Watch your step."

"My grandfather told me almost the same thing tonight. About watching my step."

Flames leaped from a fire pit in the center of the round room, smoke going up through a hole in the twelve-foot ceiling. There were a number of trunks in the living space that Jordan knew contained books; used now for tables and seating.

Fresh coffee bubbled by the fire. Several opened books lay on the rough-hewn table on which Anson set the lamp. He had been engaged in reading.

Moving closer, she saw that these books were on forensic science. That did not surprise her.

A graduate of Harvard Law School, Anson had been the young lion in a prestigious law firm in New York City before his retreat into the forests of the Quinault Nation.

"Some people work with crossword puzzles," he said, watching her glance at the open books. "My pleasure is inventing interesting murders with a complete cast of characters, then acting as the lawyer for the defense. Or the prosecution if that happens to please me."

"Do you always win the case?"

"No, sometimes I lose."

Then he laughed, a very pleasant sound. "Yeah, well, I used to play Monopoly all by myself when I was a kid, acting the part of five or six players. I guess I'm really a crowd instead of just one man. Maybe that's why I don't get lonesome."

"You should write your court cases down. I'd bet they'd make terrific mysteries. You'd become the rich and famous recluse author."

"Oh, I do, some of them, just for the hell of it. But no other eyes will ever see them."

"Why not, Anson?"

His mouth firmed. "Because I'm through with that world. It holds nothing for me. It's a destroyer of lives."

As she sipped the coffee he had poured for them both, she saw a black-and-white glossy photograph of a young man lying on the table among the books.

"Good-looking guy," Jordan said, picking up the photograph. "Who is he?"

"One of the two people I allow to visit me," he said. "Just recently taken, I understand. He just got promoted to top dog in one of those gene-splicing shops in California. Same kind of corporate garbage I got away from. Those guys won't stop until they tear up the world."

Studying the picture, she saw that the young man was dressed in typical CEO clothing, tailored to fit, not off the racks. On his right ring finger he wore an unusual ring, wide gold with stones set at angles that seemed to form a cross. Definitely a young man on his way up.

"See those stones there?" Anson asked. "They're called sun stones. Dug them myself when I spent some time in central Oregon. Had them polished and had that ring made up for my young friend when he graduated from MIT."

"Tell me, Anson, how do you receive mail? Via raven delivery?"

"Mail? Oh, I pay for a post office box in Tacoma. Have for years. Use it for correspondence to a few people who live worlds away. Far enough to keep the pests out of my hair. Far as the U.S. government's concerned I'm dead anyway. But I always liked to keep in touch with this young man. He understands me and I understand him. At least I thought I did."

Jordan sipped her coffee, wondering at the troubled expression that momentarily crossed Anson's face. Probably loneliness, maybe a case of the might-have-beens.

"Thanks for the coffee," Jordan said, rising. "Since I'm on duty I better be on my way."

He did not ask her to stay longer, but walked over and gave her a long hug, something he had never done before.

"Keep safe, honey," he said. "Come see me anytime. And watch out for the bad guys."

As Jordan entered the high country, the storm suddenly paused, leaving a dark, wet night, black as the inside of a wolf's mouth.

For hours her truck bumped across rutted gulleys, along abandoned skid roads, and places where roads had never been built.

She drove slowly and carefully, most of the time with only her parking lights on, trying not to get stuck in treacherous mud pools.

Around three in the morning, a sharp wind began to scurry along the ground, tossing damp forest debris into miniature tornadoes, wringing showers of raindrops from soaked evergreens, then fell abruptly still as if daring Jordan to stop, get out, and walk into the dark.

When she finally braked and lowered her window, the scent of rain-soaked forest and its undergrowth flooded in: the night breath of great trees, the perfumes of rich forest-floor tilth, of a hundred kinds of mosses, fern fronds, vine maple, huckleberry bushes growing from stumps, and thousands of small, wet green plants.

She sat quietly, listening to the rapturous sounds of a vast forest dancing in an ecstasy of rain, its members ranging in age from saplings whose threadlike roots clutched their nurse logs to patriarchs reaching three and four hundred feet upward, penetrating the clouds.

She listened and heard the distinctive sloshings and drippings of trees receiving the beneficence of the clouds.

There was absolute silence for a moment or two. Then vague tricklings as if a small lost creek had meandered under her truck.

Water. Water running behind her, then water running all around her. A waterfall somewhere up ahead whose thunder could be heard over the lesser sounds. The blessing of water everywhere.

Sounds and fragrances that reminded her of making love. Of Roc whispering, "Yes, again, darling. And again. I will overwhelm you with my love."

Unbidden and desperately unwanted, passionate scenes with Jordan's former husband assaulted her mind. Sternly she locked them out and forced herself to remember what he'd really been: only a self-styled master of Native American metaphysics, who was nothing more than a mushroom guru.

Roc, the womanizer, for whom one woman, even one as sensual as Jordan herself, was never enough. Jordan had left him when she was three months pregnant with Tleyuk and had willed herself never to love a man again.

Over eight long years ago.

She wiped tears from her face, knowing she wept not because she missed the lovemaking but because she could no longer want or feel sexual passion.

In the years since she had left Roc, while she was at the University of Washington, then at the police academy, and here, in the Quinault Nation, Jordan could have led a very active love life for there were plenty of men who desired her.

But she turned them all down. Roc had left her a—what? A female eunuch? Was there such a thing? She didn't know what she was anymore except a still-young woman who could no longer feel physical desire for a man.

Jordan opened the truck door to step out onto the running board. As she did so, she felt a sudden heavy weight on her heart and fell back behind the wheel.

What was *that*? she asked herself.

Something to do with the Klokwalle? Or her dead mother's hand in warning?

For several minutes Jordan sat quietly, truck door open. She hadn't thought particularly about Jocasta in years.

So why now? Why had she dreamed of the woman who was her mother? Was it because of the gold medal brought to her early that evening by Raven?

Her mind concentrated on Jocasta, who had died giving her and her twin brother birth. What had she been like?

Once, a few years ago, she'd found snapshots of her newly married mother and father in an old album. In the photograph, her mother smiled shyly, clinging to her father's arm as he stood tall and proud, dressed in his tribal sheriff's uniform.

And after Mika's death two years ago, when she and her brother, Paul, had reluctantly and sadly cleaned out his things, they'd found a swatch of their mother's hair—black and curly just like Jordan's.

"So that's where you got your curls," Paul had said.

What did I get from my mother besides my hair? Jordan wondered, sitting all alone in this cold and lonely wilderness with the trees exulting overhead. *The timbre of my voice? My skin tones? The way I hold my chin in my hands when I'm thinking deeply?*

In spite of being motherless, she and Paul both had enjoyed happy childhoods. When they were growing up, their father was gone so much it was always Great-grandfather Ahcleet to whom they had looked for comfort and advice. And she still did. Never having known a mother, she did not miss her. Until tonight.

Stop that right now! she told herself. Brooding about an unhappy past with a faithless husband or about a mother she would never know in this world wasn't doing the job she was paid to do.

This time when Jordan forced herself out of the truck, the weight of an unseen hand on her heart was gone.

When she looked around, she knew instantly why she must not stay and realized the cause of her previous inhibition. Subconsciously she must have known where she was.

Caught in the light from her torch stood a massive cedar stump from an ancient blowdown, one very like the stump in which Anson lived.

Huge, jagged, fifteen feet tall more or less, bleached gray/white by time and weather, the whorls and cavities and holes in the bark where branches once had grown formed an aghast face.

Two elongated eyes, a mouth round with apprehension, what appeared to be a splayed hand held up under the chin as if in stark horror.

This was The Guardian that marked entry into the burial grounds of the Seatco, those beings the rest of the world called Bigfoot. Mika, their father, had warned Jordan and Paul about this place many times.

When she and her brother were young and school was out for the summer, they had ridden with their father on patrol through reservation lands. Upon several occasions he had pointed out this marker.

Never, Mika said, were they to trespass here. This was holy ground, sacred to the Seatco. And he warned them never to talk about it, especially to any white person, because the *hoquat* would come sneaking around, digging up the remains to prove that Seatco existed.

She remembered staring as a child with great curiosity into an area that seemed no different from the surrounding forest except for the strange face formed by nature on the cedar stump.

Jordan got back in the truck and carefully backed out through large clumps of salmonberry bushes and deadly nightshade until she came to a long-deserted logging road.

Here she proceeded carefully, driving as much as she could with her lights off, stopping every now and then to turn on her spotlight and move it around.

So far during this night's patrol she had found nothing

suspicious, no animal remains or signs that anybody had been around.

But the reservation was a vast place and what she had covered tonight was just a very small part of it.

Lights off again, she stopped to relieve herself. Squatting, she saw a tiny flamelike flicker off in the distance.

Someone lighting a cigarette? She must investigate. No one had any legal business up here at night except herself.

Suddenly a full April moon, the moon of sprouts and buds, burst through fleeing storm clouds. By its light Jordan saw what appeared to be fresh blood on the ground in front of her.

3   Able Majors and Jack Flanagan were worried. Not that they feared discovery. That wasn't even a possibility, they felt, in this deserted wilderness at this time of the night, just a couple of hours before dawn.

What they *were* afraid of was a maddened bear.

A wounded black bear was very dangerous, could turn on its pursuers and become a hunter itself.

Being stalked in the night by a killer bear was not an experience either one of them desired.

They had baited the animal, knowing that when hungry bears emerge from hibernation, they head for the nearest place where they might expect to find food.

Black bears loved the foam rubber in automobiles and the seats of heavy logging equipment. If loggers didn't take precautions, their equipment could be torn up. And frequently was.

This particular place was the site of a closed-down logging show, one where bears, both men knew, had caused trouble the year before, eating the foam rubber out of cars and the seats out of tractors and loaders.

Four days before, Majors and Flanagan baited the place

with rotten meat rubbed with honey, and then, wearing heavy gloves, piled deadfalls helter-skelter on top of the bait so that it all looked like a natural windfall. Something heavy enough to prevent raccoons or coyotes from making off with the bait, but not too heavy for a bear to handle.

Then the two men spent the next three nights waiting and watching. And tonight a bear had come.

But it had not been their usual quick kill. Flanagan's aim was off and the animal was only wounded.

Using their flashlights, the two men blood-trailed the bear for a mile or so over intensely rough country, careful that they did not walk into an animal ambush.

"I think it's making a big circle, comin' back to where it got shot," Flanagan said after they stopped to rest.

"Yeah, trying to sneak up on whatever did the damage and tear it apart," Majors replied.

"Which'll be us," Flanagan said. "We can't let that happen."

He stopped and listened intently.

"What's the matter?" Majors whispered.

"Dunno. Got the feeling somethin's following us."

"Long as it's not that damned bear," his partner muttered.

A full April moon elbowed its way out from behind black storm clouds.

To the poachers' great relief, they spotted the bear in the moonlight, saw that weakness had forced it down in the middle of a deserted logging road, very near the spot where Flanagan had first wounded it.

Now, flooded with moonlight as if on a stage, they could see the bear turning on itself, trying to bite away the pain burning into its body.

Whining softly, the animal looked around, inhaling the flows of wind. The men knew it was studying each layer of scent, back to the place of wounding, looking for its enemy.

Panting heavily, steam rising in the cold night air from its exhalations, the bear tried to struggle up on its forelegs.

Downwind, Majors and Flanagan watched intently.

As the bear finally raised itself up, Majors drew careful aim and squeezed off a heart shot. The bear gave a hoarse, roaring scream and slowly collapsed.

Majors started forward but Flanagan stopped him. "Hold your horses, Able. Be a hell of a note to be killed by a dead bear."

They waited to make sure there was no life left in the big animal.

When they were certain it was dead, they approached, took off their jackets, threw them on the ground out of the way, placed their rifles on top of their jackets, rolled up their sleeves, and began skinning the bear out.

Flanagan slit the belly from throat to anus. "Been after this big bastard a long time," he said.

"It's a lot easier since that logging show closed down," Majors said, cutting the inside of the right hind leg above the paw, then severing the paw at the joint and tossing it aside.

"Sure as hell is."

They both laughed softly.

Flanagan decapitated the bear, leaving the hide attached. After Majors slit the hide on all four legs and severed the other three paws, they detached the hide from the body, starting at the tail end and rolling it up carefully. When they were finished, they had an intact bear skin complete with head.

"Want any of the meat?" Flanagan asked.

"Hell, no. My freezer's full."

"Mine, too. We'll leave it for the critters."

Both men wiped their hands on nearby wet ferns in the undergrowth.

Now that the bear was dead and could not detect the presence of men by cigarette smoke, Flanagan lit up Lucky Strikes for each of them.

Both men sat back on their heels to wait for their transportation, which they knew should be arriving shortly.

"Bill Hereford told me about an interesting guy the

other day," Flanagan said. "We hook up with him, we could make us some real money."

Hereford was a breeder of bear dogs with a small spread down around Humptulips. He owned several cows and a bull that he rented out for breeding purposes.

"Yeah? How?"

"Way I understand it, all we'd have to get would be gall-bladders and paws. Wouldn't have to go to all this extra work of skinning and taking the head."

"Who's the guy?"

"Beats me. Understand he's got outlets all over the world, China, Korea, places like that."

"Hereford tell you his name?"

"Nope."

"How'd he know about it?"

"Hell, Bill's always got his ear to the ground. You know that."

"Yeah, specially if it ain't legal."

They heard a pickup approaching in the distance.

"Here's Ed now," Majors said.

Ed Richter drove the pickup for them.

"Let's get this stuff together."

They stuffed the hide and head into an oversize burlap bag, then added the paws and gallbladder.

As Majors and Flanagan expected, the pickup rounded a bend in the old road with only its parking lights on. They knew their associate did not want to attract unwarranted attention any more than they did.

They both stood facing the oncoming vehicle. Just as the truck approached, its driver threw the gears into park, turned on the high beams, and slid out of the vehicle in one fluid motion.

"Cut it out, Ed," Flanagan called, blinded by the head-lights. "Kill those damn lights and give us a hand."

To their intense surprise, it was not Ed who replied.

"Hold it right there," came a cold, unfamiliar voice.

Flanagan squinted into the light. "Who in the hell are you?" he asked.

Remington pump shotgun drawn, a tall, uniformed woman moved out in front of the headlights.

"Jordan Tidewater, tribal sheriff for the Quinault Nation. You're both under arrest."

"Jee-sus H. Christ!" Majors swore disgustedly. "A damned woman."

His right hand moved slightly as if to grab the gun Flanagan knew Majors carried at the small of his back. Flanagan carried the same thing in the same place.

"Don't be a fool," Flanagan growled, suspecting his partner might be angry enough to go after the woman. "She's got a shotgun on us less than ten feet away."

Majors's hand fell to his side, his eyes fixed on the sheriff. He knew just as well as Flanagan a shotgun that close would blow out a nasty six- to eight-inch hole in anything it encountered, including his belly.

Jordan moved toward the men, remaining herself outside the circle of light.

"Lie down flat, both of you, with your arms and legs spread," she commanded.

After they had complied, she stepped behind the two prone men, released handcuffs from her belt, and cuffed each man separately.

Then she swiftly pulled a .38 snub-nosed pistol from inside the back waistband of each of the men's pants and threw the guns aside.

Jordan turned on the small tape recorder she always carried when she was on duty and read them their rights.

She got her camera and flash out of the truck and took in situ—in place—shots of the crime scene and the perpetrators.

"The hunting season for black bears in western Washington is August first through November first," she said. "According to my calendar it's the middle of April."

Neither prisoner responded.

"Just who are you men?" she asked.

Lifting his face from the dirt, Majors said with a lopsided grin, "Mr. A. Nonymous."

"Yeah, and I'm his brother, B. Nonymous."

She searched them but found no identification. "Okay, I hope you like the food in prison," she said.

Jordan knew these men would be indicted and sentenced. She'd caught them both in the act, and she suspected they were repeat offenders.

Black bear poaching was a "big game" violation as well as a gross misdemeanor punishable by a fine of up to one thousand dollars and imprisonment for a minimum of thirty days and maximum of one year.

Civil penalties would add another thousand to the fine; a second violation, jail time and a mandatory loss of hunting privileges for two years.

General criminal law in Washington allowed for up to a five-thousand-dollar fine for a gross misdemeanor.

Jordan knew it wasn't unusual for a judge to apply the maximum for a big game wildlife violation, especially if the violation was deliberate and/or a repeat situation—which she was sure this was. She suspected these two had killed a lot of bears. Cougars and eagles, too.

Jordan wondered if she should wait around and nail the driver, but decided not to because she knew he'd probably get off.

"Okay, gentlemen, on your feet," she ordered.

They both lay motionless on the ground.

She could well imagine what they were thinking: She was just one lone woman but they were two strong, although temporarily disabled, men.

They would simply wait for their buddy to show up, and warned by the presence of her vehicle, he would devise some plan of escape for all of them. They would be three men against one woman. Their license plates had been deliberately smeared with mud so that she could not identify the truck if they managed to escape.

She nudged Flanagan lightly on the hip with the toe of her boot. "I said get up!"

He groaned in mock pain but neither man moved.

She aimed the shotgun at one of Flanagan's knees.

"I've never had a kneecap shot off but I understand it's very painful," she said.

Flanagan looked up at her and smiled. "You know you wouldn't do a rotten thing like that."

"Try me," she said and blasted the underbrush near their heads.

Neither man moved.

"You two are really pissing me off," she said.

The men remained motionless and silent.

"Okay, if that's the way you guys want it."

Jordan walked to the front of her truck, unrolled the cable on the motorized winch, pulled it back to Flanagan, fastened the hook to his handcuffs, walked back to the truck, and yanked the starting lever to pull him in.

Yelling in protest, Flanagan was roughly dragged over bumpy, rocky, and muddy terrain until he reached, not under his own steam, Jordan's truck.

"Lady, you are one rough customer," he growled upon arrival, getting the words out between coughing and spitting out dirt as she helped him up.

"Only as rough as I have to be."

Opening the back door of the canopy, Jordan reached inside and pulled out a half-inch nylon rope through a pulley that was anchored in the top of the truck.

She wrapped the rope around Flanagan under his arms and pulled it up behind his neck. Using the shotgun as encouragement, she had him crawl into the back, where he sat huddled and bound, under the pulley.

Jordan strode back to his partner. "Okay now. Do you want to walk to the truck or shall I drag you in, too?"

Majors got to his feet without argument and hastily climbed in the back of the pickup to join Flanagan.

Jordan tied him, stuffed the end of the rope through a hole in the side of the canopy, pulled it tight, and wound it round and round a cleat on the outside of her truck.

"Nice and tight," she said. "That should keep you guys from falling around and getting hurt."

They both gave her sour looks.

She picked up the men's rifles and handguns, checked to make sure there were no bullets in the chambers, then placed the weapons in the cab of her truck.

She wrestled the gunnysack containing the evidence—bearskin and head, paws, gallbladder—into the back with the perpetrators, then slammed the canopy door shut.

She drove as fast as she could down the mountain and out of the wilderness.

As she did so, a gypsy sun arose, flaunting draperies of orange and scarlet and purple across the heavens.

4   In the same general area but out of hearing distance from where Jordan had just arrested the two poachers, a son of the highest places in the world waited to salute the dawn.

Arms upraised, he stood on the edge of a deep, forested ravine. Silhouetted as he was against the dawn sky, with mist steaming from the dark forested abyss below, he could have been an archangel just arrived on earth.

Or a devil, moments before descending back into hell.

5   Early that morning, when Jordan finally got home and went to bed, she lay quietly for a time mentally reviewing her night's activities.

She smiled, knowing she had made a good arrest. She had already reported the arrest and coming prosecution to the State Fish and Wildlife people and, out of courtesy, to Jasper Wright, the county sheriff.

And she thought a lot about Anson. She had seen him

once freshly shaven and discovered that he was a handsome man with great bones.

His body was lean and strong and he had what she'd
always considered intelligent hands. Hands that could do
anything, any kind of hard work or any kind of delicate
work. She wondered how he would touch a woman.

She closed her eyes and drifted off to sleep. For the first
time in her life she dreamed of cougars. Of turning into a
cougar.

Although her spirit animal was Cougar, Jordan had
never dreamed of one before.

The dream transformation was awkward and painful.
Although wearing the cougar's coat, she remained a
human female, her arms and legs squeezed uncomfortably
into the legs of the cougar, her human eyes peering out
through wide blue eyes that did not belong to her.

*The Indians of the Northwest Coast shared with their Eskimo
neighbors the belief that all animals, fish, and birds, possessed
a dual form.*

*The nucleus of their human form, the inner spirit, was somewhat
synonymous with thinking and the soul. Whenever the creature
decided to show its* inua, *it simply raised its face, beak, or wing
or parted its breast feathers. If it wished to assume human form,
it shed its feathers or fur coat and the transformation
was instantaneous.*

—JOSEPH H. WHERRY,
Indian Masks & Myths of the West

⚶

Chapter 3

1 Hannah McTavish had never seen so many foreigners all in one place in her life.

Lots of South Americans, Russians, as well as Chinese
and Koreans in addition to the contingent of American logging industry representatives.

I am hearing the Tower of Babel, she thought, listening
to the strange languages flowing about her. She wondered
why foreign languages always sounded to the untrained ear
as if they were being rattled off at tremendous speed.

The occasion was the eighty-fifth annual Northwest
Logging Congress being held this year at Lake Quinault
Lodge.

Outside in the forest service parking area were huge trailers filled with machinery and equipment exhibits from various manufacturers. Hundred-foot and more towers reached toward the sky, skidders and loaders sat quietly on their treads, as did helicopters designed for the lifting of felled timber.

Although logging had opened up just a little in the Pacific Northwest, most of the real buyers were from distant countries, intent on taking down their forests with the best of American machinery.

Hannah was nervously waiting in the lobby to great guests coming to her book party being held in one of the lodge's reception rooms.

All heads turned when two tall, fiercely handsome people, both with the striking features of ancient nobility, walked into the lobby.

The new arrivals were Jordan Tidewater and her twin brother, Paul Prefontaine, chief of police for the reservation city of Taholah.

Tonight, for this event, Jordan looked like a beautiful woman, not a police officer, although technically she was *always* on duty.

Slender, six feet tall, she wore long blue-green silk the color of the North Pacific sea when it shimmers in the sunlight.

Fastened snugly around Jordan's neck was a unique choker made from three strands of small, curved pieces of mother-of-pearl, prized since prehistoric times, and so-called because its iridescence lines the shells of pearl-bearing oysters and abalones.

Her short black curls were combed back and up, revealing her aristocratic profile with its high cheekbones.

Prefontaine himself, in uniform, was a big man, barrel-chested with lean hips and long, straight legs, who stood six and a half feet tall. Jet-black hair fell straight to his shoulders.

Prefontaine's eyes, like Jordan's, were large and dark, with pools of golden light; his cheekbones high. He had straight black eyebrows, smooth and heavy. His powerful nose overhung a wide, generous mouth.

Immediately behind these two, and even more impressive because of his age and his stature, strode their great-grandfather, Old Man Ahcleet, the ancient whaler and shaman, who was in his tenth decade.

Ahcleet's noble face was scored with a thousand fine lines and deeper indentations, an ancient scar on the bridge of his nose showing livid. He wore his long, graying hair in gleaming braids fastened with clasps made from dentalia, three-inch shells shaped like the tusks of a walrus, valuable currency in the old days.

Holding tightly to Old Man Ahcleet's hand was Jordan's son, eight-year-old Tleyuk, round-eyed with excitement, festive in brand-new jeans and a new sweatshirt with the distinctive Quinault design for salmon on its front.

Hannah hurried over to greet them. She wore a starkly simple dress of black silk with close-fitting long sleeves and a hemline just below her knee.

Her décolletage did more than hint at large, firm breasts. Sheer black silk stockings and black high heels completed her outfit.

Paul Prefontaine thought she looked good in black. Her fine porcelain skin glowed like a pearl on black velvet.

"Do I look like I'm in mourning?" Prefontaine heard Hannah laughingly ask Jordan, her luminous gray eyes glowing. Before Jordan could answer, Hannah flushed and smiled at Prefontaine.

They moved into the reception room, Hannah saying that the signs would guide the rest of her guests, although most of them had already arrived.

Hannah was a professional photographer whose work was being compared favorably with that of Ansel Adams in its clarity of line and use of light.

But Hannah's photography was unique in that it had the look of fine watercolors. One critic wrote: "Most photographers shoot what they see in nature—mountains, waterfalls, deserts, sunsets, oceans. Hannah McTavish shoots what *she* sees, which is very different. Her work is magical."

In private life Hannah was married to Michael McTavish, who owned Quinault Timber Company.

This was her first book. Copies of *Rain Forests of the Olympic Peninsula,* containing beautiful reproductions of Hannah's photographs and minimal typography, were on prominent display. Prefontaine saw that people were buying autographed copies at a satisfying rate.

Hannah busied herself making sure all the guests met her editor, Susan Greer from New York, a pencil-thin young woman with spiky hair, who invited everybody to the refreshment table but took no food herself, only sips of champagne from the fountain.

As Hannah laughed and talked with various well-wishers, Prefontaine noticed that she had thinned down at her waistline, probably for the occasion, but happily, he thought, nowhere else.

He remembered some of the other outfits he'd seen her in.

The business suit she was wearing when they discovered what they thought was her husband's dead body in the overturned loader at the logging site.

The kimono, and nothing else, when she'd received the first anonymous letter.

The long gown and robe the night he'd stayed in her living room guarding her from a mystical but very real harm.

The worn jeans and old sweatshirt that night on the beach when he'd told her he loved her and she had let him know the feeling was mutual.

He had no memory at all of what she'd been wearing the day he and Jordan had found Hannah's husband, Michael, barely alive but severely injured.

Then, shock had wiped everything out of his mind except the expression on Hannah's face when he'd told her about Michael. The look that cried plainer than any spoken words, "I love *you*! And I want *you*!"

But she had also loved her husband deeply. And even though she'd gone through much of the agonizing grief period of mourning, believing that Michael was dead, there'd been no future for Prefontaine with her except as friends.

Cautious friends at that, because Prefontaine still felt an overpowering attraction for her and he was certain she felt the same about him.

He also knew that Hannah would never be unfaithful to her husband, no matter how deep her longing for another man.

Even though two years had passed, Prefontaine still wanted her; he always would. He lusted after her.

He'd heard the Old Ones say that when a coupling was right, a matter of the spirit as well as the flesh, the overwhelming physical desire mellowed with time into an all-pervasive oneness instead of the previous lonely twoness.

Which, they said, was the best mating of all. Prefontaine wasn't sure about that; he was still young enough to settle for lust.

Perhaps not so unreasonably, Prefontaine sometimes wondered if he could ever forgive Hannah's husband for turning up alive.

And he knew one thing for damned sure: if Michael were any less of a man he'd have no compunction whatsoever about trying to take Hannah and the kids away from him.

But Michael was a good man who loved his family—and showed it—in every way a man could.

And here he was tonight standing in his rightful place beside his wife. Michael McTavish, the man who had returned from the dead.

Hannah and Michael's two children, Angus, twelve, and Elspat, ten, were in solemn attendance, dressed to the teeth, afraid to move for fear of wrinkling their new clothes or spilling something on themselves and thereby dishonoring their mother.

Prefontaine put aside his memories and his jealousy.

Smiling, he shook hands with Michael. "No tux?" he whispered with a wink.

"Hell, no. This damned starched shirt is bad enough," McTavish replied, running a finger inside his collar.

When McTavish turned his head to look across the room at a man standing alone by the fireplace, the terrible scars on the right side of his face and head from injuries he had suffered in a logging accident were revealed.

Sartorially speaking, this was the sort of gathering common to the area. People appeared in what each thought fashionable or—far more important—fashionably comfortable.

Fran Wilkerson, resident manager of the lodge, and her recently hired assistant, Joshua Little, moved about unobtrusively, making sure there was plenty of food on the refreshment tables.

"Peaches, go tell the chef those sandwich trays are a little low," Fran told Joshua. "And better check that champagne fountain while you're at it."

As Prefontaine walked up to Fran, Joshua sped away to obey Fran's command.

Joshua was one of those shining young men who move easily in their clothes; all tanned skin and white, gleaming teeth. The whites of his eyes were so white they were actually blue: just the kind of gleaming southern California good looks, Prefontaine thought, that most people in the Pacific Northwest, unreasonably enough, found highly suspicious.

"So how does he like your name for him?" Paul asked Fran.

"Peaches?" She looked surprised at what she thought was criticism. "He answers to it."

"Why don't you call him Josh?"

Fran turned to face the police chief. "Well, I'll tell you, Paul. When I first interviewed Joshua and found that only he, of all the other applicants, really was qualified, I said, 'You're a peachy-looking kid,' which he is and that's what he's been to me ever since."

Prefontaine moved away, quietly amused that Fran saw nothing chauvinistic about her nickname for Josh Little.

Ruby Campbell and his wife, Melisande, comparative newcomers to the area, had recently purchased a house overhanging the sea cliffs at Moclips.

Now they walked over to talk to Prefontaine, after first congratulating Hannah, buying an autographed copy of her book, meeting her editor, shaking hands with Michael, and helping themselves to goodies from the refreshment table.

Melisande was a splendid woman who, in her mature years, had developed a passion for working with oil paints.

Noticing the touches of cadmium yellow and hunter's green in her muted chestnut hair—which gave her the appearance of a turning autumn leaf—Prefontaine suspected that Ruby had rushed his wife out of her home studio barely in time to attend this function.

Ruby himself was memorable; a tall, erect man with hair and brows bleached by sea salt and sun, narrow eyes alert and wolf-pale, skin flushed with weather and health.

A deep round dimple in his smoothly shaven chin saved his face from looking too warlike. Tonight he wore handsomely fitted western-cut clothing and Justin boots.

Born in Kentucky, Ruby had spent his life after World War II starting businesses in the Pacific Northwest, industrial painting, commercial paving, the building of swimming pools, air-conditioning and heating, commercial insulation, heavy construction.

After Ruby built a business and it was paying off, he got bored, sold out, sometimes at a profit, sometimes not, and started another.

"He's an Aquarian," Melisande had confided in Paul. "And you know how *they* are—always with one foot in the next decade."

Everybody thought Ruby had come to the Olympic Peninsula to retire early and just have fun being a good old boy—hiking, hunting, fishing, boating, now and then shooting the breeze in local taverns.

Prefontaine and Jordan both, however, knew something about Ruby that no one else did, except his wife.

Ruby worked undercover as a timber cop, seeing that logging operators didn't take down more timber than they had contracted for.

Stealing extra trees was a game that loggers had been playing for years; something Prefontaine thought about every time he watched a truckload of logs going down the highway out of the Nation, each fifty-foot log section averaging from four to six thousand dollars and even much more, depending upon the kind of timber and its quality.

And Prefontaine was beginning to wonder if Ruby Campbell wasn't into something else, something even more dangerous.

Michael McTavish and Prefontaine walked out into the lobby. "Get a load of that guy by the fireplace, the one who looks like an eagle," McTavish said.

Glancing over, Prefontaine saw a tall, gaunt man with a sharp profile standing by himself, staring into the flames.

"What about him?" Prefontaine asked.

"He told me he's a cryptozoologist."

"What in the hell's that?"

"I thought he meant that he sold mausoleum vaults. But the guy said, no, he studies hidden animals."

Hidden animals.

Thoughts of Jordan's search for poachers flew into Prefontaine's mind. "Think I'll check him out."

Prefontaine moved casually toward the mammoth handhewn stone fireplace, greeting friends and acquaintances as he went. When he saw the stranger in full profile, he thought, *He does look like an eagle!*

Straight white hair slicked back to his shoulders from a narrow forehead, aquiline nose, glittering eyes, dark clothes like a mature eagle's plumage. He stood hunched over as if about to descend on a phantom salmon swimming upstream in the flames.

Prefontaine stuck out his hand and said, "Hello there, I don't believe we've met. I'm Paul Prefontaine, Quinault Nation."

The man straightened as if pulling his thoughts reluctantly out of the fire. He studied Prefontaine, then extended his hand. "Edward Eagleton."

When Eagleton asked about the social event going on in one of the reception rooms, Prefontaine told him about Hannah's book on the rain forest.

"Well, I'm afraid I can't relate to her excitement," Eagleton replied. "My own books, although they have fomented loud arguments and probably fisticuffs here and there, have never occasioned social activities."

"You're a published author?"

Eagleton nodded. "To save you embarrassment I'll tell you right now you've never read any of them."

"Well—"

"Unless you read books about science."

"Once in a while I do."

Eagleton did not reveal the names of the books he had authored but he did present his card. "I'm what is called a cryptozoologist."

Prefontaine looked at the card.

"In case you're wondering, and I know you are, it means the science of hidden animals."

"Hidden animals?"

"Yeah, it's a branch of zoology that focuses on the possibility that creatures like the Loch Ness monster, Bigfoot, and the yeti may actually exist."

"I see," Prefontaine said.

Eagleton smiled thinly. "I've heard that you Quinault believe in the existence of Bigfoot. Is that true?"

"Oh, I don't know. Different people believe in different things at different times. It's hard to keep up." Prefontaine looked at him levelly. "Welcome to the area, Mr.

Eagleton," he said, thinking as he walked away, *Good God! Another Bigfoot hunter.*

Jordan slipped away to the ladies' room. She thought it was turning out to be a great party, the kind where people talked interestingly more than they drank.

When she returned through the crowded lobby and into the reception room she noticed her brother in animated conversation with two men she had never seen before. Michael McTavish stood next to Prefontaine, in deep attention, arms folded across his chest.

"Jordan," her brother called, and motioned to her.

She walked over, smiling.

"These are two friends of Mike McTavish's. He just caught them coming out of the dining room," he said, then added, "I'll let him make the introductions."

"Jordan," McTavish said, "may I present Mr. Xavier Escoro and Mr. Lima Clemente? Gentlemen, Jordan Tidewater, Paul's sister. Sheriff Tidewater, I should say. Jordan is tribal sheriff for the Quinault Nation."

Immediately there were the usual flattering murmurs she had grown accustomed to regarding her appearance, especially when new males discovered that she was a law enforcement officer.

"Mr. Escoro," she said, extending her hand to the older of the two, a big, muscular personage with erupting white hair, wild black eyebrows, and a huge, flattened nose.

What a guy to meet on a dark night, she thought.

"I hope the men of this country appreciate beauty," Xavier Escoro said, bowing, his voice raspy. "Such beauty as yours, my dear, is rare." He released her hand but stood close, inhaling her presence.

Another voice, soft, seductive, broke in. "I may be forced to commit a heinous crime if you promise to arrest me for it yourself."

Xavier Escóro backed away as if relinquishing pride of position to a younger, more qualified contender.

Turning, Jordan's first impression was of two wide, ash-gray eyes looking at her out of darkness. Then she saw that standing before her was a man with a dark, brooding presence, almost brutally handsome, and slightly taller than her own six feet.

"I am Lima Clemente," he said quietly, taking her hand, not in a brisk businesslike handshake, but gently, as would a close friend. Or a lover.

She realized that his was an expressive face capable of showing the many human emotions: passion, hatred, greed, forgiveness, ferocity. And love.

He had a high, intelligent forehead, black eyebrows arched over those astonishing eyes, walnut-oil complexion, a full, sensuous mouth. Thick, straight black hair was cut above his collar. White teeth gleamed out of a friendly, dark smile.

As he touched her hand, the inside of Jordan's body pulsed and moved and she experienced a sudden flood of erotic feeling—womanly feeling—of such strength that for a moment she trembled. And thought triumphantly: *I'm still alive!*

Lima Clemente tightened his grip infinitesimally as if to say, "I understand. I feel it, too," but she knew that was her imagination.

Jordan pulled her hand away slowly.

McTavish was telling the Chileans how he obtained permits to cut timber on reservation lands.

When he had finished explaining the procedure, he said to Jordan and Paul, "Xavier and Lima are partners in a logging machinery and equipment business in Santiago. They're up here to look at new lines, meet our loggers, see how we do things."

"We want to study every aspect of your industry," Xavier Escoro rumbled. "Chile has huge forests that are starting to come down. In fact, some of your unemployed loggers here and in Oregon are moving down to Chile to go to work. We intend to sell our people the most efficient logging equipment available in the world. We're putting on a logging congress of our own next year."

Jordan noticed that her brother, who had remained silent, was studying the two Chileans with great interest.

"Let me see if I can get out of here," McTavish said impatiently, then looked across the lobby at Hannah.

When he caught his wife's attention, he signaled with his right hand and raised eyebrows; his unspoken question: *Can I leave and talk some business?*

She smiled and nodded her permission.

"Good, I've done my duty," he said, obviously relieved. "Let's go on into the bar and I'll buy us some real drinks. Come on with us, Jordan."

Jordan declined, saying she wanted to join Hannah.

As the four men walked across the lobby toward the bar, she studied Lima Clemente, noticing that he moved with the easy grace of someone who doesn't need to prove much of anything to anybody. Yoga or karate can sometimes give a person that quality, she reflected. So can money. Lots and lots of money.

He was thick and strong in the chest. There was something about his long legs that made her think he could outrun a bear if he had to. She suspected that those strong, beautiful hands of his could be extremely quick and lethal. She wondered how they touched women.

Abruptly Lima Clemente left the small group of men and returned to Jordan's side.

"I just had a thought, Sheriff Tidewater," he said. "Or, more exactly, a favor to ask."

"And what is that, Mr. Clemente?"

"Tomorrow Xavier has business of his own elsewhere. May I accompany you on your patrol, see how your people have replanted their forests? Would that be an inconvenience to you?"

She found his quiet voice extremely pleasant. And since she could not think of one reason to deny him, they arranged to meet in front of the lodge around nine the next morning.

When Lima Clemente turned to rejoin the other men, Jordan saw that his hair was not short as she had thought. It was only pulled back from his face, caught at the base of his skull, and fell from there in a shining black silk rope down his back.

Never before in Jordan's life, not even with Roc in the beginning, had she felt such sharp, hot, sudden physical desire for a man.

And she felt something else, an emotion she could put no name to as yet.

2   When Jordan came into the kitchen at home in Taholah the next morning she found her great-grandfather holding a shot glass in his right hand and telling Tleyuk stories about the old days of The People.

"Animals could change their forms whenever they wanted to," Old Man Ahcleet was saying.

"How?" Tleyuk asked, swallowing a mouthful of hot cereal, then putting down his spoon and carefully watching his great-great-grandfather.

"When they wished to become people they just pushed up the muzzle or beak in front of their heads and all at once they changed into manlike beings."

"And then what happened?" Tleyuk asked.

Jordan sat down at the table, suspecting by Tleyuk's expression that he longed to change right then into something four-footed or with wings so he wouldn't have to go to school. Or, at the very least, if he must go, arrive as a miraculous being.

"The muzzle—or the beak, in the case of birds—remained like a cap on top of their heads. It might even be removed altogether. If they took it off, though, they had to be very careful not to lose it."

"What would happen if they lost it?"

Ahcleet took a sip from the shot glass. Since he'd turned ninety he found that a little Jack Daniel's every morning made him feel more like himself.

"Think about it. Suppose you were really a wolf and

you'd become a boy for a day or two. Just to see what it was like. You wanted to return to your wolf family but you couldn't find your muzzle. You'd be stuck the rest of your life as a lonely, disharmonious person."

"I think we know one or two of those ourselves," Jordan commented.

"If they still had their muzzles or beaks, then how did they turn back?" Tleyuk asked.

"It's very simple. When they wanted to become animals or birds again, all they had to do was pull their animal faces back down."

Tleyuk looked out the kitchen window at clouds of sea-gulls hovering over their front yard. "Can they still do that, Grandfather?"

"Things have changed. Now only a few can transform." Ahcleet sighed and rubbed his face. "It's time for school, Sparky."

He reached over and wiped milk off the boy's mouth with a paper napkin. "Remember, if you see an animal or a bird that acts strange, stay away from it because it will be a person in disguise."

Both Ahcleet and Jordan kissed Tleyuk before he grabbed his lunch bag and raced out of the house wearing a very determined expression.

"How much do you want to bet he comes home this afternoon wanting to know who the crazy-acting dog up the street really is?"

Ahcleet grinned. "I'll tell him it's Old Woman Scatt."

"Grandfather—" Jordan warned, then laughed out loud.

She would soon leave for day patrol duty. Her shifts varied so that prospective evildoers could not know in advance where she'd be on the reservation at any given time.

"Anything new on why the Klokwalle is here?" Old Man Ahcleet asked as he buttered a cinnamon roll.

Jordan smiled but did not look at Ahcleet, afraid that her great-grandfather might read her mind, riotous all night and still this morning with voluptuous thoughts of the man with the ash-gray eyes.

"What about those two strangers last night?" he asked.

"Strangers? There were a lot of strangers in the lodge last night."

"I meant those men from Chile you and Paul were talking to."

"Oh, those two," she replied casually, as if she'd forgotten their existence.

"I am not so old that I cannot remember the fever in the blood," Ahcleet said quietly, then added, "Be very careful, La'qewamax."

"We don't even know them, Grandfather."

He nodded. "Good. It's best to keep it that way. They are strangers."

"Until we meet, we are all strangers, Grandfather."

The old man did not reply.

It was true that she had been uncomfortable with the older man, probably because he was so physically intimidating.

But with the younger—Lima Clemente, his name was— her response was quite different. She had been instantly drawn to him, feeling a genuine liking and a raw sexual desire for the first time in years.

Did her body respond this way because it sensed that Lima Clemente, being a foreigner, wouldn't be around long enough for a continuing relationship to develop, one where she'd be forced to make a commitment, one that could end by disappointing or hurting her?

Was she experiencing a fleeting sense of fear? Psychic warning signals from her subconscious about the dangers of falling in love again?

But Jordan knew in her deepest heart that the attraction was something very special, very different, about Lima Clemente himself.

3   Outside, Jordan walked into a dazzling morning alive with sunlight and sweeping westerly winds, just the sort of Quinault day that made her feel good to be alive.

Like the rest of The People, Jordan knew she was extremely sensitive to sea and seasons. In times past, weather forecasting and weather sorcery were essential. For countless ages her people had successfully navigated the raging North Pacific.

She smiled when she remembered her great-grandfather talking about old-time fishermen who tasted the sea to determine if whales were about. And old women who sold winds.

Before getting into her truck she stood and watched great greenish blue ocean waves, shot with sunlight, curl high, then crash on shore with impassioned ardor; plunging, powerful, moving in swiftly at fifty miles an hour, streaming white mares' tails blowing in their wakes.

Green-ankled sea stacks offshore were splashed with spume and white bird droppings. Crying seabirds floated over their pinnacles like drunken performers trying to get their act together while sea lions barked and frisked at their feet.

And now to work, to see Lima Clemente again, she told herself, breathing in deeply. First, she would pick him up at the lodge, then check things out on South Shore Road.

The lake itself belonged to the Quinault Nation and was roughly surrounded on the southeast by the Olympic National Forest and on the north by the Olympic National Park.

After that she'd go back into the reservation wilderness where she had arrested the two poachers, see if any important physical evidence had been left behind.

She entered the Moclips Highway, drove the twenty miles to U.S. 101, then went left and drove until she came to the South Shore turnoff.

4   Lima Clemente was waiting for her on the semi-circular cobblestone driveway in front of the lodge.

"A good morning to you, Jordan," he greeted her as he climbed in the passenger side of her truck, his arms loaded with camera gear and a large basket. "I can't thank you enough for your courtesy."

"The pleasure's all mine, Mr. Clemente. These long patrols can get pretty lonely."

"I've taken the liberty of having the lodge kitchen pack us lunch." He set the basket down on the floor between his legs. "I now am entirely in your hands."

Would that that were literally true! Jordan told herself, hiding a smile, then glanced over at him as he slammed the truck door shut. "We'll go up to the end of South Shore Road first," she said.

"I brought a camera. I hope that's permitted?"

She nodded. "Mr. Clemente, there's nothing around here you can't photograph."

"Jordan, may I make a suggestion?"

"Sure. As long as it's not that you drive. This wheel must remain firmly in my hands. I am the officer in charge."

He joined her in laughter.

"Nothing that drastic, I assure you," he said. "You seem to have no objection to my calling you by your first name. 'Mr. Clemente' sounds so formal. It would please me if you call me Lima."

"Lima it is," she smilingly agreed as they stopped for a herd of elk leisurely crossing the road.

Clemente admired the size, obvious excellent health, and gleaming brown and black coats of the huge animals, then asked if they could be hunted at any time of the year.

"Could I, for example, shoot for our dinner tonight that haughty bull right there with the magnificent rack?"

"I hope you are not carrying a gun," she said. "And no, you could not."

"I was just trying to make a joke." Clemente gestured with his hands. "But not a very good one, I see."

When the last elk had run across the road, Jordan stepped on the gas and said, "To answer your question, there's no season for non-Indians on the reservation but we Quinault can hunt from July 1 to December 31 on the reservation. With the exception of black bear, that is. Quinaults are allowed to hunt bear year-round. This is because of the damage they can do to second growth forest. Some feel there is a larger bear population now than in the past because the large amount of logging has created more brush areas with more available food. Also, some feel that off-reservation hunting pressure has driven more bear onto the reservation."

Her hands tightened on the steering wheel and her mouth firmed. "I get mad as hell when I find a dead elk with only the back strap and hams taken, all the rest of the animal left to rot."

"Are those the people you search for in your patrols, the ones who take the elk?" he asked.

"I catch that kind every once in a while. But the ones I'm really looking for are the big-time poachers. They kill bear, cougar, eagles."

He raised his black eyebrows. "I'm surprised to hear there are criminals in a beautiful place like this."

"We've got them," she said grimly. "I nailed a couple just the other night, literally red-handed with the evidence."

"And what had those men killed?"

"A black bear."

"How big an animal was it?"

"It probably weighed around seven hundred pounds."

"Do you like the bears, Jordan? Do you feel sympathy for them?"

She wondered how she could explain her ancestral feelings about wild animals to this stranger and decided that she could not.

Instead, she said, "I have seen a black bear sitting propped against a fir tree, staring out to sea. Who am I to say it doesn't watch and enjoy the sunsets?"

He studied her profile. "What kind of punishment will those men be facing?"

"At least a year in jail plus a five-thousand-dollar fine for each of them."

"With sanctions like that, poaching hardly seems worth the effort."

"It's worth the effort, all right, if you can get away with it. We caught one man last year who had cleared over two million dollars in wildlife parts in one year, all taken from the park, the national forest, and reservation lands. And that was only the two million we could prove."

"What do poachers do with the parts?"

"There are huge worldwide markets for bald eagle beaks, claws, feathers, bear paws and claws, teeth, and gallbladders. And the velvet from deer and elk antlers."

"Feathers?"

"Bald eagle feathers," she explained, "are spiritual agents of great power. And there's a lot of lucrative trafficking in eggs and young birds not yet able to fly. They're taken from their natural nests in the wild and upon reaching suitable size are shipped to countries in the Middle East, such as Saudi Arabia where peregrine falcons are sold for ten thousand dollars and the prize white yearling gyrfalcon for as much as a hundred thousand."

"And the velvet on deer and elk antlers? What is done with that?"

"Shortly after refugees from Southeast Asia reached this country the demand for velvet increased because those folks believe it has aphrodisiac qualities. I imagine because it's so rich in blood supply."

"What about the bears? Their paws and gallbladders?"

"The Orientals make soup out of the paws. And they believe the gallbladders are a powerful aphrodisiac. The galls are also used in Asian medicine to treat liver cancer."

"Are you talking about important money, Jordan?"

She looked over at him as she drove. "I don't know what you consider important money, Lima. But I can tell you this.

Dried bear galls are more precious than gold. They bring twenty thousand dollars each in Hong Kong. And they can be smuggled through customs in a person's pocket."

"Why are the Orientals looking to your bears, Jordan?"

"It's very simple. They've almost hunted their own to extinction."

"It sounds like you have quite a campaign going against these criminals."

Jordan sighed. "We're so understaffed it's pitiful. Sometimes I think we're fighting a losing battle."

By this time they had arrived at Graves Creek Trailhead where the South Shore Road ended. They got out of the truck and walked across a footbridge supported by two sixty-foot lengths of cedar, each cedar log five feet through.

"This is the beginning of the hike into Enchanted Valley," she said.

"How far away is that?"

"About thirteen miles."

"And what is there to warrant such a beautiful name?"

She smiled. "It's also called the Land of Ten Thousand Waterfalls."

"Is it possible that someday we could take that hike tógether, Jordan?"

She looked at him. "How long will you be here, Lima?"

"As long as necessary."

"It's possible. Let's wait and see what happens."

When they walked back to the truck, they stopped to study two posted signs. The first sign read:

WARNING—COUGARS IN AREA
- Remain Calm
- DO NOT RUN
- Stand and Face It
- Be Assertive—Wave Your Arms—Speak Firmly
- Keep Children Under Close Supervision

- Report All Sightings & Encounters to the Nearest
  Ranger Station

"What an odd sign," Clemente said. "How many strangers to this forest, upon seeing a wild cougar, would have the courage to stand and face such a beast?"

"Would you run, Lima?"

"Most assuredly. I would run away faster than anyone else."

"Then you would be caught and played with. I should caution you that cougar play is intensely rough."

He put his arm lightly around her shoulders. "Well, perhaps I can find some other form of play that will leave my body intact. Do you think I might, Jordan?"

She moved casually out from under his arm without replying and walked over to study the second posted sign:

MISSING—LAST SEEN GRAVES CREEK AREA
Sherry Lyne Adams
Weight: 70 lbs. Height: 4 feet
Age 11, Blond Hair Cut Like a Boy's
Green Eyes, Freckled Complexion
If Seen, Please Contact National Park Service
206-555-4501 or 911

Clemente came up behind her. "An unusual country," he said. "Cougars on the pathways and children lost in the forest. It sounds like an old fairy tale."

Jordan stared at the sign, left elbow cupped in her right hand, chin supported by her left hand.

"Where are you, Sherry Lyne?" she said softly.

"Do you suppose she chased a cougar and the cougar caught her?" Clemente asked.

Jordan shook her head and headed for her truck.

5   When they stopped by the river to have a picnic
    lunch, they sat on a moss-covered fallen tree. Here
the shoreline was comprised of thousands of rounded river
rocks, very clean and so smooth and shifting they were
nearly impossible to walk on without slipping and falling.

Lima Clemente got out his camera gear and took several
photographs of Jordan in spite of her laughing objections.

The lodge kitchen had prepared roast chicken breast
sandwiches with lettuce, cucumbers, honey mustard, and
mayonnaise. There were thermos containers of coffee and
hot tea, and huckleberry pie with whipped cream in a separate cooled container.

As they ate, Lima Clemente told Jordan about his business and his day-to-day activities in Santiago.

"It is a very busy city with many cultural affairs."

"It's near the sea, isn't it?" she asked.

He smiled. "Only sixty miles. But sixty miles in my
country is not like sixty miles in yours. Beyond Santiago
itself we do not have your beautiful highways. To get to the
sea would require at least a day, more likely two days, of
very difficult travel."

"You're not married?" she asked suddenly.

"No," he replied. "I've never married."

"I'm surprised."

"And why is that, Jordan?"

She looked at him steadily. "Because you are an
extremely attractive man."

"Thank you," he said simply. He did not ask about her
marital status.

6   Later in the day, when they arrived at the place
    where Jordan had apprehended the two poachers,
she saw immediately that the scavengers of the forest had
been busy.

The skinned bear carcass, minus the head and paws, and

nearly picked apart, was crowned by several large, black, disputatious ravens.

With great reluctance, the ravens retreated to the limbs of a nearby salmonberry bush from which vantage point they carefully scrutinized the humans' every movement.

Lima Clemente changed the lens on his camera, then photographed the ravens as they voiced their objections to any human presence.

When he had finished to his satisfaction and was once again replacing the lens cap—Jordan wondered why he bothered to put the cap on and off so many times; probably he was a very careful person—he told her that in Chile people believed ravens possess their excellent eyesight because they eat human eyes.

Jordan was about to reply when she spotted a narrow, fresh trail leading off the old logging road where the bear had been killed, one she had not noticed the night of the arrest.

After examining the broken leaves and stems of the underbrush, she knew that the trail had been made within the last forty-eight hours.

"Can you read trails?" Clemente asked when he noticed what she was doing.

She nodded. "I'm going to follow this. You can come along or wait for me here."

"I'll join you. You might run into some kind of trouble out there."

She looked at him and raised an eyebrow. He smiled, winked, and followed her, camera held at the ready, lens cap firmly in place.

After hiking a couple hundred yards, Jordan discovered that the trail ended at a cliff whose steep walls were heavily forested. Far below she heard the chatter of a small, busy stream at the bottom of the chasm.

On the near side of the deep ravine lay an enormous granite boulder, partially hidden by rampant undergrowth.

She knew that the only granite to be found in the Olympics, and then only at elevations up to thirty-five hundred feet, was in the form of huge boulders like this one, carted down from the north by the movements of gigantic ice floes during the last Ice Age, then left behind like cast-off baubles when the ice retreated. Many were in strangely grotesque shapes.

Suddenly the smell of wild animal reached Jordan's nostrils, a smell that was nearly visible; a wild, heavy smell, warm and raw and fearful, the sweeter, somehow, for being savage.

When she noticed an almost imperceptible flicker at the periphery of her vision, she forced herself to become quiet, willing every particle in her body to absolute stillness, moving only her eyes.

A female cougar stared at her from a fallen log near the foot of the boulder, a gorgeous animal, a study in shades of apricot and raw umber.

Great blue eyes, unusual in a cougar, looked deep into Jordan's human eyes, one intellect communicating with another.

And then the cougar was gone as if she had never been there at all.

Cougar? At this time of day? Cougars seldom showed themselves. Cougars were invisible.

Had Lima Clemente seen it?

When Jordan looked back, she saw that he was quite a distance behind her, apparently busy again with his camera.

She was pleased that he had not seen the cougar; it was special, for her eyes only. When he caught up with her, she did not mention it.

Rays from the afternoon sun poured through the upward curving branches of a huge Douglas fir, lighting a pile of ashes about ten feet from the base of the tree trunk.

"Odd place for a campfire," she murmured.

"Why is it odd, Jordan?" Lima Clemente asked.

She squatted down to examine the ashes. "Whoever made this fire was not a casual hiker, not around here."

"Who do you think it could have been?"

"Someone who knew exactly what he was doing and why."

"Isn't this reservation land?"

"It is."

"Maybe some of your people had a picnic."

"Impossible," she said, not explaining to Clemente why no Quinault would come here.

Up a steep incline from where she now stood, Jordan could see the bleached, jagged cedar stump that marked entry into the burial ground of the Seatco.

Holy ground. Forbidden ground.

She knew she must leave right now and take Lima Clemente, the stranger, the outsider, with her.

The sun moved lower.

In its lengthening rays Jordan saw something red glistening in the hollow of the boulder.

Something fresh, something that couldn't possibly be what it looked like at first glance.

Jordan caught hold of her medicine pouch through the cloth of her shirt.

Clemente suddenly rushed past her, moving up to the boulder in long strides. "Don't come any closer!" he called back.

For one terrified moment Jordan felt a stab of overwhelming dread. She hesitated, thinking seriously about turning around and leaving, not investigating any further. She did not want to find out what lay before her.

But because she was a police officer, she had no choice. She started to walk toward the boulder.

"Stay away, Jordan!" Clemente ordered, his voice strangely harsh.

When she kept coming, Clemente grabbed her arms. "Do not look at that! It is not for your eyes!"

"Let go of me!"

His grip tightened.

Jordan made a swift, smooth movement and Lima Clemente, showing amazement, sprawled on the ground.

"Don't ever do that to me again," she said.

He got to his feet, camera swinging from around his neck. "Forgive me, Jordan. At least let me help."

"You want to help me, Lima?"

"I do."

"Then just stay the hell where you are. Don't get in my way again."

"In my country we protect women."

She looked at him steadily. "You're not in your country. You're in my country. Now, please, leave me alone to do my job."

The earth never tires,
The earth is rude, silent, incomprehensible
at first,
Nature is rude and incomprehensible
at first,
Be not discouraged, keep on, there are divine things
well envelop'd,
I swear to you there are divine things more beautiful
than words can tell.

—WALT WHITMAN,
"To Foreign Lands"

Chapter 4

1   The thing in the curious hollowed-out boulder was
    the severed head of a young Indian child.

Jordan stared for horror-struck moments, then stumbled
away and vomited. As if from a great distance she heard
Lima Clemente's voice, "Jordan, what is it? Let me help
you. Please, Jordan."

Whispering a Calling-on-Guardians prayer, she held out
her arm in a gesture forbidding him to come any closer.

For a time all she could see behind her closed eyelids
were memory flashes of Tleyuk calling happily, "Watch
me, Mom! Come and watch me!" as he did whirlies on his

new bike. Then the grinning horror in the crevice superimposed itself over her little boy's smiling face.

Old Man Ahcleet's words burned in her brain: *"Something is coming. Something for which you will need more than human courage."*

How right he was! Although she had not yet performed the painful and fear-inspiring ritual of *tamañois,* or religious power, required for the Klokwalle's help, she believed that her own guardian spirit—Sta'dox!wa, the most powerful of shamanistic supernaturals and a spirit that she owned—would aid her now if she proved herself courageous.

When she wiped her face and stood up, Jordan saw that Lima Clemente remained at a distance, watching her.

"What is it?" he called out, then added, "I am here, Jordan, for whatever you need. I wait but I will not interfere."

"Thank you, Lima."

Stark realization came: *This is a crime scene.*

Jordan determined that no matter how horrible the details, she must force herself to function competently.

The boulder, which now seemed to Jordan to be a sacrificial altar, and the area of ground around it, littered with fir needles and forest debris, looked like an outdoor abattoir. There were several great gushes of blood and a number of smaller gouts.

She saw that the child's head had been completely cut off and his torso jammed sideways under the head. Both head and torso were positioned inside the boulder as if the child had been formally and carefully executed.

When she knelt to make a closer examination, Jordan realized that in addition to the general savagery of the crime scene, there was something very strange about the severed head.

She soon saw what it was.

The entire facial skin had been meticulously scalped off and loosened, then pushed up above the head, where it hung partially over the skinned face like a limp, ghoulish mask . . . as if someone had been trying to pull it back down.

Again Old Man Ahcleet's words sounded in her brain:

"When they wished to become people they just pushed up the muzzle or beak in front of their heads. When they wanted to become animals or birds again, all they had to do was pull their animal faces back down."

Two questions formed in her mind: Had an Indian with mental problems thought he was helping this child to become an animal or, thinking he had already become an animal, been attempting to return him to his humanity?

Could the child be one of Tleyuk's schoolmates? She could not recognize the face because of the careful savagery done to it.

She knew this was going to be a very unusual criminal investigation. The FBI would be in charge, of course, since this was a felony committed on Native American lands. Jordan was certain the background of this crime lay deep within ancient beliefs of the Pacific Northwest.

She took several calming breaths, feeling her guardian spirit very close, and then got down to business.

"Whatever it was that happened, happened right here on this spot," she told herself, and began to mentally review police procedure protocols.

The first step was to always try to save the life of the victim—to the exclusion of concern about the crime scene—even if a suspect was at that very moment seen running away.

"The victim must always be your number one concern," her instructor at the police academy had drummed into her head.

She didn't have to worry about suspects running away: there were certainly none around this wilderness. Not now.

If the victim was beyond hope, like this poor child, she must next verify death. She laughed bitterly.

Verify death? Under these circumstances there was no question about death. She could verify it just by looking.

"The body cannot be moved until the coroner arrives," she heard in her mind. "Do not touch the body until the coroner gets there."

Jordan knew that the coroner was the number one law enforcement officer in the county, ranking even over the

sheriff. A miffed coroner could cause a lot of trouble if
established protocols were not followed, even file a com-
plaint against her.

No body deceased under suspicious circumstances
could be moved until it had been released by the coroner.

Those were the rules.

But how could she follow them precisely? How could
she leave this lonely child in order to find an area where
her truck phone would function and she could call in?

Should she send Lima Clemente out to make the call—
or leave him on guard here while she went out?

She realized she could do neither. He was a foreign
national. His presence, if it were known, could only com-
plicate matters.

So what to do?

The rules rang in her mind: stabilize the body, protect
the crime scene, keep dogs and cats and other people
away . . .

She shook her head.

What in God's name was she thinking about? This was
not a normal crime scene in a dwelling in a city. This was
a ghastly ritual murder committed in a vast forest. No fear
of pet dogs or cats or curious neighbors getting in the way
up here.

There were, of course, natural predators: cougars, one of
which she had recently glimpsed, and coyotes; bears, too,
just coming out of hibernation and starving.

She saw both cougar and raven tracks in the softer parts
of the ground but there were no indications that a cougar
or any other four-footed wild creature had touched this
child. The ravens, of course, were different. They had
eaten the eyes.

Since she obviously could not leave the body, she would
do what she could to collect or preserve any evidence lying
around.

Focusing her mind sternly on investigative procedures,
Jordan walked back to her truck, passing Lima Clemente
as she did so. Again he quietly offered his help.

"Not now," she said, preoccupied.

"What is out there, Jordan?"

"A butchered child."

Then, noticing the look of horror on his face and realizing she had been rude to a professional acquaintance of Michael McTavish, who was logging on the reservation, she asked him, "Lima, I'll tell you about it later. Would you be more comfortable waiting in the truck?"

"Thank you, but I'll stay right here. Should you need me, I'll be instantly available."

"Thank you, Lima. Maybe you can help me later. Right now I have things I must do first."

"I understand. But remember that I am at your service should you need me."

She needed him, Jordan thought. Needed him—or someone—to hold her while she screamed out her terror at what had happened; to take charge so she could creep away and bury her head in her pillow, refusing to think about people in the world who were capable of doing such savage things to anyone—let alone a small child. A child like her own. She never wanted to become so hardened that scenes of horror did not move her.

She sighed, knowing that in spite of all her law enforcement training, she would forever be a woman with a woman's basic needs for comfort and protection. Or hoped she would.

But also with a woman's strengths. In the old days it was the women who cared for the dead.

2   Jordan went back to the truck and picked up her camera with strobe, several rolls of film, and her CSI, her crime scene kit.

Resembling a weatherproof briefcase, the kit held four sizes of both plastic and paper bags plus twelve regular grocery bags; various bottles, forceps, and vials for blood and other fluids.

Making a couple of trips, she brought a plastic ground cover and several cardboard boxes of various sizes to the boulder.

Back at the murder site, Jordan wrote down the case number and date—93/AK for all federal numbers; since the murder had obviously happened on the reservation it would be a federal case—then added Victim A-13-C.

She established a crime scene area by pounding small wooden stakes into the ground radiating out thirty feet from the boulder, then fastened yellow tape to the stakes.

Even though it was a bright afternoon, there were numerous shadowed areas because of the trees and bushes, so Jordan took all photographs using the strobe.

First she took hand-held shots from outside the perimeter of the crime scene, aiming in.

Next she conducted a walk-through, mentally dividing the crime scene into smaller areas, closely examining everything within each of those areas, shooting as she went. She took each photograph at sharp right angles.

And in one of these areas she found a small hand, crudely chopped from the wrist, partially covered with forest debris. She marked the spot and took camera shots of the small remains.

Noticing several partial human footprints, Jordan screwed her camera onto a tripod, then shot the footprints while aiming the camera straight down, first placing a ruler for size reference and an ID card next to each print.

This procedure was time-consuming because she also wrote a description of every detail pictured in each shot. After the photography was completed, Jordan drew a rough diagram of the area.

She knew from her training that at least half of the truly productive work at a crime scene was documentation. And she also knew that the more agencies that got involved, the greater the chance of catching the murderers.

Jordan wondered if the perpetrators had done the murder on the reservation knowing that the location could cause jurisdictional problems with its resultant delays.

She also wondered why she felt so certain there was more than one murderer. *Probably because it feels like ritual murder,* she told herself.

Using her Swiss army knife, she slit the ground cloth into one smaller and one larger section.

After putting on latex gloves, she swallowed hard and removed the child's head from the crevice.

Clinically, she noted that the head felt cold and was turgid from rigor. While there were no maggots in evidence, there were a number of beetles in and around the head.

The loosened facial skin, dried out along the cut edges, was partially glued back to the face by dried blood. The eyes were gone.

As she held the severed head in her gloved hands, Jordan experienced a flood of emotions not her own.

First she felt love. Then fear, terror, a brief blaze of shock and pain, and then, curiously, a peaceful sense of wonder followed by comforting darkness.

Focusing all of her psychic energies, she kept holding the head, trying to read something identifiable in the welter of feelings she was picking up. If only she could glimpse a sense of the child's killers!

She suspected that if she took off the latex gloves, placed her bare hands on the mutilated face, and looked directly into the empty eye sockets, she would receive a clearer mental picture. But she could not bring herself to do so.

Jordan placed the head in a large plastic bag—keeping it open at the top—put the plastic bag inside a grocery-sized paper bag, then loosely wrapped it in the smaller piece of ground cloth.

When Jordan moved the torso, the genitals showed that the child was a boy. And she saw that he had suffered even more damage than decapitation.

His heart had been cut out. His legs, arms, and hands had been hacked off and were missing, except for the small hand she had found.

Blood had flowed down from the neck stump over the body, and from the stumps of arms and legs. There was little blood from the crude incision in the chest, causing her to suspect that the heart had been removed after death.

The skin of the torso was white, without the usual dark spots from cyanosis, because so much blood had drained from the corpse.

"Poor little broken boy," she whispered. "Where is the rest of you?"

Jordan knew that the bladder and bowels are frequently—not always—voided at death, especially a violent one. But she could find no visible sign or odor of urine or feces either in the area or on the body. Nor was there any clothing.

She wrapped the torso as she had the head, walked carefully back to where the hand lay, wrapped it appropriately, then called to Lima Clemente to come forward, cautioning him not to step within the staked crime scene area.

"These are the remains," she said. "Please put them in the back of my truck."

He nodded gravely.

She handed him the three wrapped body part packages one at a time and he carried them with great care to her power wagon.

When Jordan examined the inside of the crevice with a flashlight, she noticed several areas of slick stone interspersed with growths of moss.

She removed a small brush and vial from her forensic case. Dipping the brush into the vial, she dusted the clear stone areas with a pale powder, very much in consistency with the ash that came from Mount Saint Helens when it erupted.

Squinting as she worked, she managed to lift several prints showing clear ridges and swirls with her fingerprint tape. She then attached each piece of tape to an individual three-by-five-inch index card.

Outside of the crevice, Jordan covered all gouts and splashes of blood on the ground, as well as the several par-

tial human footprints, with opened upended boxes to iso-
late and preserve them for subsequent coroner's office
forensic examination. She weighted each box down with
rocks to prevent it from blowing away.

3   Jordan did not speak all the while she drove Lima
     Clemente back to the lodge. He also remained
silent. Before he got out of the truck, he leaned over and
gently kissed her cheek.

Her eyes filled with tears.

"I am so very sorry," he said.

She held on to the steering wheel, tight, with both hands
and stared straight ahead. "Why would anyone do such a
terrible thing to a child?"

"Could it be a racist crime?" he asked. "I know there is
that problem in this country."

"I have no idea."

"Perhaps there is a reason beyond your present compre-
hension," he said.

"There is no sane reason for such insane cruelty."

He studied her tearstained face, touched her cheek with
his fingertips.

"I must see you again. We have much to discover about
one another. Do you suppose that can be arranged?"

She looked over at him, knowing she would need to talk
about this terrible experience later with someone who was
not family or friend.

And certainly not with a fellow law enforcement officer
who, because of too much homicide experience, could feel
only the cynicism of a professional.

She needed to talk about it with Lima Clemente because
he had been there with her. And he was not a professional
for whom dealing with death was part of a day's business.

"Yes," she whispered.

4   Jordan stopped at an outdoor public telephone to
     call Hunter Kleoh, agent in charge of the FBI
office in Aberdeen. She did not want the call going through
her regular channels.

"Have you notified the coroner?" Kleoh asked, after
hearing the details.

When Jordan explained the circumstances, Kleoh suggested she come into Aberdeen. She could call from his
office, he said; then they would go together and deliver the
remains to the medical examiner.

She told him that she would call the county sheriff right
away.

5   That night in Ahcleet's old house by the sea,
     Jordan did not sleep in her own bed. She did not
sleep at all.

As the sea winds rose outside, she lay restless in
Tleyuk's bed, one arm around her young sleeping son, the
other clutching a worn old doll made of a bundle of soft
cedar inner bark folded double and tightly wrapped just
below the doubled portion to form head and neck, a doll
that was ancient when Old Man Ahcleet had given it to her
when she was three years old.

Thinking about the murder scene, she realized for the
first time that something had been missing. Something
very important.

The scent of evil.

In spite of the horridness of the act, she had not felt any
sense of malice or hatred. Was it possible that in some way
beyond her understanding the killing was an act of love?

But that was impossible. It must have been done by
some deranged Indian who needed to be caught fast and
cared for before he could harm anybody else.

She listened for messages from her guardian spirit, from

her own subconscious, but all she heard were the crashing discords of wind and sea.

Then, like a resolving harmony, came Lima Clemente's soft words: *"We have much to discover about one another."*

And remembering, she was comforted by the genuine concern for her she had seen in those ash-gray eyes.

6   At ten o'clock the next morning the two Chilean business partners were together in their suite at the lodge, having just finished a leisurely breakfast.

Xavier Escoro, an immense figure clad in burgundy silk pajamas and matching robe, arose from the breakfast table and began to walk, back and forth, back and forth, hands clasped behind his back.

Lima Clemente sat near a window, the morning light glowing in his startling ash-gray eyes, glinting off the glossy black of his eyebrows and eyelashes, and the long braid of his shining black hair. He wore a loosely fitting black silk shirt with white cotton pants.

"Tell me of your day with the beautiful sheriff," Xavier Escoro said, then lifted both of his huge hands to make a salacious gesture.

"There was nothing like that."

"What? No lovemaking?" Xavier Escoro's eyebrows rose like embattled porcupines. "I am shocked and disappointed, Lima. The woman was ready. Even from where I stood I could smell her lust."

Lima Clemente understood that his partner could smell desire in women; had demonstrated this ability many times, even with women who appeared cold and disdainful.

Although Xavier Escoro was physically ugly, he had tremendous sexual appeal that came off him like a fragrance.

He was gifted in his way with females. Lima Clemente knew the older man had slept with many, all of whom had evidently enjoyed his attentions; most were always available for additional assignations.

"You must make love to her," Xavier Escoro counseled earnestly. "Fill her with enchantment. Her goodwill is most important to our success."

"We were busy with other things," Lima Clemente said, telling his partner about their discovery of the little Indian boy's body.

Xavier Escoro volubly expressed his shock.

Lost in thought, Lima Clemente realized that Jordan was the woman he had been looking for all over the world, ever since his beloved Eclenza, with whom he had grown up, and whom he had lost many years ago.

Jordan reminded him of Eclenza in many ways, her regal bearing, the color and shape of her eyes, most of all the inner spirit that at times seemed to quietly consume her.

Over the ensuing years Clemente had known many compliant women, his enjoyment of them hardly more than masturbation, since he could love none.

A man like himself, he felt, needed a woman with strong principles and character, a woman who was attracted to him but had the courage to resist. At first. All of his adult life he had needed a woman like Eclenza. And he had found her in Jordan.

He smiled to himself when he remembered how he had landed on the ground after Jordan's unexpected martial arts move. Magnificent!

He would carefully and slowly seduce her into falling in love with him, not for business expediencies, but because he already loved her.

Lima Clemente knew by past experience that he could cause almost any woman to fall in love with him.

He couldn't say exactly what it was about himself that so appealed to them, whether it was those unexpected gray foreign eyes in his dark face or his natural grace. Because he was a pragmatic man he strongly suspected it was his position in society and, most of all, the perfume of money.

A man who truly believed that if a thing was worth doing at all it was worth doing well, he had made himself an expert in the arts of physical love, having gone to the trouble of taking special classes on the subject from masters in Hong Kong.

He had learned enough, and was by nature subtle enough, to wait for Jordan to make the first move.

And when it came, he suspected it would be an infinitesimal and instantly fleeting sign on her part, one that he, waiting oh-so-patiently, like the master hunter awaits the prey, would instantly recognize and act upon.

"I firmly believe Jordan Tidewater is the woman for me," Lima Clemente told his uncle.

"Bravo! At last!" Xavier Escoro replied. "I wish you great good fortune."

7   The autopsy was held early the next morning. The coroner was present as was Philip Gerber, M.D., the medical examiner, and their guests: Jordan Tidewater representing the Quinault Nation; Hunter Kleoh, the FBI; Jasper Wright, the county sheriff; Leonard L. Duncan and Clarence Montgomery, two senior homicide investigators from the state.

Dr. Gerber's assistant, a slender young man, removed the green sheet from Victim A-13-C, represented by three pathetically small lumps on the examination table: a head, an armless, legless torso, and one small hand.

As he did so, Hunter Kleoh told Jordan that FBI investigators were at that moment scouring the site of the killing.

Everyone stood back while Hunter Kleoh, shooting from all directions, took a series of photographs at right angles to the body parts using first a wide-angle lens and then a regular lens.

Normally, Jordan knew, Kleoh would take away any projectiles found in the body, along with blood and hair samples. But here there was no heart; no feet to examine for scratches; just one small hand that might possibly provide fingernail scrapings.

In this case death was so obviously caused by terrible physical injury, decapitation, Jordan suspected that only the basic forensic examination would be conducted.

As if reading her mind, Hunter Kleoh said, "Phil, toxicology can work up the samples whenever they get around to it. It's pretty obvious what killed this one."

Dr. Gerber nodded. Then he began to examine the severed spinal column, complete with the visibly severed spinal cord; the trachea or "ringed" air pipe up front; the esophagus or food pipe behind the trachea; and a group of severed whitish tendons.

In addition there were good-sized jugular veins and large carotid arteries running alongside and roughly between the trachea and esophagus on either side of the neck.

Embedded in the severed neckline of the torso, Dr. Gerber found foreign material represented by several strands that appeared to be woven.

"I'd say this was the result of a blow from an ax or a machete using great force," Dr. Gerber said. "It had to be very sharp and very heavy. See? It sliced his larynx and severed his spine at the fifth vertical vertebra."

When Dr. Gerber examined the places where the missing arms and legs had joined the torso, he pointed out how severely the bones were splintered on the ends.

"It would take several chops to sever the legs, no matter how sharp the cutting instrument or how strong the arm that wielded it," he said.

After the minimal autopsy was complete, six jars filled with specimens were sealed, labeled, and boxed, ready to be handed over to toxicology, where they would be stored in a walk-in freezer.

Dr. Gerber led them into a small adjoining room where

he poured coffee for himself and indicated clean cups for the others. They all declined.

Dr. Gerber then informed them that the young boy had been alive when first his arms and legs, and then his head, had been cut off.

Hunter Kleoh's voice broke the silence following Dr. Gerber's remark. "I get sick to my stomach when I think about how that kid must have suffered."

"You know, that's a funny thing," Dr. Gerber said. "About pain, I mean."

They all looked at him questioningly.

"Back East, I worked on a case where a forty-year-old paranoid schizophrenic, long institutionalized for the criminally insane, was transferred to a unit housing an assortment of the mentally ill, one where patients were allowed to sign themselves out for several hours at a time.

"This man did so. He took a bus into town where he bought a seven-inch hunting knife at a hardware store. He then walked outside and seized an eight-year-old girl standing in a crowd on the sidewalk watching a street fair.

"He threw her to the ground, bent over her, his outstretched right arm hacking away at the child's face and neck. At first everyone fled in fear of the crazed man, who, unhindered, crouched and then sat alongside the child, all the while chopping ferociously.

"As the pavement reddened with blood, two men grabbed at the killer. But he just kept stabbing the girl. Even when the men kicked at his face with their heavy boots, he apparently did not notice, although his head was being knocked from side to side by the force of the blows. A policeman ran up and the three of them finally subdued the struggling man.

"By the time the little girl arrived at the hospital she was, of course, pulseless and brain-dead, beyond clinical death.

"She had died of acute hemorrhage leading to hypovolemic shock, having been cut in numerous places on the upper part of her body. The main source of bleeding was a completely severed carotid artery that emptied itself into a laceration of her esophagus. The blood passed down the esophagus into her stomach and was the source of a huge regurgitation."

Jordan tried to suppress a shiver.

"A specific sequence of events takes place in people who bleed to death," Dr. Gerber went on. "At first, they usually hyperventilate. It's the body's compensatory attempt to saturate the decreasing volume of circulating blood with as much oxygen as possible. The heart rate will speed up for the same reason.

"As more blood volume is lost, the pressure in the vessels begins to fall rapidly and the coronary arteries receive less and less of it. When the blood pressure and pulse rate become low enough, the brain ceases to receive enough oxygen and glucose, and unconsciousness follows, preceding brain death.

"Finally the heart slows to a stop, usually without any fibrillation, circulation is arrested, breathing ceases, there are a few agonal events, and clinical death has occurred.

"Now when a blood vessel the size of the carotid artery has been cut wide open, the entire sequence can take less than a minute. What I just told you explains how the little girl died."

Dr. Gerber took a swallow of coffee, then continued. "But it does not explain a phenomenon seen by that little girl's mother and many other witnesses.

"Suffering one of the most horrendous kinds of death and fully conscious at the time, she died without a look of terror on her face. Her expression was one of tranquillity and release. Of surprise rather than horror."

"Sounds impossible," Hunter Kleoh said.

"It is not impossible," Dr. Gerber replied. "There is far more at work than the 'fight or flight' of a rush of adrenaline. It is neither supernatural nor mystical. It is simply the human brain at work, manufacturing morphinelike opiates called endorphins.

"As I'm sure you all know, the explorer David Livingstone was a physician, a medical missionary. One day he was set upon by a wounded lion, which seized him by the left upper arm.

"He felt himself lifted off the ground and violently shaken as the lion's teeth sank deeply into his flesh, splintering the humerus and ripping eleven jagged lacerations into the bleeding skin and muscle. One of Livingstone's party grabbed a rifle and discharged both barrels, frightening the animal away.

"Livingstone was amazed at his own survival, but even more so at the ineffable sense of peace he experienced in the jaws of the beast. He said he felt a sort of dreaminess in which there was no sense of pain or feeling of terror, that it was like what patients partially under the influence of chloroform described who saw all the operation but did not feel the knife.

"Livingstone wrote that his singular condition was not the result of any mental process, that the lion's shaking him annihilated fear and allowed no sense of horror in looking around at the animal. He decided that his peculiar state was probably produced in all animals killed by carnivores and attributed it to the kindness of God.

"What we now know, of course, is that it is a result of the principles of stress-related biochemical alteration of states of consciousness, bringing a sense of peace.

"I suspect that that little boy in the next room felt very little pain, if any, as he was being killed. And I know for a fact that his death was almost instantaneous."

"Almost?" Jordan asked.

"Well, when someone's decapitated, the brain stays alive for a few more seconds."

"Are you saying this child was conscious *afterward*?"

"Probably. But only until the blood drained away and the brain was deprived of oxygen. That would have been just a moment or two later."

"Then he could have known what had happened to him after his head was separated from his body?"

"He could have known."

Jordan grew even paler.

The others moved uncomfortably.

"He was not sexually molested," Gerber said firmly, as if that information would comfort them.

8   A full-scale investigation was underway. Since the FBI was in charge of felonies on Indian reservations, Hunter Kleoh was officially the top man with all information feeding into his office.

The first step, aided by officers from various law enforcement agencies, was a several-hundred-man investigation of all of the Indian reservations and schools on the Olympic Peninsula.

This broadened into a house-to-house inquiry of all residents of the several Indian Nations on the peninsula, and was then enlarged to cover the white schools.

There was massive media coverage that instantly became nationwide and then worldwide. Not all of the details of the boy's death were released, only the fact of his decapitation.

Investigators were sent to all motels, lodges, and rooming houses on the Olympic Peninsula, seeking to find one from which a small Indian boy had disappeared.

No child was missing anywhere. All little Indian boys were present and accounted for.

The FBI was laboriously checking with Interpol into the backgrounds of the various foreign nationals who had attended the logging congress.

It was difficult, time-consuming work. Many of them had already left for home; others were touring other parts of the United States; and still others remained in the area enjoying the scenic beauty of the Olympic Peninsula.

Jordan was especially interested in the reports that came back from the Chilean federal police on Lima Clemente and Xavier Escoro.

Neither man had a criminal record. They were partners in a highly successful logging and lumber machinery business in Santiago, exemplary citizens of the highest status and important wealth.

*You will find something more in woods
than in books. Trees and stones
Will teach you that which you can never
learn from masters.*
—SAINT BERNARD OF CLAIRVAUX,
French Theologian (1091–1153)
Epistle 106

Chapter 5

1   Two days later there was a knock on Old Man
Ahcleet's front door.

"*Qatcawiqoe'cqo-icx;* go break wind!" muttered the old
man.

He had felt disharmonious all day and was determined
not to be torn from his afternoon viewing of *Oprah*.

Ahcleet heard Tleyuk in the kitchen making his regular
after-school sandwich. Even a young boy like Sparky
knew enough not to disturb Grandfather when he was
watching his favorite show, Ahcleet thought grumpily.

Ahcleet looked at the clock and realized Tleyuk was a
little late. Usually he got home before *Oprah* started.

Ahcleet decided he'd check on the boy after the program was over.

Now came a flurry of knocks.

"*Aqa,ikLigE'kiqet;* oh, go louse yourself!" he said irritably, getting up out of his worn leather chair.

When he peered from behind the drapery and saw who was waiting, Ahcleet's face grew thunderous and he cursed.

"*Lq'eyo'qt wi'qectq;* Old Woman Vulva!"

He drew himself up straight, assumed his most ferocious expression, and flung open the front door.

A dark bundle, dressed in smelly brownish rags, stood on the porch. Old Woman Scatt.

Dangling over the old woman's left arm was a rib-thin black-and-yellow cat with one malicious eye, half of an ear, and two fangs that hung down over its lower lip.

Old Woman Scatt was considered by many to be a present-day pestilence. A true ancient of days, she was older than Ahcleet; in fact, he remembered her looking about the same when he'd been a boy. And smelling the same. The old *wi'qectq* never bathed!

She'd been a slave, the daughter and granddaughter of slaves. And not high-priced slaves, either; bargain basement slaves. He didn't know which nation they'd been stolen away from, but it must have been a backward one.

Ahcleet stood behind his screen door with his nose turned away to avoid her body odor and remembered the story.

In the old days everybody knew it was forbidden to make fun of supernatural beings. If some fool did, he would be sure to die in a very short time.

Old Woman Scatt's grandfather, the one taken in slavery as a young man along with his wife, had laughed at the huge carved figure that stood on the beach long ago, made fun of its manly endowments.

The blasphemer did not die in a short time. He lived to be old and miserable, but all of his progeny were cursed with craziness and uncleanness.

Old Man Ahcleet had always believed that first Scatt survived because the carved figure standing on the beach in the old days was not really one of the supernaturals but more of a welcoming sign.

And here was the last of the line befouling his doorstep. Well, almost the last. She had one living descendant whom Ahcleet considered barely human.

"What do you want?" He would not honor her by using the old language although he knew she understood it.

"Tell that kid of yours to leave my cat alone." Her hairy face bristled up at him from a tangled nest of musty hair. Like her cat, she had only one eye.

Imperiously, Ahcleet looked down at her. "I have no kids. Kids are the young of goats."

"Okay then, that spawn of your great-granddaughter's, the policewoman. The *twin.*"

The last word was spoken with great contempt.

Ahcleet knew what Old Woman Scatt was getting at. In the old days, twins were considered the absolute worst of bad luck.

Farther up north, where Old Woman Scatt's people had come from, newborn twins had their mouths stuffed with moss so that their crying would not be an offense in the ears of the spirits. Then they were taken out into the forest to die of exposure to the elements or to be devoured by wild animals.

Ahcleet knew there'd been no horror of twins, or *tsaile'sxwil,* among the ancient Quinault, although the parents did have to observe a number of taboos.

For twenty days neither parent could fish. The father sometimes camped alone in the woods for a month after their births. He had to refrain from hunting for two years, during which period of time the couple was supplied with meat by friends.

In those days, Quinault twins were never separated. If one went for an armload of wood, the other followed. They occupied the same bed.

If girls, they both married the same man. They were

never referred to as *tsaile'sxwil*, "twins," but as *tsopoh*, "wolves," so they would not feel ashamed.

Ahcleet, ignoring the old woman's insult, stepped out of his memories and onto the porch. "Tleyuk was at your place?" he demanded.

"He was there and he touched my cat."

Ahcleet turned and roared back through the screen door, "Tleyuk!"

Tleyuk came running, sandwich in hand, mustard outlining his mouth. When he saw Old Woman Scatt his eyes grew even rounder.

"See, Grandfather, they're both together!" he whispered loudly.

"Who's together?"

Tleyuk pointed with his sandwich. "Her and her cat."

"Don't talk foolishness. Did you touch Old Woman Scatt's cat?"

"Just its face."

Old Woman Scatt's voice shrieked out, "Old Man, I know what the brat was doing. He was trying to pull the cat's face up to see who's underneath!"

"Ridiculous!" Ahcleet glared down his considerable nose.

Then he said to Tleyuk, "Haven't we told you never to go around that place?"

"Yes, Grandfather."

"Why did you do it?"

Tleyuk hung his head. "I just wanted to see something."

"What did you want to see?"

Tleyuk moved closer to Ahcleet and whispered, "It's private, Grandfather. Can't I tell you after she's gone?"

Ahcleet closed his eyes and contemplated. He was certainly not going to chastise his own flesh and blood in front of this *ga'yamoa*, this maggot.

Opening his eyes, he pronounced, "Old Woman Scatt, you may leave. And take that animal with you. I will discuss this matter with my great-great-grandson."

She remained obdurate. "You going to punish him?"

Ahcleet roared, "I said *leave!*"

Cat still hanging limp on her arm, she hobbled off the porch, glared at them both from the gravel road, and shouted, "You and yours! You leave me and mine alone! 'Specially my cat!"

"Is she a witch, Grandfather?" Tleyuk asked.

"No, Sparky, nothing that dignified. She's just a dirty, demented old *wi'qectq*. Now get me some cedar branches. Then we will talk."

Quickly Tleyuk ran to obey Ahcleet's request. When he returned with the branches, Ahcleet swept them over the porch boards where Old Woman Scatt had stood and brushed them against the side of the house and the surface of the screen door where her breath had touched.

Then he took a fresh cedar branch and brushed each of the steps, all along the walkway to the gravel road. He used a third cedar branch to brush a lengthy area of the road upon which Old Woman Scatt had walked.

After purifying his house and the road out front, Ahcleet stacked the used branches on the ground to be burned later.

He went inside, washed his hands in the kitchen sink, brewed tea, then told Tleyuk to sit down. He poured the boy a Coke and himself a strong cup of Morning Thunder tea, then added a teaspoonful of raw sugar and a large slurp of whipping cream.

After they both sat quietly for several minutes, Tleyuk gulping his Coke and Ahcleet sipping his sweetened tea, the old man asked, "Are we now at peace?"

Tleyuk said he was peaceful.

Ahcleet considered, decided he was as peaceful as could be expected.

"Why did you go to Old Woman Scatt's place?" he asked.

Excitement flushed Tleyuk's face. "Remember what you told me the other day about how animals could become people?"

Ahcleet nodded.

Now Tleyuk's words could hardly rush out fast enough.

"And how if I saw an animal that was acting funny to stay away because it was probably a person in an animal disguise?"

Ahcleet took another sip of tea and looked serene. Inwardly he groaned.

"Well, that cat of Old Woman Scatt's always acts funny. And I've been thinking. I've never seen that cat together with that old woman. So I figured, I bet she turns herself into that cat. Don't you see, Grandfather?"

Unfortunately, Ahcleet did. Wincing, the old man remembered what he'd said in jest to Jordan the other morning when he was telling Tleyuk about how animals used to be able to turn into people and back again.

"Go on, please," he told his great-great grandson.

"I couldn't think about anything else. And on the way home from school today, here comes that cat. Sort of like an invitation."

"I see," said Ahcleet.

"Grandfather, I knew it was meant to be. You telling me about animals turning into people, me thinking about it for days—"

"Two days," Ahcleet said. He would never interrupt an adult but a child was a different matter. Children must be taught.

"Okay, two days. And then today, that cat walking slow right in front of me with its tail in the air. It's never done that before."

"So what did you do?"

"Alls I could do was try to pick it up. It'd let me get just so close, then run off a little and look back at me. It went on that way until it stopped, stood stock-still, and waited for me."

"Yes?" Ahcleet continued to look elderly and wise.

"I was just touching its face to see if its muzzle would pull up, if I could find Old Woman Scatt underneath. But real gentle, you know, so as not to hurt it or anything, and here she comes yelling and running at me with a broom."

In the silence they could both hear the clock Ahcleet had

rescued decades ago from the old railroad station at Moclips ticking on the wall behind them.

Tleyuk looked crestfallen. "So it isn't really true, is it, Grandfather?"

"What isn't true, Sparky?"

"That animals can change into people."

Ahcleet looked surprised. "Why do you say that?"

"Well, that cat didn't change into Old Woman Scatt 'cause there they both were, standing side by side on our porch right in front of us. Cat and old woman together."

Ahcleet contemplated his teacup. Then he looked across the table at Tleyuk, the warmth of love—and irritation—flushing his old face.

"What I didn't have time to tell you the other morning was that nowadays only a very, very few can change. Those who can are all very powerful and very old shamans."

"Not Old Woman Scatt?"

Ahcleet made a noise with his lips that sounded like an even more explosive Quinault version of the American raspberry.

"Certainly not a crazy *wi'qectq* like that. She's not even one of The People." He lowered his voice. "That Scatt clan! They were all slaves, you know. The lowest of the low class."

Tleyuk nodded wisely.

2   When Jordan tucked her son in bed that night and gave him the ritual good night kiss, she thought he seemed troubled.

"Mom, can we talk a minute?" he asked.

"Sure, honey, as long as you want."

She sat on the bed and held his hand. By sheer power of will she banished thoughts of the butchered boy that plagued her constantly.

Ever since finding the remains she had struggled with a nausea very like that of pregnancy. When she tried to eat she couldn't keep anything down.

She couldn't sleep. Her only comfort came from thoughts of her small family—her son, her great-grandfather, her twin brother. And, like an occasional grace note, of her new friend Lima Clemente, with whom she had agreed to go for a drive later that night.

Tleyuk sat up in bed.

"Mom," he said seriously. "Don't tell Grandfather but I don't think anyone can turn themselves into animals anymore."

"Are you sure about that, Tleyuk?"

"I don't know, but I wonder if it's kind of like the white kids and Santa Claus. There isn't any such thing." Brilliant dark eyes stared into hers searchingly. "What do you think, Mom?"

Seeing the youth and life embodied in the young figure before her, Jordan thought again of the meaning of his name in the old language: Tleyuk, "spark of fire."

Jordan took his other hand in hers. She knew enough not to do motherly things like run her hands through his hair, not when an important subject like this was up for discussion. Tleyuk would find that demeaning.

"Honey, in life there are many meanings to things. Like layers on an artichoke."

"Yuck," he said.

An unfortunate comparison, she thought, knowing her son hated artichokes almost as much as he hated broccoli. But he did kind of like artichoke hearts.

"You know about all the outer leaves?"

"Yuck again."

"And the heart?"

"Sure. That's not so bad."

"As you peel each layer of leaves away, the next layer down gets more and more sweet, until you're at the heart, or you might say the truth, which is the sweetest of all. In important matters, never take the most obvious, the outer, meaning."

"Like what?"

She thought a moment. "Well, like expressions we use. Say you're reading a book, and the author writes about the hero, 'He dropped his eyes.' You know his eyes didn't really drop out of his head, don't you?"

"Oh, sure." In the lamplight, her son's momentarily haughty expression reminded Jordan of Old Man Ahcleet at his most regal.

"If you took the first meaning, the poor guy would be scrambling around on the ground trying to find his eyeballs, wouldn't he?"

Tleyuk giggled. "Mom, that's crazy!"

"And so is life, Tleyuk. It's an intricate puzzle. That's what makes it so much fun. The happy people are those who try to figure it out, to see the patterns."

Tleyuk brightened. "I'd sure like to believe it, Mom. You know, about people and animals. It sounds great."

"You and Grandfather and I will discuss this later. At a better time. It's very important, honey. But go to sleep now."

She kissed Tleyuk again and softly closed his bedroom door.

3   "He told you about what happened this afternoon," Ahcleet said when Jordan came into the living room.

"No, but I figured something important had."

Ahcleet described the scene with Old Woman Scatt and her cat. When he was finished, they both laughed softly.

Ahcleet lay his head back in his favorite old leather chair and closed his eyes. "Now that Tleyuk is eight years old I must begin his training."

Traditionally, when a young Quinault entered his eighth year, the boy's father began his special training. Since Tleyuk's father was gone and his grandfather was dead, this duty must fall on Old Man Ahcleet.

"I want him to question everything, Grandfather," she warned.

He opened his eyes. "Of course you do. Like you did. Like I myself did. This is right. This is good. Blind belief is for fools, too lazy to think for themselves."

He studied her. "Are you going to tell me what is wrong?" he asked gently.

She told Ahcleet, then, about her hideous find in the forest. She hadn't been able to talk to him about it before. So far only the most basic details had been released to the local press.

"Now I know why I've been feeling bad. That child's death has caused great disharmony. Did it have anything to do with the poachers you're looking for?"

"I can't imagine how. Poachers creep about silently. They certainly wouldn't advertise their presence with a gaudy murder like that."

"One never knows what's in the heart of a stranger," the old man said.

Jordan remained silent.

They both watched as the fire in the hearth transformed solid driftwood into blazing orange and purple tongues of flame. And then smoke and ashes.

"Transformation," Ahcleet murmured. "That is what life is all about. Every day we are transformed into someone just a little different from the day before."

He coughed, then raised up and spat into the fireplace. "Except *ia'qeXEle*."

Jordan lifted an eyebrow. "Excrement, Grandfather?"

"Yes. Shit like those Scatts."

Smiling, she shook her head at Ahcleet. Then they both fell silent and studied the fire again.

After a while, Jordan said, "Did Tleyuk ask if you could change, Grandfather?"

"No. I guess he didn't think about it." Ahcleet looked over at her. "I suppose it's hard to think of your great-great grandfather, someone you live with every day, as being a magical person. He will, though, when he does think about it. Maybe he'll ask me tomorrow."

"And what will you tell him?"

"The truth."

"Is he ready?"

"If he asks, he's ready."

"I wonder if I could transform," she said slowly.

"Have you ever tried?"

"No."

"When it is time, and necessary, you will."

4   Both bundled up, Jordan and Lima Clemente sat on a log on Moonstone Beach, near the pilings of the old hotel and dance floor that had washed out to sea many years ago during a horrendous storm.

Now, at ten-thirty, the moon was just rising.

Having brought newspaper and gathered driftwood, Lima Clemente built a fire. When the flames were tossing and turning in the sea winds, he asked, "How are you feeling, Jordan?"

Even though it had only been a couple of days since he'd bidden her farewell in front of the lodge, he thought she seemed thinner. And there was something lost-looking about her beautiful dark eyes.

"Not too good," she said.

"You know, Jordan, that it is quite common to have physical problems after receiving a shock, particularly one of the magnitude of the other day."

"I've heard that," she said absently.

"*Are* you having physical problems?"

She looked at him for a moment or two as if offended by such a personal question.

"Don't be angry, Jordan," he said. "I am truly concerned about you."

The words burst out as if against her will. "I can't sleep. If I do manage to drop off, suddenly there's that scalped face staring at me. Last night it was lying on the pillow right next to my head." Her voice broke. "I could smell it."

His voice was calm. "Are there other difficulties?"

"If I try to eat anything, I throw it right back up."

"Can you keep anything down?"

"Just water."

"Have you consulted a physician?"

She shook her head.

"Do you plan to?"

A scornful expression crossed her face. "Of course not. What kind of law enforcement officer has to go to the doctor every time she discovers a dead body?"

Clemente knew her beginning expression of anger was a good sign that she was coming back to life. And he was very grateful that he was the one to whom she could express the feelings that disturbed her so deeply.

He would be the cliff against which the waves of her emotion could exhaust themselves. He would encourage her to do so; in that direction, he knew, lay the beginning of intimacy.

He was very careful not to touch her.

"How many dead bodies have you had to deal with in your work, Jordan?"

She stared into the fire. "Several. But the people were very, very old and I knew death was a release for them. This was my first bad one."

He sighed. "It is very difficult. It never gets easier."

Now he knew he had her complete attention. She looked over at him curiously. "Have you been in police work?"

"Not police work, no. But political unrest. In the past there has been much brutality, much violent death, in my country."

"Are you a mercenary, Lima?"

He smiled. "I am only what I seem. Just a dull business-man from Chile who wants to sell more logging machinery and equipment to cut down our forests."

She nodded, apparently satisfied.

"Jordan, may I ask you a personal question?"

"Go ahead and ask."

He was aware mentally of her unspoken qualification: *I don't have to answer.*

"Do you have a faith, a religion, to fortify you in times like these?"

For a few moments there was only the thunder of the sea. Then Jordan's voice. "I have my own beliefs."

He could see sorrow on her face as she turned to him. How he longed to take her in his arms! But he would make no untoward move.

"I myself could not exist without my faith," he said, lifting the crucifix at his neck and kissing it. "I pray your beliefs are enough to comfort you."

She did not reply directly. Instead, she said, "See how the fog is rising. Fog is when the supernaturals come."

He smiled. "My people believe that fog is the devil's breath."

They listened to the thunder of the sea. Lima Clemente said, "I feel a yearning coming from you, Jordan. If I am not being too bold, what is it that you long for?"

She replied with small sparks of amusement showing in her eyes, "An island, I think. Somewhere off our coastline. One I could go to whenever I wanted. But only for a day or two. I'd always come back home."

Lima Clemente realized at that moment that Jordan had an ancient, mystical bond with this place. With this land and this sea. As he had with his homeland.

"Alone?"

"I'm not sure."

They sat for a time, not speaking, simply watching the night sky, listening to the breakers, inhaling the sea's fresh breath.

"Jupiter is still brilliant over there in the west," Jordan murmured. Then she turned to him. "Lima, are you homesick?"

"Only when I look up at the stars. The night sky here is so strange."

She touched his hand.

"It is time to go," he said softly.

5   Later, after Jordan returned to Old Man Ahcleet's house, she took a sweat bath in the backyard.

As she sat in the hot enclosure, her skin slick and rosy with steam, she reflected upon the last hour or two with Lima Clemente.

To her great relief, he had made no pass, no approach of any kind, although she was certainly vulnerable. Even when she touched his hand, he had not seized the opportunity to move closer.

Although strongly drawn to him, she understood herself well enough to realize that undue haste on his part would spoil the energy already flowing between them.

Because of his restraint, she was beginning to feel safe with him. Already she was lighter in her spirit, as if just a small part of the horrible nightmare of the mutilated child had been drawn from her.

Although they had not even talked directly about the murder, it seemed to her that now Lima Clemente shared some of the burden with her.

And he had asked to see her again.

That night, although Jordan slept very little, there was no scalped face on the pillow next to hers.

When she did sleep, she dreamed again of cougars, one special cougar curling and winding about her legs, the beautiful smiling face with the startling blue eyes uplifted to hers.

What I am trying to say is hard to tell
and hard to understand . . .
Unless, unless . . .
You have been yourself at the edge of the Deep Canyon
And have come back unharmed.
Maybe it all depends on something within yourself—
Whether you are trying to see the Watersnake
Or the sacred Cornflower,
Whether you go out to meet death or to Seek Life.
    —ELDER OF THE SAN JUAN PUEBLO,
        "Out of Chaco Canyon"

Chapter 6

1 Very early the next morning, but still late enough that the loggers who usually occupied the large U-shaped back booth in Denny's restaurant in Aberdeen had already left for work, Ruby Campbell sat alone, waiting.

It was a booth where billions of dollars in timber deals had been hammered out over the years. Lawyers were all right when it came time to sign the necessary papers, but the logger talk had to come first.

Campbell was dressed in snug-fitting bleached Wrangler jeans, a long-sleeved, striped oxford-cloth shirt open at the neck, and a western-style tweed blazer. He wore black cowhide leather Justin boots and a black felt river gambler's hat, which he had carefully placed on the seat beside him.

The man he was waiting for arrived within five minutes, dressed in a three-piece dark suit, including a buttoned vest, gray-and-white-striped long-sleeved shirt with starched white collar, and shoes Ruby would bet were handmade.

They each ordered the breakfast special: two eggs, three pieces of bacon, three pancakes, crisp fried potatoes, biscuits, and coffee.

"One thing our company needs to ascertain, Mr. Campbell," the other man said.

"What's that?"

"Why you are willing to represent us."

"I need something to do," Campbell replied, his voice showing remnants of a Kentucky drawl. "Something that interests me. I've got to keep busy."

"We understand you already work undercover as a timber policeman."

Campbell shrugged. "Yeah, a timber cop. That doesn't take up much of my time."

"As you already know, what we require is strenuous and not without danger."

"I like hard work and I've never seen anything yet that I'm afraid of."

Campbell's tone of voice was that of a man to whom money didn't mean much. One who thought the thrill of the hunt, the smell of danger, was everything.

"Have you had military training?" the other man asked.

"I was a sergeant, master sergeant, in the Rangers."

"Vietnam?"

"World War II. Eight campaigns and three landings. North Africa, Italy, Omaha Beach. When the war ended in Europe I served in the military police."

"World War II? That's hard to believe. You look to me like a lean and healthy fifty-year-old man, at the very most, fifty-five."

"You want to see my discharge papers?"

Noticing the color rise in Campbell's face, the other man

held up his hand. "Please, sir, please. No offense was meant."

"None taken," Campbell said shortly.

But he reached inside his blazer for his wallet and handed his driver's license across the table. The other man glanced at the license, at the date of birth, then politely handed it back.

"It's very hard to believe that you're in your early seventies," the other man said consideringly.

"You know, of course, that the part of our company business that concerns you is considered illegal. Does that trouble you?"

Campbell frowned. "Let me tell you something. I fought for my country, that's true. But the United States I fought for doesn't exist today."

The other man nodded once. "I am in total agreement."

Then he asked, "Are you yourself a hunter?"

"Sure as hell am. Ever since I was five years old and had to prop my daddy's rifle up on a stump to fire it. And I had better hit what I was aiming at with the first bullet because bullets were expensive. Cost a penny apiece."

The other man smiled, then grew serious. "Now what is the legal position in the area, Mr. Campbell? I understand you've researched all that."

"I have and this is the way it works out. If we're smart, we'll be damned careful not to attract the attention of any law enforcement agencies.

"We'll have to watch out for state and local police agencies, sure. And there are a couple of federal law enforcement agencies that could cause us a lot of trouble."

"Such as?"

"The FBI, for one, as I'm sure you already know. They'll definitely be involved, especially if we get caught on Indian lands."

"And the others?"

"Park Service and the Fish and Wildlife Service. When we work in the Olympic National Park, we'll have to keep our eyes peeled for the resident park rangers and the park police. But their patrols are predictable, so we shouldn't have any trouble there."

"And that's it?"

"Not by a long shot. As for the Fish and Wildlife Service, they have a division of law enforcement that's made up of less than two hundred special agents scattered far apart in one- or two-man duty stations. Those boys are only interested in wildlife violations within their respective regions."

"Do we have to worry about them?"

"If we're sloppy, we could get into trouble with their Special Operations Branch. It's made up of two five-agent teams that are covert. They've got their own intelligence capabilities and the authority to conduct their investigations anywhere in the country. Their investigations are limited strictly to wildlife violators—the killing or commercialization of endangered species."

After several moments of silence, the other man asked, "Do you have a family, Mr. Campbell?"

"My wife."

Campbell understood what the pleased expression on the other man's face meant: *Good, that's at least one hostage to fortune.*

"Because of the nature of our business it's best that your wife know nothing of our arrangements."

Campbell waved a hand in dismissal. "Melisande never questions my comings and goings. Never has. She's too busy with her own work."

"And what work is that?"

"She paints."

"Excellent." The other man made a gesture showing approval of Mrs. Campbell's activities. "An artist. My mother painted small watercolors. They were very good."

Campbell's mouth firmed. He remained silent as if to reproach the other man for trespassing into a personal area of what was to be, if it became anything at all, a business-only relationship.

Feeling the snub, the other man said, "I find it strange you haven't asked about the financial rewards."

"I figured we'd get to that when the time was right."

"Your share for the first year's supervisory work will be five hundred thousand dollars in cash, tax-free."

"Sounds okay," Campbell said. "Tied in with quotas, is it?"

"Later, yes. And if things work out, the rewards will be greater. But this first year you are guaranteed your five hundred thousand, regardless of quotas."

Campbell nodded.

There was a look in the other man's eyes that told Campbell: *He's inclined to like me. But he still wonders if I can be trusted.*

As if making a sudden decision, the other man motioned for the waitress. When she arrived, he said with a smile, "Mr. Campbell, how about a refill on the coffee to seal our bargain?"

"We have a deal?"

"It's yours if you'll take it."

"I'll take it and the refill."

The other man took a silver flask from his pocket and added a dollop of brandy to each coffee cup.

After they had toasted each other and their upcoming project, the other man said, "To show our good faith our company will pay you, almost immediately, one hundred and twenty-five thousand dollars cash in used American currency."

"*Almost* immediately?" Campbell asked.

"We have one preliminary requirement."

Campbell looked interested. "Yeah?"

"We ask that you participate in a small ceremony that must take place in the forest. Very private, just you and me."

Campbell's narrow wolf-pale eyes smiled. "We cut our fingers and become blood brothers, is that it?"

"Nothing's cut, Mr. Campbell. It's a superstition carried on since the days of our founder to insure success in any new business undertaking."

"Like breaking a champagne bottle on the prow of a newly commissioned ship?" Campbell asked.

"A good comparison."

"Just see there're no champagne bottles broken over my head, okay? So when do you want to see me again?"

"Meet me at Amanda Park at eight tonight. And wear old clothes. Something loose."

"I'll be there," Campbell said.

After shaking hands, Campbell left the restaurant wearing a hard, calculating look.

So far, he was satisfied with his progress. He knew a lot more about the other man's company than any of them suspected.

Certain of Campbell's inquiries had revealed that the other man was a smooth, dangerous character, representing a company suspected of controlling an empire responsible for filling eighty percent of the global wildlife parts market—monetary value in the billions.

If he played his cards right, Ruby Campbell thought, they'd all find out that this here old, transplanted Kentuckian was just a little bit smarter. And even more dangerous. If he was successful in nailing this other guy and the members of his company, his own financial reward would be well worth the effort involved. Several million, tax-free.

As he drove back home to Moclips for lunch with his wife, Ruby fired up a cigar and thought about the past that had brought him to this place at this particular time.

2   A man who continually needed frontiers to push back, a Louis L'Amour sort of character, Ruby Campbell had felt for most of his life that he'd been born by an error of cosmic timing into the wrong century.

Tall, erect, with well-built shoulders and lean hips and flanks, he'd always moved with an inborn elegance, even as a colty kid. Campbell grinned when he remembered that his wife still called him A.G., short for Amazing Grace.

Like his father before him, whose parents had come from Scotland, Ruby had roamed the Kentucky hills while growing up.

Walked and stalked with his young beagle hound every wild animal, every scuttling insect, every decrepit old Indian within a thirty-mile radius.

"Ruby, yur fiddle-footed," said his father, a superintendent in the coal mines during the bad old days of John L. Lewis (killings, fighting, dynamitings, when a man had to carry a gun to work and back, and during working hours, too).

"Always wantin' to see what's over the next rise. Ya'll never amount to a hill a' beans."

Until the young Ruby's overwhelming thirst to see what was on the other side of the next ridge drove him ever further.

Something else drove him, too. Something even more powerful than wanderlust.

And that was his father, who had one bad habit that Ruby could not tolerate, in spite of his mother telling him that things were better when he did not interfere.

Occasionally his father came home drunk and beat on Ruby's mother. When that happened again the night after Ruby's twelfth birthday, he waited until his old man was in a drunken sleep, then tied his arms and legs to the bedposts, got a two-by-four, and beat hell out of him until his mother managed to stop him.

Very early the next morning Ruby left Harlan County riding the rails.

Down into the Texas oil fields he went, where he passed for eighteen, worked like three strong men, and fought in the Golden Gloves.

Then a little long-haul trucking, but that required sitting still for too long at a time.

Still later he said good-bye to the disappointed tobacco farmer who promised to give him his daughter and will him·

the farm if he'd stay and run it but Ruby was too restless for that.

Now, as he braked, allowing a bear to lumber across the road, he thought fondly of those sweet old whores *(Old! They were around thirty to his sixteen)* up over the restaurant where the tobacco men ate, the ones who'd taught him the Big Secret about women: if a man takes the time to do it right, the ladies love it.

In Ruby's memory, it became World War II again and the rises grew steeper—up the exploding hills of Italy, Sicily, North Africa; up the White Cliffs of Dover for D-day training.

Already a bloodied combat veteran at nineteen, up Ponte de Hôte with the rest of his Rangers on that bloody Omaha Beach predawn.

And where was the damned beach? he still asked himself. There was no beach, just razor-sharp black cliffs rising nine sheer stories high out of a heaving black sea into a demon-black night.

Ruby was the first one going up, thank God not seasick like the others from the long wait on the ship, where their quarters were slippery with vomit.

Thought he'd been killed when his body came awash with blood, blood in his eyes, his hands gloved with blood, tunic and bandolier soaked with blood; heavy, red, running warm, but it was only an injury and not the death of himself.

Up he went, through intense fire, and the noise was the sound of the world exploding, God sounds, sounds of a universe being formed and torn apart.

"Christ!" he whispered softly as he took the cigar out of his mouth, remembering the 225 Rangers who started up. Sixty made it, but some of those were torn fragments of men and soon died.

Then there was the liberation of Paris and soon the surprise Battle of the Bulge, the single biggest and bloodiest battle in U.S. military history in which eighty thousand Americans were killed or wounded in the worst winter

Europe had seen, and he was holding a bridge for forty-eight hours, the only man left alive on a machine-gun emplacement because his buddy's arm froze and broke off and he couldn't help him because his own legs were frozen to the gun and his buddy died.

And he had to keep on raising the gun sights because it seemed like the land was rising and the snow was falling but it was not the land, it was the enemy's casualties piling up, and the German soldiers charging and screaming like fighting men do over the bodies of their own dead.

Later, in the field hospital they told him he'd killed a lot of men at that spot but the information was meaningless because they also told him they were going to amputate both of his legs; gangrene had set in.

Hell, he already knew that by the stink.

But he wouldn't let them cut off his legs and he told them if they came any nearer he'd break their necks and they knew he could, even as sick as he was, because he was a trained killer, so they said you'll die and he said fine, he'd rather die than be a man with no legs.

They gave him a drug nobody'd ever heard of before called penicillin and left him alone and he started talking real soft and gentle to the man in the cot next to him, who'd been screaming all day because he'd been gutshot and even all the morphine they gave him couldn't kill the pain and they were just waiting for him to die.

The guy did die, finally, and after he died Ruby remembered how he saw him for a couple of days after that standing at the foot of his own cot, smiling at him. And then he was gone to wherever the dead go.

Funny thing, the only other time he'd seen a man with his own eyes after the guy had died was that German lieutenant walking patrol. Lieutenants didn't usually walk patrol but in the Bulge rank got lost in the business of war.

Ruby knew he couldn't creep up and stab him in the back because the German's clothes were too thick, looked like he had on a couple of greatcoats at least. And the usual slit throat from the rear wouldn't work because he was wearing one of those high, stiff collars that a knife couldn't slice through without a lot of hassle and outcry.

So Ruby sneaked up in the darkness, grabbed the guy's chin from the rear, sealing his mouth shut with the same move, stabbing his knife up under his chin and into his brain. A good, quick kill. But after he was dead that German hung around him for days.

With all the men he'd killed in war and never seen again, he never could figure out those two.

And he didn't lose his legs. They stank and hurt and turned black and peeled and itched like holy hell but by God today, fifty years later, he still had them and they'd given him damn good service. Only thing different about them was that they were smooth and hairless.

Just goes to prove if you believe in yourself, if you really believe, you can do anything you want to until it's time to die.

After that, he didn't know what happened. He didn't think anybody else did, either. Dying was like the war. You had to have been there to know what you were talking about.

The fact that he personally had killed a lot of people did not rest heavily because he refused to think about it. The creed of war was Kill or Be Killed.

Anyway, he finally got back home after five years and then started out again, westward this time, across the Great Plains, the Rocky Mountains, the Grand Tetons, up and over the Cascade Range, until he ended up in Portland, Oregon.

He stood one glorious windswept Saturday in early spring on top of Rocky Butte, where he saw spread out before him the peaks of four great mountains all glistening with fresh snow: Mount Hood; Mount Saint Helens in all her pointed splendor as this, he recalled, was thirty-five years before the 1980 eruption; Mount Adams; and even Mount Rainier over a hundred miles to the north as the crow flies.

A brisk wind blew down the Columbia River Gorge

while out on the mighty river itself a few brave sailboats tacked crazily.

"I think this is the place," Campbell announced to his beagle, a great-great-great granddaughter of the original. "Seems to me a man can breathe out here."

At that very moment, balancing precariously on the rocky parapet directly in front of him, appeared a slim female, chestnut hair wildly blowing.

A sudden updraft lifted her skirt and Ruby saw long, straight legs and a proud movement to her hips, the kind of proud that comes with being a creature young to the earth.

Campbell, who had lived an awful lot in a very few years, didn't believe in wasting time.

"My name is Ruby James Campbell," he announced in his drawl, so slow and thick the girl could hardly understand him.

"You talk funny," she said. "Where are you from?"

"I'm from Kentucky and it's not funny."

When the girl turned her head against the wind and gazed at him, she saw tousled reddish blond hair and a jaw as square as an oak plank. Plunk in the center of that jaw was a dimple big enough to bury her thumb.

Over his shoulder he carried a duffel bag on which appeared the worn letters CAMPBELL. R. J., US 36865222. A small cinnamon, brown, and black dog sat at his feet.

"What kind of name is Ruby for a man?" she asked scornfully.

"A right good name. I was named by my daddy for a favorite aunty of his," he replied, then added, after studying her, "Say, you got hair just like my granny's."

She tossed her head. "You probably think I'm as old as your granny, too."

"No-o. Don't appear to me you've been around long enough for gravity to have settled in." He lifted her down from the parapet. "You're quite a girl. Got a lot of bottom."

"Bottom?" she asked, drawing away.

"Yeah, you know. Spunk."

Her eyes glinted dangerously. "I just may have more bottom than you're ready for."

"You're not afraid of me, are you?" The expression on Ruby's big open face showed genuine curiosity. "I'm a Campbell, you know. We're a warrior clan."

She pulled her wind-driven hair off her face. "Why should I be afraid of you? I'm as tall as you are."

"Why, that you are," he said admiringly. "Almost."

They stood studying each other for long minutes, glowing amber eyes looking up into electric-blue eyes; each searching the other's face, noting the arch of brow, the curve of lip, each scenting the sweetness of the other's breath.

"My name is Melisande," she said, uttering, as she did so, an unspoken pledge.

"That's a real fine name."

Ruby James Campbell, born attuned to all living creatures—the wild things came to eat out of his hand—found he was especially attuned to this one.

As she moved closer he took her in his arms. When she returned his embrace, a great gust of wind blew her long chestnut hair around them both.

They clung to each other then, passions rising, each uncourted yet by the other. No preliminary takings-out-to-dinner, no sacrificial givings of corsages and candy. Just the giving of self to self that, Ruby still thought to this day, was the best giving of all.

He smiled when he remembered how Melisande, blooming with a blush he was pretty sure encompassed her whole body, had pulled down her skirt. "Is this the way they do things in Kentucky?" she asked.

"It's the way things should be done between a man and a woman. When it's right, that is, and when it's not bought. Only thing is," he added warningly, "I'm not the marrying kind."

"Don't worry about it," she said. "Neither am I."

That was a lot of years ago.

He and Melisande were still deeply, passionately in

love. He smiled when he thought how their sex life would put that of many young couples to shame.

In fact, he told himself as he entered the driveway of their cliffside home, *I'm going up to that tower room, snatch Melisande baby-ass naked, and make passionate love to her right on her studio floor.*

As he got out of the car, Ruby decided maybe not on the floor; Melisande would probably be a whole lot more comfortable on the bed.

Then he laughed, knowing he would not disturb his wife when she was deep in her work. He had too much respect for her talent. They'd both simply have to wait until night.

3   Melisande Campbell stood on a five-foot ladder using a palette knife to lay in splashes of sunlight on the sea cliffs in her sixteen-foot painting.

Actually it was a mural but she thought of everything she did, no matter the size, as her paintings. And this one, she'd already decided, she would not sell.

She called this work "Welcoming Spirits." It depicted one of the dramatic beaches of the Olympic Peninsula. Light-saturated waves pounded against the cliffed headlands at each end of the painting.

Three gorgeously painted Quinault ceremonial canoes had just put out to sea. The center one, a mortuary canoe partially engulfed by flames, carried the body of a high dignitary.

On the beach stood Native Americans from ancient times. To one side of the group, several split sides of salmon were cooking over a fire.

A vigorous green forest was visible above the cliffs. In the sky overhead flowed and formed the ancient spirits, the Listening Ones—bear, salmon, whale, eagle—awaiting the spirit of man beginning to ascend from the death canoe.

In the sea a whale spouted and its spume rose to become the Whale Spirit. A bear stood in the forest; its exhaled breath became the Bear Spirit.

Eagles soared overhead and their flight patterns wove into the Eagle Spirit. Smoke from the cooking salmon ascended to become the Salmon Spirit.

Melisande loved working on huge canvases, imagining the painted sea winds on her face, hearing the screech of eagles, the people talking, seeing the spouting whale, smelling the salmon cooking—while beyond and below her studio tower lay the actual beach with its thundering sea and the northwest winds whipping against her windows.

When Melisande heard the grandfather clock downstairs chime noon, she realized it was about time for Ruby to get home. They had a date for lunch.

Luckily, she had reached a point where she could climb down off the ladder, move off, and take a good look at the whole thing.

She sat on a stool about fifteen feet away from the painting and studied it, her attention focusing on a young couple, their faces solemn, standing in the group of Native Americans.

In the painting, the young woman leaned slightly toward the man while his left hand, unseen by the others, gently cupped her buttocks.

They both gazed out to sea with serene expressions but the viewer knew exactly what was in their minds. Life with a capital L as expressed in the lovemaking they had done and the lovemaking they were both looking forward to.

Like us, Melisande thought, *Ruby and me.*

When she heard women her age and younger talk about others who "certainly should be beyond that sort of thing by now," she felt sorry for them.

They had never known life if that's the way they felt about love. Certainly they'd never been lucky enough to know a man like Ruby, a man who embraced life with great energy and passion.

Smiling to herself, she recalled the first time she'd ever seen him, down there in Portland when she'd been just a kid out larking around on Rocky Butte. Ruby and his hound had looked at her then as if they were both seeing the same apparition.

And when they first embraced, she'd felt the strength and gentleness of his hand on the back of her neck, on her arms, on her breasts.

In his arms she'd experienced an emotion that had totally shocked her at the time. She'd felt *complete*.

Which was an astonishing revelation to Melisande because she'd always been a very independent girl, one who knew absolutely she didn't need anybody else. Certainly not a man.

She also remembered how Ruby had told her he wasn't the marrying kind. Fine, she'd said; she had no intention of marrying until she was at least forty or fifty.

But it wasn't long after that he insisted on a marriage ceremony, looking red and outraged, and wearing his dress kilt that revealed well-shaped, muscular, but hairless legs.

At the reception following the ceremony there'd been a great imbibing by all parties of Jim Beam whiskey. The dance was a boisterous affair in which Ruby whirled Melisande exuberantly around the floor, whooping loudly.

"Imagine marrying a man who wears a skirt!" one of Melisande's neighbors had sniffed.

Sixty-five herself now, Melisande laughed out loud as she remembered what her then eighty-three-year-old great aunt had wistfully replied.

"I just wish he'd kick a little higher. I'd like to see what's under that skirt."

Melisande had been a virgin (what an old-fashioned word that seemed nowadays) on her wedding night. And for a few hours she'd thought she was destined to remain in that condition.

For although her new husband had held her in his arms during what was left of their wedding night, he'd whispered that he wanted to wait until morning; it would be her first time and he'd drunk too much to do it right.

She'd never forget how he had introduced her to sex, so

lovingly and gently; she was amazed that a big rough and
tough war veteran had such gentleness in him. As if she
were a young fawn he was taming.

Now, a lifetime later, Ruby still had the stark remains of
a Kentucky drawl. He couldn't pronounce the word *film;* in
his mouth it became "fim." And the expression *kind of* was
always "kindly," which at first led to some misunderstand-
ings.

Although childless—perhaps *because* childless, there'd
been no growing kids to fight over, take sides with against
each other—they were still deeply, passionately in love.

The truth was that not only was she in love with her husband, she was in love with his body.

While his face and arms were wind-and-sun-scoured,
the parts of his body where he was usually clothed were
white and fine-pored, skin many a young woman would
kill for—except for the white-on-white jagged bullet scars,
of which there were a number. Skin he'd inherited from his
Irish mother.

Fine, still-golden hair grew on his chest and at his
crotch. He had a well-formed, strong body, flat belly, tight
hard balls—not big old sloppy ones—and a lovely, lovely
delicious penis.

The only white hairs anywhere were just a few in his
mustache. She'd painted him in the nude several times but
those paintings were for her eyes only.

When Melisande heard her husband's step on the spiral
staircase leading up to the tower room, she stood and
wiped her hands with her paint rag.

Glancing across the room at a mirror in which she was
reflected, Melisande saw that she looked as if she had just
stepped out of the mural she'd been working on.

But she, the originator, was a shrilly discordant note, not
nearly as beautiful as the characters she portrayed.

Her hair flew around her head in what Ruby called her
"Mrs. Einstein style," her old jeans bagged at the ass and
were ripped at the knees, her long-sleeved sweatshirt,

streaked with various colors of paints, looked as if she'd used it for a year or two to mop floors.

The door crashed open, as doors always did when Ruby was around. "Hi, ducks," he called. "Ready for lunch?"

"Right now, A.G.?" Melisande replied, knowing that she glowed with the joy of successful creation. She could feel the energy zapping around her body.

Ruby took a good long look at her, then said softly, "By God, lunch can damn well wait."

She began to undress, throwing her clothes around the tower room.

"Your bed or mine?" she asked, glancing back at him over her shoulder with the smile of a seventeen-year-old girl.

4   That night the other man waited for Ruby Campbell in a rented Jeep Cherokee outside the café in Amanda Park. When Campbell drove up, he beckoned for him to get in the Jeep.

Following instructions, Campbell had worn old, loose clothing and tennis shoes.

His baggy pants concealed a balanced throwing knife at his ankle. At the small of his back, under his loose shirt and jacket, was a Smith & Wesson automatic with a fifteen-shot magazine plus one in the barrel.

Campbell loved this new 40 series; small, it could lay in the palm of his hand, but it carried as much stopping power as his .44 Magnum.

He didn't know what was coming but he felt mentally alert and physically prepared for anything. He lit a cigar and leaned back in the seat.

With the other man at the wheel, they drove north on U.S. 101 for some distance, then turned right off the highway and onto a one-lane dirt road that wound for miles up into the forest.

Campbell stared out the window trying to recognize landmarks but it was too dark for him to see anything except the winding road immediately in front of their headlights.

After fifty-eight minutes by Campbell's watch, they arrived at a tumble-down log cabin.

"Welcome to our field headquarters," the other man said as he got out of the Jeep, taking with him a small overnight bag.

The other man lighted gas lanterns on the floor of the cabin's roofed porch. Then he built a campfire outside on the ground.

For a time the two men sat on logs around the fire talking and smoking. The sky was overcast and it smelled like rain but none had fallen as yet.

"We needed a man experienced in both war and business to oversee the operation we're setting up here," the other man said. "The company feels you are that man."

Then he added, "There is great wealth in these forests yet to be taken and I'm not talking about timber."

"Good," Campbell said. "I hope it works out."

"Now I have a question. Do you plan to recruit men who are already in the business?"

"Hell no," Campbell replied. "Guys like that are too careless, too sloppy. They get picked up all the time. I'll set up my own crew, men I know can be trusted. And I'll train them my way."

"Will you have a selection to choose from?"

"Are you kidding? There're a hell of a lot of unemployed loggers around here. Men with families to support, house payments to make. Men who know the woods and how to keep their mouths shut."

"At all costs?"

"At all costs."

"In some of our other international operations we've been forced to have the talkative eliminated."

I'll bet you have, Campbell thought.

He rolled his cigar around his lips, then took it out of his mouth and gazed at the burning end. "I'll have no loose lips on my team."

"We have found that is the best way to operate," the other man said, then opened the overnight bag that had been at his feet. "It is time for the ceremony, Mr. Campbell."

He reached inside the bag and from a small plastic container withdrew a physician's tongue depressor covered with what looked to Campbell like a thick, hard coating of aged varnish.

He scraped some of the material from the tongue depressor into the palm of his hand, then mixed it with his own saliva.

Campbell saw that the resulting preparation had the consistency and color of greenish mustard.

"Please roll up your left sleeve," the other man said.

Campbell complied.

The other man pulled a smoldering twig from the fire, took hold of Campbell's left wrist, and burned the inside of his forearm. Showing no reaction except curiosity, Campbell saw that the burn mark was about the size of a dime.

"Once again," the other man said.

"Okay."

Ready to go the distance with this man to whom he had committed himself, Campbell stood stock-still and permitted his arm to be burned a second time, enlarging the first wound.

The other man held the blade of his opened knife in a flame, then used the cauterized blade to carefully scrape away the burned skin on Campbell's arm.

As Campbell silently watched, the other man carefully spread the green mixture over the raw, exposed flesh.

Now what? Campbell thought.

In one shocking instant he found out.

Campbell's body heated up like a flash fire. In seconds he was in agony—burning from the inside.

He grimaced in pain, silently cursing himself for having allowed the other man to administer a drug he knew nothing about.

He began to perspire.

Sweat poured down his face, his belly, his crotch, his arms and legs.

His blood raced. His heart pounded.

He became acutely aware of every vein and artery in his body, could actually feel them opening, widening, to allow for the fantastic tidal wave surging in his blood.

What if an artery doesn't open wide enough?

If it didn't, Campbell knew he'd have a stroke.

But fear of stroke—all coherent thought—swiftly flew from Campbell's mind as wrenching stomach cramps hit him with the brute force of sledgehammer blows.

He vomited violently and uncontrollably.

Again and again, over and over.

Realizing he was about to lose total control of his bodily functions, Campbell managed to struggle out of his pants and briefs—the throwing knife showing at his ankle, the gun at his back falling with his clothing—moments before he started to urinate and defecate in what seemed endless bursting streams.

After fifteen or twenty minutes, weakened by his body's explosive discharges, Campbell collapsed on the ground.

For seemingly endless hours there was only a hollow, echoing silence . . . and then there was nothing at all.

When Ruby Campbell came around, he feared he'd gone blind and deaf.

The only part of him that functioned were his nostrils. An impeccably clean man, he smelled with disgust the fluids expelled from his body.

Suddenly, without warning and totally beyond his physical control, he began to shriek and growl.

Then, as if powered by some all-compelling outside force, he moved lumbersomely about on all fours, pawing the earth, blindly lifting his head to read the odors of the forest.

With a sudden terrifying surge upward, he felt himself rise in the air. He spread his arms as if they were wings, then seemed to soar on the thermals.

He retained enough sense of self to realize with breathtaking disbelief that hordes of animals—bears, cougars, eagles—were passing through him, trying, one after the other, to form themselves with his human body.

And it hurt. God, how it hurt!

For hours, it seemed, he ran and flew with the beasts, groaning and screaming in mind-rending agony.

Finally all grew black again, and Campbell was neither human nor animal, but something strange and sentient caught between the two life-forms.

Gradually he became aware of the painful rushing of his blood, a sensation so intense it rocked his whole body and he thought his heart would burst.

The flash flood inside his body moved faster and faster until Campbell writhed in agony.

Tears streamed from his eyes, mucus from his nostrils.

He gasped and gasped, repeatedly, for breath.

Slowly, the pounding became steady and rhythmic like a great tolling death bell.

When at last it finally subsided altogether, Campbell was overcome with pain and exhaustion and he passed out.

When Campbell awoke he had no idea who or where he was.

As he became more aware of himself, he remembered the so-called ceremony he had undergone, the pain of it, and the subsequent strangeness. Moving his head around, he realized he was inside the old log cabin.

He had been cleaned up, dressed, placed on a cot with a mattress, and covered with a blanket. A candle burned in a dish on the kitchen table.

Turning his head he saw that his knife and gun lay on the seat of an adjacent kitchen chair, handy to his reach.

He stood up carefully, fully expecting to stagger from weakness after his unbelievable ordeal.

But, surprising himself, he was not at all weak. Instead, he felt invigorated and extremely strong. He dressed, walked to the open doorway of the cabin without difficulty, and looked outside.

The night was deep and dark and wet. A wistful rain had come. There was something about the sound that reminded Campbell of a woman weeping softly, trying to get control of herself, then weeping again. The rain reminded him of one particular woman.

Where had he heard that sound before? And then he remembered. In France. The Frenchwoman who was about to shoot one of his men in the back because her German lover had been killed.

He remembered how he gentled her out of it, thinking that in a sane world she and her German young man could have married and had a life together. That was so long ago, but sometimes it seemed more real than what was happening now.

Filled suddenly with strength and feeling clearheaded, he walked outside where spits of wind struck his face, followed by a lash of tearful rain. Looking up, he saw the stars seeming to race by as moisture-laden clouds passed overhead.

Campbell soon realized that he could hear the tiniest sounds coming to him from the forest, sounds he could never have heard before, even a banana slug groping its determined way across a distant moss-covered log.

Although it was the middle of a dark night, he could see *into* the forest, see the needles on branches far away, smell every scent exhaled from the damp forest floor.

His vision, his sense of smell—everything about him—seemed larger than life. His body felt immensely strong, as if even a hail of bullets could not fell him.

When the other man stepped up onto the porch, Campbell asked, "What the hell was that stuff?"

"A secret preparation acquired by our founder."

"Now tell me about the aftereffects?"

"Your present feeling of strength will not diminish," the

other man said. "You can go whole days without being hungry or thirsty. You can move through the forest for hours without tiring. Every sense you possess has been heightened."

"What's the point?"

"It has put the rhythm of the forest into your blood. It will show you where the animals are."

At first Campbell wondered what the other man was talking about. Then he realized that he now had crystal-clear mental pictures of where the animals were moving through the forest.

He could see in his mind the geographic locations where the eagles were nesting, the bears coming out of hibernation, the cougars hunting.

The other man went on. "After you set up your organization, you may want your key men to have some. It sharpens the senses and increases stamina during long hunts when carrying food and water is difficult. It makes the human hunter invisible to poor-sighted but acute-smelling forest animals. It kills the human odor."

The other man smiled. "So my friend," he said, putting his hand on Campbell's shoulder, "you are now one of us."

He handed Campbell a package and asked him to open it.

When Campbell did so, he found a large quantity of American money in small denominations.

"The first payment on your contract," the other man said. "When you count it, you will find a hundred twenty-five thousand American dollars in used untraceable bills."

Campbell nodded and took the money.

5   When Ruby Campbell arrived home at six in the morning, he drove into the garage and parked. He got out of the car and stepped to his workbench, where he carefully wrapped the package of money in heavy plastic and fastened it with freezer tape.

Taking a shovel from the wall, he went outside and headed for Melisande's rose garden, planted in a sheltered ell of the house to protect them from salt-laden sea winds.

Here he buried the sealed package three feet deep between two newly planted English rosebushes, Heritage and Perdita, which had recently arrived from a world-famous Oregon rose grower.

Campbell knew the money would be safe there. Although Melisande fed, watered, and pruned the rose plants, no one dug in the rose bed except him.

He went inside the house, showered, and climbed naked into bed with his sleeping wife.

She turned in unconscious welcome, cradling his penis in her left hand and placing her right hand on top of his head—their favorite position when sleeping together. He loved the feeling of her breasts up tight against his back.

Campbell sighed and closed his eyes. He knew he should try and get some rest but he wasn't at all tired. Probably the effects of that stuff in his system.

He forced himself to remember that no matter how good he felt, he was still seventy-three years old.

Campbell's doctor, an experienced Seattle internist, had examined him only last month and found him as fit as a young man. "But use your head," the doctor had added. "Slow down a little. Don't tempt fate."

Then, his mind back on business, Campbell wondered if the deal he was now in would prove as dangerous as international drug dealing. Experience and the instincts of a hunter informed him it could turn out to be far worse.

Melisande stirred in her sleep and he knew she was waking up. He felt himself beginning to swell in his wife's hand like a spring seed.

Soon those exquisite pleasures known only to longtime lovers drove all other thoughts from Ruby Campbell's mind.

Nomadic groups of hunters were the first to reach the Northwest Coast. Over a period of time they changed into fishing societies, although it is not entirely clear when this transition took place . . . the Northwest Coast has seen human habitation for 12,000 to 15,000 years.

Settlements on the coast developed from south to north, as plateau hunters followed the Columbia River to the coast and, becoming a fishing society, gradually extended their territory northward. As the archaeological site at The Dalles on the lower stretch of the Columbia River and the remains of a mastodon hunt found on the north side of the Olympic Peninsula indicate, this process must have occurred 10,000 to 12,000 years ago.

—MAXIMILIEN BRUGGMANN AND PETER R. GERBER,
Indians of the Northwest Coast

Chapter 7

1   In spite of tireless work on the part of the law enforcement agencies involved, the investigation into the bizarre death of the young Indian boy remained frustratingly stalled.

So far, it seemed the little boy had belonged to no one. No one had seen or even heard about him while he was living. Inquiries were sent to all Indian Nations and organizations in the United States. He was simply unknown.

What description was available, scanty as it was, along with forensic details, had gone out over the Law Enforcement Telecommunications System to national and international police agencies.

There were no relatives, friends, or even acquaintances to be found. Old Man Ahcleet said the little boy had come from the stars.

When reporters called Hunter Kleoh, special agent in charge of the FBI office in Aberdeen, Kleoh politely said he was awfuly sorry he didn't have any further information, but they might try the state boys.

Leonard L. Duncan and Clarence Montgomery, senior homicide investigators for the state, had no news. Nor did the coroner's office.

"God, I wonder if they even found a damned body!" the crime reporter for the *Aberdeen Daily World* exploded to his boss. "There're sure a hell of a lot of people around here who don't know anything!"

Since Jordan was on patrol most of the time, she was difficult to get in touch with, especially when she didn't wish to be reached. Her telephone at Old Man Ahcleet's house was unlisted. In fact, very few people outside the nation even knew where she lived.

Frustrated reporters then called Paul Prefontaine, chief of police at Taholah. He referred them to Hunter Kleoh at the FBI, at which loud sighing was heard coming from the other end of the line because the old fruitless circle was forming again.

Jordan met several times with Hunter Kleoh to exchange thoughts and review developments, of which there were none. Only hurricanes of paperwork. Other than that, she continued to do her regular job.

Occasionally she saw Lima Clemente. She hadn't invited him to the house yet but always met him elsewhere—usually on the beach, regardless of the weather. By mutual unspoken consent, neither mentioned the butchered child.

During their times together, Lima Clemente asked many questions about the beliefs of her ancestors, many of which he came to understand Jordan still followed. He said he found them beautiful and meaningful. She did not tell him she was a shaman.

On her part, Jordan felt comfort in his presence and realized the natural barriers between them of gender and background were gradually coming down. Waking or sleeping, Lima Clemente was always in her mind.

So was the scalped face of the butchered boy.

One day when Tleyuk was at school and Old Man Ahcleet out visiting, Jordan removed the damaged gold medal and bright woven ribbon from her locked desk drawer.

As she held both medal and ribbon in her hand, she experienced once more that original bone-deep chill and suddenly realized it was very like the shock of terror and pain she'd felt when she'd touched the boy's severed head.

Could there be a connection? she wondered. *If so, what could it possibly be?*

She'd found the medal shortly after it had been dropped on the beach by Raven. Raven the trickster.

She'd found the child's body far away, up in the high country, several days later.

Then she remembered something.

She called Hunter Kleoh at his Aberdeen office. Although there was a question in his voice, he agreed to meet her at the log loading dock in Aberdeen in one hour.

Jordan didn't want the two of them to be seen together. These days the log loading dock in Aberdeen was about the emptiest place around.

In the past there'd been miles of log decks stacked fifteen feet high, log trucks roaring in and being unloaded, forklifts scurrying around, ships waiting in line to take on cargo. Now there was mostly silence.

When Kleoh arrived, Jordan watched him fondly as he got out of his car and waved to her.

He was a tall, heavyset man with thick, graying hair, deep vertical lines in his face, and a sudden bright smile that made him look at least ten years younger than his true age.

She knew several things about Hunter. One was that he

had to go on a brutal diet for two or three months every year before his medical examination came up.

And when he passed the test, Hunter invited those he considered his best friends to join him in fabulous celebration feasts, after which he quickly put back all the lost weight, and even more.

She knew he'd recently lost the wife he adored to a cruel death from ovarian cancer. Although he kidded around a lot, Jordan suspected there was really only one woman for Hunter.

And that one woman was now gone.

Jordan knew also that Hunter Kleoh was a very kind and thoughtful man.

After he climbed into her truck, Jordan drove around the deserted dock until she found a stack of logs behind which she parked. She turned to the FBI man.

"Hunter, does Dr. Gerber still have the remains of that Indian boy?"

Kleoh shook his head. "Phil sent those on to the state lab."

"He has the reports, doesn't he?"

"Oh, sure. And the forensic specimens the reports were made from."

"If I remember correctly, Dr. Gerber found several strands of what he said appeared to be threads embedded in the boy's severed neck."

"Yes, you're right. He did."

"If I gave you some threads, could you have Dr. Gerber see if they match the ones he found?"

Kleoh looked at her curiously. "Sure, Jordan."

"I'd like this to be unofficial, Hunter. Just between you and me. At least for the present."

"What have you got, Jordan?"

"That's the problem. I don't know if I've got anything."

"I can ask Phil to take a private look. No paperwork." He looked at her sternly. "On one condition."

"Which is?"

"That you'll have dinner with me at Ocean Shores."

"When you get the answer for me I will. I promise."

"You don't think I'm a dirty old man?"

"Hunter, no matter how hard you tried, there's no way you could ever be a dirty old man."

His face fell. "I don't know whether to take that as a compliment or an insult."

Jordan squeezed his hand. "Believe me, Hunter, coming from me it's a compliment."

She gave Hunter Kleoh a sealed envelope with her initials and the date scrawled on the front, then drove him back to his car.

Part Two

*Every year a given tree creates absolutely from scratch ninety-nine
percent of its living parts. Water lifting up tree trunks can climb
150 feet an hour; in full summer a tree can, and does, heave a ton
of water every day. . . .*

*A tree stands there, accumulating deadwood, mute and rigid as an
obelisk, but secretly it seethes; it splits, sucks and stretches; it heaves
up tons and hurls them out in a green, fringed fling.*

—ANNIE DILLARD
Pilgrim at Tinker Creek

Chapter 8

1 Two miles up Fire Road Six, which meanders north
off the Moclips Highway, an early-morning sky had
fallen down around the loggers' ears, wrapping both standing and fallen trees, men, machines, and waiting trucks in
a blur of misty fog.

Since mist alters everything, neither men nor machines
appeared to be what they were. Only the trees, although
specters of themselves, were recognizable as standing timber in this veiled world.

Ornamenting the muted scene, colorful blue curses
exploded into damp fog the color of crushed mother-of-
pearl.

Michael McTavish, from whose mouth the expletives were issuing, had discovered that once again, despite all their efforts, several feet of water covered a section of the rough road over which his trucks must pass to get the timber out of the woods and transported down to the Aberdeen docks.

Shortly after his company began hauling logs out of this show, McTavish realized that two hundred feet of Fire Road Six had been built over a bog, while fifty feet of *that* was an actual sinkhole.

Upon his first knowledge of this disconcerting fact, McTavish wanted to do the sensible thing: move that part of the road in question around the quicksand.

He'd inquired from Jordan Tidewater about getting the necessary permits to do so.

And found to his dismay that he must first obtain 185 signatures from the various Quinault owners of timber through which the proposed section of new road would pass. These particular allotments, although few in number, had numerous owners.

Many of these people were not only out of state, they were out of the country, some in South America, some in Europe.

By the time he got the last of the signatures—if he ever did—McTavish figured he'd be dead of old age. Or at least out of business.

So the battle—man and machines against quicksand—continued. Every morning they'd have to rebuild the road before they could run any trucks over it.

Two men would come out to the job three hours before the first load was scheduled to roll, take the skidder and go up into the logging operation and pull down the slash from the previous day's work, cut it loose, and drag it back to the bog and sinkhole.

Buck Trano would then direct the rest of the crew in the additional filling of the bad part of the road with brush, old snags, and hastily cut pieces of skinny peckerwood as a loose fill. Now they were having to cut up merchantable second growth and throw it into the pit.

And every morning a disgruntled McTavish, operating the company dump truck, hauled several loads of gravel from a pit three miles away and poured them into what the crew now called the Burma Road.

Usually this refilled section of road held during the day. But after eight hours of loaded log trucks compacting it down, by the next morning there'd always be more water, with an impassable quagmire underneath.

Along about the time the third truck and trailer of the next day, loaded with an additional fifty thousand pounds of raw logs, encountered the Burma Road, it gradually sank up to its running boards into the quagmire, despite the most valiant efforts of skilled drivers.

Because of this apparently insurmountable problem, Quinault Timber was now running only their four company-owned trucks.

The company had lost all of its freelance drivers, each of whom departed with his individually owned vehicle. "Get Burma Road fixed and we'll be back," they'd said, almost to a man.

Freelance drivers were paid according to the board footage they hauled through the scale. When production slowed down for any reason whatsoever, the drivers lost money they could be earning elsewhere. Besides, they didn't think it was good for their trucks to be jerked back and forth through the swamp.

Even the shake blocks weren't getting out. Shake blocks were made from cedar logs that had been buried for years. Disease and insect resistant, the buried trees were pulled out of the ground, then cut into chunks roughly the size of firewood, about sixteen inches long.

These chunks of nice, clear wood were taken out of the woods on a pickup or packed on a pallet and helicoptered out, headed for a shake mill where they were sliced into cedar shingles.

* * *

On this particular foggy morning, a DC-9 tractor, stationed between the Moclips Highway and the swampy area of Fire Road Six, was furiously attempting to pull yet another loaded log truck out of the sinking roadbed.

McTavish, frustration written all over his no-nonsense face, stood with his logging superintendent, Buck Trano, watching the desperate scene.

Both men wore standard woods' working gear: hard hats, calked boots, long-sleeved gray-striped loggers' shirts, red suspenders, and wide-legged, black denim pants cut off raggedly at the bottoms.

The ragged cuts at the bottom of loggers' pants were there for a specific purpose. If a man caught his pants on down timber or debris, the pants would rip—rather than stay whole and cause a fall that could seriously injure or even kill.

"I've been thinking about corduroying this damn road," McTavish said.

"Won't work," Trano said.

"Why not?"

"A road builder I met the other day tells me other guys around here have tried it and no matter how much crap you throw in, the quicksand just keeps on sucking it up."

"Then they're not doing it right."

The two men fell silent as they watched the herculean efforts of the big tractor and listened to the shrieks of the loaded truck as its driver tried desperately to pilot it through the muck.

McTavish turned and saw Jordan Tidewater driving up through the fog. She parked her power wagon in a weedy area off-road, waved to the two men as she got out, then approached them with her long-legged stride.

"Looks like you're still having trouble with Burma Road," she said, putting on a hard hat.

McTavish scowled. "I sure as hell wouldn't have contracted for this timber if I'd known about that quicksand."

This eighty-acre patch contained Douglas fir, Sitka

spruce, hemlock, and some western red cedar. Valuable stuff. But they had to be able to get it out.

Now, on this chilly April morning, with fog dripping from trees, equipment, and human noses, Jordan said, "I talked to my great-grandfather about your problem up here. Ahcleet told me to tell you that when the old-time loggers ran into quicksand like this they used to corduroy their roads."

"And it worked?" McTavish asked.

"Ahcleet says it did."

"We've fought this thing for nearly three months and it's cost us plenty. Every morning we're throwing in stumps and rubbish and gravel. God only knows how far down that sinkhole goes. It eats up every damn thing we put into it."

In reply, Buck took off his hard hat and ran a hand through his tightly curled chestnut hair. "You're the boss, Mike."

McTavish turned to the sheriff. "Jordan, thanks for the tip and be sure to thank your great-grandfather. What does he drink?"

"Jack Daniel's, but only for breakfast."

McTavish chuckled. "You tell that old man for me that if this works I'll buy all his breakfasts for the rest of his life."

"I'll be happy to give him your message," she said, smiling.

Trano said, "Hey, Jordan, there's talk around that the little Indian kid you found in the woods was all chopped up. Is that right?"

"Buck, you surprise me. I thought you'd know better than to listen to wild rumors."

As she walked back to her truck, Trano said, "Have you ever noticed what a great ass that gal has on her?"

McTavish looked at Jordan appreciatively. "She's a good-looking woman, all right. What always surprises me is how well she gets along with men, manages to keep them at arm's length without any hurt feelings. All kinds of men, and you sure get all kinds around here."

"I'd sure like to have a piece of that. How about you?"

"Everything I want I've got at home." Michael slapped Trano on the shoulder and laughed. "Buck, you'd better find a woman of your own and settle down. I think it's time."

McTavish made his way along the edge of the sunken roadbed until he reached the place where the road became a hard-packed surface again.

Since the trouble with the road, the company had kept an old pickup on this far side for convenience in running errands up to the landing or out where the fallers were working. In the way of loggers, the men named the old junker "Betsy."

Now, Mike got into the pickup, battered and scratched from its many long, hard days in the woods, turned the key in the ignition, and bounced ferociously up the rough, rutted roadbed in search of his chief faller. He knew Matthew Swayle was working alone this morning.

He reached the landing, a large, cleared area where both skidder and tower dragged in logs that had already been limbed and bucked; here to be sorted and hot-and-cold decked in preparation for loading onto trucks.

He drove past the landing to where the rough road ended, braked, climbed out of the pickup, and began walking in to where he could hear the screams of the chain saw followed by the crackle and deep-throated thud of falling trees.

When he reached his destination, he stopped and stood absolutely still, hands on hips, watching Matt Swayle as the faller prepared to bring down six big trees at one time. One tree was a Sitka spruce, a couple were hemlocks, and the rest were Douglas firs.

Right in the path of descent was an old cedar, whitened by an ancient death, and with only one limb, and that a stovepipe growing out at a ninety-degree angle like the chimney of an ancient cabin.

McTavish saw that this dead tree's one and only limb was about seventy-five feet from the ground. Trees like these made fine places for eagle nests. Apparently there was one there; he saw something dark in the crotch.

If it was an eagle's nest it had to be an abandoned one. Otherwise they would not be allowed to fell the tree.

Swayle was a lean, quiet, self-contained man with dark hair, bleak eyes, and a look of great, paced strength.

Some years ago he had lost his wife and three young sons in a house fire, had driven up just in time to see his entire family, still living at that moment, perish in the hellish flames. He still carried the scars on his body from desperately trying to rescue them.

Watching this man at work was always a pleasure to McTavish. It seemed to satisfy some kind of an artistic thirst within himself.

The study of wind and weather, McTavish knew, was a great part of a faller's specialized knowledge. He must figure wind flow and strength, must execute the right cuts for each particular tree.

Swayle was a master faller, one who could make the trees flow any way he wanted them to. Like a symphony conductor, McTavish thought, and apparently with no more effort.

McTavish knew, however, that it took physical and mental strength, patience, and an encyclopedic knowledge of weather patterns as well as intense familiarity with the trees themselves.

An inexperienced man could easily get himself and others killed. Or, at the very least, end up with such a mess on the ground that half the timber would be ruined in trying to get it untangled.

Swayle, unaware of McTavish's presence, studied the five still standing trees that he'd already notched, then made the final cut on the sixth one, a somewhat deeper cut than on the other trees.

At that very moment, the northwest wind trumpeted in as if from stage left, dispersing the fog but bringing with it gail-like sheets of hard, cold rain.

Swayle turned his back to the slashing rain, cried, "Timber!" then stood waiting as the sixth tree fell onto the fifth, knocking that into the fourth, the fourth falling and knocking over the third, and so on until all six trees lay in a neat, overlapping pile on the ground.

But something wasn't right.

McTavish saw Swayle start to run when the sixth tree was halfway through its descent.

After the thunder and thump of its falling had ceased, Swayle approached the downed timber with McTavish close behind him.

"What's wrong, Matt?" McTavish called as they ran along the lengths of the fallen trees.

"Christ Almighty!" Swayle said. "Look at that."

They both stopped abruptly when they realized something was bound to the crotch of the sixth tree, the old cedar with the stovepipe limb.

It was an eagle's nest, all right. And something was in the nest.

About seventy-five feet along the old cedar's prone length, through the flooding rain, a dead child gazed at them out of empty eye sockets.

Momentarily speechless, McTavish and Swayle stared back, the rain beating hard on their faces.

"My God, it's a kid!" McTavish whispered.

The two men looked at each other in shocked silence, then back at what was tied in the nest of the tree.

"Think we should cut him loose?"

"Don't touch him, Matt. I'll see if I can still catch the sheriff."

McTavish ran back through the woods to Betsy, where he crawled inside the truck and radioed down to Buck Trano, who told him that Jordan Tidewater was just about ready to leave.

"Let me talk to her, Buck. Now."

Down on Fire Road Six, Trano handed Jordan the radio.

"What is it, Mike?" she asked.

"We've got a dead kid up here."

"A *child*?"

"Sure as hell is."

"Girl or boy?"

"A boy, I think, but I'm not sure."

"Okay, I'll get in touch with the coroner's office."

"Wait right there, Jordan. I'll send one of the choker set-ters back down with Betsy."

Jordan phoned in to the Enforcement Center at Taholah, reached Prefontaine, who said he'd call the coroner's office for her and tell them what was going on.

Battling wind and great surges of rain, Jordan and Buck Trano walked around the sinkhole and stood shivering as they waited for the woods' pickup.

After Betsy noisily arrived, splashing mud every which way, they both crowded into the battered one and only seat. The driver, a young choker setter, was soaking wet, white-faced, and very scared.

At the end of the road, Trano told the choker setter to stay in the truck. He and Jordan climbed out and slogged their way into the timber-falling site.

Jordan politely asked McTavish, Swayle, and Trano to keep themselves and others away from the fallen tree that was holding its terrible burden.

As she approached the crime scene, she gagged, nearly overcome by the awful stench of evil rising above the sweet fragrances of falling rain and the things of the for-est. She realized that it was an odor others could not detect.

She remembered the missing person notice posted at Graves Creek on the south shore of Lake Quinault: *Blond hair cut like a boy's, green eyes, freckles, seventy pounds, four feet tall.*

She couldn't tell about the eyes; they were gone. Ravens, of course.

She was certain this was not a young boy. It was undoubtedly the body of Sherry Lyne Adams, who had been eleven years old.

Sheltering under the nearest standing tree, Jordan started the paperwork on this new homicide, writing down the date, then 93/AK since it would be another federal case, and adding Victim A-13-D.

Then she established the crime scene with difficulty, sloshing around in the ever-deepening mud.

She took a number of in situ photographs at sharp right angles. She unzipped her jacket, sheltering her notepad under it, and wrote complete descriptions of every detail shown in the photos, then drew a rough diagram of the area.

When she gently touched her bare hands to the dead girl's face, she did not sense the welter and extremes of emotion she had felt when she'd placed her gloved hands on the butchered face of the Indian boy.

Instead, she was overwhelmed by such a hopeless, dark despair that she wondered if this child had not died a swift death. What nightmares had she lived to endure?

Deep in thought, she left the body where it was, strapped to the fallen tree, until the coroner and the medical examiner arrived from Aberdeen.

Frenzied rains were making the road problem even worse. With the weather the way it was, and the expected turmoil of police and medical personnel coming and going, McTavish closed the job down for the rest of the day. But the men could not go home. They had to remain for questioning.

Trano said he'd go back down the road in Betsy, wait at the sinkhole for the law enforcement officials, and ferry them up into the timber as they arrived.

Both men knew it would be a long wait. Even if Paul Prefontaine had been able to get in touch with the medical examiner immediately after Jordan's call, Fire Road Six was at least one hour away from Aberdeen. Probably a lot longer in this hellish weather, Trano said.

An hour and a half later, Jasper Wright, the deputy county sheriff, arrived first, followed closely by the state police.

The coroner and Hunter Kleoh came up from Aberdeen in the same car.

Their vehicles had been parked a couple of miles away between the quicksand sinkhole and the Moclips Highway. They'd walked around the sinking roadbed, then been taken up to the crime scene by Trano in rattling Betsy.

When the ambulance arrived, Trano decided to have the DC-9 pull it through the sinkhole. It would be unseemly, he thought, for the dead child to be carried over two miles on a litter in this beastly weather.

After his arrival, the coroner, head bent, big black umbrella up, slogged through the mud to the dead body.

Kleoh pulled Jordan aside and told her under his breath that he didn't have any information yet on the contents of the envelope she'd given him. She said she hadn't expected anything so soon.

"Think this one has anything to do with the boy?" Kleoh asked as the rain poured off the brim of his hat.

"It seems unlikely, Hunter," she replied, wiping the rain off her face. "There's nothing about it that's the same."

Soon there was a milling group of law enforcement personnel clad in waterproof raincoats and streaming rainhats. Several of the officers began questioning Quinault Timber's crew.

Most of the new arrivals were not wearing galoshes or heavy boots. Some lost their shoes as they sloshed around in the mud, and cursed quietly.

There were mutterings, some shouting, and frequent losses of tempers while a sea of mud expanded around them like a rising tide.

Upon cursory examination of the corpse, the coroner found that the child had been tied to the stovepipe crotch of the tree and positioned in the nest with several strands of heavy rope.

The hands of the victim were bagged by the coroner's assistant. Paper bags were placed over the hands and taped at the wrists to ensure that any microscopic evidence under the nails was not lost—fibers, tissue, hairs—anything that might have indicated a scuffle or struggle by the small victim prior to death.

This procedure also protected the hands from becoming contaminated by trace evidence during transportation.

En route to the ambulance, the paramedics slipped and dropped the body, then fell into the mud themselves.

Finally, the muddy paramedics got the muddy corpse back onto the muddy litter and into the muddy ambulance, which then took off screaming at the top of its Klaxon voice.

"Why in God's name the siren?" Kleoh muttered.

"Probably to vent the driver's frustration," Jordan said, shivering from the chill.

After the ambulance's dramatically loud and mud-splattering departure, drawing yet more curses from those working the scene, the coroner, walking carefully in the mud, approached Jordan and Kleoh.

"I can tell you right now the body is that of a skinny young female around ten or eleven years old," he said. "We're awfully busy with a twelve-car pileup but as soon as I get back I'll see that Phil does the autopsy. You two are invited. Consider it a command performance."

"I think that young girl might be Sherry Lyne Adams," Jordan said. "I'll get in touch with the park ranger, find out who her parents are."

The coroner nodded. "If we're pretty sure that's who it is, they'll have to come in and identify her."

A small, thin man, he took a white linen handkerchief out of his coat picket and mopped the moisture off his face. From his appearance, Jordan suspected there were human tears mixed in with the rain running down the man's cheeks.

"Was she sexually molested?" Jordan asked.

His reddened eyes looked off into the distance. "In every way possible," he said.

2   Immediately before the autopsy, which was con-
    ducted that same afternoon, Jordan reached Sherry
Lyne Adams's father in Seattle.

"Mr. Adams, can you tell us what clothes your daughter
had on when you last saw her?" she asked.

When she heard the father say Sherry Lyne had been
wearing a red insulated jacket, and green cotton overalls
with a Beauty and the Beast T-shirt, she turned and nodded
to Philip Gerber, the medical examiner.

"I'm afraid I have some very bad news, Mr. Adams. We
have found the body of a young girl who may be your
daughter. Is it possible that you could come to Aberdeen
and see if it is Sherry Lyne?"

They all heard the man's deep cry over the telephone.
After a few words of sincere but ultimately meaningless
consolation, Jordan hung up and said quietly, "He and
his wife will charter a small plane and fly in this
evening."

Unlike the unknown little boy, this young girl had not been
dismembered. Except for the missing eyes, Dr. Gerber had
an entire body to work with.

Shooting from all directions, his assistant took a series
of photographs at right angles to the body using first a
wide-angle lens and then a regular lens.

There were obvious rope burns on both wrists and
ankles made before death.

Dr. Gerber examined the body for rigor mortis and livor
mortis, the latter being the settling of blood due to gravity. He
found livor mortis on her back and on the back of her legs.

"Livor mortis is usually fully developed after ten hours,"
he said. "While livor is of little evidential value it does
show that this body was moved after death."

Fingernail scrapings were taken, as were anal and vagi-
nal swabs. Stomach contents. Samples of head hair were
plucked in order to obtain the roots.

Her sparse pubic hair, heartbreakingly just beginning to

show, was combed and plucked; these could provide vital clues in identifying the perpetrator.

The usual autopsy cuts were made, the physical parts that made up what once had been a living, laughing young girl dispersed for further laboratory study.

Her heart's blood was taken using a turkey baster. Urine was collected from the bladder. Slices were taken from the liver, the bladder, the kidneys, the brain, a fillet from the lungs.

As the approximate quarter-inch slices dropped down, Dr. Gerber examined each piece, ending up with eight jars marked with the case number and the victim's name. The jars were labeled, sealed, boxed, and handed over to toxicology.

She had been abused in particularly horrible ways, her orifices torn and sexually entered. Her body, scabby from smeared, dried semen, looked as if a group of men had surrounded her as they ejaculated.

"She drowned," Philip Gerber announced. "That's what caused her death."

"Drowned?" Hunter Kleoh asked incredulously.

Dr. Gerber looked up. "In semen. One hell of a lot. In her vagina, her rectum, down her throat. She aspirated some of that into her lungs."

A great wave of nausea burst over Jordan and she swallowed hard to regain control. Kleoh handed her a mint, then took one himself.

"Does the amount of semen mean more than one attacker?" Kleoh asked.

Gerber shook his head. "I won't know until we do the tests. See if it came from one secretor or several."

"And if it all came from one man?"

Gerber chewed on the earpiece of his glasses. "If it all came from one man, I'd say he kept this little girl alive for quite a while before she finally died."

"God, what are you going to tell the parents?" Jordan asked.

"As little as I have to."

*   *   *

Jordan and Kleoh both waited with Dr. Gerber for Mr. and Mrs. Adams who, after they arrived from Seattle, experienced every parent's worst nightmare.

They had finally found their missing child.

As Jordan heard their brokenhearted weeping, she was filled with melancholy.

She and Hunter Kleoh stepped out into the hall with Dr. Gerber to give the parents a moment or two of privacy with their daughter, who had been cleaned up, before a police officer drove them back to the airfield.

Looking out at the night, Jordan whispered, "I wonder who weeps for the little boy with the scalped face."

"Maybe no one," Kleoh said.

"Old Man Ahcleet says he came from the stars."

"I'm almost ready to believe that."

"Hunter, something mystifies me."

"What's that?"

"Why did the man or men who abused that little girl in such a brutal way bother to put her clothes back on? Why was an act of the greatest disrespect followed by an act of respect?"

3 Following the discovery of the young girl's violated body, parents on the entire Olympic Peninsula became more watchful of their children, some no longer trusting school buses but bringing their youngsters to school in the morning and meeting them at school in the afternoons.

4 There were the usual number of false confessions to both murders.

In each case, the police, as is customary, held something back. With the little Indian boy, only the law knew how he had been disfigured. With the young girl, only they knew that she had been dressed again after the numerous violations done to her.

5   Michael McTavish's Quinault Timber got busy corduroying Burma Road.

The crew cut a series of sixty-foot-long timbers and laid them five feet apart over the swamp, so that the ends of the timbers were on solid ground.

They filled the area in between the crossing logs with brush, toppings, anything they could get ahold of. When all was firmly packed, they graveled the entire length of swampy roadway.

To McTavish's delight, Fire Road Six was now passable and the logs started rolling out.

Once again, I set down the core of what I continue to believe.
Nature is a part of our humanity, and without some awareness
and experience of that divine mystery man ceases to be man. When
the Pleiades and the wind in the grass are no longer a part of the
human spirit, a part of very flesh and bone, man becomes, as it
were, a kind of cosmic outlaw, having neither the completeness and
integrity of the animal nor the birthright of true humanity. As I
once said elsewhere, "Man can either be less than man or more than
man, and both are monsters, the last more dread."

—HENRY BESTON,
The Outermost House

Chapter 9

1   It had been a day with entirely too much weather,
Jordan thought wearily as she parked her power
wagon late that night in front of Old Man Ahcleet's house.
Weather of all kinds, from atmospheric storms to human
emotional outbursts.

She longed for her bed and her special pillow with its
calming herbal mixture of flaxseed, lavender, roses, wild
orchids, mugwort, and oak moss.

Tonight she did not feel like a law enforcement officer.
And certainly not like a shaman of The People. She felt
like what she was: a tired, discouraged young woman at
the end of a particularly bad day.

Before she went into the house to face family conversations with her great-grandfather and her young son, Jordan needed to sit absolutely still for a moment or two, gather enough strength to even get out of the truck.

First thing this morning she'd made the trip out to Quinault Timber's logging operation on Fire Road Six to tell McTavish about Ahcleet's suggestion that he corduroy the road over the quicksand bed.

Then came the discovery of the murdered girl tied in the eagle's nest in the stovepipe cedar.

Who had done such a thing? And why, having committed the crime, would the perpetrator go to the trouble of carrying an inert body seventy-five feet up a standing tree and put it in an eagle's nest?

A tree that was marked for felling.

One fact was clear, she realized. Whoever had carried that girl up the tree must be in the logging business.

The average man does not shinny up and down tall trees; does not know how, for one thing, and does not have the necessary equipment.

Or perhaps it was an inharmonious Indian trying to re-create in some sick, offbeat way the ancient rituals.

Like the ritual of the Indian boy's scalped face?

Jordan could understand someone trying to dispose of a body that way in a part of the forest where people were not likely to be around. After all, even the most remote ground burials were frequently found and dug up by wild animals.

But in an area that was obviously being logged? And in a tree that was marked for immediate harvesting? It didn't make sense.

Then she sighed. Right now she was too tired and too wet and too depressed to think of anything except a deep, hot bathtub with mounds of fragrant rose-scented bubbles and her warm, comforting bed with its special pillow.

She stepped down out of the truck into darkness and a cold, slashing rain and ran up onto the porch.

* * *

Perfume?

Jordan smelled it while she was still outside dripping on the mat. She threw open the front door.

And saw a stream of bubbles moving sensuously down the hall to meet her. In the background she heard the sound of cascading water and Tleyuk's young voice raised in treble clef song.

The aroma of roses was overwhelming. What kind of bubble bath had she bought?

She walked carefully down the hall through soapy bathwater and found Tleyuk in the tub surrounded by clouds of steam and billows of bubbles that were even then overrunning the tub and swirling at her feet.

"Tleyuk!"

He looked up quickly through a mask of bubbles. "Gosh, Mom, I didn't know you were home."

"Turn off the water and get out of that tub!"

He obeyed immediately, pulling the plug as he arose through the steam covered with thousands of bubbles.

"You look like a spitbug in its nest," Jordan said, undecided between laughter or anger. "Dry yourself off and clean up this mess in here and out in the hall."

She started to leave, then turned back. "Is there any hot water left?"

"Well, the last of it was getting kind of cool."

"Dare I ask about my bubble bath?"

"I guess I got carried away, Mom," he said, holding up the empty bottle.

She crossed her arms. "And where was Grandfather while this bathing marathon was going on?"

"Remembering by the fire. You know, about the old days."

"I wish he'd remember he has a small boy to watch."

Tleyuk was offended. "I am not a small boy anymore, Mother," he said with dignity. "I am practically a teenager."

She gave him a mother look, then splashed back down the hall toward the living room, telling herself she would not yell at Ahcleet. He was old and wonderful and didn't deserve her anger. Still—

The fragrance of roses grew even stronger. Had Tleyuk anointed the whole house with her bubble bath before he got in the tub?

She stood in the doorway into the living room and saw that Ahcleet sat in his old leather chair watching her.

"It's a good thing I don't have hay fever," he said.

As she glanced around the darkened room, lit only by light from the television screen and the fireplace, Jordan's eyes opened wide in astonishment.

She saw roses, hundreds of roses, thousands, everywhere. Spilling from vases, jars, bowls, pans; from anything that could possibly be used as a container for water.

"You'd better look in your room," he said.

Jordan ran into her bedroom. Roses were so thick she could scarcely make her way to her bed. And here in her own private space the roses were all contained in varying sizes of crystal bowls.

On her herbal pillow lay several profusely blooming branches of the same kind of rose that filled the house.

A gilt-edged card with her name written by hand in ink on the front was attached to the branch. Opening it, she found a message printed in gold ink on the inside:

> ### FLOWN TO YOU FROM FRANCE
> ### FOR YOUR PLEASURE
> *Autumn Damask*, Rosa gallica bifera, *was the first known rose in human history. Used in the cult of Aphrodite, it grew on the Island of Samor during the tenth century B.C. and flowered twice a year. It is the only kind of rose grown in the Balkans and the Near East for the production of attar of roses.*

Attar of roses, the most heavenly fragrance in the world. Still in her wet, muddy clothes, Jordan sat down heavily on the edge of her bed.

The expense involved in this profusion of rare roses and collector's crystal was enormous. All this could not be for her. Surely someone had made a mistake!

She looked at the card again and it *was* her name written on the front by someone's hand.

She turned the card over and there on the back, in the same hand that had written her name on the front, appeared this quotation: *"Une rose d'automne est plus qu'une autre exquise."*

She remembered enough of her high school French to translate the meaning: "More exquisite than any other is the autumn rose."

And where had the roses come from? GROWN IN FRANCE, the card said.

She looked again. No, it read, FLOWN TO YOU FROM FRANCE.

Who knew her well enough to want to do such a thing? Who had the money? This was the act of a very rich man for a woman he needed to impress. Or one he truly loved. No one loved her. Not in that way.

She got up and went back into the living room, passing Tleyuk who was down on his hands and knees cleaning up bathwater and bubbles with a mop and what looked like all the towels they owned.

"Grandfather, how did these roses get here?" she asked.

"Thunderbird brought them." He sniffed approvingly. "They sure smell good, don't they? Reminds me of all the wild roses that used to grow around here when I was a boy."

She crossed the room and sat down on the sofa opposite the old man.

"Please. It's been a hard day."

"I'll tell you what I know. That's all I can do."

She leaned forward.

"It happened this afternoon before Tleyuk got home from school."

"What happened?"

"A helicopter landed on the beach. Three men dressed in

some kind of uniforms got out. I thought we were being invaded." His eyes twinkled. "Probably by the Makah."

"Uniforms?"

He nodded.

"What kind of uniforms were they? Army? Navy? Marines? Coast Guard? Boy Scouts?"

"La'qewamax, I did not recognize them," he said sternly.

She smiled. "Okay, Grandfather, I'm sorry. Please go on."

"One of the uniformed men ran up the beach and onto the road. I saw him looking around until he found our house. He blew a whistle and the others came up through the rain, all carrying big boxes. They made several trips."

"Were there any markings on the boxes?"

Ahcleet shook his head. "None that I could see."

"How did the roses get inside the house?"

"One of the men knocked on the door. When I opened it he said in kind of a cracked English that they had flowers for Jordan Tidewater."

"And what did you say?"

"I didn't say anything at first. The men looked like warriors but they seemed harmless enough. I couldn't see any weapons."

"And then?"

"I told them to come in but to wipe their feet first. They did and arranged the flowers as you see them. When they were finished they cleaned everything up and left. They were very polite."

"Didn't you ask them who the flowers were from?"

"I did."

"What did they say?"

"One of them said you would know."

"So there was no message for me?"

"Just the flowers. Seems to me that's a pretty strong message."

Jordan could feel questions rising in Ahcleet that she did

not want to answer. Not at the moment. What she wanted to do was go somewhere where she'd be alone to think.

She stood up. "Since there's no hot water left I'm going out back to take a sweat bath."

"You look very tired. Should I come out and help you?"

"No, Grandfather, but thank you anyway."

"Be sure you keep awake. Don't fall over on the hot rocks."

She smiled at him, regretting her recent displeasure, and thankful she had not voiced it aloud. What would she ever do without this lovely old man?

Because Jordan knew—and feared—he was not immortal, sometimes she tried to imagine life without him. Death must come to him someday. But the thought of Ahcleet's death presented a forbidding wall in Jordan's mind, one she could not surmount.

Life without her great-grandfather was unimaginable. Which would make it all the harder on her, she knew, when the inevitable happened.

Old Man Ahcleet had lived through many changes. From being an honored whaler, a *hoachinicaha,* as a young man— the livid scar on the bridge of his nose proved his prowess— through the discarding of the old ways by most of the Quinaults due to white teachings and accusations of devil worship, to becoming a powerful shaman in his middle years.

Some of The People, even now, were ashamed of the old ways. But not Ahcleet. And not Jordan.

The devils that missionaries had accused the Quinaults of worshipping were in the whites' own minds, Jordan thought, and represented the intruders' personal fear of anything or anyone different from themselves.

In the peculiarly limited manner of most organized religions, the love their missionaries claimed to bring was tainted with racism and hatred. A sort of "follow my God but clean my toilet" mentality.

Those who understood the old Smokehouse Religion—

with its old ways and old beliefs—would also know how truly beautiful it was.

"And still is," Jordan whispered to herself, "for those of us who open our minds."

She thought again of her dead mother. How in the world could Jocasta have forsaken the beliefs of her ancestors?

But Jordan knew how, when she really thought about it. Hadn't she herself, not too long ago, followed the same path of disbelief, of striving for the white man's values?

Probably Jocasta, like so many others, had been laughed at, made fun of, spit upon by whites she was trying to emulate, not realizing the strangers were empty vessels full of ignorance and noise, signifying nothing.

Jordan leaned over and kissed her great-grandfather, then went outside through the driving rain carrying one Autumn Damask rose.

2   Now that she was alone, Jordan cried a little to relieve her tension and tiredness as she prepared the sweat bath.

As she worked, she reflected that the sweat bath was not as important in the ancient Quinault way of life as it had been with other Native American people.

Probably, she thought, because her ancestors bathed twice a day, and sometimes more. They'd always been surrounded by water, in the sea, in the rivers, in the waterfalls, falling from the sky.

But when you've got an eight-year-old son who beats you to the hot water and the bubble bath, it's kind of nice to have a sweat bath in your backyard.

When the rocks shimmered with heat, she splashed water on them, creating clouds of steam, then sat back on her heels, holding the rose, and wondered if she really liked being female.

While in the sweat bath Jordan acknowledged to herself that Lima Clemente must have sent the roses. Was it possible that he was as deeply attracted to her as she was to him?

What kind of man makes such an opulent display of his wealth to a woman he's barely met?

A helicopter, men in uniform, thousands of the most expensive roses in the world flown in from France, numerous Waterford crystal vases . . .

Was it simply a matter of the peacock spreading his tail? The arrogance of a man who always gets what he wants, because no matter how high the cost, he can well afford it?

Did this mean he wanted her?

For all Lima Clemente knew there might be someone in Jordan's life with whom she was deeply in love.

Jordan herself, of course, knew there was no such man. Not anymore. And only she knew the powerful feelings that had arisen within her when she'd first met Lima Clemente.

Then a police officer's thought intruded: How much money does a man make who sells logging equipment in Chile and the rest of South America? Was Lima Clemente a very wealthy man? Perhaps he came from a wealthy family.

Although she had no answer to those pragmatic questions, there was one thing Jordan understood now with absolute certainty. And a feeling of breathless anticipation.

Lima Clemente was destined to become extremely important in her life.

She herself was a woman of spiritual power. She sensed that Lima Clemente was also a person of great power. Power that had nothing to do with the Christian symbol of the cross he wore around his neck.

Power different from hers, but just as strong, and certainly as ancient,

With a great uplifting of her spirit, Jordan wondered if perhaps at last she had found the man who was in all ways her equal.

* * *

When she emerged from the sweat bath soothed and strengthened, the storm had passed. Everything outside smelled deliciously rain-wet.

Jordan gathered up her clothing and moved carefully so as not to step on the tiny green tree frogs she heard jumping around after the rain.

It was a shadowy night, and looking up into the sky Jordan saw that the stars were coming out. She inhaled deeply, smelling the promise of spring all around her.

At that moment, something separated itself from the blackness of the bushes and made its way silently to the road in front of Ahcleet's house.

A stealthy figure that hurried swiftly along, it was wearing a long black robe that fell from humped shoulders.

The Klokwalle, Jordan breathed to herself.

And then it was gone, so suddenly that in immediate retrospect it seemed to have been only an apparition.

She watched the now-empty road, illuminated somewhat by starlight, then went into the house knowing she must soon prepare herself for the painful and fear-inspiring ritual of *tamanois.*

But not quite yet.

First Jordan wanted to think about the force of love she could no longer ignore, the one she knew she was now ready to welcome.

She lifted the Autumn Damask to her nostrils. Wilted from the heat of the sweat bath, close to death, its fragrance was even stronger.

There is a pleasure in the pathless woods,
There is a rapture on the lonely shore,
There is society where none intrudes,
By the deep sea, with music in its roar:
I love not man the less, but Nature more.
　　　　　—LORD BYRON,
　　　"Childe Harold's Pilgrimage"

Chapter 10

1　　Morning came with a blaze of sun and the movements of young breezes, agitated and uncertain as if they were just learning to fly.

Congregations of seagulls rose as one body through the sparkling air, sounding like newly washed bedsheets flapping in the wind.

Gone were the rain clouds and gales of the day before, the thunder and lightning, the sense of apocalypse descending.

To make life even sweeter, it was Saturday, with no school for Tleyuk. And, as it happened this week, it was also Jordan's day off.

A nursling gust tickled the hanging chimes on Old Man

Ahcleet's front porch, where noisy Northwest blackbirds yelled at scarlet-breasted finches over the contents of the bird feeder. There was more than enough food for all, but the blackbirds stubbornly refused to share.

"What a bunch of nags!" Jordan laughed to herself as she sat watching them.

On this informal morning she was wearing jeans, thongs, and one of her brother's floppy old white shirts, open at the neck, long sleeves rolled up to her elbows.

While the blackbirds did not actually attack the finches, one particularly hormonal male raised his red-striped wings just enough so that they looked like humped black shoulders, then hung down his menacing head between them, glaring at the smaller birds, who took one look and fled. A perfect imitation of Snoopy doing Dracula! Jordan thought.

Or the Klokwalle.

Disturbed by the latter comparison, she stood up, stretched, and decided that today she would distribute her roses among the older generation of Quinaults, people she knew would enjoy having them.

Activity of a different nature was going on out on the back porch. Unbeknownst to Jordan, Tleyuk had been up to more than just getting into his mother's bubble bath. But the fault was not entirely his.

Improbable as it seemed, Old Woman Scatt's cat had fallen in love with the eight-year-old boy.

The scraggly black-and-yellow animal lurked around Old Man Ahcleet's house, hiding in the bushes when it caught sight of the old man or Jordan, weaving seductively between Tleyuk's legs, meowing with hoarse passion when they were alone.

At first Tleyuk had tried to chase the cat away, fearing his mother's displeasure and his great-great-grandfather's loudly voiced wrath.

He didn't even think about the cat's owner, Old Woman Scatt, or her anger. Tleyuk knew she was a low-class person, a descendant of slaves, not important enough to bother with.

Despite the disapprobation of Tleyuk's family, the cat was a persistent and thoughtful lover. It always arrived bearing gifts: a shed snake's skin, a headless mouse . . .

("And where's the head?" Tleyuk had asked, peering suspiciously down the cat's throat.)

. . . a large black beetle with its dead legs sticking straight up; the broken-off wing of a seagull; a small, bedraggled starfish.

Its gift list also included objects such as a tiny cracked pot from a doll's porcelain tea set, an empty mussel shell, a shiny beach agate.

Helpless before such feline adoration, Tleyuk began to secretly feed the cat leftovers: bits of crisp fried salmon skin, the fat, limp parts of bacon, cold potatoes, a small moldy piece of huckleberry pie.

This clandestine friendship between cat and boy reached joyous fruition when Tleyuk discovered that the animal would eat just about everything except broccoli.

Wow! We're brothers under the skin! Tleyuk thought excitedly. *Maybe someday I can turn into him. Or he can turn into me. Or together we can turn into each other!*

"I just had to get out of the house," Tleyuk told the cat this particular Saturday morning as they both sat on the lower steps of Ahcleet's back porch, Tleyuk in his pajamas, the cat in its usual fur. "The smell of those roses in there was killing me."

The cat closed its one eye in a knowing way and rumbled understanding.

"Hey, what's that you got hanging out of your mouth?"

The cat opened its eye wide, looked furtively around, then placed at Tleyuk's bare feet its best and brightest gift yet: a length of ribbon.

Tleyuk picked up this latest gift and examined it carefully, noticing there was rust or something on one end.

"Where'd you get this, Cat?" he asked. "It's kinda pretty."

Instead of replying in his usual throaty growl, Old

Woman Scatt's cat looked up, laid back its half ear, screeched, exploded off the step with its fur standing on end, and streaked into the bushes.

At what seemed to Tleyuk to be the exact same moment, the sounds melding together and pronouncing *disaster* in his ears, Jordan threw open the back door and began yelling.

"*Tleyuk!* What did we tell you about *that cat?*"

"Gosh, Mom, how come you're up so early?" Tleyuk asked in his most innocent voice.

"Don't answer *my* question with *your* question—"

Abruptly Jordan stopped yelling and stared at what Tleyuk was holding in his hand. Then she ran down the steps and sat beside him.

"Where'd you get that, honey?"

"Old Woman Scatt's cat brought it to me."

"Tleyuk—" she said warningly.

"It did, Mom, honest. It brings me stuff all the time. Bugs and mice and beach agates—"

"All right, Tleyuk, please give it to me, okay?"

"What for?"

"Because I need it. At least for a while."

"Can I have it back?"

"I'm not sure. Depends on what I have to do with it."

"That doesn't make sense, Mom."

"Yes it does. That ribbon could be important evidence in a case I'm working on."

"Okay, I guess."

Reluctantly, Tleyuk handed the tattered ribbon to his mother.

"Thank you, honey. Would you like a receipt?"

Tleyuk looked at his mother consideringly, then ran back into the house, returning shortly with a pad of paper on which he had printed in a firm hand: *Receeved of T. Tidewater one peece of ribbon. Signed by Jordan Tidewater, His Mom.*

He gave the pad to Jordan, who corrected his spelling, scribbled her initials, and added the date.

"You should always date everything," she said, handing the receipt back to him. "Papers without dates don't mean much."

"Okay. Thanks, Mom. When's breakfast?"

"How about you making it for a change?"

Tleyuk's round eyes grew rounder. "Can I?"

"I don't know whether you can, but you surely may."

He shook his head in childish confusion, then rushed up the steps and into the kitchen, hollering as he went, "Explain it to me later, Mom."

"If you cook you have to clean up after yourself," she called.

But Tleyuk was already making so much noise clattering pans and dishes, she suspected he probably hadn't heard her. Or hadn't wanted to was more like it.

Jordan remained seated on the back steps, examining the ribbon, noting the indentations of feline teeth.

Once again she felt that same bone-deep chill, but faintly now, ever so faintly, like the fading memory of an almost-forgotten nightmare.

She stood up and went inside the house with the ribbon in her hand.

In the kitchen Jordan asked Tleyuk what was on the menu for breakfast.

"French toast?" he said with a question in his voice.

"Sounds good to me. Have we got the ingredients?"

Tleyuk rummaged in the refrigerator. "There's milk, margarine, and eggs."

He slammed the refrigerator door shut, checked the bread box, and found a full loaf of uncut French bread.

Jordan, meanwhile, looked in one of the cupboards. "And we're okay on powdered sugar."

"Then French toast is okay, Mom?"

"It is with me," she said, smiling assent. She walked into the living room, where she picked up the telephone and called her brother at his house on Cape Elizabeth.

"Are you on duty today, Paul?" she asked.

He yawned. "No. What time is it?"

"Seven. I'd like to see you."

"When?"

"Would right away be too soon?"

He laughed. "I could be there in half an hour, I guess."

"How about breakfast with us?"

"What's to eat?"

"French toast."

"I could make it in fifteen minutes." He paused, then asked cautiously, "Who's doing the cooking?"

"Well, Tleyuk, actually."

"Oh. Maybe I'll pick up breakfast on the way."

"Come on, Paul. What can he do to French toast?"

"I don't know what Tleyuk can do, but I sure as hell remember what you and I used to do with it."

They chuckled together, recalling bizarre childish experiments of their own. Finally, Prefontaine assured her that regardless of who the chef was, he'd be there as soon as he got dressed.

Jordan wandered back into the kitchen. "Your uncle's coming for breakfast," she said.

"Great!" Tleyuk was so busy beating eggs he didn't look up.

Jordan glanced in the bowl and suggested he add six more. "Want me to slice the bread?" she asked.

Tleyuk stopped beating eggs and gazed off into space, taking mental inventory of things he had yet to do in the preparation of breakfast for three grown-ups and himself, who ate like two grown-ups.

"Okay, Mom," he said slowly. "I guess it would be okay."

"Thanks a lot," she murmured, giving him an amused sidelong glance, then began converting the loaf of French bread into thick, absorbent slices.

When Paul Prefontaine, freshly shaved and showered, walked into Old Man Ahcleet's house at seven-thirty that morning, he looked around in amazement at the thousands of roses.

"Did somebody die?" he asked.

"They are from an admirer," replied Ahcleet, who had just arisen.

"An admirer of yours, Grandfather?"

"Hardly, Kla'xeqlax. An admirer of your sister's."

Kla'xeqlax, meaning "the hunter," was Paul's real name, the one Ahcleet had given him at birth, just as the old man had given Jordan her real name, La'qewamax, "the shaman."

Prefontaine and Ahcleet went into the kitchen where they found the table neatly set for four. A full shot glass of Jack Daniel's waited at Ahcleet's place.

Jordan opened the kitchen windows to let out the fry smell. The sound of the surf roared in, so everybody shouted a little in order to be heard.

"Hi, Unc! Morning, Grandfather!" Tleyuk called, grinning from ear to ear, but too careful to take his eyes off the smoking pan in which he was frying the first slices of French toast.

Prefontaine moved to the stove and tousled his nephew's gleaming black hair with his great hand. "Looking good there, kid," he said with a smile.

Then he turned to Jordan. "So who's your conquest?" he asked.

She blushed and got busy filling two bowls with powdered sugar that she placed at each end of the breakfast table.

Prefontaine sighed theatrically. "Okay, Sis, who do I have to go out and beat up this time?"

They looked at each other and both laughed out loud, remembering when as young teenagers a protective Paul had gotten into many bloody-nosed fights trying to whip older men of twenty, twenty-five, and even thirty, who'd cast what he thought were unseemly covetous eyes on his beautiful sister.

"Relax, Paul," she said. "You don't have to defend my honor this time."

"Well, who's the guy?"

She shook her head.

"I'll bet it's that Chilean, isn't it?"

Now Tleyuk turned from the stove. "What Chilean?"

"We'll talk after breakfast, Paul," Jordan said firmly. "Just the two of us. Privately. Okay?"

"Guess it'll have to be."

Ahcleet glanced at Jordan, then closed his eyes, opened them again, and, instead of sipping the contents of his shot glass, his usual practice, gulped it all down in one swallow.

Tleyuk served up the first of the French toast, puffed and nicely browned.

"Eat it while it's hot," he said authoritatively, then dashed back to the stove.

Prefontaine spread margarine and powdered sugar on his helping, took a big bite, chewed, swallowed, then said, "Sparky, how about coming to live with me? I'll let you do all the cooking."

Tleyuk, busy at the stove, was silent for a few seconds while he reviewed his options. Then he asked, "What about the cleaning up?"

"If you cook like this, I promise I'll do it all."

"Put it in writing, Unc, and it's a deal."

"And don't forget to date it," Jordan said with a smile.

2   As a reward for Tleyuk having done such a good job with breakfast, Ahcleet helped him wash the dishes. Then they both sat down in the living room to watch Saturday morning cartoons.

Jordan and Paul went for a walk on the beach where the earlier promise of fine weather continued; a splendid dawn had grown into a bright, glorious day.

The agitated young breezes of early morning, matured now into fresh west winds, flung mist into their faces from smoking mares' tails.

The air was full of the smell of saltwater, cedar, and woodsmoke; the roar of the ocean a symphonic background to the cries of seabirds, which somehow managed to sound lonely even when moving about in gangs of hundreds.

The tide, not quite at the full, was surging in. Great ocean breakers rushed toward Jordan and Paul, then strained their misty heads back toward the sea before crashing in watery green crystals on the sand, one on the heels of the next, each higher than the last.

Until the seventh wave, more or less, after which the sea was quiet for nearly a full minute. Then the ever-escalating onrush of waves began all over again. Night and day. Month in, month out. Year after year. Decade after decade. Century after century.

"It's almost like riding the rapids!" Jordan laughed, turning sideways to wipe her dripping face.

Prefontaine put his arm around her shoulders, laughing with her. Then his expression changed,

"Jordan, tell me the truth. Could you really live anywhere else?"

Jordan's smile faded as she looked into eyes so like her own, eyes that were dark with pools of golden light, glowing now with an incandescent brilliance.

We are like the sea, Paul and I, she thought, *eternal like The People who live by the sea.*

And for the briefest of moments she almost understood the custom of the ancient Egyptian rulers, whose brothers married their own sisters. Who else was worthy?

"I don't think so, Paul," she said.

"You almost left us once."

"I know. But when it came right down to it, I couldn't go."

As an honors graduate of the University of Washington and the police academy, Jordan had been accepted a couple of years before for FBI training at Quantico, Virginia.

At the last moment she had changed her mind and decided to stay on working for the nation. It was a time when she had just returned to the old Smokehouse Religion and had entered into her shamanhood.

Obviously relieved, Prefontaine hugged her and said, "I'm sure glad to hear that!"

They started walking again.

After a while he asked, "You want to talk to me about this new man in your life?

"No, I don't. And he's not in my life. Not yet, anyway."

"If he sends you thousands of roses when he's not in your life, what's he going to do later on? Buy up the nation?"

"I don't want to talk about love, Paul. I want to talk about murder."

Prefontaine studied Jordan's face. "Okay, honey. Sure," he said.

Jordan explained the sequence of recent events, starting at what she assumed was the beginning:

First, the evening on the beach when Raven had brought her the torn woven ribbon with the attached broken gold medal.

Next, her happening on the body of the butchered boy with the scalped face, not mentioning that Lima Clemente had been with her at the time.

Then, her giving some threads off the ribbon she'd found to Hunter Kleoh for forensic comparison with threads the medical examiner had removed from the boy's neck, results of which she had not as yet received.

The discovery of the dead girl tied seventy-five feet up an old dead stovepipe cedar in Michael McTavish's logging show on Fire Road Six.

And finally, the piece of torn woven ribbon presented to Tleyuk by Old Woman Scatt's cat just this morning.

"Did the coroner find any woven ribbon or threads with the dead girl's body?" Prefontaine asked.

"No."

"Obviously, the ribbon and its threads are connected only to the boy's murder in some way but not to the girl's."

"So it would seem. But where could the cat have gotten that piece it brought to Tleyuk?"

"From any place in the cat's territory. It could even pick up stuff dropped by people driving through."

"I wonder how far afield the cat goes."

"Who knows? Maybe the rest of the ribbon that you

have came in on a later tide and Raven found it on the beach just like you did."

"Or maybe since it's Scatt's cat, it found the ribbon where it lives."

"That's a distinct possibility, Sis."

Prefontaine stared out to sea, obviously deep in thought, arms folded across his chest, looking as if he were confronting the spray being flung in his face.

Watching this proud and handsome man whose heart had beat with hers for nine months in their mother's womb, Jordan could easily imagine their ancestors, as far back as time went, standing in this same position, looking out at the same sea, the same thoughtful expression on their faces.

What did people do, she wondered, who did not know who their forebears were, who had no sense of the continuity of their bloodlines? How lonely they must be!

Prefontaine turned away from the sea, took Jordan's hand, and headed up the beach toward dry sand and an immense pile of whitened driftwood.

When they were both seated on a dry log, bark peeled from it and buffed satin-smooth by surf and sand, he asked, "You think we should look around the Scatt place, is that it?"

"It might be a good idea. But what reason would you give?"

"Reason? I don't need a reason with that guy!" He barked out a laugh. "Whenever anything's missing we always check Scatt's first. And usually find it there, I might add. Jack Scatt is not exactly a sterling character."

"Do you think he could have killed those kids?"

Prefontaine shrugged. "I don't know what Jack's capable of. I do know that a few years ago when you were away at the university he was involved in a big mess around here."

"Involved how?"

"Gossip, mostly, when it came right down to it."

"What happened?"

"Some aging stripper married a Quinault man she'd met

in a bar down on the Seattle docks. He'd just sold a timber claim and was bragging about how rich he was."

"How romantic."

"Oh, you bet. It was one of those marriages where everybody sobers up the next morning and wonders who in the hell that is in bed with them."

"What's that got to do with Jack Scatt?"

"Well, the woman had a twelve-year-old daughter and all three of them came to live here on the reservation for a while. Before long it was evident that the daughter was pregnant. The woman started claiming that Jack had been messing with the girl."

"Did the girl's mother press charges?"

Prefontaine shook his head. "No. And there was nothing except her word. No proof that the girl had ever been around the Scatt place, or that Jack had ever been around her. The girl herself wouldn't say a thing. Kept her mouth shut tight. Suddenly all three of them left town and I've never heard from any of them again."

"Couldn't you have charged Jack Scatt?"

"With what?"

"Rape? Contributing to the delinquency of a minor?"

"Sis, you're not thinking. There was nothing to substantiate a criminal charge. And if we ran around arresting people who look guilty, half the country would be in jail."

Jordan said she had to agree.

"My hands were tied. There was no proof whatsoever that Jack Scatt had ever seen the girl, let alone that he had contributed to her delinquency. As far as that goes, in my personal opinion it happened when she was still with her mother in Seattle learning the business."

"What business? Stripping?"

"Whoring."

"When did they leave Taholah?"

"Right after I said I wanted the girl examined by a doctor to find out how long she'd been pregnant."

"Kind of suspicious."

"Yeah, isn't it."

They both stood up and brushed the sand off their backsides. As they walked slowly up the beach, Jordan asked what Jack Scatt did for a living.

"Not much. Steals shake blocks and yew bark when he can get away with it. And anything else he can lay his hands on. Probably grows pot back up in the woods. When you can get him to work an honest job he's really good at fixing cars. Old junkers, especially."

"What's the relationship between Jack and the old woman? Do you know?"

He shook his head. "I'm not sure. God knows how old she is. Jack's around forty, so he could be her great-grandson. Or great-grandnephew."

"Grandfather says she looked just the same when he was a boy."

"I know he does but I think that's stretching things."

"Where're the rest of the Scatts?"

"There're only the two of them left. As far as I'm concerned, that's enough."

3   Later that morning, both wearing casual clothes, Jordan and Paul headed purposefully toward the Scatt place, which they smelled before they reached.

Jordan carried a bouquet of her Autumn Damask roses, stems wrapped in damp paper towels, intending to present it to Old Woman Scatt.

Fortunately for the neighbors, none of whom lived close, the Scatt place was set off by itself and surrounded by a ring of closely growing alder trees, rampant vine maple, and a sagging fence put together with miscellaneous pieces of driftwood. The big timber had been logged off long ago.

Broken, rusted automobile bodies, mostly veiled by blackberry vines, weeds, and poison ivy, lay collapsed on what passed for the yard. Somewhere in the distance Jordan and Paul could hear the sound of wood being methodically chopped.

To one side of the property crouched a tumbledown outhouse, whose rank stench joined the congress of smells seeping from ground and buildings.

At their approach, wild-eyed chickens ran in circles squawking dementedly as if momentarily expecting the ax. A gaggle of upright geese tried unsuccessfully to warn the humans off with strident hisses and militantly extended necks.

Seventeen wriggling piglets screamed and ran toward their mothers, two big brown sows that had recently given birth; the cords were still hanging from the young. In a far corner, several hugely expectant white sows lay in the sun.

"Have you been here before, Sis?" Prefontaine asked.

"Not since I was a little kid charging around where Grandfather warned me not to go. If I remember correctly, and I do, I got my bottom spanked when Ahcleet found out."

"You'd better follow me. Be careful where you step."

Looking down, Jordan decided to take her brother's advice literally. She swallowed hard and stepped high.

The ground was slimy and odorous with chicken droppings, geese splats, pig shit. There were flies everywhere.

When Jordan and Paul reached the house, an indefinable style that looked loosely held together by poison oak and blackberry vines, Prefontaine knocked on the front wall near the open doorway.

A sudden silence descended; even the animals stopped their hissing, cackling, and screaming.

Prefontaine knocked again, harder.

Something short and dark materialized just inside the doorway.

"What?" came a cracked voice.

"Is Jack home, Mrs. Scatt?" Prefontaine asked.

"Who wants to know?"

"Come on now, you know who I am."

When the figure inside the doorway moved out into the light, Jordan saw that it was a very old woman with a face like a shriveled butternut squash.

Thin, dusty hair sprouted from her scalp. She was dressed in what looked like layer upon layer of smelly brownish rags.

Her one dark eye squinted up at them, staring first at Prefontaine, then moving to Jordan. There was an eye patch over the woman's other eye.

"So it's the twins, eh?"

"Mrs. Scatt, I came here to see Jack," Prefontaine said. "Is he home?"

"If you'd been born to my people, you would have been dead long ago. Both of you. Dead right after you was born. Your mouths stuffed with moss and left out for the wild animals. My people knew how these things should be done."

"Even your people don't do things that way anymore," Prefontaine said with a surprising gentleness in his voice.

"That's 'cause there's none of my people left. You people took us all in slavery."

Jordan extended the rose bouquet. "Mrs. Scatt, please accept these fresh roses. I brought them for you. They smell absolutely wonderful."

Fear tightened the old woman's face. "Don't you set your witchy feet acrost my doorway!"

She spat on the ground in front of them, then turned and shuffled back inside the house, mumbling as she went.

Jordan bent down and placed the roses on the lintel, hoping that the old woman would view them as a peace offering.

As she did so, she noticed that the front doorway was open because there was no door. Glancing up, she saw a length of hide rolled up and held in place above the doorway with two lengths of rope.

The old woman turned back and saw the roses. "Don't

you put none of your curses on me!" she screeched, and disappeared into the depths of the house.

Looking toward the direction of the ancient voice, Jordan drew in her breath sharply, then wished fervently that she had not inhaled.

She saw that the floor inside was thick with garbage: eggshells, potato peelings, coffee grounds, a putrefying detritus that beyond those recently placed items she could not even identify.

In the middle of what had been the single-story living room when the house was first built, a huge hole had been chopped through the floor, apparently right down to the ground, then lined with rocks to form a cooking space.

Overhead, she saw that another hole had been chopped in the roof as an escape route for smoke. The walls were grimy with old smoke and grease.

In a far corner, comparatively neat, stood a twenty-six-inch television set with an upholstered rocking chair in front of it.

"My God, Paul," she whispered. "Should we allow people to live like this?"

"It's their choice, Jordan. You know yourself that every community has two faces. The acceptable one it shows to the world and—the other."

Prefontaine started around toward the back of the house. Jordan followed, walking carefully in her brother's footsteps. She held her arms across her chest, ducked her head, and tried to hunker down into herself so she would not touch anything unclean.

She paused to examine the only patch of garden on the property. When Paul noticed that Jordan was no longer behind him, he stopped and walked back to her.

"What are you looking at, Sis?"

"That." Jordan pointed to the cultivated area.

"What is it?"

She lowered her voice. "I think it's a poison garden."

"A *what*?"

"I'll explain when we get out of here."

The sound of chopping stopped.

They moved on. Some distance behind the house they found a large, three-sided woodshed with an overhanging shed roof.

In front of the shed stood an enormous chopping block made from a Sitka spruce tree stump. To one side of the stump lay a helter-skelter pile of dry alder freshly cut into stove-size lengths.

A lean, powerfully built man watched them approach, a two-headed ax held loosely in his right hand. His hair was nicely trimmed, and he wore, surprisingly, a clean white starched shirt with black pants.

As they drew closer, Prefontaine called out, "Hey, Jack! Smells like a rotting whale around here. Why don't you clean the place up?"

"That's the old woman's job," Jack Scatt answered, his voice a low rumble.

"Don't you think she's a little beyond that now?"

Scatt shrugged. "Not my affair. She's got her business, I got mine."

"How about hiring some of our young people to come in, give her a hand?"

Scatt ignored Prefontaine's suggestion as if deeming the question unworthy of a reply. Instead, he asked his own question.

"What you looking for today, Chief?"

"Just passing by, Jack. Jordan brought Old Woman Scatt some fresh roses."

"Nothing missing around town?" Scatt asked sarcastically, then turned his attention to Jordan, studying her with a slow, amused smile.

When Jordan looked at Jack Scatt close up, she seemed to see for just a moment or two, as if a stage curtain had been inadvertently raised a few inches and then quickly lowered, a psychic darkness in his eyes, not of dull despair, but a living darkness filled with an unpleasant glee. Unconsciously Jordan touched the medicine pouch at her neck.

When she looked at him again, his black eyes shone with an intelligent, kindly light.

All three fell silent.

Jack Scatt's mouth turned down in sudden contempt.

"Go on, then, both of you," he said. "Look around all you want. Can't fool me; I know that's what you're here for."

"I guess we might as well," Prefontaine said. "Anything we shouldn't see?"

Scatt turned his back on them and began to chop wood again, his strokes slow and steady, the sharp blade cleaving the dry wood with insistent accuracy.

Watching him, Jordan remembered the medical examiner's words about the cleaving of the little boy's head, legs, and arms from his body.

"I'd say this was the result of a blow from an ax or a machete using great force. It had to be very sharp and very heavy."

Deep in thought, she moved around to the north side of the woodshed as Prefontaine walked off in the opposite direction.

After a stunned moment, she stepped back and called to Prefontaine. When he joined her, she pointed to what was nailed to the exterior wall of the shed.

Faces. Animal faces. The gray of weathered cedar planks looked back at Jordan and Paul through numerous empty eye sockets.

Faces of several dogs, raccoons, foxes, a bear cub, two cougars, even a couple of rats. Just the fur faces, severed and scalped from the animals' heads and nailed into place.

"What do you think, Paul?" she asked quietly.

"It's interesting," he said.

"Doesn't it tell you anything?"

"It tells me that Jack Scatt likes to keep strange trophies."

He called out to Scatt, who stopped chopping wood and walked over.

"This is quite a display," Prefontaine said.

Jack Scatt shrugged. "Don't know nothing about it. That's the old woman's doing."

4   As Jordan and Paul passed the house on their way off the property, Old Woman Scatt's cat peered at them from the open doorway, one Damask rose petal hanging from its mouth. The bouquet still lay where Jordan had left it.

"Now tell me about that poison garden," Prefontaine said.

"Nothing else around there except that one piece of ground looked as if it received regular attention."

"I noticed that. And the plants looked in pretty good shape to me." Prefontaine grinned. "Of course, I'm not an expert."

"Do you know what those plants are?"

"Are you kidding? About the only plant I'm on speaking terms with is a dandelion."

"Old Woman Scatt is growing hellebore, aconite, deadly nightshade, henbane, laburnum daphne, clematis, white poppies, foxglove, larkspur, morning glories, buttercups, and bluebells."

"So?"

"Paul, they're all capable of causing illness and death if taken by mouth. Belladonna, for example, comes from deadly nightshade. It produces hallucinogenic effects such as flying. It can be a real killer."

"Maybe they're just plants the old woman happens to like."

"But they're all very peculiar plants. Tea from fox-gloves, for instance, when added to the water in vases, helps preserve the life of cut flowers."

"So?"

"It's deadly poison to humans. As is tea made from the stems of clematis. And larkspur has exceedingly poisonous seeds which in the old days were used to destroy lice and their eggs in people's hair."

"What about morning glories? There's nothing wrong with them, is there?"

"It's true that a tincture of morning glory flowers can be used for headaches, rheumatism, and inflamed eyes. But every part of the morning glory except the roots contains a dangerous hallucinatory drug. Even the seeds, if worn as bracelets or necklaces, can cause a rash."

"You think Old Woman Scatt set out deliberately to cultivate these plants?"

"I have a strong suspicion that she did, Paul. She had monkshood, or aconite, and that contains a deadly poison. And buttercups with their wonderfully varnished golden flowers? They'll blister and inflame the skin."

"Buttercups grow wild all around here, Sis. Why would she bother to cultivate them?"

"Maybe for convenience. Have them right at her back door. And I noticed bluebells. Their fresh bulbs are poisonous."

"I guess I'll never look at a flower the same way again, Sis," Prefontaine said.

As they got into his cruiser, Jordan said, "You know, Paul, there's something else strange around here."

"There's a lot strange about those Scatts."

"I didn't see any dogs. Live ones, I mean. People around here usually have dogs. For guard duty if nothing else."

"Well, Sis, there's a kind of unwritten law that the Scatts can't have any dogs."

"Why not? Doesn't the old woman like them?"

He started up the motor. "That's the problem. She likes them too well."

"I don't understand."

"She likes to eat them."

"*Eat* them? Good God, why?"

"The people she came from considered dogs a delicacy. I guess she just never lost her taste for them."

·

5   Later that afternoon Prefontaine and Tleyuk helped Jordan deliver roses to the older people in Taholah. When they found they still had a number of flowers left, they drove into Aberdeen and presented the remainder to the hospital.

Now the Autumn Damask roses were all gone from Old Man Ahcleet's house, except for the branches Jordan had found lying on her pillow.

These she tied by their stems and hung up to dry while the flowers were still fresh and highly scented . . . these, she knew, she would treasure forever.

That night, after Tleyuk and Old Man Ahcleet were asleep, Jordan received a telephone call from Lima Clemente.

"Are you free tomorrow afternoon?" he asked.

She said yes, this week she had Sunday and Sunday night off.

"Will you meet me on your beach at noon tomorrow? I will be in my helicopter."

When Jordan asked him why, Lima Clemente told her there was something out in the ocean he particularly wanted her to see.

"Why don't I meet you on the beach at Moclips?" she suggested, not wanting the entire population of Taholah to be aware of her comings and goings with a strange man.

He said that would be fine. Then he asked if she had liked the roses.

"I loved them, Lima. So did a lot of other people."

Lima Clemente was silent for a moment, then he said softly, "Until I see you tomorrow, Jordan."

"Until tomorrow."

*The mountains seem to rise from the
edge of the water as though Nature
had designed to shut up this spot for
her safe retreat forever.*
—EUGENE SEMPLE,
Governor of Washington Territory,
The Seattle Press, 1888

Chapter 11

1   When the telephone by Jordan's bed rang early
     the next morning, she grabbed the receiver and
mumbled, "Hum-m-m. Hum-m-m?"

"I know it's Sunday and it's too early for a decent person to be calling, but I'm not a decent person." A good-natured male voice chuckled in her ear. "Are you?"

Dimly, Jordan recognized the fine baritone voice of Hunter Kleoh.

"Am I what?"

"Decent. Are you decent, is what I said."

Jordan tried to swim up to full consciousness, to understand what Kleoh was talking about. She heard him laugh.

"Forget it, Jordan. I was just kidding around."

"Hum-m-m. Hum-m-m?"

"Hey, are you awake?"

"Hold on a minute."

She put the phone down, threw her legs over the side of the bed, stood up, did seven knee bends, yawned hugely, cleared her throat, stretched her arms out as far as they would go, waggled her hands, moved her head from side to side, drank from a water glass, sat back down, and briskly picked the phone back up.

"Okay, Hunter, go ahead." Fully awake, Jordan's voice was now strong and clear.

"I'm calling to invite you to dinner tonight."

"Thank you, Hunter, but I can't make it tonight."

"When, then? You promised, remember?"

"Maybe some night this coming week. I've got to see my schedule first, find out when I'm on duty." She tried to sound enthusiastic.

"Okay, Jordan. I'll call you in a day or two."

"Wonderful, Hunter. And thanks so much."

She hung up, feeling guilty.

It would be a kindness on her part to have dinner with Hunter Kleoh. He was a very nice man; since his wife's death, a lonely, bereaved man trying to make the best of things. She wondered why socializing with him even on a professional basis seemed to be such a chore.

Maybe it was because Hunter reminded her of a pet, an aging, dignified Great Dane, perhaps, who, after years of two-way affection and care, had lost his beloved owner and desperately feared he would never find another. She felt sorry for him.

Suddenly Jordan realized that she did not like feeling sorry for grown men; her pity diminished them in her eyes. She was uncomfortable with that diminishment.

2   Jordan drove to Moclips, arriving shortly before
     noon, and parked in the public access to Moon-
stone Beach.

Soon she heard the *whoppity-whop* of a helicopter overhead. It was a French-built Puma. Old but obviously well
maintained, it descended onto the hard, wet sand with all
the grace of a fat lady lowering herself onto a lavatory seat.

As the pilot cut the motors, the rotors slowed and
stopped. Jordan got out of her truck, locked it, and ran
across the road and down the beach toward the machine.

Lima Clemente made a motion with his hands. She
thought he meant for her to use the boarding ladder, which
she did, climbed inside, and slammed the door shut behind
her.

There were no signs of the uniformed men Old Man
Ahcleet had seen and spoken to when the Autumn
Damasks were delivered.

Today, Lima Clemente himself smiled at her from in
front of the controls, his ash-gray eyes glowing.

Jordan smiled a return greeting, then leaned back and
tightened her shoulder harness.

"Thank you for coming, Jordan," he said, speaking
through the com link between them.

Both wore headphones so that they could communicate.

"I could hardly wait," she surprised herself by saying,
although it was the stark truth. "So where are you taking
me, Lima?"

"Out to sea."

"I've been there a lot in my life," she said with a whim-
sical smile.

When Jordan saw Lima Clemente's look of puzzlement,
she realized he did not understand the American
metaphoric expression. Rather than trying to explain, she
said, "The sea's a big place. How far are we going?"

"Would you enjoy flying up the coast for a little time
first?"

"I'd love to."

"After that I have a surprise."

"Weren't the roses surprise enough?"

"Not nearly enough for a woman like you."

"I hope I've thanked you for them, Lima."

"Very graciously, from which I can assume you found them pleasant."

"I loved them! After I got over the shock, that is. And I was a lot more than just surprised, Lima. I was amazed."

"Surely you've received flowers from admirers before."

"Not by the thousands."

"There was no question in your mind that they came from me?"

"Who else? I don't know anyone who can afford to spend that kind of money. You must be a wealthy man." Having said that, Jordan wondered if she had been too outspoken.

Evidently not offended, he replied, "I am comfortable enough to do the things that are important to me."

"Then you are a man many people would envy."

He smiled.

As before, she wondered: Was the business in Santiago that lucrative? Had he, perhaps, inherited old family wealth?

Lima Clemente turned back to the controls.

There was a roar of engine followed by a storm of blowing debris as the helicopter lifted off, spun 180 degrees to the left, and sailed out in a northerly direction.

Relaxing in her seat, Jordan realized that it made her very happy to be with Lima Clemente. She felt lighthearted; uplifted physically, mentally, spiritually.

She watched as he piloted the helicopter and decided that Lima Clemente's relaxed position at the controls spoke a lot about him; here was someone born to be in control. She'd never have to feel sorry for this man.

"I understand there has been another distressing discovery for you to deal with. The body of a second child, if my information is correct."

"Yes, I'm afraid so."

"I am sad that you must endure such experiences, Jordan."

"Well, it's all in a day's work, I guess. At least lately it is."

"Was the second like the first?"

"No. I'm sure you remember the notice of a missing eleven-year-old girl we saw at Graves Creek?"

"I remember."

"That's who it was. Someone had sexually abused her, horribly, then tied her dead body seventy-five feet up a tree in a logging show."

As Lima Clemente frowned, the blood seemed to come up under his eyes, making his face even darker.

"Sexual abuse? A child? There is nothing more heinous, more despicable. When you discover the murderer you must not waste money and time on a trial. He must be summarily executed with no ceremony and none of the publicity Americans so love to give their worst criminals."

"I share your feelings, Lima, but it doesn't work like that in this country."

"Perhaps it should."

They were silent for a time, looking at the view. This was the sort of country that people photographed endlessly, talked about, wrote about, and gazed at with wonder.

It was another glorious day, although so far not as riotous as the day before. Nature was at rest after yesterday's wild exuberance.

Scattered below them off the coastline were sea stacks and small islands of various shapes, sizes, and elevations, all of which were the peaks and plateaus of undersea mountains. Some of the islands were ghosts of prehistoric headlands; some, little more than rocky islets.

The winds were down, as was the sea. Now at its lowest ebb, the ocean flashed in the early-afternoon sun like a single sheet of polished silver.

There were no breakers, simply a slow, breathing surface undulation as if the great waters slumbered and dreamed.

Today the only whitecaps visible lay to the east ,where

the snow-drenched Olympic mountain chain rolled like the waves of a turbulent sea.

The triple peaks of Mount Olympus, frigid home of the gods, rose in lordly view over a mile into the sky, not one summit but several: east, middle, and west, the highest.

Thrusting up chaotically from deep valleys and canyons, hundreds of smaller snowcapped mountains, many of them unnamed, added to the oceanlike welter.

From the height and angle at which the helicopter was flying, the mountains seemed an undecipherable jumble.

There were no groups of parallel ranges, no solitary, majestic spires. Just a welter of snowy peaks and icy ridges, as though the choppy waves of a gale-tossed sea had been flash-frozen in midstorm.

Following Jordan's gaze, Lima Clemente said, "Beautiful. Hundreds of extinct volcanoes in one area."

"Actually, the Olympics weren't created by volcanic eruptions like the other mountains in the Pacific Northwest," Jordan told him.

"How then?"

"What you're looking at, Lima, is the wreckage of an ancient undersea collision. The Olympic Peninsula is what geologists call 'exotic.' That means it has a different origin than the rest of North America."

"Somehow that doesn't surprise me," he said with a smile.

She told him that sixty-five million years ago the peninsula had been born as part of an offshore oceanic ridge. At that time, what is now called the Juan de Fuca Plate was thickly layered with sedimentary rock and lay at the bottom of the sea.

"In a tectonic collision, the edge of the continent moved and, under enormous compression, forced the Juan de Fuca Plate down even deeper, at the same time scraping its rock sediment up, out of the sea, and thousands of feet above the surface of the earth. The resulting pile of cracked, twisted rocks formed the original Olympics."

Lima Clemente whistled. "What an earthquake that must have been!"

"Defies the imagination, doesn't it?" Jordan's eyes shone. "Geologists have recently discovered that the tectonic plates are thinnest under Puget Sound. And they're thickest under the Coast Range Mountains in Oregon."

"Is that the end of the story about your beautiful Olympics?" Lima Clemente asked.

"Not quite yet," she said, smiling. "Those original Olympics were subsequently worn down by erosion, covered by the sea, raised up at least twice again—maybe even three times more—and after all that we have the present Olympics, more or less."

"More or less?"

"Four times in the Pleistocene epoch that ended ten thousand years ago, ice flooded down from the north to cover the Olympics so that all but the highest peaks were engulfed."

She said that glaciers carving the channels of the Strait of Juan de Fuca, Puget Sound, and Hood Canal had cut the peninsula off from the migratory paths of many animals.

"Which is why we have very few snakes, and the ones we do have are harmless varieties. Also missing are grizzly bears, wolverines, bighorn sheep, and other animals found in upland habitats in nearby Canada and other parts of the West."

"But you do have black bears, cougars, deer, elk, bald eagles?"

"Yes, and a lot more."

"I've heard men around here talking about mountain goats," he said.

She groaned. "Those damn goats! We have them, all right. Too many!"

"And how is that?"

"Back in the 1920s, somebody had a bright idea that we needed mountain goats, so a dozen were transplanted from Canada and Alaska."

"What exactly was the reason for this transplantation?"

She shrugged. "Who knows? Anyway, the herd now numbers twelve hundred voracious animals chomping up the native plants. The Park Service is trying to control or even remove the herd and restore the mountains to what has been called, and I quote, 'a vignette of primitive America.'"

"Fascinating," Lima Clemente murmured.

"There are sixty glaciers up there, creeping their way to the sea," Jordan said, looking to the east. "Have you ever heard the voice of a glacier, Lima?"

"No. Not that I remember."

"If you had, you would remember. They creak and crack and issue awful groans."

He shivered theatrically.

"Anyway, in that short thirty-mile distance, from the mountains to the beaches, there are more zonal regions than any other place in the United States."

"You know well and love well your beautiful land," he observed.

"It is where The People live. It is my home," she replied. "Tell me about your homeland, Lima."

"My homeland?" He glanced off into the distance. "In my homeland you would find enormous, smooth, treeless slopes, some ending in sudden various edges below which hang pleated curtains of rock. The air is thin, there are more and more mountains, barren and desolate. Here and there are sudden sharp ridges of rock that look like the dorsal plates of a petrified dinosaur."

"I thought you lived in Santiago."

"Santiago is where I now live and do business. My homeland"—he named a village—"is on a vast plateau high in the Andean mountains between Chile and Argentina, where it is very cold."

He repeated the name of his village and described the usual way to get there—by donkey cart, adding that occasionally trucks made the journey.

"But I can assure you the vehicle, if it survives, is never quite the same after such a trip."

"Are there many cars in your village?" she asked.

"There is one. The priest, Father Lavate, has a derelict old truck."

"It sounds lonely, Lima."

When he looked over at her, Jordan saw shadows in his ash-gray eyes and an expression she could not put a name to.

"I am a very lonely man, Jordan."

They'd turned out to sea and had been flying for some time when Jordan noticed small white clouds forming along the western horizon, each one seeming no larger than a man's hand.

She looked down and saw that they were approaching an island about four miles long and two or three miles wide.

The island's northern end formed a high plateau covered with tall, shivering grasses, and lay atop steep basalt palisades rising directly from the sea.

There was something about the island that reminded Jordan of photographs she had seen of the open grassy savannahs of Africa; she almost expected to see lions lolling about.

The center of the island was timbered, with patches of evergreen forests floating in seas of grass through which ran several creeks.

The southwestern side ended abruptly in huge piles of basalt boulders, then flattened into a wide, white sand beach edging a windward cove.

Lima Clemente landed on the sandy beach, shut off the engine, and asked Jordan to please remain seated.

He waited for the blades to stop whirling, unfastened his seat belt, jumped out, ran around to Jordan's side, where he opened her door and prepared to help her out of the helicopter.

"You didn't give me a chance to do this earlier," he said with just the softest touch of chagrin in his voice.

"Do what?" she asked as she unbuckled her seat belt.

"Help you into the machine. Now I must help you out."

Jordan, genuinely puzzled, said, "Why would you want to help me?"

"It was my wish."

"I'm not handicapped, Lima."

"It is one of the things a man does for a woman."

She was astonished. "Lima, I'm totally capable of going through doorways and getting in and out of machines by myself."

"Will you allow me the privilege?" he asked quietly.

She looked at him and saw that he was serious, then realized that what she was experiencing was a gentleman's sense of courtliness to a woman he respected, old-fashioned words and actions in a modern age too busy for what used to be the common courtesies.

She herself was a very busy woman with several roles. She worked in law enforcement, dealt with the ancient spirits, cared for her great-grandfather, and was trying to raise a young son.

As a police officer she saw and dealt with things that many times turned her stomach. As a shaman, in spite of her faith in the Smokehouse Religion, she was often terrified. And sometimes just the thought of her family responsibilities exhausted her.

It was pleasing to be treated with care and courtesy as if she was special, needing protection herself, instead of always giving it.

"Well, of course I will, Lima," she said.

There was a small contretemps as Jordan took his hand, then caught her foot and stumbled, made awkward by the undue attention focused on her descent from the helicopter.

"I had no idea this island was here," she said after she'd finally alighted and was standing on her own two feet. "It's a beautiful place."

"Would you like to explore?" he asked.

"Would I ever!"

She took a deep breath, inhaling the freshness of the place. He reached back inside the helicopter and lifted out a large metal container, then shut the helicopter door.

They headed for a pile of driftwood, Lima Clemente carrying the container effortlessly on his shoulder, Jordan swinging along beside him.

When they reached the driftwood, he set the container down between two sea-peeled, bleached logs.

"For a small supper when we grow hungry," he said.

He lifted the lid off the carrier, removed two water containers, and handed one to Jordan.

"Now we shall explore," he said.

They hiked around the island as far as they could, passing through wide pastures of grass, jumping over a meandering creek, and through a small forest where the huge size of the trees told her they were passing through an untouched ancient forest.

Jordan asked if they could climb up to the grassy plateau on top of the rock palisades rising from the sea.

"When I saw it from the helicopter it reminded me of the African savannahs," she said.

Lima Clemente studied the palisades. "I suppose it could be managed with climbing equipment. But not, I'm afraid, with what we've brought today."

Then he changed the subject.

"Did you know that some of the islands off your coast are privately owned?" he asked.

"I've heard that."

"Most of them belong to the state their waters surround."

"You've been researching islands?"

"Yes."

"Why, if I may ask?"

"Because they interest me. Did you know, Jordan, that in times past, nations claimed ownership of three miles out to sea and the ground beneath?"

"Why three miles, I wonder."

"Because that was the distance a cannonball could be shot."

"I see," she said.

"But today, because the world's last unexploited riches lie

in its oceans, nations want ownership of 12 nautical miles out to the sea off their shores and the ground beneath."

When they returned to the seaward beach and the pile of driftwood, Lima Clemente opened his carrier and removed three large blankets, one of which he handed to Jordan, commenting, "For when the winds change."

The second blanket he laid aside, and the third he spread out on the sand in front of the driftwood, anchoring the edges with rocks.

He built a fire, and invited Jordan to seat herself in whatever place she found to be the most comfortable.

"Let me help you," she said.

"No thank you. Today I am your servant."

She laughed, somewhat embarrassed. "I am not accustomed to servants, Lima."

"Well, you should be. And I am yours."

As he busied himself opening various packages of food, he began to hum. Jordan listened, then asked, "Isn't that from Verdi?"

He thought for a moment, hummed a few more bars, then said, "You are right. It is 'Ah! Si Ben Mio.'" He looked up at her. "Are you a lover of opera?"

"I like some of it. Not all. In fact, not much. But I do like Verdi."

"What is your favorite music?"

"My very favorite music of all? Why, the voices of the river and the sea, the wind in the trees, the cry of gulls, the scream of eagles."

"There is another music that you did not mention."

"Tell me, Lima."

He studied her. "Do you not enjoy the sighs of love?"

She turned her head and looked away.

The food Lima Clemente provided was delicious: four baked quail stuffed with brown rice, minced elephant garlic, bits of dried cranberries, grated fresh ginger and orange peel, melted butter, and chopped filberts.

He poured the juices from the quail roasting pan into a small cast-iron pot, added salt and pepper, then placed the pot on the fire. He poured cognac into a second pot and placed it near the flames. Into a third pot he poured water.

When the quail juices were steaming, he ladled the mixture over the stuffed quail, followed by warmed cognac, which he ignited and served at once.

"Whatever happened to hot dogs on a green stick?" she asked.

"That kind of food is for peasants," he said.

After they finished eating, Lima Clemente handed Jordan a linen napkin, the corner of which he had first dipped into the warm water heating by the fire.

"What a feast!" Jordan said, wiping her mouth and hands.

"There's more to come," he said as he presented her an individual silver dessert dish. "For your pleasure, Coffee Bavarian Creme."

Then he handed her a china cup and saucer, the cup filled with hot, black Colombian coffee, and on the saucer, a cinnamon stick.

"What's this for?" she asked, picking up the rolled spice.

"For additional flavor, you may wish to stir in your coffee."

"Lima, did you prepare all this yourself?"

"Truthfully, I had help. You see, I have made it a point to become excellent friends with the chef at the lodge. He prepared our meal today with my assistance and under my closest scrutiny. My hope is that it pleased you."

"Pleased me? That's the understatement of the year."

"Then I am happy, Jordan."

Once again refusing her help, Lima Clemente cleaned up, putting things back in the carrier. Then he sat beside her.

"I do love islands, Lima," she said, leaning back against a driftwood log.

"That is why this island is now yours."

She sat up straight and stared at him. "This island is *what*?"

Lima Clemente removed an envelope from an inside jacket pocket and handed it to her. "This will explain."

She opened the envelope, removed and read the papers she found inside. There was a deed to this island, along with an attached surveyor's description. To Jordan's amazement, the owner's name on the deed was her own.

She looked at him in confusion. "I can't take this, Lima."

"But I have purchased this island and given it to you, whether or not you accept the documentation."

She remained silent. How could a foreign national buy an island and give it away? She was beginning to wonder if Lima Clemente was just a little mad.

Then she remembered that he was a very wealthy man, certainly accustomed to doing things on a scale far different and more grand than she was used to.

"Yes, this island is yours," he said. "Whenever you wish to visit here, perhaps to be alone with your thoughts for a time, perhaps with a friend, I will bring you."

"But if you bring me, I wouldn't be alone, would I?"

"Of course you would be. I would simply drop you off and return again for you whenever you wished to come back."

The tide had turned and was rushing back in as if to make up for lost time, breakers haughtily lifting their spumed heads high before crashing onto the beach. Seabirds, fleeing to their nests, seemed to be blown off course by rising winds.

"It's getting colder," Jordan said as she wrapped herself in the blanket Lima Clemente had given her and moved closer to the fire.

Lima Clemente draped himself in the third blanket before walking over to sit beside her.

"When do we have to leave?" she asked.

"Not for a while."

Spellbound by the magic of the evening rising all about

them, Jordan said she really didn't want to go. Not now anyway.

"Nor do I," Lima Clemente replied.

The small clouds of early afternoon had grown into huge, white, towering edifices, castles from a fantasy. The sky burned, looking as if a frustrated artist had flung away his color-stained palette.

For a few timeless moments, the great sphere of the sun, touching the western horizon, appeared to stop in its descent before stretching into an elongated shape, as if the gateway to night was impossibly narrow.

Then, suddenly, seemingly all at once, it sizzled into the North Pacific and was gone, staining the waters vermilion, purple, gold, and a feathery green.

The southwest wind quickened, the evening star came out, and a young moon, curved like a scimitar, sliced through the incandescent sky.

Jordan broke the silence. "Lima, why did you give me Autumn Damasks? I mean instead of any other kind of rose."

He took her hand, turned it over, and slowly pressed the palm to his lips. Looking into her eyes, he said, "Because, Jordan, like the Autumn Rose, you are more exquisite to me than any other."

Thrilling to the firmness of his grasp, the feel of life pulsing in his strong fingers, she did not remove her hand from his. But she was curious about a question that had been in her mind ever since she'd received the roses.

"With all the women that you must know in your own country, why me?"

His grasp tightened lightly. "I would not expect you to understand."

"Try me. I may surprise you."

"I will tell you then if you promise not to laugh. And not to interrupt me until I am through with my explanation."

"I promise." She held up her hand in the Girl Scouts' oath.

"This will be hard for you to believe, but it is the truth. For decades I have sought you in all the corners of the world."

"How could that be? We met only recently."

He shook his finger at her reprovingly. "You promised to hear me out."

"I'm sorry, Lima. Go ahead."

"It may seem to you that we met only recently. But on the contrary, I knew you in my childhood and my youth. Long ago I lost you. For decades my heart has lain heavy within me, fearing that I would never find you again. Fearing also that if ever I saw your face, in its living beauty and not in enchanted memories, I would fall on my knees, speechless, out of longing for you."

No man had ever spoken to Jordan with such deeply felt emotion, such antique grace. Perhaps it was the translation of his thoughts from the Spanish language into English that made his words seem so old-fashioned.

For long moments those ash-gray eyes looked directly, unhesitatingly, into hers. In his searching glance she felt an indefinable power calling to her.

Jordan knew absolutely, then, that a great part of the glamour and mystique she found in Lima Clemente was his differentness, his quality of being alien from anything she had known in the past.

She realized how it pleasured her to look into the chasm of his eyes, to see the desire, the longing, coiling there like smoke. She knew that no matter how different he was, *because* he was so different, she wanted him.

But should she indulge her longing? Would it be wise?

"Remember, I am your servant in all ways," he murmured, moving closer.

Jordan felt herself grow weak as a tide of desire swept over her, one so strong she was almost helpless against it.

But even as she turned to him, she became suddenly chilled by what one writer called "an awful amorous fear." Slowly, she drew away. Why was there so much doubt connected with newly forming love?

He looked into her eyes, saw what was written there, kissed her hand, this time as if in regret, then pressed it against his face.

"You know that I love you, Jordan. You felt the chord

between us, as did I, that night we first met, so real others could sense it, too. But do not fear. Never will I force you. The decision must be yours."

"I don't play sexual games, Lima. With me it's all or nothing."

"I understood that about you the first time I saw you."

"If we started with love, I would care too much."

"Can one care too much?"

"Lima, there are too many obstacles between us. Soon you must return to your homeland. My home, my work, is here but yours is far away. I have a young son and a very old great-grandfather to care for."

"Love finds a way, Jordan."

"Does it?" she asked softly.

"I will teach you that it does. But only when you are ready to learn."

Her heart racing, her mouth dry, Jordan knew that if Lima Clemente took her in his arms, she would yield. But he did not.

They both fell silent.

The evening sky shaded to lavender and rose, then cooled to mother-of-pearl. The only sounds were the rush of the sea, the cry of the wind, and the songs of the trees. Gently she withdrew her hand from his.

Lima Clemente remained silent, hands on knees, staring at the darkening sea.

"Unfortunately, we must go now, I am sorry to say," he said at last.

As his helicopter rose into the night and headed east toward landfall, Jordan looked back at her island. Although the young moon was curved and thin, giving off little light, the stars were exceedingly bright.

By starshine she saw a strange humped figure moving across the high grassy plateau. "The Klokwalle," she breathed.

Evidently Lima Clemente had not noticed the figure nor heard Jordan speak. He sat behind the controls, silent and remote, his Incan profile silhouetted against a field of stars.

3   Jordan went to bed that night and listened to the
     sea winds crying around her great-grandfather's
old house.

She could not go to sleep. She lay restless and feverish,
wondering if she'd had too much sun or too much Lima
Clemente.

Visual images of the man rose up before her. In her
mind's eye she saw again those strong, tanned hands with
long, spatulate fingers, each black hair on his wrists gleaming individually . . .

Saw him sitting on a driftwood log fully lighted by the
westering sun, one strong leg thrown over his knee, one
hand lying carelessly on his booted ankle . . .

Saw how the fabric of his clothing stretched taut over his
leg, and knew again that sharp desire she had felt to touch
his muscled thigh, to move her hand slowly up his body, to
be lost in his arms.

Montages moved disquietingly before her; a flash of
white teeth; black, gleaming brows; the faint lines that
ran vertically on each side of his sensual mouth when he
was in deep thought; the high cheekbones that spoke of
Incan ancestry; the unexpected ash-gray eyes betraying a
northern enrichment somewhere along the ancestral lineages.

And the expression in those eyes: mystical, desiring,
showing an experience of pain, a troubling knowledge of
cruelty.

And a great cry for love. Jordan's love.

Why had she not loved him tonight? What had held her
back?

She thought of the seabirds blown off course by the
strength of the sunset winds. Would that happen to her if
she allowed herself to become involved with Lima
Clemente? Would her entire life be thrown off course?

Jordan knew she was not a woman for whom sex was a
sport, an activity to be engaged in when there was nothing
better to do. She hated talk of "having sex." She had never
"had sex" but she *had* made love.

In spite of Jordan's attempt to be rational, her heated thoughts seemed to call Lima Clemente to her.

She sensed him with an awareness that was sharply physical, felt him forming all around her like those dancing motes of dust that only became visible under certain conditions of light.

When finally Jordan allowed her self-restraint to crumble—that dam she had so carefully constructed over the years—the physical desires she had kept at bay so long, so successfully, broke rank and came streaking in upon her, howling for release.

Succumbing, she permitted herself to imagine Lima Clemente unclothed and splendidly hard, entering her slick, hungry silences, making long, measured love until they spilled together in great hot bursts.

She cried out as she came with his imagined presence. But as furious as her lonely climax had been, Jordan found no relief; her body still ached so with longing that it hurt. It was not only men who had wet dreams, she told herself bitterly.

Emotionally exhausted, she fell into a light sleep, only to hear a voice calling softly to her on the sea winds blowing through her open window.

"Jordan, my beloved," it whispered, then called again and again, with ever-increasing urgency, until the cry became the wail of a four-footed creature.

It was Lima Clemente's voice.

When Jordan awoke in the morning, her pillow was damp and she realized she had wept during her troubled sleep.

4   Fresh spring winds shouted over sea and land for four days and four nights without ceasing, screaming up the beaches, whistling at window cracks, lavish with caresses, fondling even the dignified ancient trees into sophomoric dances of energy.

There was something strange in the swiftly moving air that quickened Jordan's nerves so that she could not bear to sit still but must be always up and doing things.

Her thoughts were constantly on Lima Clemente. She seemed to have no control over her growing feelings for this strange, compelling man.

Mentally, she played back their time together, trying to interpret every word, always with a sense of opportunity lost, of having been given a glimpse of a strange country of the soul, of high, dark, treeless places and stealthy, dangerous creatures.

Her thoughts exercised a fascination so powerful that she began to grow frightened by her feelings of fierce attraction, of desperate need.

Jordan performed her job like a skilled automaton, patrolling the two hundred thousand acres of the Quinalt Nation, dealing with law enforcement matters with cool, professional dispatch.

But on another level she seemed to see Lima Clemente everywhere. And nowhere. She saw him moving through the trees as she drove through the forest on patrol. She saw him passing into the evening fog as she walked the beach. When she hurried to investigate she discovered only shadows.

During this unhappy period Jordan realized she was in a state of disharmony. She took no sweat baths, experienced no connection with her guardian spirit.

She felt stale, ordinary, cut off from the divine vigors of life. No longer could she see the glowing world beyond the world of human sight—her real world—nor sense the presence of the Listening Ones, those great animal spirits of ancient times.

Nor did she see the Klokwalle.

At home with Tleyuk and Old Man Ahcleet, she was distracted, not herself. When her great-grandfather asked her what was wrong, Jordan told him that she was simply tired.

"Remember that I am always here, La'qewamax," the old man said softly.

"Thank you, Grandfather," Jordan replied, thinking, *But what will I do when you're not?*

Later that same evening, as the three of them sat before the fire, Old Man Ahcleet turned to Tleyuk.

"I will tell you a story about Grandmother Bear," he said, discreetly making sure that Jordan was present and listening.

"Okay, Grandfather."

"*Anqa,* long ago, when white people first started coming around here making trouble, they lived in tents. They brought cast-iron stoves to prepare their food instead of cooking over open fires.

"One day, during the Moon of Berry Time, every member of such a white group went into the hills, leaving their cast-iron stove with fire still burning in it.

"While they were gone, Grandmother Bear walked into their camp, having caught the foul smell of white man but also the pleasant odors of food. When she saw the stove, a device she had never seen before, she was naturally curious.

"Because the fire was enclosed in the belly of this contraption and she could not see the flames, Grandmother Bear did not know she could be hurt.

"She reached out with both her front paws and picked up one of the stove lids to examine it. To her surprise and anger, the lid burned her because it was very hot.

"Now, as we all know, a bear's defense against something that is hurting it is to hug that hurtful thing tight, crush the life out of that thing that it knows to be an enemy.

"Grandmother Bear, being a bear, did just that. The more that stove lid burned her, the tighter she hugged it to her body, and the tighter she hugged the stove lid to her body, the worse she was burned."

Old Man Ahcleet was silent for a while. Then he spoke. "What should Grandmother Bear have done, Tleyuk?"

"She should have dropped the lid."

"What does that story tell us?"

"Not to hug any hot stove lids."

"It tells us more than that."

"What, Grandfather?"

"It tells us that we must not keep hugging to ourselves those thoughts or memories that make us sad or angry, that hurt our hearts. We must throw them aside, forget them, let them have no part in our lives. It tells us we have the power to stop the hurt."

Silently, without comment, Jordan stood, then bent and kissed her great-grandfather, and walked out of the room.

Jordan had not heard from Lima Clemente since they had been on the island together. Hunter Kleoh called toward the end of the following week and invited Jordan out to dinner.

This time she accepted pleasantly. She told Kleoh she could meet him the next evening at Ocean Shores, adding that she needed to be home early on account of Tleyuk.

She breathed a quiet sigh of relief when the FBI man didn't ask why Old Man Ahcleet couldn't stay with the boy as he always did.

Their dinner destination had changed. Kleoh explained that yes, he *had* originally planned on taking her to Ocean Shores, but had subsequently changed his mind. He'd decided on a place quite different, but one with superb food.

When Jordan suggested they get together at the restaurant of his choice, Kleoh insisted she come into Hoquiam where he would meet her in the Safeway parking lot and drive her to their destination.

As Jordan got ready for her evening out, thinking as always of Lima Clemente, her emotions boiled. She felt resentful one minute, hurt the second, and defiant the next.

She told herself that talking police business in sophisticated surroundings with Hunter Kleoh, a law enforcement officer himself, was a good idea; it would probably allow her to forget about Lima Clemente, the man of her dreams and nightmares, for at least a couple of hours.

She dressed in cocktail-length rose taffeta with a matching taffeta coat, smoke-gray silk stockings, rose suede shoes with slender heels.

Before leaving, she dabbed Ysatis de Givenchy at her pulse points, and took a final glance in the mirror, admitting quietly to herself something she would never say aloud: Jordan Tidewater was beautiful.

Then she whispered derisively, "All this for Hunter Kleoh?" But she knew better—she hoped to run into Lima Clemente at the restaurant.

When Jordan said good-bye to Tleyuk and her great-grandfather, Old Man Ahcleet studied her.

"You're looking very white, La'qewamax," he said enigmatically.

"Grandfather, you know that I live in both worlds."

"Don't get trapped out there in the wrong one," he warned.

She kissed him and Tleyuk, took off her heels, slipped into a dilapidated pair of Nikes, walked out of the house, down the stairs, and across the rutted gravel road carrying her heels in one hand.

She opened the door of her power wagon, leaned in, pushed her notepad and handcuffs to the floor, dusted off the seat, then got in and put her heels carefully beside her. Her guns were in place and she did not remove them.

Hunter Kleoh watched Jordan appreciatively as she got out of her power wagon and into his car.

"You are one gorgeous lady. You smell gorgeous, too!"

Jordan wondered if she had overdone things by dressing up; she didn't want to give the FBI man the wrong idea about any romantic intentions she might have.

To offset his loudly spoken and continuing appreciation of her attractiveness, she made a point of grumbling, "I don't understand why we couldn't have met at the restaurant."

"I was afraid you wouldn't come if you knew where I was taking you."

"Well, lead on, then. As you can see, I'm dressed for the best."

Kleoh looked at her with a strange expression on his face. He had just passed his annual physical and was in his slender period. When he gave her his sudden smile, Jordan realized again what an appealing man he could be.

He wore a new suit, or at least one she'd never seen before, and a white silk shirt with gold cuff links at the long sleeves. Also, a narrow necktie that had been the height of fashion in the seventies. Then she was ashamed of her private criticism; the tie may have been one his wife had given him and he now treasured.

His hair was styled, and he was redolent with Old Spice, a male fragrance she remembered her ex-husband couldn't wear because it always gave him a crawly rash.

To her surprise, Kleoh headed north on U.S. 101, eventually wheeling in front of a ramshackle two-story building badly in need of paint and fronted by a graveled parking area, a place Jordan had passed many times but had never stopped at.

"Why are we stopping here?" she asked.

"Only for the greatest tenderloins in the world," he replied, coming around the car to open her door.

So much for sophisticated surroundings and the possibility of running into Lima Clemente!

Jordan once more took off her heels and put on her Nikes to walk across the gravel. Inside, she changed shoes again. She saw Kleoh smiling at her.

Jordan discovered that the café was an anachronism from the late forties. There was a wooden counter scrubbed dull, twelve stools, five high-backed wooden booths painted bright blue with tables covered in blue-checked oilcloth.

As Jordan stared at an ancient jukebox, singing now about someone looking over a four-leafed clover that he'd overlooked before, Kleoh said, "Believe it or not, you can still get three songs for a quarter."

"Unbelievable," she murmured.

"The coffee is out of this world and Ethel's pies—well, all I can say is that you'll have to see for yourself."

A sad, cadaverous man, wearing a large bleached flour sack as an apron, stamped over to take their order, his one wooden leg thumping out his passage.

"Hi yah, Hunter," he said mournfully.

Kleoh returned the greeting, then said, "Clyde, this is my friend, Jordan Tidewater. I brought her here for the best meal on the peninsula."

"You sure came to the right place," Clyde said, nodding at Jordan. Then he addressed Kleoh again. "I near fell asleep counting log trucks today."

"How many?" Kleoh asked.

"A lousy fourteen. Not too long ago I recall three hundred or more going by every day." He sighed loudly. "I don't know what we're all coming to around here. Death and destruction is about all I can figure."

"Stop being such a Gloomy Gus," came a rich female voice from behind the counter.

"What are your pies tonight, Ethel?" Kleoh called.

"French Silk and Huckleberry Cream."

Kleoh looked at Jordan. "Why don't we have a piece of each and share?"

Jordan nodded. "And I'll pretend I've never heard the words *calorie* or *cholesterol*," she said, wondering as she spoke if they were only having dessert.

Now came a full-blown laugh from behind the counter. "My pies won't hurt you. Been eatin' my own cooking for fifty years and it ain't killed me yet."

"Ethel, come on out here and meet Jordan Tidewater," Kleoh called.

He smiled at Jordan's carefully controlled expression as she was introduced to the cook, a pleasant woman with a very pretty face who verged on four hundred pounds and managed to get around by propelling herself on a tall wheeled stool.

"Yup, I was real smart," Clyde said, looking at Jordan

and managing something with his face that could have been an expression of agony but was certainly a smile.

"Years ago, when I lost this here leg of mine, I married the cook in the logging camp. Now I get fed real good and I sure am warm and cozy on cold nights."

Ethel laughed heartily when Jordan praised Clyde's foresight.

"Want me to bring the pie now?" Clyde asked.

"Of course not," Kleoh replied, looking severe. "We've got to have our dinners first."

Elbow on the table, Jordan covered her eyes with one hand and laughed quietly to herself.

"What's funny?" Kleoh asked.

"Hunter, the only other person I've ever heard order dessert first is my eight-year-old son."

Kleoh nodded. "Intelligent young man."

First, Clyde brought in a Caesar salad, preparing it at their booth in a large wooden bowl oiled with the juice of fresh garlic, then cracking the raw egg and sprinkling coarse ground black pepper with unexpected gusto.

The tenderloin steaks were superb; back strap of elk carefully prepared, Kleoh's rare, Jordan's medium, both so delicate in texture they could be easily cut with a fork, and served with a sauce made from juniper berries, shallots, madeira, and truffles dug in the Olympic national forest.

Over their dessert—each had half servings of both French Silk and Huckleberry Cream pie—Hunter Kleoh handed Jordan a sheet of computer paper.

At her questioning glance, Kleoh said, "Just came in today. It's a copy of a report on the threads Gerber found in the boy's neck. What they are is strands of bright hand-woven ribbon and they do match the threads in that envelope you gave me."

Jordan studied the report.

After a while Kleoh asked, "Jordan, would you like to tell me how you came by those threads of yours?"

Jordan told him about the ribbon she had found on the beach a couple of days before she'd come across the body of the murdered boy. She did not mention the gold medal.

"Got any ideas about the connection?" he asked.

She shook her head, then said, "We've never had any child murders on the reservation or around the lake before."

"Suddenly, within a period of days, you've got two."

"And each so different. I can't believe they're connected in any way."

"They're not, Jordan. I'd bet my pension on that. It's just one of those crazy synchronicities."

"I think the boy's death was some kind of a sacrifice."

"There aren't any satanic cults in the area that we know about," Kleoh said.

"I don't think it was satanic, Hunter, not anything that commonplace. I don't quite know how to express what I feel, probably because it's not yet clear to me, but somehow I think the boy's killing represents something larger, more meaningful, than satanic tomfoolery, as bad as that can be."

"What, then?"

"I haven't a clue."

The coffee they had both requested be served after the meal arrived, hot and aromatic.

"In the girl's case," Kleoh said, "maybe the guilty man is a tree topper, a guy who runs up and down trees. Or maybe he works in a small logging operation where they use a limbed standing tree for a high lead."

"Carrying a seventy-pound burden?"

"Hell, Jordan, those loggers carry around a hell of a lot more than that. As far as I'm concerned, the girl's murderer is someone in the logging business."

"Or that's what we're supposed to think."

Kleoh said, "Regardless, whoever put her there had to know how to get that high up in a tree and how to get back down again safely. And had to either own or have access to the necessary equipment to do it." He was silent for several moments, then he said, "Does it fit in with any old Indian lore? Anything like that?"

"I've been thinking about that," Jordan replied. "Only two things ring a bell with me at all. The first is that in the old days a man who was skilled at climbing trees to cut off the top limbs for firewood owed his ability to the fact that Raccoon was his guardian spirit."

"That sounds pretty remote."

"Yes, it does. The second is that a long time ago, in the villages nearest to Lake Quinault, new fathers took the placenta and lashed it to the top of a tall tree."

"The placenta? As in newborn babies?"

She nodded. "The afterbirth. In those days it was called the 'baby's grandmother.'"

"What about the villages on the lake?"

"There weren't any. In the old days The People didn't live on the lake."

"Why not?"

"It was too holy."

"Jordan," Kleoh hesitated, then went on. "Jordan, there's something else I need to talk to you about." He paused again.

"What?"

"I didn't want to earlier because it's not exactly a nice thing to talk about while we were eating."

"Well, Hunter, I'm waiting."

"It's about the little girl. I just got back a report on her injuries. I was afraid that semen might be too old for a valid sampling. It wasn't. All of it came from one secretor. We know that much at least."

"Good God." An image of the girl's body rose up in Jordan's mind, smeared, caked, and flaking as if her murderer had tried to encase her in a cocoon woven of spermatic fluid.

"Unless he was a damned incubus, he had to have kept her alive for quite a while."

"An incubus, Hunter?" she asked, her tone of voice just a little sarcastic.

"Yeah, you know, like Pan and Priapus in the old Greek and Roman legends, or the sons of God, the giants, that are mentioned in the Bible. The ones who mated with the daughters of men."

"I'm not familiar with them."

"The incubi were metamorthropes. Shape-changers. They could change their shape and size, control muscle tone and strength. They were supposed to have members like mules, and to discharge semen by the cupfuls. Their whole purpose in existing was to breed with humans. Their problem was that most times their mating killed the woman, although not always."

"Your idea, I suppose, is that some male around here who looks more or less normal can change his shape and is actually an incubus in disguise?"

He shrugged.

"I find it hard to believe that an FBI man is telling me this with a straight face."

"God, Jordan, even you have no idea of the weird worlds we get pulled into. You haven't been in the business long enough."

"So tell me."

"You know, stuff that's never on TV or in the newspapers because we make damned sure it isn't. There're an awful lot of nuts out there. Frankly, and I wouldn't say this to anyone except you, I'm not sure that all of them are exactly human."

A memory of Jack Scatt rose in Jordan's mind to be quickly banished. He looked neat and clean enough, surprisingly so for where he lived. But she felt something around him, something dark, that as yet she could put no name to. She was certain, however, that he was no shape-changer.

"I don't think there's anything like that in our mythology. Of course, there *was* the woman who married a dog."

"A *dog,* Jordan?"

"That's no weirder than your incubus."

"So tell me the story."

"A long time ago in a certain village lived a young girl who had a dog of which she was very fond. She took the dog with her everywhere and at night, as was the custom at that time with young girls, the dog slept at the foot of her bed."

"To guard the maiden against teepee creepers?"

Jordan smiled. "No teepees, Hunter. Cedar plank houses. Anyway, every night the dog changed into human form and lay with the girl. Every morning, before it was light, he changed back into his dog shape, so no one knew anything about what was going on.

"The girl became pregnant, and when her parents discovered that the dog was the cause, they were greatly ashamed."

"I can imagine."

"Anyway, they called The People together, tore down the house, put out all the fires, and moved the whole village a long distance away across the water, leaving the girl to die where she was."

"Rough parents," Kleoh said.

"Rough situation. Anyway, Crow, taking pity on the girl, placed some coals between two clam shells and told the girl that after a while she would hear a crackling. She was to go to the place where she heard the crackling and there she would find a fire. The girl sat very still listening for the crackling and when she finally heard it she went to the place and found the fire as Crow had said.

"Not long after this the girl gave birth to five dog pups but as her father had killed her lover, she had to look after them by herself. She was what today we would call a single mother. The only way she could live and care for them was to gather clams and other shellfish on the beach.

"There were four male pups and one female and with the care their mother gave them they grew very fast. Soon she noticed that whenever she went out, she heard singing and dancing which seemed to come from inside the house.

"Four times she heard this and when, on going out again, she heard it for the fifth time, she stuck her clam digger in the sand and put her clothes on it to make it look as if she were busy gathering clams.

"Then she stole back by a roundabout way, and creeping close to the house, she peeked in through a crack to see what the noise might be. There she saw four boys dancing and singing and a little girl watching the place where the mother was supposed to be digging clams.

"The mother waited a moment and watched, and then coming in she caught them in human form, and scolded them, saying that they should have had that form in the first place, for on their account she had been brought to shame before The People.

"Now the children felt really bad. The mother tore down the dog blankets which were hanging about and threw them into the fire.

"They remained in human form after this and as soon as they were old enough, she made little bows and arrows for the boys and taught them how to shoot birds, beginning with the wren, and working up to the seagull. Then she taught them to make large bows and arrows, and how to shoot fur-bearing animals, and then larger game, right up to the elk.

"And she made them bathe every day to try to get *tamanois*—"

"What's that?" Kleoh interrupted.

"The word means spiritual powers. They needed *tamanois* so that they could successfully hunt the whale."

"I got it. Okay, go ahead."

"She had them begin by hunting hair seals to make floats of their skins. The mother made harpoons for them of elk bone and lines of twisted sinews and cedar. At the end of the lines she fastened the sealskin floats. And when everything was ready, the boys went out whaling and brought in so many whales that the whole beach stank with them.

"One day Crow noticed, from far across the water, a great smoke rising from where the old village had stood, and that night Crow came over secretly to see what was going on.

"Before she neared the beach, Crow smelled the dead whales, and when she came up she saw the carcasses lying all about, and there were so many that some of them had not yet been cut up.

"When Crow reached the house, she found the children human and grown up. They welcomed her and gave her food, all she could eat, but gave her nothing to take back, telling her to come over again if she wanted more.

"When Crow started back, the young mother asked her, when she reached home, to please weep so that The People would keep on believing they were all dead and leave them alone.

"But Crow, on arriving home, instead of doing as she was requested, described how the beach was covered with seagulls feeding on the whales that had been killed by the boys.

"Crow had brought with her secretly a piece of whale meat for her children, and after putting out the light she fed it to them; and one of them ate so fast that she choked, and coughed a piece of meat out on the ground. And some of The People saw it, and then believed what Crow had told them, as they had not done before.

"The People talked it all over, and decided to go back. They loaded their canoes and moved back to the old village. And the boys who used to be dogs became the chiefs of the village, and always kept The People supplied with whales."

"I think your story's better than mine," Kleoh said. "I wonder what it means."

"It has many meanings. Perhaps one is that people are not always what they seem to be," Jordan replied.

She looked around the café. "Do you realize that we've been the only customers here all evening?"

He smiled broadly. "That's because I rented the restaurant just for us."

Kleoh got up, walked to the jukebox, inserted several quarters. Soon the poignant words, "I'll be loving you, *always,* with a love that's true, *always,*" floated through the café.

Kleoh sat back down and gazed at Jordan soulfully, his expression reminding her of Tleyuk when he wanted a special favor from his mother, face washed, hair carefully combed. Jordan pointedly looked at her watch.

"It's certainly been an interesting evening, Hunter, and I'm sorry to break it up, but I really do have to go."

"Just a few more minutes, Jordan?"

She shook her head firmly. "My little boy, you know."

He sighed. "I understand."

Jordan expressed her appreciation for the superb meal to both Ethel and Clyde, promised to drop in again, left the café on Hunter Kleoh's arm, her thoughts on Lima Clemente as the strains of forties' love music followed in their wake.

On the way back, when Hunter Kleoh braked for a traffic light as they entered the city of Aberdeen, Jordan thought she saw Lima Clemente, head bent, studying the window of a small shop specializing in rare books.

"Stop!" she told Kleoh. "Stop right here."

Startled, he replied, "I am stopped. For the light."

He looked over at Jordan as she threw open the car door and ran across the sidewalk to the bookshop.

There was nothing there except shadows from the streetlight. She walked back to Kleoh's car, climbed in, and huddled against the door.

Kleoh touched her arm. "Jordan, is something wrong? Can I help?"

She shook her head.

When they got out of the car at the Safeway parking lot, she thought she saw a man with long, braided, black hair walking slowly toward them through the darkness.

She grabbed Kleoh's arm. "Hunter, who is that? Do you know him?"

Kleoh peered intently into the darkness. "There's no one there, Jordan."

Then, to be certain, he walked around the empty parking lot, examining every corner, every shaded spot.

"Nope," he said, striding back to Jordan and his car. "Nothing but shadows."

He escorted Jordan to her power wagon, where they stood talking.

"Are you in some kind of danger, Jordan?" he asked, his voice serious. "Has some pervert you put away been released? Is there some nut on your trail?"

"No, Hunter."

"Would you tell me if there were?"

She studied him. "Yes, I believe I would."

"Well, something's wrong. I can see that."

"I don't know if it's wrong or right. All I can say is that I have to figure it out for myself."

"I hope you know me well enough to understand that if anyone wants to hurt you, I will personally kill the bastard and fill out the forms later."

She took Hunter's hand, wanting to kiss him for his concern.

But when Kleoh trembled at her touch, Jordan, knowing her own fragile emotional state, immediately understood that such an innocent act as a kiss of thanks could quickly lead to something far more intimate, which she did not want. She would only be taking advantage of the man.

So she thanked him again, climbed into her truck, changed out of her high heels and back into her grungy old Nikes, and drove away, tears running down her cheeks as she headed for her great-grandfather's house by the sea.

O love is the crooked thing,
There is nobody wise enough
To find out all that is in it,
For he would be thinking of love
Till the stars had run away
And the shadows eaten the moon.
—WILLIAM BUTLER YEATS

Chapter 12

1 One of the unique attractions at Lake Quinault Lodge is that there are neither telephones nor television sets in the rooms of the lodge itself.

Guests, it is correctly assumed, come to enjoy the amenities of the establishment, the superb food, and the beauty of nature while in retreat from the vociferations of everyday life.

For those who find instant communication absolutely necessary, there are two pay telephones situated discreetly in a hallway leading to the rest rooms and the cocktail lounge.

Since Jordan could not reach Lima Clemente by telephone without members of the lodge staff knowing of her call, she wrote a note, folded it into an envelope, addressed the envelope to him in care of Lake Quinault Lodge, and mailed it at Moclips.

Unsigned, the note was brief, consisting of only five words: "I am ready to learn."

2   One week later, on an early afternoon in late May, a time when out in Olympic forests the black bears were mating and the elk were calving, Jordan stood once more on her island with Lima Clemente.

En route there had been little conversation. It was as if each had nothing more to say to the other; all doubts had been swept aside, all questions would soon be answered. Now their combined energies were focused on what was to come.

"May I ask why you changed your mind, Jordan?" Lima Clemente said.

"It was the seabirds."

"I beg your pardon?"

"I remembered the seabirds being blown off course when we were on the island before."

"Yes?" He looked over at her and raised a questioning eyebrow.

"When I thought about it, I realized something I had always known. The seabirds only seemed to be blown off course. But they weren't. Not really. They were simply accommodating themselves to the force of the wind and later arrived safely in their nests."

"I am thankful to the seabirds, Jordan."

This time, after they landed, Jordan waited decorously inside for Lima Clemente, the old-fashioned young man, to come and help her down.

Which he did, with grace, then led her to a shore-cliff cave, one they walked past on their first visit but had not explored.

"I have made some small provisioning for our comfort," he said, inviting her into the cave.

She saw that he had prepared a large couch by placing several fur robes on top of hemlock branches piled two feet deep.

"How did you know I love the smell of hemlock branches?" Jordan asked.

"I know a lot about you."

"Whenever I got the chance I used to sleep on them when I was a child."

Lima Clemente smiled.

A fire was laid to one side. Numerous candles, unlit as yet, were carefully positioned on every surface irregularity in the cave large enough to provide a base to support them.

When he saw her looking at the large metal container placed against the wall of the cave, he said, "We will dine later."

But now that the time had come for love, Jordan felt a nervous anxiety building up within her.

"Lima, if you don't mind, I'd like to walk around outside for a while by myself."

"Take as long as you want, Jordan. I will be here when you are ready to rest," he said gently.

Ready to rest! she thought. *Ah, yes.*

She walked slowly down the sand to the tide line. Here and there were great whitened accumulations of driftwood, the debris of trees seized from forests by the encroaching sea.

Their hulks lay immovable, ten to twelve feet tall above the high-water mark, all asprawl like the whitened bones of prehistoric giants fallen in the very act of battle.

When the ocean rose again, driven by storms or high tides, the logs would be picked up once more like weightless toothpicks, swept out to sea, then hurled back with the force of battering rams.

Jordan saw the milky luster of a moonstone glowing from a scattering of beach pebbles. Bending to pick up the pearly white gem, she became suddenly dizzy and nauseous and was afraid she was going to throw up. The bad moment passed. She inhaled deeply, then dropped the moonstone into her trouser pocket.

"What's wrong with me?" she whispered.

It had been her wish to be here. She *wanted* to make love with Lima Clemente; she had grown sick with longing for him.

And now that the hour was at hand and all was in readiness, when she had perfect privacy, alone with the man she wanted, her body turned against her.

She had become so nervous that the palms of her hands were ice-cold and wet, her mouth dry. Her heart pounded thunderously.

She told herself it had been so long since she'd engaged in the act of love she'd forgotten how and was simply terrified of making a fool of herself.

After all, there were certain things to consider. Who would make the first move? Should she simply go back to the cave, fling off her clothes, collapse on the fur and hemlock couch, spread her legs apart?

And what would she do about the nervous sweat pouring off her body? Had she bathed this morning? Yes, as always, she had. She'd taken a long soaking bath followed by a brisk shower. Had she used deodorant? What a silly question. Of course, she always did.

The physical realities of making love swept into her mind. Had Lima Clemente brought condoms? She had not thought about it. Would he, like her ex-husband, make rude comments about the woman scent between her legs? What if she suffered flatulence as a result of her upset stomach?

"Why didn't I think about these details before I came out here?" she asked herself.

She knew she must go back to that cave, head held high, wearing the same look of strength and confidence that she wore when confronting a suspect.

She must get done what she had come here to do.

Determined, mouth firmed, she strode back to the cave, and suddenly realized what she was really afraid of.

She feared that when Lima Clemente first touched her with the hands of love, and she yielded, her intense physical response would terrify him, make him feel less than a man.

That was one of the things that ruined her marriage with Roc Tidewater. When she married him she loved him and was delighted by the pleasure her body was capable of giving her.

He called her "oversexed," accused her of having many lovers because "certainly no one normal man could satisfy a woman with your appetites." When she became pregnant he laughed and asked how in the world she would ever know who the father was.

The truth was that she had been absolutely faithful to Roc Tidewater, a man who least deserved such loyalty. Heartbroken because of his refusal to admit fathering the child in her womb, his scorn of her multiorgasmic ability, and his affairs, she left him.

3   "Why waste any more time?" she said brusquely, standing in the entrance to the cave, backlighted by the sun so that her shadowed body and her black curls were washed with a golden flush.

Astonished at her attitude, Lima Clemente hurried over to her.

"My dear Jordan, what is wrong?"

"Nothing's wrong." She coughed.

"You are hoarse. May I give you some champagne?"

"No thanks." If she took anything in her stomach she would immediately throw it back up.

"Your throat seems dry."

"I found this on the beach," she said, digging in her trouser pocket for the small gem and thrusting it at him.

"A moonstone! A wonderful sign for our future!"

She did not reply.

"Do you not know that these stones protect travelers on dark nights? Through dangerous forests and over stormy seas?"

When he saw that she had started shaking, he said, "Jordan, you're cold! Let me warm you."

As he approached her, she folded her arms, bit her lip, and stood staring down at the floor of the cave.

"Why, you're not cold, you're anxious. Dear Jordan, are you afraid that I will hurt you?"

"No."

"Do you still want to make love?"

"Yes," she whispered.

"With me?"

"Yes."

"Are you sure?" His voice was teasing.

"Yes."

"Would you like to lie down?"

She glanced at the couch and nodded.

"Would you like me to lie down with you?"

She nodded.

"All right, Jordan. I will lie down first. You may step behind that small alcove of rock and remove your clothing in privacy. Then you can join me. We will relax quietly together and listen to the sea."

She stood oddly-still, watching Lima Clemente as he undressed with his back to her. When he had finished, he folded his clothes neatly and placed them to one side. When he unbound his black hair, it fell loose to his waist.

As he turned to face Jordan, heat flooded her face and her eyes filled with tears from the strength of her emotions. His body was unashamedly beautiful. She swallowed hard, once, then swallowed again.

As if conducting a ceremony, he moved around lighting all the candles in the cave. When that was concluded, he spoke.

"I will lie down, Jordan, and you may come to me whenever you wish. No matter how long it takes I will be here."

She went behind the alcove and undressed. But she could not walk out in front of him naked, so she tried to cover herself with the T-shirt she'd been wearing.

He smiled as she approached the hemlock couch. "I knew you would not appear before me naked, Jordan. Not the first time."

When he threw the furs open, she tossed aside the T-shirt and joined him, then lay as still as a carved effigy, her hands folded below her breasts and her eyes closed.

She felt his light kiss on her forehead and then on her eyelids. He lifted her left breast and held his lips above her swiftly beating heart.

He stroked her body with touches so silken she wondered, eyes still closed, if it was truly Lima Clemente's hand or an errant breeze.

Gradually she grew calm and opened herself the slightest bit. As she did so, she felt Lima Clemente move his hand between her legs as gently as if he were touching a tender wound.

Her eyes flew open at his intimate touch and she said, "No."

He removed his hand and let it lay lightly on her hip. "Jordan, darling, please relax. I will not hurt you."

"I know that, Lima."

She took his hand from her hip and placed it once again between her legs, opening herself a bit more.

Feeling the liquid of her fierce readiness, he covered her and placed himself at her inlet. But he could not enter without using force. Her body had locked itself tight against him.

Moving gently away, he asked, "You are not a virgin, are you, Jordan? You have a child, I believe?"

"I have a child."

"Relax, darling Jordan, fall asleep in my arms if you wish. There is no hurry, dearest girl. We have all the time in the world."

Suddenly Jordan realized what she had overlooked in her weeks of passion and unfulfilled longing. Something important.

She had forgotten that she was more than a woman. She was a shaman, and as such had a life beyond the mere physical.

"Put your arms around me," she said.

He moved quickly to obey.

"All the way, Lima, put all your weight on me. Your face against my face, your belly on mine, your legs entwined with mine. Then lie perfectly still."

Clasped together, Jordan allowed her spirit to flow into him, into his solar plexus, through his lower body, down his legs, up through the top of his head, down through his body again.

Her spirit found no evil within him, found only hungry passion and a genuine love for her.

And something else. A spiritual belief so strong it was like a great rock cliff.

Freed now from her fears, she said, "Kiss me."

He kissed her passionately and she opened to him, her body taking his length and fullness with incredulous delight.

At first they found it difficult to establish an exquisite rhythm, for she could not prevent her body from climaxing, one orgasm right after the other, like small magnetic storms.

"Ah, my beautiful hungry girl," he whispered, and then played her like a harp; at his slightest movement, his barest breath, she came and came again, he accommodating her with careful patience until at last they moved together with a long and luscious ease.

4   Hours later, as they grew tranquil after the fatigues of love, long after the candles had burned down and only firelight remained, they arose from their furs and walked naked, hand in hand, onto the beach and into the waves, their way lighted by a marigold sliver of moon.

They laughed and danced, ran and splashed, the two first

people on earth, until she led him back into the shallows where they lay down and came together again, the heat in the depths of their joined bodies made even more incandescent by the cold surging waters of the North Pacific sea.

"At the next full moon I will place the moonstone you gave me in my mouth," he told her, wiping the sea from her face. "When I do so, I will know our future. That is one of the powers of the moonstone."

"Don't talk about the future," she said, clinging to him.

She already knew she was his. Forever.

And he was hers. Forever and ever.

When the moon slipped away, darkness fell around them both like a sweet black veil.

5   Jordan arrived back home late at night and plunged into sleep as if falling off a cliff.

She dreamed again of cougars. This time they were all around her; playing, chirping, rolling in ecstasy.

One of them, a gorgeous female clad in fur the colors of apricot and raw umber, raised her smiling blue-eyed face to Jordan as if awaiting her kiss.

Northwest Coast Indian art is one of the most distinctive of all the arts of man. When one has come to know the components of this dynamic style, it is impossible to confuse it with art from any other part of the world.

—ALLEN WARDWELL,
Objects of Bright Pride

Chapter 13

1　At seven o'clock in the morning Hannah McTavish was alone and hard at work in the A-frame office of Quinault Timber Company at Moclips.

Michael in his pickup and the crummy, a dilapidated old bus full of workers, had left for the woods before first light.

Since the company logging trucks had not been able to haul timber there were no scale tickets to post, so she busied herself on the quarterly payroll reports.

Looking outside, she saw that four of the trucks sat in the mill yard, trailers hunched up over their backs like vast primordial insects.

They would sit there until Fire Road Six became passable

again. If it ever did. She didn't know where the fifth truck was. Michael had probably rented it out to haul for somebody else.

Hannah was one of those women with a directness of look that was as good as a handclasp.

She possessed the kind of figure that appealed to men who genuinely liked women.

Her breasts were large and firm; her legs, long and shapely. Her husband had once told her, "None of those skinny females for me. When I make love I like to know I'm holding on to a real woman, not a bunch of bones, and she's holding on to me."

Ordinarily, health and vigor gave her a strong attractiveness. Now, however, she was not her usual groomed, collected self.

Her soft brown hair, which she usually wore shoulder length and carefully brushed, was carelessly pulled up on top of her head and held in place, more or less, with several combs.

She'd overslept, awakened feeling bloated and achy, checked her calendar and found it was almost time for her period, had an argument with her ten-year-old daughter Elspat, who'd been sassier than usual, and left the house, upset, without eating breakfast.

Hanna realized she had a roaring case of PMS. Today she was definitely not a woman to be trifled with.

At half past seven the front office door opened and Ruby Campbell walked in. She liked this older man with his easy, upright carriage, electric-blue eyes, and ghost of a gentle Kentucky accent.

She knew that he liked her and her family, and certainly their dog, Kirstie the Beagle. He'd once told her that beagles were bonds between people.

"Hi, Hannah," he said. "What's the good word?"

"The good word today is a word of warning. This is a bad hair day. A very bad hair day," she said with a smile.

"Guess I better just slide on out then."

"No, stay awhile and tell me what you're up to."

"Oh, just moseying around. Thought I might look in on Michael, see how he's getting along out there on Fire Road Six."

She groaned. "Burma Road? Every day I expect to hear that the whole crew has fallen into that sinkhole, never to be seen again."

"That bad, is it?"

"Worse. But they've started to corduroy, so maybe that will solve our problems. At least we haven't found any more dead kids."

They talked about the horror of finding the dead girl and wondered if the police had made any progress in the investigation.

"Think I'll take a run out there, see how they're getting along." Ruby started to walk away, then turned back. "Say, come to think about it, Melisande wants me to give you a message."

"I haven't seen Melly since the book party."

"She wants to know if you can come to the house for lunch tomorrow. You and Binte both. She says to tell you that if you can't, give her a call. If you can, just show up."

2   Shortly after Ruby Campbell left, the phone rang and Hannah picked it up. The male voice on the other end sounded harsh, irascible.

"Let me talk to the bull of the woods," the voice demanded.

"Who?" Hannah cleared her throat.

"The bull of the woods. The guy that runs the place."

"Michael McTavish is not here," she said repressively. "Who are you?"

"I'm the wife of the man who runs the place."

"Well, all I've got to say is that I kinda like to decide when and where to slaughter my own livestock."

Hannah's patience, never at high tide before noon, ebbed to a historic low. "Sir, I don't know who you are or what you're talking about."

"I'll make it short and sweet. One of your people just killed one of my cows."

Killed a cow! Hannah was silent. She remembered being told at some point in her life that offense was the best defense.

"What was your cow doing in our timber?" she demanded.

"You trying to tell me a cow don't have no right out in the woods?"

"I'm telling you that we have no liability if your animal was interfering with the operation of our business."

Hannah had no idea whether or not such a statement was legally true but she thought it sounded good.

"Carelessness is carelessness out in the woods or any-place else," the voice declared.

Hannah's gloom deepened. One of their men must have been doing a little out-of-season hunting on company time. Shot old bossy instead of an elk.

If so, the employee was liable, not the company. She hoped. Also, if so, that employee was going to have his vision checked and his pay docked. Maybe she'd urge Michael to fire him.

The caller's voice increased in volume. "Besides, my cow wasn't out in your woods."

"Where was it?"

"Walking down U.S. 101 minding its own business."

Hannah groaned, then covered the groan with a hasty cough, envisioning multiple lawsuits zinging her way with the accuracy of night-feeding bats.

"Has there been an accident?"

Breathing heavily, the caller seemed to deliberate. "Well, I thought it was an accident, but maybe it wasn't. Maybe it was intentional. Now if your man ran that cow of mine down with malicious intent—"

Hannah inhaled, then slowly exhaled, four deep breaths, and tried to calm her racing pulse. It didn't work. She took four more deep breaths, wishing she'd gone in for meditation in her younger days so she'd know how to do it. If she could somehow project an air of calmness, false though it was . . .

"Look, sir, I don't even know who you are. Or where you are. Or what really happened. Could we start all over?"

"Reckon we could."

She put a smile in her voice and asked, "Could you tell me your name?"

"Name's not important. Not right now."

Exasperated, she demanded, "Then what do you want?"

"Lady, I want you to come out here and talk this thing over—"

"Look, I'm awfully busy right now. And I'm alone in the office."

"—or my lawyer will be banging on your front door first thing in the morning with a writ."

A *writ*! What kind of a writ, for God's sake?

"Yes. Well, perhaps I can make it."

"Good decision."

"Where shall we meet?"

"Know where the Black Rooster is?"

"I do."

She couldn't bring herself to ask what a cow had been doing walking down the highway in front of a tavern at this hour of the morning. Or at any hour, come to think about it. Or what the cow had to do with Quinault Timber.

But these were litigious times and she and Michael could not afford any more trouble, not with the way things were going up on Fire Road Six. Hannah knew she had to go and find out what this was all about.

"How long will it take you to get here?" the voice demanded.

"Well, if I leave right now, about forty-five minutes to an hour, that is if the road—"

"Then leave right now."

"Just a minute! Who do you think you—"

Hannah found herself talking to an open line. The man had hung up on her!

"Jerk!" she breathed.

Who in the world was her caller? Some kook out there in the wilderness? Had the "accident" even happened? She wasn't about to leave the office on a wild goose chase.

But maybe he wasn't a kook. Maybe he was simply an impolite old man fearful about a loss he could not afford.

On impulse, she looked up the telephone number of the Black Rooster and called.

When a woman's voice answered, Hannah said, "This may seem like a peculiar question, but do you know anything about someone hitting a cow this morning?"

"Oh, sure," came the reply. "Logging truck hit her. Right out in front."

"Do you happen to know who the truck belonged to?"

"All I can tell you is that the name Quinault Timber and a funny-looking bird was painted on the door."

It was their truck, all right. Their company name and that stylized eagle in four colors.

"Thank you."

So the accident was real. The cow had died. Now she knew where that fifth logging truck was. Out running over some poor old man's cow.

Hannah unplugged the coffepot and the wall heater, turned on the answering machine, left a big note scrawled in black felt pen that read GONE TO SEE A MAN ABOUT A DEAD COW followed by four scare points in red felt pen, and left immediately.

Delayed by construction work on the Moclips Highway, she didn't arrive at the Black Rooster until over an hour later.

A butcher's van stood in the parking lot. A state police car was just driving off. The only sign of a cow was a large, irregular area on the blacktop that had been sprinkled with sand. Miscellaneous men ambled about with their hands in their pockets.

"Come on now, let's get this over with!" Hannah ordered herself after sitting still for several minutes contemplating the scene.

She hated this sort of thing. Michael now, he was good at

negotiating tricky situations. He always remained cool and kept his temper. Maybe she should have left it for him. But no, he had enough problems to handle as it was. Serious problems, like getting the damn timber out.

She climbed out of the car, slammed the door behind her, and with a large and what she hoped was a charming smile, walked over to the group of men.

"Which one of you is the gentleman who owned the cow?" she asked.

Nobody admitted to holding that position.

"Do any of you know where the owner is?"

After spitting judiciously, several of the men shook their heads while the others maintained a dignified silence.

Irritated, Hannah stamped into the tavern where a scrawny woman with glittering white-blond hair piled improbably high on top of her narrow head asked Hannah what she wanted to drink.

"Hemlock," Hannah muttered.

"Pardon?" The barmaid stared at her, one long black false eyelash dipping perilously low.

"I'm sorry. Nothing, actually. I'm looking for the owner of the cow that was run over."

"Oh, him. He went home." Using a damp towel, the woman began mopping the bar with long sweeps of her arm. "You want to see him?"

"Not particularly."

"Oh."

"But I have to. Do you know where I can find him?"

"Sure. Go down that side road over there until you see the sign." The woman pointed to a narrow alley that ran perpendicular to the main highway.

"What sign?"

"Only sign there. You can't miss it." She leaned across the bar and lowered her voice. "Watch out for him. He's a ladies' man."

Ladies' man? What in the world was a ladies' man? It sounded like an expression her grandmother might have used.

Having given the nonspecific directions along with a woman-to-woman warning, the barmaid disappeared into the back regions of the tavern in response to a male shout.

Hannah called out a "Thank you!" ran outside and down the steps, jumped into her car under the unflickering eyes of the men in the parking lot, and drove down the alley as directed, leaving a trail of damp dust in her wake. *Damp dust?* she thought. *Only I could raise damp dust!*

She'd gone about an eighth of a mile when she saw a crude sign nailed to a fence post. Bright purple block letters announced:

BULL SERVICE AHEAD

Directly under those words, also in purple but in flowing script rather than block letters, appeared the single word: *Hereford.*

So. The man she was to meet offered the breeding services of a Hereford bull. She supposed with a sigh that the deceased cow had been impregnated by the very expensive bull, making the loss that much greater.

Following an arrow on the sign, she turned right and drove onto a wide gravel apron fronting an old house with a large porch.

Several outbuildings lay to one side of the parking space. One of the buildings had a well-built dog run attached to it. Directly opposite was a fenced pasture that contained one enormous and boldly masculine bull.

Hannah eyed the animal carefully as she got out of the car. How solid was that fence? Good Lord! Were those his— what did the Mexicans call then?—*cajones*?

"Big old bastard, ain't he?"

She turned quickly. She'd been so engrossed with the bull that she hadn't noticed the man's approach.

"Oh, hello there. I'm Hannah McTavish from Quinault Timber."

"Figured as much."

"I came to talk about your cow."

"Sure you did. Come on in. This is where I do my business."

He walked into the house, not looking back to see if she was following. Hannah stood her ground.

The only sign of life, other than the man himself, was the bull, which was now evincing a great interest in her.

Hannah took another good look at the animal. *That fence seems pretty feeble,* she thought, and ran up the steps of the house, then walked sedately inside.

"Have a seat," the man said.

Hannah looked around a living room filled with over-stuffed furniture covered with cotton throws. Everything seemed neat, although the light was too dim to really tell. Two dogs lay quietly together in front of the fireplace.

"Handsome animals," she said. "What kind are they?"

"They're redbones, ma'am. Bear dogs. Worth a fortune. Names are Sally and Old Griz."

When their names were spoken, the two dogs got up and walked over to Hannah, then stood politely looking at their master as if waiting to be introduced.

"This here is Hannah McTavish," the man told them. The dogs gazed quietly up at her.

Hannah solemnly patted each head.

"Okay, Sally, Old Griz, you've met my company. Now go back to your places."

The dogs returned to their rugs by the fire.

"Is your wife home?" Hannah asked.

The man laughed shortly. "She hasn't been home since 1983."

Beginning to feel distinctly uncomfortable, Hannah sat down in a straight-backed chair, one nearest the open front door, and carefully crossed her legs. There was something about this man that made her glad she'd worn trousers. Loose ones.

"I hope we can conclude our business soon," she said. "I need to get back to the office as soon as possible."

He was standing in a doorway she assumed led into the kitchen. "Like a cup of coffee?" he asked.

"No, thank you." She would have loved coffee, but she would not eat or drink anything in this man's house.

"Guess we need a little more light on the subject." He walked around the room turning on table and floor lamps.

The atmosphere brightened with the addition of light. When he sat down in a chair directly opposite her, Hannah saw that he was one of those ageless individuals who could be anywhere from the early forties to the late seventies. He had a friendly face but there was something in his eyes she did not like. Something . . .

"I've brought you the name and number of my insurance company which I will be happy to give you after you tell me exactly what happened and how our company is involved."

Having fired the first shot, Hannah sat back and awaited his response.

"Say, I do admire a businesslike woman. Not many of them around."

His eyes traveled her body, stopping obviously at the high points, smiling in approval of what he saw.

Hannah did not like that look, either. *Who the hell are you to approve of me?* she thought with ferocity.

"Before we go any further, sir, I would like to know your name."

"It's Hereford," he said. "William Hereford."

She frowned. "Hereford? But I thought your bull—"

"Was a Hereford? No, lady. I'm the only Hereford around here. And just as much a bull as he'll ever be, if I do say so myself. Main difference is, there's no charge for me."

He bent his head and laughed quietly as if modestly accepting accolades for services more than satisfactorily rendered.

Hannah did not like that laugh, either. She swallowed, uncomfortable with the man, the place, the situation.

"Some of us don't believe in artificial insemination, you know. It's not fair to the animals," he said, trying, she suspected, to draw her into a discussion of breeding practices.

"So what happened out there today, Mr. Hereford?" she asked crisply.

He studied her before replying. "From what the witnesses tell me, my cow was walking down the side of the highway when your log truck came barreling along and hit her a good one."

"Where is the animal now?"

Hereford looked at his watch. "I suspect that right about now what's left of her is cooling off in the butcher's refrigerator. No use wasting good meat. That's what my lady friends tell me all the time."

"I see." Hannah stood up. "Here is my card, Mr. Hereford. The name and number of the company's insurance agent are written on the back. If you'll give him a call, he'll take it from there."

"Now, just a minute, missy." He got up leisurely, hands in his pockets. "This don't have to go to no insurance company. That can get pretty complicated."

Hannah paused, her hand on the screen door. "What do you propose?"

"Oh, I only proposition." He chuckled softly and moved closer.

Hannah stood up straighter and stared at him.

He moved even closer. "I think we could work this thing out in a friendly way, all things considered."

Before she realized his intentions, Hereford grabbed her buttocks with one hand and fondled her left breast with the other.

"You could let me ravage your body," he muttered into the curve of her neck. "I'd even let you have some of the cow meat."

"Old fool!" she shouted and hit him in the face as hard as she could.

He gave her breast a painful wrench, then let go and held his nose, which had begun to bleed. "Bitch!" he mumbled.

Hannah ran out of the house and down the steps. The bull bellowed in its enclosure and rammed against the fence. She leaped into her car, praying for it to start on the first try, which it did.

She raced back up the gravel road and screeched to a stop

in front of the Black Rooster, bereft now of its male audience, thank God!

She tumbled out of her car, ran inside the tavern still gritting her teeth in fury, and dashed into the women's room where she washed her hands and scrubbed her face with a number of dampened paper towels until the skin that normally glowed like fine porcelain was red, tender, and sore.

"Guess you've met William Hereford," the barmaid said, placing a foaming glass of beer in front of Hannah when she stamped back out to the bar.

"Somebody ought to beat that guy to a pulp!" Hannah muttered, drinking down the beer in two gulps.

"Came on to you, did he?" The barmaid filled a second glass and set it on the counter. "Want another after this?"

Hannah nodded, too hot-eyed with rage to think straight, and drank down the second glass.

"Well, I'll tell you something," the barmaid said, placing two more glasses of beer in front of Hannah. "That William, he operates on the percentage principle. Figures that if he makes a lot of passes, a certain number of women will accept his advances."

Hannah gave a scornful laugh. "Who could be that hard up?"

The barmaid shrugged. "Well, from what I understand, some are, I guess."

Hannah gulped down more beer, wiped her mouth with the back of her hand, and said, "Asshole!"

"That he is. But every now and then he snags himself one. Personally, I think his technique leaves a lot to be desired."

Lifting her face from the beer, an interesting foam mustache curved above her lips, Hannah said, "You've had a run-in with him, have you?"

The barmaid pulled another beer for Hannah, then added one for herself, which she began to sip companionably.

"I don't know whether I'd call it a run-in or not. More like a fatal collision. I was married to the creep for a couple of years. How about another one on the house?"

Hannah shook her head. "Better not. I've got to get back to work."

She stood up shakily, glanced in the smoky mirror behind the bar, not even seeing the disordered hair that hung around her face, the combs having fallen out in her fevered comings and goings.

"When you see that old goat you can tell him for me that if I ever hear from him in any way, shape, or form, I will kill him."

"Can I quote you on that?" the barmaid called as Hannah stalked across the floor heading for the door.

"Forget it!" Hannah yelled back, remembering she had not left William Hereford her business card with the insurance information on the back. "I'll tell him myself!"

She ran to her car, started it up with a roar, and with the door on the driver's side still hanging open, sped back down the gravel lane to Hereford's house.

She screeched to a stop near the pastured bull, gravel flying every which way, jumped out of the car, and ran up the steps.

When she looked through the screen door and saw Hereford holding an ice pack on his nose, a new surge of anger flooded through her.

"Listen, you old fool!" she yelled. "That kind of stuff might work with the women you know but if you ever try anything like that again with me I'll have every goddamn policeman in this state on your ass! Believe it!"

Hereford moved closer to the screen door and stared at her balefully.

"Trouble with you, missy, you need to be taught a damned good lesson." He laughed softly.

Hannah opened the screen door, attempted to throw her business card on the floor at his feet, found to her displeasure that the damned thing would only float, slammed the door shut, and ran back down the steps. The wide-eyed bull remained silent in his enclosure.

She leaped into her car, remembered to shut the door on the driver's side, and raced off.

Shaking with anger, Hannah headed back up U.S. 101 toward the Moclips Highway. The more she thought about her recent encounter, the heavier her foot became on the gas pedal.

"Ravage my body! I'll ravage his with a sledgehammer, the old goat!"

Then she remembered the look on William Hereford's face. One thing for sure—she'd made an enemy. In William Hereford's world, she suspected, nothing was over until it was even.

Glancing in her rearview mirror, she saw the blinking lights of a state police cruiser gaining on her. When it came abreast of Hannah's car, the officer inside motioned for her to pull over with a lordly wave of his hand.

"Oh, shit!" she said.

She watched in the mirror as the officer got out of his cruiser, hipless and sleek as a trout, not a wrinkle showing anywhere, and strode up to her window, which he signaled her to open. Gazing at her through the lens of his opaque aviator sunglasses, he asked to see her driver's license.

After she gave it to him, he walked back to his cruiser with the license in his hand, came back and returned it to her, then stood by her open window, ticket pad in hand.

"Are you satisfied that I'm not driving a stolen car or wanted for any criminal offenses?" she asked.

He did not reply.

"Tell me something, Officer. How can you sit on your ass all day and not get your uniform wrinkled?"

He stared down at her, obviously deciding to ignore this question, too.

"Didn't you see that speed limit sign back there a couple of miles?" he asked.

"I was going too fast to see it," she replied morosely.

"I guess you were. Ninety-five miles an hour in a fifty-five-mile zone." He glanced at her oddly, then wrote out a ticket and handed it to her. "Will you try to hold your speed down, Mrs. McTavish?"

"You know who I am?" she asked.

"Ma'am, I saw your driver's license."

Hannah looked at the ticket he'd given her. *One hundred and fifty dollars!* And all because of that fool with the cow! Damn William Hereford to hell and back! And that went for his bull, too!

Hannah drove off, slower now, but still seething and swearing. *Ravage my body! Stupid old retard! One hundred and fifty dollars! Damned cop!*

Come to think about it, that business with the cop *was* her fault for driving too fast. Had she had that much beer? Course not. She'd only had one glass. Well, maybe two.

She groaned. Talk about a bad hair day. This one was not only bad, it was the mother of all bad hair days. Then she had a brilliant idea; she knew precisely what she'd do.

She'd drive up to Fire Road Six and find her husband. Michael was always so positive, so full of energy, so optimistic, even when he was pissed off.

In fact, when he was angry he had even more energy and more optimism. Seeing him always got her blood circulating, cheered her up, made her feel better.

3   When Hannah glanced in her rearview mirror again, she saw that the state police cruiser was driving sedately behind her about an eighth of a mile. Not following her, nothing like that, just proceeding leisurely on his way.

She turned left onto the Moclips Highway. And so did he. Well, maybe he was on his way to Moclips. Who knew what these state cops were up to?

Driving with exaggerated caution, she proceeded carefully along, the trooper not passing her, simply remaining behind at what he probably considered a discreet distance.

When Hannah saw the small nearly obliterated sign indi-

cating the entrance to Fire Road Six, she turned in with the
state cop now right behind her.

She would have recognized Fire Road Six even without
the sign. It was obviously a fire road in current use; the
entrance torn wider by crushed greenery, dust all over everything, holes in the road filled with muddy water, gravel piled
along the side. Logging was so damned *messy*!

She drove two miles in over a very rough roadbed with
the cop bumping right along behind her. *Hope he breaks his
goddamned axle!* she thought uncharitably, and wondered
why she felt so mean.

Then she remembered the cow and its poor old owner;
yeah, sure, that asshole with the grabby hands. And the *hun-
dred-and-fifty-dollar ticket*!

She rubbed one hand over her face, tried to push the strag-
gly hair back up on top of her head but could find no combs
to anchor it, so she wound it behind her ears, letting it fall
messily as it would.

What difference did her hair make? She wouldn't be seeing
anybody except some muddy, sweaty men who didn't give a
damn what she looked like. And she'd see Michael, of course,
but he loved her no matter what she looked like. She wondered
fleetingly if she was drunk. On one or two beers? Hardly.

Suddenly she slammed on the brakes and slewed off the
roadbed into a big puddle of standing water, splashing mud
all over the windshield of the state cruiser that had crashed
to a stop right behind her, its nose, she was certain, about
half an inch away from her bumper.

Directly ahead was most of the logging crew, working
like maniacs on the road. Some of the men stopped momentarily and looked up when they saw Hannah's car lurch into
view, but most of the men kept on working as if she wasn't
even there.

Looking around, Hannah saw the crummy and Michael's
truck; also Ruby's pickup and another car.

It was a Rolls-Royce, parked with care on a gentle mound
of wild grass. How in the hell did this limousine get over
that awful road? Hannah wondered, climbing out of her car.

She smiled when she saw Michael hurrying up to greet her, but after he gave her a kiss and a hug without saying anything about her appearance, Hannah backed away angrily.

"You make me so mad," she said.

Genuinely confused, he asked the fatal question, "What's wrong, honey?"

"You wouldn't know anything was wrong if I came crawling up naked on all fours with my head shaved."

He grinned. "If your head was shaved I might begin to wonder."

"You are an exasperating man."

Hannah turned away. He hadn't even noticed how upset she must be with her hair all scraggly, her face scrubbed raw, and wearing no makeup.

She wanted to scream. She wanted to slap him. God, men were so dense! Then she knew she must get control, not make a fool of herself in front of all these people.

She saw Michael stride over to the state cop, who was just getting out of his cruiser. The cop said something to her husband that Hannah couldn't hear. Michael glanced back at her, said something to the cop, the two men shook hands, the cop got back in his cruiser, backed around, and drove off.

"What was that all about?" Hannah asked as Michael walked back to her.

"Have you been drinking?" he asked, eyeing her carefully.

She shrugged. "I had a beer at the Black Rooster."

Michael looked at his watch. "What were you doing at the Black Rooster? It's not even ten in the morning."

She lifted both eyebrows and tried to look dignified. "Is there some magical hour when it's proper for your wife to be seen in a tavern?"

"Come on now, Hannah, don't be like that. You know you don't hang around beer joints. What's going on?"

"What's going on is that our fifth log truck was out killing a cow this morning in front of the Black Rooster."

"Yeah, Tim, the state cop, just told me about that."

"The cow's owner, understandably upset, called up the office and insisted a company representative come over and work things out. Why wasn't that truck parked in the yard with the other trucks where it should have been?"

"Because Buck's brother-in-law was driving it down to his place for some work it needs done on it."

"What's Buck's brother-in-law got to do with it?"

"He's a mechanic, a damned good one, and he happens to need the work."

"That cop was following me, wasn't he? Why was he doing that, Michael? He'd already given me a ticket. One hundred and fifty dollars, I might add."

"He was following you, Hannah, because he knew you'd been drinking and he wanted to see that you got where you were going safely."

"What made him think I'd been drinking?"

"That mustache of foam on your upper lip might have given him a hint."

"Then why didn't he arrest me and haul me off to jail?"

"Because he's a friend of mine."

They were interrupted by the approach of two men who had been previously standing to one side with Ruby Campbell, talking and watching the work going on.

"Hannah, here comes our customer," Michael said.

One of the men was Japanese. He wore a dark three-piece suit, a white shirt with starched collar and cuffs, a slender black necktie, and low black oxfords covered with mud.

His companion, a broad-shouldered blond male walking with the carelessly exuded vigor of youth, was dressed in Danner hiking boots, an L.L. Bean safari jacket, and jeans so tight Hannah had to stifle a compulsion to pinch one of his buttocks, hard, just to see his reaction.

"Hannah, this is Andy Bennett, Cliff's younger brother," Michael said. Cliff Bennett was their timber broker.

Hannah shook hands with Andy, checking at a glance everything about him that was male and desirable, but, like most women, pretending not to.

"Are you in business with Cliff?" she asked, forcing a smile.

"I'm thinking about it. I just got out of Harvard and I'm kind of looking around."

The Japanese man listened to the conversation with interest, his cigarette held backward between his thumb and forefinger, the burning end sheltered in the cupped palm of his hand.

"The first thing Andy here acquired was that Rolls-Royce over there," Michael said.

"Yeah," Andy said seriously, "I've wanted a Rolls ever since I can remember. And this one's a beauty. Course, she's twenty years old, but that was the best year for Rolls. Mrs. McTavish, do you know anything about classic cars?"

"I try not to," Hannah said.

Seeing that their Japanese customer was being left out, Michael hurried to introduce him.

"Mr. Smith, I'd like to present my wife, Hannah McTavish. Hannah, Charles Smith from the Seattle office of . . ." he named a huge worldwide Japanese buying conglomerate.

Charles Smith bowed graciously to Hannah, then acted surprised when she extended her hand, which he managed to accept but seemed not to know exactly what to do with. He dropped it uncertainly and soon he and Michael walked off to where the crew was working on the road, heads together in conversation.

"Charles Smith," Hannah said musingly. "I met a Charles Smith from the Japanese buyers a month or so ago but he didn't look anything like this man."

"He isn't the same man," Andy Bennett told her. "The reps take American names when they come over here, and each name follows a certain client. For example, the rep that works with my brother will always be Charles Smith. Cliff said he's dealt with six Charles Smiths so far."

"What's the point?"

"I suppose so that we Americans won't be upset by continuing changes in personnel. Somebody probably told the top brass that Americans like continuity in their business dealings."

"Do they?"

He grinned. "I don't know yet, but Cliff thinks so."

"So what's Mr. Smith here for? To see if we can ever get this road fixed and his timber delivered to the docks on time?"

"Only partly."

Hannah looked at him curiously. "What then?"

"What he really wants to do is hunt bear."

"Not for a bear rug to take home, I hope."

"No, he wants the bear's gallbladder."

Hannah made a face. "Yuck! What for?"

Andy, having been very well brought up, and being a very young man talking to an older woman, could not prevent the blush that flooded his face.

"Some Oriental people believe that the juice in a bear's gallbladder is, well, good for them."

"Good for what?"

Andy Bennett jammed his hands in his pockets and looked off into the distance, calling, Hannah was sure, upon the memory of all of his extensive MBA training and finding no answer.

"Well, you see, Mrs. McTavish, there's a lot we don't know about Oriental medicine."

"Oh, he's sick. What's wrong with him?"

"I wouldn't say that Mr. Smith has anything wrong with him. Nothing like that. It's just that bear gallbladders are considered well, strengthening, particularly for a man."

"I see." Hannah was beginning to get the point. "In other words, the good that Mr. Smith will get out of a bear's gallbladder will also be good for his wife. Do I understand you correctly?"

Relief flooded Andy Bennett's youthful face. "Exactly, Mrs. McTavish. Exactly."

By now they had reached Michael and Charles Smith, who had also been joined by Buck Trano. Ruby Campbell stood off to one side watching the ongoing work.

Michael was saying, "Charley, I'm real sorry, but I can't help you out. It's just not the right season."

"When is that?" Smith asked, a fresh cigarette burning in the palm of his hand.

"I'd have to check but I think it starts some time in August."

"August first through November first," Buck Trano said promptly.

"Yeah, a couple of months is all. That's not too far away. Besides, this is a bad time. The bears are starting to mate."

Charles Smith grew excited. "That is best time. The blood is up. The male juice is up. The"—he used some Japanese word that Hannah suspected meant penis—"is up."

Michael laughed and put his hand on Smith's shoulder. "Charley, I'll get this timber out for you if it kills me. But honest to God, I just can't help you with the bear. I'm really sorry. Now I'm sure we can arrange something if you want to wait till August—"

"Can't wait. Going back to Japan in two weeks."

Hannah walked slowly to her car and got in. Her head hurt, she felt nauseous; dull, heavy pains invaded her lower belly and back, and her legs throbbed. If only her period would start, get the damned thing over with.

She had turned on the engine and was just about to back around and drive out when Michael came running up, slogging through the mud.

"What?" she mouthed through the windshield.

He opened the door on the driver's side and said, "Move over. I'm taking you home."

"You can't leave. What about all the work out there?"

"If those guys don't know what to do by now I might as well give up."

4   It was one o'clock when they got home. Michael left his muddy clothes on the back porch and had a quick shower in the downstairs bathroom.

When he emerged with a towel tied around his middle, he

found Hannah slumped in one of the kitchen chairs staring out at the lake.

"Take off your coat," he said.

"I haven't got the energy."

"Here, I'll help you."

He hung up her coat, then opened and heated a can of chicken soup, poured the soup into a bowl, put the bowl on a plate along with crackers, and set it all down on the table in front of her.

"Eat a little soup. You'll feel better."

He went upstairs. She heard water pouring into the tub, then smelled the fragrance of her favorite bubble bath.

He came running back down, urged her to eat more soup and crackers, then went back upstairs with her. In the bathroom he got her out of her clothes and into the tub, and while she soaked and drowsed, he busied himself in their bedroom.

She heard him run back downstairs, then up again. He came into the bathroom, helped Hannah out of the tub, dried her back, then rubbed body powder all over her—even in her hair, in his gentle enthusiasm—then got her into bed.

"Why'd you change the sheets?" she asked, snuggling down. "The old ones were still clean."

"Because I know you like fresh sheets, especially when you don't feel so good."

Hannah loved clean sheets. Whenever the weather permitted, Binte Ferguson dried them outside on the line instead of in the dryer to get that good outdoors smell.

He threw his bath towel aside and got into bed beside her, leaned over and picked up a tray from the floor on his side of the bed, poured tea from a steaming pot into two cups, and handed one to her.

She took a few sips of tea, leaned back on her stacked pillows, and sighed. "Want to talk?" she asked.

"After you've rested."

She turned over on her side and he snuggled up close, one large warm hand holding her sore belly. As she fell asleep she felt him growing hard up her back.

When Hannah woke up, she didn't know what time it was but the house was quiet so the kids must not be home from school as yet.

She yawned, sighed, and rolled over.

"Awake, honey?" Michael whispered in her ear.

"What time is it?"

"After four."

"Where're the kids?"

"Sent them off to Audie's. Told them they could stay until I picked them up."

She got up, went to the bathroom, and came right back to bed.

"How are you feeling?" he asked, gently cupping one of her breasts.

"Better." She stretched. "A whole lot better."

"Want anything?"

"You."

"Are you sure?"

"Never surer."

He entered slow and gentle, holding his weight off her body, responsive to her every movement, careful not to hurt, only to caress. When she came, the coming enveloped her whole body, and as it gradually subsided it took with it all of Hannah's aches and pains, all her crabbiness. She was totally relaxed, inside and out.

"You're the best cure in the world for PMS," she said.

He smiled. "Want to farm me out?"

"I want you all to myself."

They were silent while he held her gently.

"Do you love me, Michael?"

"Do you have to ask?"

"I like to hear you say the words out loud."

"Saying doesn't mean much. Doing is what counts."

"It is a fact, rarely admitted by women, that when PMS strikes, no man can do anything right. Unless, that is, he knows exactly the right thing to do."

After being silent for a time, she asked drowsily, "How is

it, Michael, that you always know exactly the right thing to do?"

"Because I love you. You're my whole life. Haven't you figured that out yet?"

5   At eight o'clock the next morning, Binte Ferguson stamped up the steps of the McTavish house on Lake Quinault in her size-two shoes and hurriedly entered Hannah's kitchen. She carried a large brown paper sack.

"Sorry I'm late," she announced to the house at large. She usually arrived an hour earlier.

"That's okay," Hannah called from the living room.

Hannah's pleasant voice was preceded by the rushed arrival of Kirstie the Beagle, who lifted her face to Binte and received enthusiastic tickles behind both silken ears. Hannah appeared in the doorway, smiling and brushing her hair.

"I brought the cow pies."

"Thanks, Binte. I'll make the tea a little later."

Binte put the paper bag on the table.

"Would you like to go with me to Melisande's for lunch today? You're invited."

"Sure. Sounds fine to me. Say, I didn't see the goslings out there. What happened?" Binte asked.

A month earlier Michael had given Angus and Elspat four baby geese and had built a pen for them near the house.

Binte told the whole family there should be a cover over the top of the pen to protect them from the eagles, a warning that had gone unheeded.

"You were right. The eagles got them."

"Well, I told you. All of you. Where're the kids? The eagles didn't fly off with them, too, I hope."

"Not as yet. They're supposed to be out playing on their raft."

"I didn't see them either when I drove up. You've gotta be careful about that raft."

"I know. Both kids are wearing their life jackets and I know that they stay close to shore."

"They've already eaten?"

"Those two bottomless pits? Of course they have."

"Where're their dirty dishes?"

"In the dishwasher."

"You didn't have to do that, Hannah."

"I didn't. They did. This happens to be a morning when I feel like puttering around the house. Except for lunch with Melisande, I'm staying home."

"That mean you're going to be underfoot all day?"

"What if I am?"

"Well, if you are, I'll wash windows."

"That's great, Binte." Hannah smiled, thinking, *What a treasure this woman is!*

Binte took off her ancient navy wool sweater, hung it over the back of a kitchen chair, and went into a small storage room off the pantry to get the necessary equipment for window washing.

Hannah sat down at the kitchen table to have a cup of coffee and gaze out the window at Lake Quinault, at this moment a shimmering kaleidoscope of colors. Today she felt wonderful, like a whole new woman.

"Got myself another job," Binte said as she banged back into the kitchen with a plastic bucket filled with ammonia and water in one hand and a large sack full of crumpled newspapers in the other.

Hannah looked up in shock. "What! You're leaving us?"

"Course not. You couldn't get rid of me that easily."

"Then what are you talking about?"

"Couple of foreigners moved into that empty house down the road. Two men. Business partners. The young one's very nice. Very polite."

"What about the other one?"

"Him? He looks like a grouchy old bear with a toothache. Acts like one, too."

"What are you going to do for them?"

"I'll get dinner every night and straighten things up

once a week. Mr. Clemente said they liked their privacy and didn't want household help around all the time. If it had been an all-the-time job, I wouldn't have been available. I told him that. Anyway, it won't cut into my time here at all."

"If you get dinner for them it will."

"No, it won't. Their dinner is more like our midnight snack. Can you imagine, they don't eat until ten at night."

"Where are they from?"

"Chile. Santiago, the young one, Mr. Clemente, said."

"I remember those two. I saw them at my book party at the lodge. Michael knows them. Quite an interesting pair. Incidentally, what are *we* going to have for dinner tonight?"

"How about new red potatoes from my garden with fresh peas in a garlic cream sauce along with broiled salmon steaks?"

"Any dessert, you suppose?" Hannah asked.

A new voice spoke up, that of her twelve-year-old son, Angus, who appeared like a genie out of a bottle at the mention of food.

"What about those cow pies Binte brought?" he asked.

Binte turned, a smile quivering about her mouth. "Thought you were supposed to be out on that raft. What are you doing in here listening to grown-ups' conversation?"

"I wasn't on the raft. I was down in the basement. I heard Mom saying she was going to make tea to go with the pies."

"Where's your sister?" Hannah asked.

"Up in the bear tree, reading."

An old apple tree in front of the house had for decades been the favorite spot of visiting bears. Now the bears had pretty much gone into the high country because of encroaching humans, but every once in a while the McTavishes still had a visitation.

Hannah walked to a window where she could see the tree with Elspat perched on a stout limb, deep in a Nancy Drew mystery. Now that Elly was ten, she needed periods of time by herself, which Hannah fully understood.

"Just what kind of cow pies do you think I brought?" the old woman asked Angus.

Angus looked surprised. "The only kind there is. You know, Binte, the ones made with butter and milk chocolate and real creamy caramel and pecans. And shaped kind of like turtles."

"You might find these cow pies a little different."

"Binte." Angus looked at the old woman with the pitying compassion of superior young knowledge. "There's only one kind."

"Is that right? Well, Mr. Know-It-All, if you're so smart, look for yourself."

Angus opened the paper bag, sniffed, then looked inside and gagged. His face dropped and he stared at the two women, puzzled.

"This stinks! What is this stuff?"

"Cow pies," Binte said.

"Looks to me like dried cow poop. Smells like it, too."

"That's what cow pies are. Your mother's going to make manure tea."

"Manure tea! What's going on round here? Mom, why would you make something as revolting as that?"

"Because Binte tells me manure tea is very good for my roses."

Angus looked at Binte, who was trying hard not to laugh. "I'm sorry, Binte, I guess I was wrong."

"I forgive you, Angus," she said with dignity.

Now Angus's curiosity had been raised. "Need any help with that manure tea, Mom?"

"I can always use help. Come along."

So while Binte got busy washing windows and talking to herself, Hannah and her son went outside where a large, mossy rain barrel full of water stood under one of the eaves of the house.

She put three of the dried cow pies into the water and watched them slowly sink to the bottom of the barrel.

"That's all there is to it, I'm told," she said. "We'll give it a few days to dissolve, then you can help me stir it up and pour it around my roses."

"Gosh, I learn something every day around here," Angus said.

"I'm glad to hear that," Hannah said, giving her son a big hug that, since no one was looking, he eagerly returned, along with a fond kiss.

6   Tall Hannah, with short Binte at her side, rang the doorbell at Melisande's, whose wonderful house with various rooms and nooks at surprising angles, hung partially down the sea cliffs at Moclips.

The two women had survived the drive from Lake Quinault, although the palms of Hannah's hands were still wet.

"Let's go in my car," Binte had said before they set out on the journey.

Binte's 1920 Model T automobile named Tilly was no doubt extremely valuable from a collector's standpoint but as far as Hannah was concerned it was an imminent death trap, at least in Binte's hands.

When Hannah so obviously hesitated, Binte asked, "Something wrong?"

"To tell you the truth I'm a little afraid to ride in that car of yours," Hannah replied with as much kindness as she could muster.

"Afraid of my driving?"

"Not your driving," Hannah lied hurriedly.

"Then what are you afraid of?"

"Of Tilly, actually. She's a really old car."

"That she is. And like a really old woman, she knows what she's doing. Which is more than I can say for these newer automobiles. And some of these new women, for that matter." Binte studied Hannah. "You afraid she'll just suddenly give out and stop running?"

"I'm afraid I'll be killed. I've got to stay around for a while. I still have a couple of kids to raise."

Binte laughed out loud.

"Don't be silly. I've been driving Tilly since 1920 and I haven't been killed yet. Get in. I'll go around the front and crank her up," which she did with energy.

"Do this the wrong way and you can break your wrist," Binte shouted. "Go on now, get in."

Hannah opened the door on the passenger side, then climbed in with some trepidation, stepping over the running board while cursing herself silently for lack of willpower.

"Pull out the choke and press your foot down on the third pedal if she starts to fire," Binte commanded

Suddenly the engine caught, spluttered, nearly died but not quite. Hannah, caught in the spirit of the occasion, revved the motor loudly, making sweet music to Binte's ears.

"Keep it going, keep it going," Binte yelled as she climbed in and settled herself behind the wheel. "We'll sit here while Tilly gets warmed up."

"How can you tell?"

"Because I know her and she knows me."

"What are those three pedals on the floor?" Hannah asked.

"One's for going forward, one's for going backward, and one's for braking."

"They look funny."

"Funny or not, they're all you need in a gearless car. What other direction would you need to go?"

"You don't have a radio in here or an air conditioner."

"No radio, that's true, but plenty of fresh air." Binte rolled down her window and pushed the windshield open.

"Actually, we're waiting for Tilly to get a hot flash. Then we're outta here."

Hannah asked when Binte had gotten the car.

"In 1920, when my husband gave it to me."

"Husband? I didn't know you'd ever been married."

"Sure was. I was just a girl working at the hotel that was over there across the lake before the lodge was built, and he was a traveling man.

"Came though here from St. Louis. My, that Jason was a handsome one, I'll have to give him credit for that. An ardent suitor, too. But I kept my wits about me and there wasn't no hanky-panky under the sheets until after the minister from Port Angeles came down and said the words over us—"

Binte stopped talking and listened carefully to Tilly's engine.

"She's not quite ready yet. Where was I? Oh, yes. Jason. He told me I didn't have to work no more, which was fine with me. He wanted to take me back to St. Louis, but I said no. Told him before we was married that the only way I'd ever leave my house was in a pine box and then just up to the cemetery.

"Jason thought he'd humor me, I guess, so he agreed to move in at my house, where I'm living now. I was born there, you know. And that's when he bought me Tilly. She was a brand-spanking-new 1920 Ford Model T, she was, and I almost died from pleasure. Paid five hundred twenty dollars for her, he did, and I've loved this old darling ever since."

Binte's house rose up in Hannah's mind. Two stories tall, unpainted since it had been built from cedar over a hundred years ago, it always reminded Hannah of an oversized planter. Binte herself had been born in the house almost ninety years earlier.

The roof was covered with green moss two feet thick out of which sword ferns waved gracefully. Moss grew on the outside of the windowsills, on the north side of the house, and lay on the tops of fence posts like drifts of green snow.

Inside, most of the walls were lined with homemade shelves filled with often-read books. The floors were bare and neatly swept. There were no collections of framed photographs, Hannah recalled, no lace doilies, no knickknacks or crewel footstools. Just books everywhere.

"How long were you and Jason married?" Hannah asked.

"About three or four years. It's been so long ago I can't rightly remember. We didn't get along too good."

"What was the trouble, if I'm not being too nosy?"

"To tell you the truth, Hannah, I've never been one to fuss much around the house. Never been interested in house-work. Now, working outside, digging in the dirt, planting and growing things, that's a whole different kettle of fish. In those days I worked from can till can't. From first light when a person can just begin to see until it's so dark he can't."

"How did Jason feel about that?"

"He didn't like it one bit. Got so he was on me all the time, night and day, nag, nag, nag, saying I should stay inside and cook and clean and sew like a real woman. I said, 'If you didn't think I was a real woman, why ever did you marry me?'

"I'll never forget how he said, 'Miss Binte, when I saw you working at the hotel I thought you knew all about a real woman's work.'

"I said, 'You sure think I'm a real woman in the bed. You're after me all the time.'

"He turned beet-red and said that was different, he was just trying to do his duty as a husband. So I told him he didn't have to do his duty by me no more and moved him out to the barn. By then I'd realized he wasn't much of a man anyway. Just flash. Flashy clothes and a flashy smile."

"How long did he live in the barn?"

"Oh, not long, as I remember. Came the Fourth of July, 1923, it was, he and some other young fellas set fire to one of the big old cedars on the place just to watch it explode and hear the crackling and popping. Could have set the whole valley on fire, damn fools. Like I've told you before, those cedars shoot out like giant firecrackers when they're dry and on fire.

"Anyway, when I saw what he'd done, and him knowing

how I felt about my trees, I marched into the barn and threw all his clothes out on the road. When he tried to get into the house, I set the dogs on him. And that's the last I seen of Mr. Big Smile Jason Jewett of St. Louis, walking down the road into the sunset with the dust puffing at his heels."

"Have you ever heard from him since?" Hannah asked.

"No and I don't want to. He's long gone to Glory now, I expect. Or maybe he hasn't. Probably gone the other direction. But I'm still here and I got trees near a hundred feet tall that I planted from seeds when he was burning down my cedar."

Hannah knew that Binte was not exaggerating. The old woman had a forest of her own, hand-planted by herself from seeds ever since she'd been a child. Most of the trees were native species such as western red cedar, Douglas fir, western hemlock, and Sitka spruce, but some were exotics like her cedars from China.

Binte sighed. "You know, Hannah, a man's got to be pretty substantial for a woman to put up with him all her life."

"You mean a man should have a lot of money?"

"Money's okay but it's the least of it. Any hardworking fool can grub around and get money. Or any tightwad can save it."

"You never married again, Binte?"

"Nope. And I don't regret it. Oh, I've always had men friends. I like men, most of them, anyway, like the way they think. But men are funny. Seems a man is either a great guy or a complete jackass. No in betweens."

Her expression grew thoughtful. "I always thought if I'd had more education I could have been a botanist or something like that. Plants grow for me. Always have—woops, I think Tilly's ready."

And she was. The ancient vehicle was trembling with suppressed energy, like a hound eager to follow the scent.

Without further ado, Binte depressed one of the three pedals and they were off accompanied by farting *pow-pooms!* and great clouds of black smoke.

That was when Hannah started to perspire and only stopped when they arrived safely at their destination.

"I'm so glad you both could come," Melisande said, and ushered them into a comfortably furnished ocean-facing room with floor-to-ceiling windows.

Outside, a gauzy midday moon, pale as a gull's wing, hung over the sea while huge breakers, riding an incoming tide, devoured a shore the color of apple blossom honey.

Hannah noticed that Melisande looked flushed.

"Did we catch you in the middle of something?" she asked.

"Only fighting my disease," Melisande replied.

"Your disease?" Binte asked, astonished. "What disease is that?"

"I'll tell you about it, but sit down first and make yourselves comfortable."

When they were seated, Melisande said, "Years ago my mother warned me that after fifty I'd get the furniture disease."

"Furniture disease?" Binte shook her head. "I've lived a long time but I've never heard of that."

"What in the world is it?" Hannah asked, puzzled.

"It's when your chest starts to fall into your drawers," Melisande replied, solemn-faced.

Binte howled with laughter. "It's too late for me. I don't even know where my chest is anymore."

Hannah laughed a little, but looked serious, as if contemplating the disease in relation to her own still-beautiful body.

"There's a price for lunch today," Melisande announced.

Both Hannah and Binte looked at her with raised eyebrows.

"I want you gals to spit as much as you can into these," she instructed, handing each of them a cup.

"Spit?" Hannah asked, unbelievingly.

"If you want us to spit you should give us a spittoon," Binte said.

Without answering, Melisande walked into another room and returned holding a carved totem pole sixteen inches in height.

"Ruby got this from some Indian he'd done a favor for," Melisande told them. "It's about two hundred years old."

Hannah and Binte saw that the small totem was exquisitely done and in good condition. The painted surface, although grimed with smoke, seemed stable. There was no flaking, cracking, or chipping.

Hannah said, "I repeat: What do you want our spit for?"

"Well, I'll tell you. I wanted to get the grime off the totem pole but I didn't know how to clean it without damaging the surface.

"Because of the softness in tone of the paint and the age of the pole I suspected the paint was made in the old way using saliva and chewed-up salmon eggs.

"I almost used Ivory soap but then I thought I'd better consult an expert and do it right. So I wrote to the Museum of Anthropology at the University of British Columbia.

"The conservator very kindly wrote back saying that the cleaning of old wooden objects is generally avoided unless absolutely necessary.

"But she went on to say that if I really wanted to do it, she suggested I use a Q-Tip swab lightly moistened with saliva. Evidently saliva contains enzymes that make it a useful cleaning agent.

"Told me to test an inconspicuous area first, like around the base, and to apply the swab in a rolling manner over a very small area at a time. Never to rub, which could damage the surface. And to only use each swab once because reapplying a dirty tip would spread the grime. She added that this method is time-consuming and will use up a great number of swabs."

"Not to mention an awful lot of spit," Binte said.

"How did it get so grimy?" Hannah wanted to know.

"From hanging many years in a smoky lodge," Melisande replied. "Now the question is this. Will we have more saliva before or after lunch."

"Before lunch," Binte said. "I'm drooling with hunger already."

"Well, let's get busy." Melisande set the example by spitting into her own empty cup.

Soon the three ladies were very busy, their spitting endeavors interrupted now and then by gales of hilarious laughter.

"Melisande, now you got all my spit," Binte said. "I'm dry as a bone. Not even sure I could swallow a bite of lunch."

"Let's go in and find out." Melisande rose and gathered up the cups, walking into the kitchen where she wrapped each one in a clear plastic and placed them in the refrigerator.

On the way home, Hannah was too exhausted from spitting, laughing, and talking to worry about Binte's driving.

They arrived safely. Binte dropped Hannah off at home, then rattled away to her own house.

7   Hannah found Elspat home alone with Kirstie the Beagle.

"Where is everybody?" Hannah asked.

A very polite young girl, not the sassy one of the other morning, replied that her dad had called and would be working late and Angus was at Audie's house.

Then Elspat started crying, ran over, and flung her arms around her mother's neck.

"Mom, I'm so sorry. Will you forgive me?"

"For what?" Hannah asked, genuinely confused.

"Day before yesterday."

"What happened?"

"You know, Mom, when I was such a beast."

Ah yes, Hannah thought, the infamous day of PMS, the Hereford on two legs with clutching hands, the *one-hundred-and-fifty-dollar* speeding ticket, and Michael's gentle love.

"I forgive you, honey. In fact, I forgave you right away."

"You mean you forgave me and here I've been worrying about it all this time?"

Hannah smiled.

"I know what my trouble was. What was yours?"

"It's the Giggle Gang, Mom. They were being mean. But everything's okay now."

Elspat had founded the Giggle Gang the first of the year. The gang's purpose was to pick up any loose candy, ice cream, or gum wrappers found around the school and bury such sloppy leavings with appropriate ceremonies.

The Giggle Gang was comprised of girls only, seven of them, to be exact. No boys, ever, under any conditions and no boyfriends.

All seven members took a solid oath on *that* subject. They all knew that a person could get "boy cooties" from even associating with girls who had boyfriends.

Hannah sighed in sympathy. How well she knew that any member of a group of girls around the age of ten was subject to fits of jealousy, insecurity about the development or nondevelopment of their bodies, suffering abject fits of dejection.

"You got it all worked out now, honey?" Hannah asked.

"I straightened it out. Twila got the idea she wanted to have a boyfriend. Some of the girls took her side. Can you imagine, Mom? After our solemn oaths? I felt like kicking them all out and starting over."

"And who was this desired boyfriend?"

"Ernie Laycock."

"*Ernie Laycock*? He's a nice little boy, Elly, but he looks like he belongs in second grade. He's one of those kids who's going to take a long time getting his growth. Somehow I can't imagine Ernie being anyone's boyfriend, not for a couple of decades at least."

"Twila's got *her* growth, all right," Elspat said. "Her mom's got her in a training bra, and Twila told me herself she's already got hair growing you know where. Wanted to show it to me, for God's sake."

"Honey, please watch your language."

"I'm sorry, Mom, the whole thing's just so yucky. Why do us girls have to be made the way we are?"

"I've often wondered that myself."

"And she just keeps talking about her *hair* and her *boobs,* as if she's the only one in the world who ever had them before."

"Boring."

"You bet." Elspat's voice took on a melancholy tone. She pulled the front of her blouse away and looked down at her chest.

"I'm flat, Mom. I haven't got anything anywhere."

"Neither did I at your age." Hannah drew her daughter close. "Want to hear about how I spent my afternoon?"

"Sure, Mom."

"You won't believe this but it's God's truth."

"Isn't that swearing?"

"No, not when the word is used that way."

"So how did you spend your afternoon?"

"Spitting."

"How disgusting. I thought only men spit."

"It depends on the circumstances."

And Hannah went on to tell the beloved young girl snuggled up close to her all about spitting for Melisande Campbell so she could use the saliva to clean off a small ancient totem pole.

They laughed until they cried and each had to rush into the bathroom before it was too late. Elspat made hot chocolate for them both and they sat in the bow window watching the winds stir Lake Quinault's paint pot of sunset colors.

Finally Elspat solemnly pronounced, "I guess men are all right if you keep them in their place."

Hannah tried not to laugh. "Sometimes that's a lot easier said than done."

Part Three

I have noticed in my life that all men have a liking for some special animal, tree, plant, or spot of earth. If men would pay more attention to those preferences and seek what is best to do in order to make themselves worthy of that toward which they are so attracted, they might have dreams which would purify their lives.

Let a man decide upon his favorite animal and make a study of it, learning its innocent ways. Let him learn to understand its sounds and motions. The animals want to communicate with man, but Wakan-Tanka does not intend they shall do so directly—man must do the greater part in securing an understanding.

—BRAVE BUFFALO
Frances Densmore, 1918.
Teton Sioux Music.
Bureau of American Ethnology Bulletin 61
Washington, D.C.: U.S. Government
Printing Office

ᚮ

Chapter 14

1 Walking like a human on the flat of his feet, the black bear meandered through the forest, talking to himself in a series of rumbling grunts, stuffing his long snout into anthills or helping himself to a bounty of sweet blackberries.

He swatted annoying mosquitoes from his nose and swung his shiny black head to and fro as if the very motion itself gave him momentum.

Every once in a while he stood on his two hind legs, threw his snout into the air, and sniffed carefully. Not long before he had faintly scented a female.

When he found the female he would remember to slouch,

flatten his ears, act playful, and take care not to stare at her aggressively.

Like many animals intent upon courting, he would try to seem anything but dominant to avoid frightening the female being wooed.

When he was born he could have fit in the palm of a man's hand. Now he weighed six hundred pounds.

As a cub he had instinctively feared only one thing—the bear trees clawed by huge males. Perhaps he knew genetically than an adult male will kill a bear cub, even his own, if he finds it in his territory.

His mother had taught him what else to fear.

He had traveled over one hundred miles to reach this particular berry patch in the Olympic National Park, grazing along the way.

Although it was not yet late fall, a time when he would feed twenty out of twenty-four hours, consuming twenty thousand calories a day in preparation for his winter hibernation, he liked to eat and ate a lot.

While grizzly bears fed principally on other animals, the black bear's main diet was sweet grasses, berries, and nuts. If he came across a dead deer or elk, he would eat it, but he would not waste energy killing the animal himself.

It was evening when the black bear first heard the baying of hounds in the distance. He stopped, sat down, and listened carefully.

When the wind changed and he could no longer hear the dogs, he got up and continued his leisurely walk, humming and rumbling as he went, looking for berries and perhaps a female.

2   Two pickup trucks, lights off, crept along a remote fire access road somewhere in the western vastness of the Olympic National Park.

Alert, dressed in brand-new camouflage gear, Charles

Smith, soon-to-depart Japanese representative of the huge international company to which Michael McTavish sold his logs, sat next to William Hereford, the driver of the first truck.

Smith's expression was carefully placid, but his eyes shone with barely concealed excitement.

The hood of this first pickup was covered with a specially fitted canvas on which crouched William Hereford's two lead redbone hounds, bear dogs, both tethered to metal fittings in the canvas.

The dogs' open mouths dripped saliva, while hanging tongues and flared nostrils caught and accurately interpreted each of the thousands of complicated odors moving along the layers of air.

Noses and tongues tasted the damp foliage fragrance of near and far forests; the cold wet smell of a banana slug, the tang of a nearby waterfall, the cool of frogs, the warm meaty smell of moving elk.

They identified many other scents, accurately judging the proximity of the source of each odor. But these were not the scents for which they were searching. What they sought was the hot stench of living bear.

As he slowly drove along the fire road, Hereford whispered quiet words of encouragement through the open window to his hounds.

"C'mon now, Sally, show me how much you love me. Atta girl. Just smell out that old bear. He's out there, darlin', just waitin' for you. Hurry up now, Sally. You want Old Griz to sniff him out first?"

The muscles in both hounds' legs tightened as they heard their master's voice and they seemed to try even harder to distinguish the smell of the bear.

The truck behind William Hereford and Charles Smith held six more anxious hounds carefully tied in its covered bed, all whining softly. These dogs represented the rest of Hereford's team and would not be released until the lead dogs proclaimed the scent.

"Are you certain you'll find a bear, Mr. Hereford?" Charles Smith asked. "This is very big country."

"Don't worry, Mr. Smith, you'll have your animal tonight. I promise you that."

"You understand that all I want is the gallbladder?"

"Yeah, I know."

"Is there any chance of our being delayed?" Smith asked.

"You worried about getting caught?" Hereford asked, looking over at his client with a superior smile. "I'll tell you right now, the answer is we won't. I been in this business a long, long time and I know what I'm doing—"

Abruptly Hereford stopped speaking and studied the dogs on the hood of his truck.

Now Sally and Old Griz both stood straight-legged, trembling with excitement, each pointing in the same direction, bodies taut, ears lifted, eyes intent with purpose.

"They got the smell." Hereford spoke with quiet assurance.

He stopped the truck, slipped quietly out, and released both bear hounds. When he made a small sign with his hand, the driver in the pickup behind him released the dogs in the bed of his pickup.

Hereford leaned back inside the truck. "Okay, Mr. Smith, now we move."

Charles Smith scrambled out of the truck and followed Hereford and his assistant over what seemed like miles of rough country, with always the baying of the hounds running along ahead.

Hereford had previously explained to Smith what would happen. The hounds, experienced as they were, would work very hard until eventually they were able to surround the bear and force it into a tree, holding the animal there to be shot at Hereford's convenience.

Moving through this wild land, Smith wondered how the dogs would be able to maneuver a bear to do anything at all that it did not wish to do.

For this was the bear's own country, and bears were strong, wild beasts. It was also mating time when the males were filled with anger and raging hormones to insure that only the strongest among them be allowed to pass on its genes.

Smith considered himself very lucky to go on this hunt. Of course, he had paid dearly for the privilege.

In Asia bear galls had become more precious than gold. He and his relatives and friends, as well as thousands of other Asian peoples, strongly believed that ingestion of bear gall juice could cure every ailment from cancer to gum disease. They also believed it could make a man sexually powerful. Consequently, the Asian bear population had been nearly wiped out.

Smith realized that what would soon happen to the bear they were chasing would never be done by true hunters. But, legitimate or not, he wanted that bear gall. He *would* have it.

The sound of the dogs' cries changed and it seemed to Smith, in his private life a writer of haiku, that the animals were now singing.

A strange harmonic song, and beautiful; full of wildness, longing, and impending death. The poetry of a successful hunt . . . the Japanese words began to form in his mind.

He came upon William Hereford and his assistant standing near a large Sitka spruce with the hounds milling around its base.

Hereford turned and caught sight of the young Japanese.

"So there you are. Thought we'd lost you. Come on over here. You're about to get what you paid for."

Smith tried to catch sight of the bear he knew was huddled high in the branches of the spruce but was unable to do so.

Hereford took careful aim with a 30.06 rifle. The hounds fell silent. A single shot rang out.

There was the tumble and crash of a large body falling through many layers of branches, and with a loud, echoing *W-O-O-F!* six hundred pounds of snorting black bear thundered to the ground at their feet.

The mature male animal was not dead, but he was mad as hell. Smith saw that Hereford's bullet had gone through the bear's right eye, missing the brain.

Growling and shrieking, the wounded bear, surrounded by attacking dogs, stood up on two legs with amazing swiftness and prepared to defend itself.

The savage fight that followed was long and ferocious. Although wounded, the bear was in top form and ragingly angry.

Before the yapping, growling, grunting, and shrieking ceased, two of the younger dogs were dead; one's neck broken from being tossed thirty yards by the bear, the other from having his belly ripped open.

At last the hounds were successful in the kill, the stench of blood and severed intestines soon filling the air.

When the animal was well and truly dead, Hereford asked, "You want the paws, Mr. Smith? Understand you people make soup out of them."

Smith, whose blood was up after witnessing the slaughter, thought for a moment or two, then said decisively, "No, but thank you very much. Since I'm leaving your country next week it would be too complicated."

Using his hunting knife, Hereford reached into the mess of fur, gore, and slime, slitting several internal connections. Then his bare hand extracted a bloody organ about six inches long, the size of a baby yellow squash, with a bulb containing the bile on one end, the bulb being an inch and a half in diameter.

"Here's what you came for, Mr. Smith," he said, and handed the slimy, dripping organ to the young Japanese.

"When dried, the bile crystallizes into a brown powder," Smith said. "But I will have some now."

He cut a slit in the still-warm gallbladder and lifted it to his lips, tipping the organ so that a tiny bit of the bile flowed into his mouth. He swallowed with relish.

Then very politely he held out the gall to Hereford and offered some of the bile to him. Hereford shook his head, grinning lopsidedly.

Smith took a self-sealing plastic freezer bag out of one of his camouflage jacket pockets, placed the raw gallbladder inside, sealed it up, and returned it to his pocket. Then he reached into a different pocket, extracted a small package of damp wipes, and carefully wiped his hands.

"Tell me something, Mr. Smith," Hereford asked curiously. "Does that gallbladder stuff really work?"

Charles Smith smiled. "Oh, yes. I will make my wife very happy when I get home. I will also please a lady friend or two."

Poor fool, Smith thought. *He actually thinks this is for me. Not likely, when I can dry it, carry it in my pocket through customs without challenge, and sell it for twenty thousand American dollars in Korea, which is my next stop.*

Hereford shook his head. "I've heard of guys with limp pricks getting implants and putting splints on it but by God this is the first time I've seen anyone drinking a bear's juice. Does it really make it hard?"

Without a change of expression, Smith replied, "So hard you could use it to pound nails."

"Wonder if the doctors know about it?"

"The Oriental physicians have known about it for thousands of years."

Except for Sally and Old Griz, Hereford's assistant got the bear dogs back in the second truck, then threw in the bodies of the two mangled hounds.

"We'll stop at the first creek we come to and wash some of this blood off," Hereford told Smith.

Hereford removed the canvas from the hood of his pickup, folded it carefully, and placed it in a special compartment built under the driving seat of his pickup. Then he invited Sally and Old Griz to sit in the front between himself and Charles Smith.

"Very dignified dogs," Smith said admiringly.

"Yeah, they know their business all right. Their place, too," Hereford replied, then muttered under his breath, "which is more than I can say for a lot of people."

Mr. Smith smiled serenely.

Bloodied man and beast, they all drove away, leaving

behind them the carcass of a fine, healthy animal, stripped of its life.

Its pelt would not make a rug or a covering for any human, its meat not feed the hungry, its ivory teeth not adorn a worthy chieftain.

Already the death beetles were beginning to gather.

Chapter 15

1   Orca, queen of the sea, her one-hundred-pound baby tucked close under her left flipper, was leading her pod, or family, of fifty-five individuals away from their home in the waters of Puget Sound and into the North Pacific, both sea and Sound being two of the earth's richest marine habitats.

The killer whales of Puget Sound have special beaches, used by generations of their kind, where they rub themselves in the sand. This is where Orca was headed, to her pod's own rubbing beach.

Along with the bear, raven, salmon, eagle, and beaver, the

killer whale was one of the predominant animal spirits in the pantheon of the Pacific Northwest Coast Indians.

The Old Ones knew that the spirits of all human hunters of the sea became killer whales; consequently no one in his right mind would even think of killing one of these mammals.

Orca's pod, according to scientists the largest in the world, was one of five known families whose home was Puget Sound, a place unlike any other in the world, a vast estuary where fresh waters from a thousand mountain streams and rivers gush into the salty sea.

It is here, under the Sound, that the tectonic plates are thinnest.

Orca and her people are members of the species *Orcinus orca,* once thought of only as ruthless killers, which by nature they are, but now cherished as performers worthy of human enslavement and forced performance for audiences.

They grow up to thirty feet long, can weigh up to ten tons, and are given to roaming one hundred miles a day. No cage and certainly not the swimming pools where they are confined in all oceanariums, could provide them satisfaction, let alone joy in living.

They have the life expectancy of a human, yet at Sea World in San Diego, the oceanarium with the best record for keeping orcas alive, they live an average of only eleven years.

From birth to death, Orca and her kind travel in clans, communicate with squeals and grunts, screams and high frequency squeaks, their dialect different and distinct from all other pods.

Gorgeous, fearsome creatures, killer whales have no natural enemies and are masters of their environment, their powers far eclipsing those of the great white shark. Huge, fast, enormously smart, they are the greatest hunters in the ocean.

Killer whales have been known to attack rafts, dinghies,

even big boats. Nobody knows why, because there's never been a true case of an orca eating a human, although a man who lives in Portland felt the killer whale's bite while swimming with seals off California's Point Sur.

There was no second attack. The man flailed for shore, caught an inbound wave, and body-surfed forty yards to the beach. His left thigh was sliced to the bone in three places. The teeth narrowly missed a major artery. A surgeon laced his left leg with one hundred stitches. The surfer said "the bites were so clean it was like someone chopped me with an ax or a machete."

It is thought he was attacked because killer whales eat seals, and to a killer whale a human swimmer paddling around on a surfboard looks like a seal.

Other sea creatures fear killer whales the most; they create absolute terror wherever they go. Sixty-ton whales have been known to run themselves aground on reefs or shoaling beaches in vain attempts to escape this savage pursuer.

Stalking prey like a pack of twenty-thousand-pound wolves, their entire lives are spent in the pursuit and capture of food.

The only known whales that habitually prey upon other warm-blooded animals, their diet includes seal, walrus, other whales and porpoises, fish, squid, seabirds.

Like the bald eagle, they need salmon, whole schools of which they first stun with volleys of sound, and then devour.

In contrast to great white sharks, there is no known case of an orca fatally attacking a human in the wild, although they eat anything in the sea from large fish to giant whales, dolphins, seals, birds, and even, upon occasion, polar bears.

Given what they do eat, not eating humans could suggest genuine fellow feeling. Those who study killer whales wonder: Is this restraint compassion? Does it entail recognition of commonalty? Or is it that humans just don't taste good?

Killer whales can be easily identified by their tails, triangular-shaped dorsal fins, and by the conspicuous white markings on their otherwise jet-black bodies. They average twenty to thirty feet in length. Each jaw is armed with a dozen pair of strong, large teeth.

In the sea, males live up to fifty years; females, up to seventy-five years. Males, whose dorsal fins are six feet high, are much larger than the females.

A female leads each pack.

Orca sang to her baby as they entered the hazy blue-green expanses of the North Pacific.

Her great black body with its dramatic white livery moved without apparent effort through the awesome currents, among the swiftest in the world, attaining speeds up to sixteen knots.

She guided her pod around a roughly fifty-acre massing of bull kelp bladders. Below the surface kelp growth, from which the bladders sprang, created a serene and cathedral-like underwater forest, wealthy in carbohydrates; so rich, in fact, that some of the kelp grows eighteen inches in a single day.

She led them past numerous looming sea stacks, many of them huge, others seeming to be as thin as darning needles, some with eye holes, all having giant mussels attached to them with threads as strong as steel.

Infant snuggled close, Orca took care to guide her pod around Plumosa anemones, which resemble Grecian columns surrounded by plumes, tower fourteen feet in height, and are capable of injecting poison into any creature that strays their way.

They passed over crimson anemones clinging to ocean rocks below, some having done so for decades; busy now stinging tiny prey, hurling it into flowery mouths in the centers of their bodies, then retracting their tentacles to digest and doze at leisure.

They swam over king crab with shells one foot across,

and over brilliant orange sunflower sea stars more than three feet across.

And past a seven-foot wolf eel peering up at them from a watery cave with its agonized manlike face, glowering eyes, gaping jaws, ferocious in appearance, truly a creature from a nightmare, but a doting parent.

Below the swiftly moving pod, a presence stirred cautiously

It was the great Pacific octopus, thirty feet in length, weighing six hundred pounds and more, silky smooth to the touch, surprisingly soft, coyly gentle.

A shy, retiring creature, relative of the garden snake and the mollusk, this individual and others of its kind haunt the groves and canyons of their undersea domain, never knowing that the first writing ink was made from pigment found in the octopus's ink sac.

Possibly realized by Orca, who had a great brain herself, the complexity of the octopus's brain placed it at the head of the class in intelligence among invertebrates.

It was capable of learning. In experiments, the creatures were trained to distinguish between shapes and also to recognize objects by touch.

The great soft roily thing was well equipped for loving, hunting, or battle. When it chooses, its eight arms, all fitted with suction cups, secrete a poison to paralyze its prey, after which it feeds. And if the octopus damages one of its vital arms, it grows a new one.

Unconcerned by the sea's other inhabitants, Orca, her baby, and the pod passed through a grouping of enormous misty white moon jellies, the jellyfish that were not fish. Five to six feet in length, they were composed ninety-five percent of water and salts.

By contracting the bands of muscle fibers encircling their bells, the jellies slowly descended and ascended like white chiffon parachutes, floating through seas and the dreams of others with no brains, no spines, no bones, and no hearts.

Orca and her kind swam on, peaceful, joyous, even, for all was well in their world and they were headed for a place they all loved and needed, their own special rubbing beach, where grooming would be attended to, old attachments strengthened, possibly even new ones formed.

> Tyger! Tyger! Burning bright
> In the forests of the night,
> What immortal hand or eye
> Could frame thy fearful symmetry?
> In what distant deeps or skies
> Burnt the fire of thine eyes?
> On what wings dare he aspire?
> What the hand dare seize the fire?
>
> —WILLIAM BLAKE,
> "Songs of Experience"

Chapter 16

1   As the killer whales swam in a southerly direction, a cargo helicopter landed on their age-old rubbing beach, now, by human law, a part of Jordan's Island.

When the machine lifted off an hour or so later, a magical creature veiled in an aura of wonder was left behind.

Murderously angry, it paced the island shore like fire on four legs, back and forth, back and forth, biting the waves, lashing its tail, frequently lifting its voice in screams of fury and homesickness that contended in volume with the roar of the sea.

Solitary by nature, possessed of a terrible burning beauty, it was a four-year-old male Siberian tiger named Amba,

which means "great sovereign" in the language of its homeland. It measured ten feet in length from nose to tip of tail
and weighed 850 pounds.

This largest of all the cats, the rare Siberian tiger, got its
name from its cold homeland that is covered in snow for
much of the year.

Its range was larger than any other tiger subspecies and it
frequently embarked on long journeys in search of food.
Ranges of more than four thousand square miles have been
recorded.

Amba belonged to a declining species that was once the
symbol of the Russian Far East. The largest of seven subspecies of tigers, it was one of a dwindling number of about
only two hundred surviving so far in the region of Primorsky
Krai.

Amba had been stolen from his home, a wooded, moun-
tainous country covered by the taiga, the largest forest
remaining in the world.

Coveted now by the global wood products industry, the
temperate mixed coniferous and deciduous forest was
renowned for its high level of biodiversity.

Russians in this region six thousand miles from Moscow,
where unemployment is high and those lucky enough to
work earn little more than twenty dollars a month, have
recently begun to flood nearby Asian markets with animal
parts sought by hundreds of millions of Chinese, Japanese,
and Koreans for use in traditional medicines.

Such parts are also used in untraditional ways. Four sex
glands of the male kabarga, a type of gazelle, will trade in
Seoul evenly for a new Jeep Cherokee. Twenty years ago
they fetched two bottles of vodka.

Belief in tiger magic is still very powerful all over the
world. No animal is more coveted than the Siberian tiger,
whose skin, bones, eyes, whiskers, teeth, and internal and
sexual organs are in continual demand for everything from
skin cures to tooth medicine.

It is possible to buy a healing plaster containing tiger
bones at the airport on the way out of Vladivostok.

In the lobby of the Hotel Vladivostok gallbladders from black bears can be purchased for a mere ten dollars a gram, a steal when compared to the one thousand dollars a gram charged in Hong Kong and Korea.

If one knows where to go, it is also possible to buy tiger parts for medicinal uses in Los Angeles, San Francisco, Portland, and Seattle.

Ten years ago there were about five hundred Siberian tigers in the Pacific Coast regions of Primorsky and Khabarovsk. With a dead tiger worth as much as twenty-five thousand dollars on the open market, there are presently fewer than half that number still living.

The loss of the tiger has affected the entire ecosystems of Primorsky and Khabarovsk. Now the region is packed with wolves, which the tigers had previously kept at bay.

The wolves, having picked the area clean of deer, reindeer, and many of the boar, are now without prey, and are spreading out to seek new territory.

Because the man who acquired Amba was a person of vision with far more substantial plans for the animal than the receipt of a mere twenty-five thousand dollars, Amba had been taken alive instead of being shot and dismembered, his difficult capture causing the death of several Russian poachers.

The next day the cargo helicopter would deliver two live goats for Amba's consumption and would do so twice every week, for there was nothing on the island to feed a Siberian tiger, which must eat over twenty pounds of meat a day to sustain itself in the cold climate of its homeland; is capable, in fact, of eating over one hundred pounds of meat in one sitting.

But this island had not the cold of Siberia. And Amba's life expectancy could be measured in weeks, so such deliveries would not be required for long.

The goats would provide adequate nourishment, but not so much that Amba would grow fat and lazy and his anger lose its edge.

For pragmatic reasons he must be kept a worthy opponent.

There exist wealthy men and women who would pay almost any amount of money for the opportunity to kill a fierce, truly wild animal.

Some have been known to pay fabulous amounts for the chance to shoot a sick or aged animal as it crawled from a cage, these pathetic animals having been purchased from certain zoos by animal brokers of ill repute.

Amba, however, was truly wild and in excellent physical condition, capable of putting up a good fight, although confined to an island where the human hunter was almost certain to win. But not necessarily.

Being healthy, he had great strength and was capable of dragging prey that would take more than a dozen men to move, truly a worthy adversary.

Consequently, his capture and future demise had been orchestrated more carefully than most armed invasions or political coups d'état of small inflamed countries, and would net his present owner two million American dollars.

2   As the killer whales approached their island rubbing beach, Orca lifted her head above the waves and saw a strange four-legged thing making a lot of noise and pacing back and forth along the shore.

She warned her baby to keep close, studied the scene, then called to her companions to take a look, which they did.

Using their special language, Orca communicated to her pod that attack was unwise. Confrontation was not worth the effort: they had recently fed and were not hungry.

They would simply wait out the creature's presence. Surely it would soon leave and the pod would have their beach to themselves once more.

3   When Amba caught sight of the creatures looking at him from the sea, he stood stock-still, golden eyes staring at them with the intentness of a world-class hunter.

Although he could be almost invisible when stalking prey in his natural element, the great Russian forest, here on the island shore his orange and black stripes flamed out, the orange so bright it seemed to bleed into the salty air surrounding him.

Undaunted, the sea creatures stared back at him. Amba issued an earthshaking roar, one designed to frighten away the most vicious of predators.

He stood motionless, awaiting the flush of victory at watching the strange ones turn and flee in terror of his majestic voice and presence.

They did not turn and they did not flee.

Puzzled, he saw that the leader remained in position, her pack surrounding her in a giant semicircle, all heads above the sea as if daring him to attack.

Angry and confused, somewhat sick from the air journey and the residue of tranquilizers in his blood that his captors had forced on him, Amba charged into the waves and began to swim out to the heads, now closing ranks, massing together.

Not one turned to flee.

On the contrary, one of the creatures dived and came up under Amba, its great jaws wide open, ready to shear the Siberian tiger in half.

But missed by inches.

For Amba had already reached one of the whales, and claws extended, fangs exposed, he struggled up onto the animal, then sprang from one head to the other, leaving damage in his wake: bleeding eyeballs, torn hides, a partially detached dorsal fin.

In the ensuing watery turmoil, with the tiger charging from back to back, and the killer whales alternately plunging deep, then ascending to break the surface, vying for best attack positions, Orca's baby was shoved out from the safety of its mother's flipper.

Almost by accident, one of the tiger's claws ripped into the baby's body, which remained skewered on the great claws.

Although tigers, unlike other cats, enjoy water and are excellent swimmers—frequently mating in water—Amba finally grew bored fighting in an unfamiliar element.

He swam back into the shallows, stood up on his hind legs, roared, then tossed the impaled infant off his claw and up onto the beach where it lay bleeding and feebly moving.

All of the killer whale heads instantly disappeared.

Amba was striding over to inspect the baby whale when, with a tremendous rush of noise and water, hordes of the sea creatures, Orca herself foremost, slithered up onto the dry beach.

Puzzled and startled, Amba grabbed the baby orca in his jaws and took several long, flying leaps up onto a nearby overhang of earth covered with tall sea grasses.

For nine hours the killer whales assaulted the beach, huge bodies wriggling back into the sea, then charging again, Orca always in the forefront.

For nine hours Amba roared back from his higher position, guarding his food and watching the amazing antics on the beach below.

At last, he began to feed on his small prey.

4   When Orca realized that her baby was well and truly dead, she emitted a shrill sound, an order to the others of her pod to retreat.

All of them wriggled back into the sea and disappeared beneath the waters.

Except for Orca herself, who rose higher out of the sea than ever before and stared at the tiger.

For a time they eyed each other, the queen of the sea shrieking out her strange cries, and the great golden sovereign of forest and icy mountain pass roaring back at the limit of his lungs.

A bond of hatred passed between them before Orca's head slowly disappeared into the sea.

Amba turned away, a string of baby orca meat hanging from his great jaws.

He walked to an ancient Douglas fir tree with its huge branches sweeping the ground and lay down. His stomach was full, and his need to vent his anger had been satisfied with those long hours of roaring.

Since tigers cannot purr, he remained silent, watching the water. He knew the strange creature from the sea would not forget him for he had taken her young.

And he would not forget her.

*Unlike the Europeans of recent centuries, the Quinault did not divide
the world between mind and matter.*

*For a lone, hungry boy in the night in the sighing forest, the moment
of encounter with his future guardian could be when some animal-
human with unusual noise and powers signified with a short song that
the child had a place in the world, that it was part and parcel of the
powers that animate nature, that the child was not an alien in the
world but rather directly chosen to be assisted. For the rest of his life
he would carry that assurance.*

—DAVID H. CHANCE,
Land of the Quinault

Chapter 17

1   Blowing like the pages of a wind-tossed calendar,
     each of Jordan's days swiftly burned itself into the
charcoal of night.

In the circle of time, each day lived, died, and lived again,
flaming into a new day drenched with sun or graying into
one of sea mists and rain.

Drawn by the moon, conquering tides raged landward and
in their appointed time crept back to the ocean's heart, each
tide seizing yet more land.

The beach at Taholah was a world of endless motion.
Trumpeting breakers scoured the sands, churning up the bottom.

Twice daily the tide fell, leaving pools containing scallops, green abalone, eyehole limpets, hairy tritons, purple sea urchins, mussels, buffalo sculpin, and exposing fish-eating anemone to sun, wind, and predators.

The great green trees, those that had not yet been felled, grew in their immutable way, seeming to be the one element that held sea and land and sky, life itself, together.

2 Lima Clemente and his business partner were away from Lake Quinault, visiting machinery companies in Seattle and Vancouver, B.C. Jordan worked and longed for Lima Clemente's return.

So far none of the law enforcement agencies had made any progress at all in the investigations into the cases of the two murdered children.

3 Now approached the time of the summer solstice, a perfect June day except for a strip along the coast where the frequent summer fog bank lay over Moclips and Taholah.

Walk inland a hundred feet or so and the sky was an exultation of blue, clear as the star-shaped blue flowers of the camas.

But this year the June midday was different.

Strange things were happening in the forest.

Birds stopped flying and sought their nests, small creatures ran for cover, bears hurried to their dens. Bees returned to their hives in great golden clouds.

Julie the Beagle, McTavish's dog who always went to work with him, started baying and running around and around, so fast that her long soft ears stood upright with the wind from her circling.

Even Matt Swayle's dignified hound dog Blue, with him

where he was felling timber up on Fire Road Six, began a mournful howling that he kept up all afternoon.

"Shut up, Blue, you're giving me the spooks," Swayle told his dog, watching alertly as six trees came down, one after the other, in a neat pile.

Blue looked intently at his two-legged friend (humans were *so* difficult to communicate with about anything important) and began howling again.

When the men quit for the day it was eight hours before the time of the solstice, the turn of the season into summer.

4   A lavender evening was slowly rising from sand and sea on the beach at Taholah. Violet shadows crept out from under piles of bone-white driftwood.

A pool of deep purple gradually formed around the base of a bench-shaped rock on which Old Man Ahcleet sat with Tleyuk at his side.

It was the longest day of the year. The sun would set at 9:03 P.M. daylight saving time.

"This rock is the seat of the shamans, where they always came to watch for the summer and winter solstices," Ahcleet said.

Unlike many of his fellow Quinaults, Ahcleet had refused to abandon his traditional Smokehouse Religion and his shamanism.

Tleyuk thought about what the old man had said, then asked, "What about when it was raining or foggy? How could they see anything?"

"It didn't matter. They still watched. What they could not see with their eyes they saw with their spirits."

"What did they watch for, Grandfather?"

"They watched to see what the coming months would bring. They sighted from this seat right here to a pole placed in the ground or to a tree that is no longer there. But I remember where it was."

"How could they tell anything just by watching the sun go down?"

"Because they were wise. You see where the sun will soon set?" Ahcleet pointed out to sea.

Tleyuk nodded.

"This year's sun has traveled farther north than in ordinary years. Last night's moon was waning."

"What does that mean?"

"The moon has moved but little each day because it's heavy. It's loaded with food for the months ahead. Last night's moon with this sunset means we'll have a good year with a heavy run of salmon."

Ahcleet went on to explain that a solstice that occurred during a waxing moon with the sun traveling far each day foretold a lean year ahead with sickness and famine certain to come.

"We always observed the summer solstice in the same way as the winter solstice. But we have no word for it and I don't know why."

"Do we have a word for the winter's solstice?"

"Yes. That word is *Xa'ltaanem*. It means 'comes back, the sun.' Whale hunters used to watch very carefully for the winter solstice."

"Why, Grandfather?"

"Because the winter season, with its very high and very low tides, was the time when we met the guardian spirit connected with whaling. That spirit's name is Slao'ltca."

"Mom told me the Old Ones didn't keep track of time like we do now," Tleyuk said.

"Naturally they called the months by different names."

"Tell me."

"I will tell you, Tleyuk, if you memorize the words after me."

Tleyuk beamed. "Okay, Grandfather, but go slow so's I can keep up."

"All right then. *Panklich,* what we now call December, was the time of darkness, of winter."

"*Panklich,*" Tleyuk sounded out carefully.

"*Panpamas,* what we now call January, was the time of cold."

"*Panpamas,*" Tleyuk repeated.

"*Panlaleah-kilech* was the time of the beach willow. February, that would be."

"*Panlaleah-kilech.*"

"*Panjans,* that's March, was the time of sprouts. And April was *Pangwuh?am Huhnsha?ha,* the time when the geese go by."

Tleyuk dutifully repeated the old name for April.

"And May, or *Panjulashxuhtltu,* is the time when the blue-back return."

Ahcleet told Tleyuk about *Pankwuhla,* or June, the time of salmonberries; July, *Panklaswhas,* the time to gather native blackberries; August, *Panmuu?lak,* the time of warmth; September, *Ts okwanpitskitl?lak,* when leaves are getting red on the vine maples; October, *Pan?silpaulos,* the time of autumn; and November, *Panitpuhtuhkstista,* the time when the clouds are covering.

The boy carefully sounded out each syllable after his great-great-grandfather, now and then being corrected on his pronunciation.

"That's an awful lot to remember," Tleyuk said uncertainly.

"Not for a smart young Quinault like yourself," Ahcleet said. "And it's only the beginning of what you must learn. Now that you are eight years old, your special training will begin."

"Who will teach me?"

"Under normal conditions," the old man continued, "it would be your father who guided you through these important matters. But your father is not here, nor would he be qualified if he was.

"Your grandfather and great-grandfather are dead. That

leaves me. Later, when you are a little older, you will go on a vision quest and, if all goes well, obtain your song."

A fleeting, lonely look crossed Tleyuk's face. "I've never seen my father. Alls I know about him is that his name was Roc Tidewater."

"That was his name. He was a stranger. He was not one of us."

"Where did he come from?"

"From outside the Quinault Nation. He appeared ten or eleven years ago talking a lot of metaphysical stuff of which I soon discovered he was truly ignorant. But he put on a pretty good show. At first some of our people were favorably impressed and he was popular for a time. He made a play for your mother and she married him. You were growing in her belly but not nearly ripe when she left him."

"Why did she leave him?"

"That is her business. Someday she may tell you. Or she may not. But do not ask her for such a question would be very rude."

Tleyuk was silent for a time, then he spoke in a quiet, worried voice, as if he feared the answer. "Was he a low-class person?"

Ahcleet studied the boy.

"I understand the seriousness of your question," he said. "You wonder if you are the son of a father who has descended from slaves.

"I cannot tell you the truth of this because we know nothing of the man's background, not even where he came from. He said he was Cherokee but when I asked your Uncle Paul to have the Cherokee Nation check their tribal rolls they could find no Tidewaters."

Expecting the concerned expression he saw on Tleyuk's face, the old man took the boy's hand in his.

"Do not worry, Tleyuk. My blood and your mother's blood run so strong in you that the man who fathered you does not matter."

Then, to change the subject, Ahcleet pointed down the beach and said, "Did you know that Tsadjak lives in that huge pile of driftwood?"

"Who's Tsadjak?"

"He is a kind spirit whose dances were devoted to curing the sick in the old days."

"What does he look like?"

"When he takes shape he has the form of a man and he paints his body red. He has great influence on the weather. He lives in driftwood on the beach and the sound of the surf is his song."

"I remember what you said about our songs, Grandfather," Tleyuk said. "Each one of us gets a special song that comes when we've found our guardian spirit."

The old man shook his head. "Not everyone gets a song," he warned. "It takes effort and belief and patience."

"Suppose I don't get mine?" Tleyuk was worried.

"You will get your song. When you do, it will be one of the most valuable things you'll ever possess. Your song is living, special, and private. It will belong only to you and can be passed down from generation to generation."

"Will I get your song when you go to the Land of the Dead?"

"Only if you prove worthy and have already gotten your own song."

Old Man Ahcleet looked at sea and sky and sand. "I wonder where the birds are?"

"I don't know."

"The seabirds are not flying. They have gone to their nests very early."

"What does that mean, Grandfather?"

"Something, I know not what, is coming. Something besides the solstice."

Tleyuk snuggled closer to his great-great-grandfather and they both fell silent, watching the sun die in the sea. As the lavender twilight darkened, the long, sandy Taholah beach grew misty and seemed even more endless than it actually was.

"Do you think I would have liked living in the old days, Grandfather?" Tleyuk asked suddenly.

"I do not know. There was no television. But you would have been living real adventures, not viewing make-believe ones on a screen."

"If right now it was a long time ago, what would The People be doing?"

"This time of year? Well, the women would be digging camas roots on one of the prairies. Very special men, the whalers, would be at sea hunting for whales."

Tleyuk's round dark eyes glowed. "If I do good in my special training could I grow up to be a whaler?"

"You know that we do not hunt *ek-oale* anymore."

There was an undertone of sadness in Ahcleet's voice as he fingered the livid scar on the bridge of his nose.

"Did you do a bad thing when you hunted whales, Grandfather?"

"No. It was a good thing, a brave thing. We were the only whale-hunting people of Salishan stock. The new people today don't understand how it was. In my day the whales gave themselves to the bravest men to feed The People.

"That is not to say that whale hunting was easy," Old Man Ahcleet went on. "It was not. Many whalers died. We had to have courage and tenacity. We had to own the right guardian spirit, and we must be willing to die."

"What kind of whales did we hunt?"

Old Man Ahcleet smiled and nodded approval at Tleyuk's use of the world *we.*

"We hunted the humpbacks, as I have told you before. They are baleen whales, which means they have a great curtain of fringed bone along their lips which is used like sieves to capture small creatures and plants from the water."

"They're awful huge, Grandfather."

"The last one I harpooned was forty-six feet long. It was covered with barnacles, which had attached themselves to the whale's skin when they were tiny larvae and then began to build shells. Actually, it is a sensible thing for the barnacles to do."

"Why, Grandfather?"

"By riding on the whales the barnacles can travel through oceans wherever the whales swim, feeding as does the whale itself, by filtering microorganisms out of the sea."

"Do whales like the barnacles on them?"

"I don't think so. They probably make the whale feel itchy. Whales leap high in the air and splash down very hard trying to shake the barnacles loose. And they rub up against rocks for the same reason."

"Did you like to eat whale meat?"

"Of course I did. But it's been a long, long time since I've eaten any."

"What's it taste like?"

"Like a fine, mild pork."

"That sounds good."

"Oh, there are those now who claim they did not like it. They say the taste was pale and nauseating. But that's a matter of opinion, like most things. Personally, I've always thought the taste of broccoli is pale and nauseating."

Tleyuk was astounded. "But you eat it. And you make me eat it. How come, Grandfather?"

Ahcleet frowned. "Because your mother makes me eat it. And she makes me make you eat it. Says it's good for our blood. Does that answer your question?"

Tleyuk did not reply, lost as he was in the stunning news of his mother being able to make a man such as his great-great-grandfather, an elder of The People, an honored whaler and a powerful shaman, do anything at all, let alone eat something he did not like.

Certainly there was a mystery here, but by the expression on Ahcleet's face Tleyuk thought it would be best if he changed the subject. Already the boy had noticed that there were things between men and women he just did not understand.

"I've seen pictures of humpbacks," the boy said. "I think they're beautiful."

Ahcleet smiled. "And even more beautiful on the inside.

All *ekoale*'s organs are pale blue like a winter sky. The lining shines white as the foam on those breakers out there." He pointed seaward.

"Droplets of golden fat hang down from the kidneys," he went on. "The liver is smooth and glistening and is streamered in maroon. The lungs are two pearly colored sacs. All around the stomach is a thin membrane in colors from pink to indigo blue. *Ek-oale* is truly a creature of the sea. Inside its body the colors are the colors of the sea."

"How do you know what the insides look like?"

"Because in butchering the whale, the time came when we could walk around inside the animal."

"Did you have to duck your head when you stood inside?"

"No. Even as tall as I am, I had to look up."

"I wonder if it was the same in the real old days," Tleyuk asked.

"As I've told you before, in the real old days The People carved dugout canoes out of gigantic cedar logs and used harpoons with long lines and sealskin floats attached.

"The harpooner, like myself"—Old Man Ahcleet rubbed the livid scar on the bridge of his nose—"was a person of high rank who passed down the magical and practical secrets that made for successful hunting.

"For four nights the whaler would bathe, rub his body with hemlock branches, and then enter what was called the Whaler's Washing House to pray.

"The next four days he wandered around the lake. Every four steps he would stop and pray. An assistant followed him to help him return home when he could no longer speak properly due to cold and fatigue. The whaler would not eat or sleep during these four days."

"Wow, Grandfather. How long did he have to do that?"

Old Man Ahcleet placed his hand on Tleyuk's head and smiled into the boy's round dark eyes.

"This particular ritual lasted for four waxing moons. Now if someone died during this period, the whaler would steal the body. Personally I always had one of my slaves do this particular chore because I did not like to do it.

"And even though the family of the dead hid the corpse, we would, through bribes and the like, usually find it. The body was brought to the beach where it was laid facedown over a stone.

"A stake was driven through the base of the skull and out through the mouth. A hollow tube was placed in the hole, and standing behind the corpse, I shouted through the tube, asking that the whales come and drift ashore."

"You were the harpooner, Grandfather weren't you?" Tleyuk asked.

"You know I was. It was also my duty to eviscerate and dry the corpse and, when it was ready, place it in the whaler's shrine."

"Eviscerate? Isn't that like cleaning a fish?"

"Very similar."

"You never before told me about that last part," Tleyuk observed. "I'd sure like to go whaling, Grandfather, but I don't know about cleaning out a dead guy."

Old Man Ahcleet smiled. "There were rules, many rules. Before the whaling expedition, the whaler did not sleep with his wife."

"Yeah, I've heard about that. Didn't she get cold?"

"I'm sure she did. He got cold, too. The whaler had to bathe every day in a freshwater pond and rub his skin with hemlock branches until it bled.

"After that a corpse was attached to the back of the whaler—"

"Yuck!" Tleyuk whispered.

"—and he entered the water and spouted in imitation of the whale. He put himself into a trance to envision a dream of the whale and then sang a quiet song to the whale."

"Will you sing me the whale song, Grandfather?"

With a smile, Ahcleet began to softly sing.

"Whale, I want you to come near me, so that I will get hold of your heart and deceive it, so that I will have strong legs and not be trembling and excited when you come and I spear you.

Whale, you must not run out to sea when I spear you.

Whale, if I spear you, I want my spear to strike your heart.

Harpoon, when I use you, I want you to go to the heart of the whale.

Whale, when I spear at you and miss you, I want you to take hold of my spear with your hands.

Whale, do not break my canoe, for I am going to do good to you. I am going to put eagle down and cedar bark on your back."

"That's a very nice song, Grandfather," Tleyuk said politely.

"Yes, it is. And when the whale heard the song, the harpooner and his crew of eight set out in search of him. Sometimes as many as ten canoes went along, so sometimes eighty men were in pursuit of a single whale.

"As I've told you before, the whaling gear consisted of harpoons, lines, lances, and sealskin buoys, all of the men's own workmanship.

"In the old days the cutting edge of both lance and spear was made from the thick part of a mussel shell or of abalone.

"The lines were made from cedar withes, twisted into a three-strand rope. The buoys were all handsomely painted and those belonging to each boat had their own distinguishing marks.

"The harpoon pole was made from the heavy wood of the yew tree and was about eighteen feet long. With the lance attached it was a formidable weapon."

"Tell me about the hunt, Grandfather."

"Again? Don't you get tired of hearing about that?"

"No."

"All right. During the hunt the crew was naked except for their woven hats. They sang sacred hunting songs to drive the whale toward the shore. They carried fire with them in large seashells as they never knew when they would get home.

"Sometimes they lanced a whale that towed them for many miles before it grew tired. Sometimes they lanced a whale that killed them. Sometimes the whale killed them before the harpooner struck.

"The men tried to approach the whale from the left side in order to thrust the harpoon into the whale's heart. Those harpoons were too heavy for most men to throw, so they had to get close enough to the whale to stab it. I, however, was strong enough to throw the harpoon from a distance.

"Once the first harpoon had been planted, other harpooners did the same. When the whale was exhausted or weakened from loss of blood, its tail tendons were severed with a blade on a long pole, and it was killed with an elk-horn lance.

"To prevent the whale from filling up with water and sinking as they towed it to shore, one of the crew members dived overboard and sewed its great mouth shut. While towing the whale to shore, the men sang, '*Go into the bay, that is your place,*' and, '*Hurry, you are great and swift.*'

"When the whale had been successfully brought to the beach, a festival was held with much singing and dancing. The head of the whale was returned to the sea for regeneration, and as much of the meat as could be consumed was eaten on the spot."

"Why did they eat so much at one time, Grandfather?"

"You must remember that our Old Ones had no way of preserving the meat. The blubber was boiled down and the oil stored in skins or bladders. The most important men got the best eating oil and the best cuts of meat. Some of The People made war clubs and other implements from whale bone."

"And that's how you got that scar on your nose, isn't it, Grandfather? For being a great whale hunter?"

"Yes, Tleyuk. It was a great honor." The old man fingered the whitened scar. "This is the sign of Thunderbird himself."

"Was there a ceremony when you got the scar?"

"A very great ceremony."

"Will you tell me about it?"

"When you are older."

Tleyuk studied his great-great-grandfather. "You miss going whaling, don't you, Grandfather?" he asked.

"I miss it."

There was a look in Ahcleet's eyes that Tleyuk could not fathom; one that only a person who had lived through perilous times to a great old age could understand.

"Whatever's coming hasn't come yet, has it?" Tleyuk asked.

"It has not." The old man arose from the stone bench. "But we have watched the arrival of the summer solstice. The tide has turned," he said. "It is time to go home."

Tleyuk gazed at the ocean. "How do you know it's turned? It looks the same to me."

"It is not the same. Those of us who live our lives by the sea know when the tides change, even if we are blind or locked in underground cellars. Perhaps even within our graves and in the Land of the Dead.

"There is a different quality to the salty air, something beyond freshness, electric, nearly tangible. Pay attention now. Can you not smell the difference? Can you not feel it?"

Tleyuk took several deep breaths. "I think I can, Grandfather. Almost."

"You will learn to know it when you begin to pay attention."

Tleyuk stared again at the wild, familiar sea.

"Let us go," Old Man Ahcleet said. "Your special training starts tomorrow morning. Are you ready?"

Enthusiasm glowed in Tleyuk's round, dark eyes. "I am ready, Grandfather."

"It will not be easy," Ahcleet warned.

"That's okay. I can do it. I'm of your lineage."

Ahcleet smiled.

As the very old man and the very young boy got up off the ancient seat of the shamans, there came a sudden impossibly loud, sharp noise as if the entire earth had cracked in half.

The ground beneath their feet shook and rumbled, throwing them onto the sand.

"Jeez!" Tleyuk yelled. "An earthquake!"

"That's what was coming," Ahcleet muttered. "Those damned old devils."

As the earth continued to shake, rattle, and roar, Tleyuk crawled into Old Man Ahcleet's arms. They both lay prone, afraid for a while to try to get up as the ground trembled and rumbled, threatening to open up beneath them.

Finally, when it seemed that the earth had quieted down, Tleyuk got up and helped his great-great-grandfather to his feet.

"What old devils were you talking about?" Tleyuk asked.

"Those old devils that live deep within the waters of our sea. They're the ones who cause the earthquakes."

"Grandfather, is that true?"

"Yes."

"Tell me about the devils."

Ahcleet put his hand on the boy's shoulder. "Tleyuk, I am tired. That will be another lesson."

5   During that same lavender evening, echoes of groans and sighs filled the bedroom of the Campbell house on the sea cliffs at Moclips. Ruby and Melisande had gone to bed before dinner to make early evening love.

"You're the best lover in the world," Melisande said, after she'd gotten her breath.

"And how would you know? Just how many have you tried?"

"I don't need to try any others. I know I've got the best."

"And so have I, honey," Campbell said, kissing his wife again.

He lay on his back, hands behind his head. "I remember hearing my dad when he was eighty-five or so tell an old friend that while he could still plow as deep a furrow, he couldn't go as many rounds."

"You can still do it all," Melisande said, running her hands over her husband's flat, muscled belly.

Campbell smiled, knowing that the abiding physical love between his wife and himself was a great part of what kept them young in spirit and happy.

Pleased with himself, his wife, his marriage, Campbell drifted into that special deep after-love sleep.

Suddenly he was awakened by a sound he had not heard for fifty years, one that once heard was never forgotten.

He grabbed Melisande and rolled them both out of bed, sheltering her with his body on the floor.

She struggled in his arms. "What was that terrible noise? Let me go, Ruby."

"A German mortar. Sounds like it went off on our front deck."

"Ruby, what's wrong with you?"

She was worried. It had been at least ten years since he'd had war nightmares. But it had been a terrific noise, like the world splitting in half.

She finally managed to extricate herself from her husband's arms. She stood up, turned on a lamp, and looked closely into his face. He seemed fine.

He got up then, shaking his head. "God, it sounded just like a German mortar. Every gun has its own sound. I could always tell a German eighty-eight fieldpiece, a big gun mounted on a tank, anytime it fired."

"Ruby, I don't think there are any German tanks around here. So what was it?"

"An earthquake, that's what it was. Just an earthquake."

Melisande put on her nightgown. "I don't know about you, Ruby, but I'm starved. How about some scrambled eggs?"

"Fine, I'll make some biscuits to go with the eggs." Naked, he followed her out of their bedroom and into the kitchen.

The next morning they heard on the news that the earthquake of the night before was a 5.8 on the Richter scale. Seismologists said the tremendous noise accompanying the quake was the sound of the tectonic plates twelve miles deep in the earth beneath Puget Sound rubbing together.

6   Early the same morning Binte called the McTavish household to see if they were all right. Michael answered the phone.

"We're fine, Binte. Some of Hannah's collector plates flew off the walls but that's about it. How about you?"

"Most of my books are off the shelves and I might as well admit that my bed hasn't shaken like that for a long, long time."

7   Before the break of day, Old Man Ahcleet got up, dressed, and went into Tleyuk's bedroom.

"Tleyuk, wake up. Wake up, son."

Tleyuk rubbed his eyes. "Is it another earthquake?"

"No, nothing like that."

"Why do I have to get up now? School's out."

"Your training starts today. Have you forgotten?"

"It's awful early, isn't it?"

"I told you the training would not be easy. Hurry now. Dress for the outdoors."

With one determined leap Tleyuk jumped out of bed and quickly put on his clothes. "Where are we going?"

"To the river. Put on a jacket."

"You mean we're going right now?"

"Yes."

"We gotta eat first."

"We will eat when we return."

"But I'll starve."

"Perhaps."

"Why do we have to go so early?"

"Because you must bathe."

Tleyuk managed an incredulous look. "With my clothes on?"

"You will take them off before you get in the water."

"But, Grandfather, why do I have to dress to walk into the bathroom to take a bath?"

"You will bathe in the river. Did you wish to walk through Taholah naked?"

Having asked that question, Old Man Ahcleet went purposefully down the hall toward the front door. Tleyuk hurried to catch up.

"We're really going to bathe in the river, Grandfather?" the little boy asked uncertainly.

"*You* are going to bathe in the river. And you must do it now while the water slumbers. After the river wakes up, the water will be much colder."

Tleyuk was trying to figure that out as they proceeded through town to the Quinault River, crashing and roaring along.

Having originated from Anderson Glacier in the Olympics and already run some sixty-eight miles, it was still icy cold and impatient for the sea.

As they walked through town Old Man Ahcleet began the first of his lectures to his great-great-grandson.

"There is power in the in-between places," he began.

"What are in-between places?" Tleyuk asked.

"All that is not clearly one thing or another. In-between places are rivers and borders and all edges, verges, brinks, rims, fringes, dividers. It makes no difference if these are borders of space or of time."

Ahcleet went on. "Caves, thresholds between open air and the solidity of earth, are often entrances to the world of spirits.

"Wells link the visible world with subterranean realms and have an enchantment that might give awareness of the future. In the space dividing foam and water or bark and tree, devils can be confined by those who know how.

"Some things hold magic because of their borderline nature. Dew, for example. Although water, it does not come from the sea, river, or spring. It comes from the air. It does not flow with gravity but rests lightly on leaf or blade of grass.

"And it comes and goes at another borderline, the division between night and day. Fog also is magical. During fog is when the supernaturals come. Dawn and dusk are magical times. They divide day from night, light from darkness."

When Old Man Ahcleet paused, Tleyuk asked about the importance of owning guardian spirits.

"It is absolutely crucial. Without the aid of guardian spirits, even those of noble blood cannot aspire to great things and are likely to lose the wealth and prestige they already have.

"Even a man poor in the goods of the world and of low class can rise to a position of wealth and influence if he owns strong helpers from the other world.

"In the old days, everyone knew how important it was to have control of supernatural power and all but a few sluggards worked diligently to get a guardian spirit."

"It sounds like hard work to me," Tleyuk said.

"It is. Training for the quest begins at eight years of age, your age now, and continues for several years.

"You will not stop your search for power with the acquisition of one spirit, but you will continue until you control a number of guardian spirits. Spirits may continue coming to a man at intervals until middle age or later, but the earlier spirits remain his mainstays.

"Except for the powers that come from submerged logs, from forked trees, or from the bones of the dead, all spirits and powers are ageless and usually sexless. They never die."

"Tell me about a shaman again, Grandfather. You are a shaman."

"Yes, I am. A shaman is a man or woman who has been particularly fortunate in acquiring the most powerful guardian spirits which enable him or her to perform deeds ordinary mortals could not do. Now listen carefully to me, Tleyuk. What I am about to say is very important."

"I am listening, Grandfather."

"A man who controls many spirits does not have to go on a vision quest for each spirit. Possession of certain powers makes the shaman attractive to other spirits. Some, of course, come to him after the death of the relative who had owned them."

They had arrived at the river of their destination.

"When you die, Grandfather, will your spirits come to me?"

"You must get your own spirits first. Now take your clothes off and jump into the river. I will remain here on the bank."

Tleyuk looked doubtful. "How long do I have to stay in the water?"

"Don't worry about that. Just jump in and stand there while I teach you the *tame'xa,* the special prayer to use when you talk to the world. After the first plunge, you must do it all over again four more times."

"You mean five times this morning?"

"You must do it five times every morning," Ahcleet said sternly.

Naked, Tleyuk jumped into the river and stood shivering as he watched and listened to Old Man Ahcleet who instructed, "Now do exactly what I do and say exactly what I say."

The old man lifted up his face, blew his breath toward the

sky, then shouted in his loudest voice, "I want you to help me."

Tleyuk yelled the words and repeated the gestures, then splashed back out, teeth chattering, body covered with gooseflesh.

Ahcleet handed the boy a length of braided hemlock bough and instructed him to scrub his body with it until his skin burned.

"You must do this after each plunge, Tleyuk, and keep doing it until the blood comes through your skin and the water feels hot. Remember, you must perform this ritual five times every morning."

"Even in the winter?"

"Yes."

"But I'll freeze."

"If you freeze you'll thaw. When I was very young, icicles formed in my hair and on my eyelashes, and the frosty stones on the riverbank stuck to my bare feet as I walked back to my house."

Tleyuk did not look happy. But he gritted his teeth and plunged back into the river, intoned the prayer, came back up to the bank, scrubbed himself with the braided hemlock. This he did the required five times.

Ahcleet handed Tleyuk his clothing and told him to put it back on.

"Did Mom go through all this?" Tleyuk asked, shivering, as they began the walk back home.

"Yes. And so will you."

So cold his mouth trembled and he could hardly get the words out, Tleyuk stammered, "Grandfather, I'm freezing to death."

"Walk faster. You'll thaw out."

"I don't know about this stuff." The words were tear-filled.

"What don't you know?"

"Whether I'll be able to do it."

"Have no fear. You will. Are you not part of me? And part

of your mother? We have both gone through this and much, much more. You must develop the strength of will to overcome your body. But all in good time. Hurry, now. I'll make you a German pancake when we get home."

The Quinaults, one of the most sophisticated tribes on the coast, had great intellectual curiosity. Their abundance granted them the time to question from the viewpoint of physical well-being. As a result, unlike many of the world's old cultures (even today), the Tribe could and did believe in a good and omnipotent creator, not a terrorizing supernatural being. He was Kwantee, the creator of all the world, the people, and the animals.

JACQUELINE M. STORM,
Land of the Quinault

Chapter 18

1   True North American rain forests are found only in the canyons and valleys of the Olympic Peninsula, a whale's tailpiece of land thrust into the North Pacific sea from the northwestern edge of the continental United States.

The peninsula is "geographically exotic," which means that its origin was entirely different from the rest of the North American continent, having been formed sixty-five million years ago as part of an offshore oceanic ridge.

It was a time when the bedrock of the ocean was in turmoil. Where the tectonic plates collided, the bowels of the earth burst into the sea. In such fiery turmoil was the Olympic Peninsula born.

Covering nearly seven thousand square miles of stunning beauty, the peninsula's seaward expanses are almost continuously saturated by rains and fogs that shroud coastline and forest.

When the fogs lift and the rain stops, which they frequently do, one is surrounded by a verdant mystique as if Kwantee made this place first and, finding that He was capable of doing such a good job, went about to create the rest of the world.

Here are some of the world's largest trees, fattest salmon, most dramatic coastlines, and wettest weather.

The perpetually snow-covered mountains are so rugged that less than a century ago people believed a tribe of man-eating savages lived in their trackless peaks.

Rain is the life's blood of this region, resulting in a soaring emerald kingdom far more productive of life than any tropical rain forest in the world.

These true temperate rain forests are the Bogachiel, the Hoh, the Queets, and the Quinault.

The life-giving rains are as varied, as different, as the faces, both human and animal, upon which they fall.

Some Olympic rains drift around as scarcely perceptible mists that one can inhale, sweet and soft, barely there; others belly flop down as big, fat, slow, wetter-than-wet splats.

Some rains sound like the feet of tiny, happy children running through dry, fallen leaves; some like the cautious whispers of secret lovers who have a lot to lose if they are discovered; some rains hurl themselves to the ground with the sound and fury of ancient warriors in ferocious battle.

Individual raindrops vary in size from a hundredth of an inch to one full inch in diameter.

Without the rains, or even if the rains lessen, these majestic North American rain forests will die.

2   Ruby Campbell, who lived with his wife in a house
     hanging over a sea cliff at Moclips, listened to the
pouring rain as he shaved after dinner using a straight-
edge razor, a boar's bristle brush, and lots of hot shaving
cream.

He did not like electric razors, did not think they shaved
closely enough. The few times he had used one, his face
never felt really clean afterward.

Melisande walked in just as Ruby had finished shaving.
She took one look and opened the window to air out the
room.

"Coming down pretty hard out there," she said, sitting on
the closed toilet seat.

"Sounds like a cow pissin' on a flat rock."

He looked at her and grinned, knowing she loved his old
hillbilly expressions.

Ruby was glad it was stormy. Such heavy rains would
make his meeting tonight private and safer. There would be
less chance of running across people he did not wish to
encounter, which included the members of his team. He did
not expect to see any of them. No arrangements had been
made to get together, but one never knew.

He had successfully recruited five men to work for him,
all laid-off loggers who knew the woods like the backs of
their hands.

All were men he felt he could trust, mature men who
could keep their own counsel, not a loudmouth or a braggart
among them. Just down-to-earth hardworking men who
needed money to support their families. So far they were
doing excellent work.

A man named Irv Mason was Campbell's main man.
When he'd made the deal with Irv, Ruby had told him,
"Don't ask a lot of questions. The less you know the better
off you'll be."

"But what if we get picked up by the law?" Mason wanted
to know.

"If you follow my orders, do what I tell you, you won't.

But if by any chance you do get picked up, I'll fix it for you. I've got connections."

Probably the best testament to Ruby's effectiveness in dealing with men was the fact that Mason and the others believed what he told them. And there wasn't a stupid man among them.

They all knew the work was illegal.

But they were also of the collective mind that while there certainly was real honest-to-God crime like murder, there was also such a thing as bureaucratic crime, technical law-breaking, the latter being okay if you were smart enough to cover your tracks and keep your mouth shut, at least if your family's welfare was at stake.

The kind of men, Ruby believed, who used to operate stills back in the ridges of Kentucky, the ones who made that flawless white lightning, the good stuff that looked clear as spring water and cured everything that ailed you, including life, if you drank enough of it.

Campbell closed the window, then rinsed out his shaving brush.

When he looked at himself in the mirror, he saw, as he had for nearly half a century, his disfigurement. The right side of his face was not quite in line with the left.

"Has this ever bothered you, Melly?" he asked his wife, pointing to the right side of his face.

"Never," she said.

In Belgium he had taken a bullet that had neatly cut through most of his right cheek and left it hanging by a piece of flesh near his ear. The bullet had then jumped under his helmet, circling it completely, ripping out the lining, but doing no further damage.

When he'd taken off his helmet and seen the miracle that he'd lived through (although Ruby had never considered it a miracle), he'd discovered that his right cheek was hanging down and his teeth showing, exposed to the terrible cold.

He'd quickly poured sulfa powder into the wound, pushed

up the hunk of flesh that was his cheek, tied an old rag around his head in an effort to hold his cheek in place, put his helmet back on, and kept on fighting. He didn't get to a field hospital for over a week.

"Wonder if I should have had that plastic surgery they offered to me after the war."

"Why didn't you?"

"After nearly five years of war without ever coming home even once, I didn't have time for stuff like that. I wanted out of the damn army, wanted to get on with my life. Besides, I'd seen some of the work those plastic surgeons had done on my buddies."

Melisande looked him over. "I didn't even see it when we first met. It didn't bother me then and it certainly doesn't bother me now. As you've gotten older it's become much less noticeable."

It was true. After all these years the scar blended into the natural curve of Ruby's cheek. The only aftereffect he still felt was a numbness on the right side of his face.

Ruby looked at himself in the mirror again and for just a moment the corners of his full, pleasant mouth pulled down as if hooked by a ghostly fisherman.

For, as had happened several times during the many years since his war, he saw in his own face the face of a killer.

It was true that he had killed one hell of a lot of men, all of whom were trying to kill him.

As a ranger in the Sixth Army during World War II, he had been trained to reconnoiter, stalk, silence firearms, and kill with weapons that ranged from bare hands to rocks, piano wire, and knives.

He had survived that war as a decorated, skillful, creative, and deadly soldier. The decorations never had meant anything to him; now he didn't even know where they were.

The way Ruby looked at life, he'd simply done his job as well as he could. He told people he'd been lucky.

But he knew it was a lot more than luck. It was that sixth sense he'd developed as a boy in the Kentucky hill country, what he'd learned from his father.

And from an ancient Indian who lived in a cave, the last of his tribe, the one who taught Ruby how to sense things before he saw or heard them, how to see things that seemingly weren't there, but could kill him in the next instant or two.

All that had been long ago.

Ruby knew from experience that a well-trained military man never forgot how to kill. And it wasn't just sophistry to say that under the right circumstances, anybody could kill. Because they could. Or at least try to.

Killing was, after all, one of mankind's basic instincts, and Ruby had been well trained to do the job.

He still wore piano wire on the inside waistband of his trousers. He never knew what he might encounter, especially in his present line of work.

Ruby suspected that some people probably figured him for a chauvinist, an unsympathetic man, since he hated any kind of weakness, having only contempt for drunkards, drug addicts, adulterers, wife beaters, child abusers. In his code there was no excuse whatsoever for such behavior.

There wasn't anything complicated about it. On the contrary, it was very simple. You had your own personal rules and you stuck by them.

If you couldn't handle liquor, don't buy it or have it in your house or make a habit of going to booze joints. Leave drugs alone altogether.

If you could not be faithful to one woman, don't get married. And if you were the kind of slime that liked to hurt little kids or beat on women, go put a loaded gun in your mouth and pull the trigger. Save everybody a lot of trouble.

"Guess I'm just an old redneck son of a bitch," he said, following his train of thought out loud as he wiped his face clean with a hot, damp towel.

"Redneck? Who's a redneck? I'll have no rednecks in this house," Melisande said, rising from the toilet seat and gathering up damp towels. "Getting all spiffed up, I see. Going out to see your new girlfriend?"

"Yeah, I'm afraid so, honey. Think I'm spreading myself too thin?"

"As long as I get my share, it's all right with me." There was a dangerous glint in her eyes. "And if you believe that nonsense, you're getting senile."

He turned and embraced her, rubbing his face against hers, knowing that she loved the smell and feel of his freshly shaved cheeks.

"Smooth as a baby's bottom," she murmured for the three-millionth time in their marriage. "Where are you really going?"

"I got a tip that Ole Olson is taking out more logs then he's paying for. I'm going to drop in on his show."

Melisande pulled away.

"Ruby, nobody would be out working on a bad night like this," she said.

"Honey, it's just the kind of night for them to do things they don't want anybody else knowing about."

"In this storm? With this wind? How could he cut any trees?"

"They're already down and yarded in. All Olson has to do is get them loaded on his trucks, branded with his brand, and then rush them to the loading docks first thing in the morning."

"I hate it when you go out on a night like this."

"What are you afraid of? I can handle myself all right. Been doing it for a damn long time."

"What I'm afraid of is that one of these nights you'll catch a logger who will shoot you for interfering."

"I don't approach them that way, honey. As far as they're concerned, I'm just driving by and stopping to shoot the breeze. Nobody knows I'm working as a timber cop. Even the guys I've already nailed. Nobody except Paul and Jordan, that is. And you, of course."

"How long are you going to be gone?"

"Maybe all night. Maybe only a few hours. It all depends on what happens out there."

"As usual, I'll expect you when I see the whites of your eyeballs."

She walked out of the bathroom with the towels and down the hall to the utility room where she stuffed them in the washing machine.

After Ruby finished dressing in his outdoor clothes, he went into the living room and asked Melisande what she had planned for the evening. Would she be working in her studio?

Not tonight, she told him. She was going to watch some Arnold Schwarzenegger movies, starting with her favorite, *Red Heat.*

"So, you go for those big guys with pumped-up muscles, is that it?"

"Generally not. But I do like Arnold."

Ruby built his wife a fire in the fireplace, carried in additional firewood from the garage, made sure all the windows and the outer doors were locked, kissed her soundly, and told her he was leaving her in Arnold's care.

"Any other men coming around here while I'm gone?" he asked with mock sternness.

"Only Arnold," she said, fluttering her eyelashes.

They laughed, hugged, and he walked out of the house and into the garage where he put on his oilskins, then stepped into his truck, still chuckling.

What a woman she was. He couldn't even imagine life without her.

Sometimes he felt guilty about not telling Melisande about his other work, his deal with the international poaching combine, but he simply did not want her to have anything else to worry about.

Melisande was developing into a fine artist. He wouldn't be at all surprised if she went big-time. Her energies should be focused on her talent, and not exhausted by worrying about what possibly dangerous activities her husband was involved in.

To make himself feel better, make at least part of his story to Melisande authentic, he drove past Ole Olson's logging show where all was shut down and dark.

Everything was noisily streaming with rainwater; stand-

ing trees, machinery, downed timber in the hot deck, the
stack of logs scheduled to be hauled out immediately, and
the cold deck, the stack of logs held for later handling.

He knew Olson was taking out logs he had not contracted
for, most of the logs in the hot deck as a matter of fact, but
Ruby hated to have to expose him.

He'd considered putting a bug in Olson's ear, warn him
to back off, but he hadn't decided yet whether or not he
should do that. For one thing, if he did, it might blow his
cover.

The man had a lot of problems and Ruby was sorry for
him. Still, theft was theft.

3   After he left Ole Olson's, Campbell drove carefully
    through the storm for several hours, up into the vast-
ness of the Olympic National Park. Most of the time only
his parking lights were on for he did not wish to attract any
attention.

There were a number of old shacks in the rain forest built
over a period of years by people wanting to escape. From
what, nobody asked. When the human owners had gone,
bears liked to use these shabby structures.

On the reservation, when previous tribal policemen had
come across them, they heard their stories, and if they liked
them, the people were usually left alone.

"Time catches everybody, one way or the other,"
Campbell was fond of saying.

Most of the shacks were falling-down ruins, their former
occupants long gone.

But Campbell and his crew had found one still in pretty
good condition because the builder had built it well. It was
near a glacial stream, down an old fire access road that had
not been in use for a couple of generations. So it became his
warehouse.

Built of still-sound cedar logs, the building was well insulated between each log. They brought in a generator for power. If the park rangers found this structure, there'd be hell to pay, Campbell reflected. He needed to get his work finished and out of here before that happened.

So far his crew had harvested a number of bear gallbladders as well as paws and claws, bald eagle beaks, claws, and feathers, and cougar skins. They had also collected a pile of velvet from deer and elk antlers.

Soon he'd have enough for the first shipment.

Campbell's head man was Irv Mason. He was assisted by a man named Josh Henley. Both men had been given the treatment—their wrists burned, the burns anointed with that stuff that looked like green mustard.

Campbell knew for sure the stuff really worked. Those two could go out and find animals with no trouble at all. As could he.

When he reached the rustic warehouse, he was surprised and displeased to find both Mason's and Henley's pickup trucks parked under the trees.

Dammit! he said under his breath, wondering what these guys were doing. He did not want them here. There had been no plans for any of them to meet tonight.

He also saw the broken branch, which meant the man he had come to meet was here, too. But upon seeing that a couple of members of Campbell's crew were present, he was wisely remaining hidden.

Using a generator, Ruby had installed low-voltage nightlights inside the building so they could see their way around without emitting a great amount of light. In addition, regular lighting was also available in the ceiling, but was used sparingly.

He parked and got out of his truck.

As he did so, he heard several shrill screams that seemed curiously near at hand. Cougar, no doubt, but he was surprised that the animal was so close.

Cougar, he knew, gave humans a lot of room. Occasionally,

if they were overpopulated or starving due to an unusually cold winter with a heavy snow pack, they were known to appear around human habitations looking for food.

Come to think about it, those screams weren't exactly like the voice of a cougar. What was different? A somewhat hoarser quality, he realized, then wondered if it was possible for a cougar to catch a cold.

As Campbell approached the building, he saw immediately there was no need to unlock the door.

A sliver of dim light told him it was already slightly ajar. He was puzzled that any members of his team, especially Henley and Mason, were that careless. Something must be wrong.

He walked inside and found the two men sitting at a large wooden table. Both of their faces were smeared with black grease and both were wearing their camouflage hunting outfits.

"What are you guys doing here tonight?" he asked.

"Boss, you'll never believe what happened!" Henley exclaimed, standing up, his face scarlet with excitement around the edges of the black grease. "Not in a hundred years."

"I'm not sure I believe it myself," Mason said consideringly.

He was the calm one, thin and tall, hatchet-faced, a man who ruminated long and thoughtfully before making any decision.

"Believe what?" Campbell asked, looking at both men with arms on hips.

"We got ourselves a Bigfoot, that's what!" Henley's high voice cracked with excitement.

"A *Bigfoot*?"

"It's a Bigfoot, all right," Mason agreed, nodding his head judiciously. "It's a young one, but it's the real thing."

Campbell looked skeptical.

"Yup, an honest-to-God Bigfoot," Henley went on.

"Sure is," Mason said. "No doubt in my mind at all."

"Ruby, we're going to be rich and famous," Henley said, his voice going higher. "Just think about it. We've got the first real live proof that Bigfoot exists."

"Now we've got to figure out how to keep the little fella safe until we break the news. And afterward. What are we going to do with him afterward?" Mason asked.

"After what?" Campbell asked.

"Well, after the stories on TV and in the newspapers all around the world. We'll go down in history as the true discoverers of an animal most people don't even believe exists."

"How do you know that's what it is?" Campbell asked quietly.

"Take a look for yourself," Mason said, his steely eyes glinting from under dark brows as he stood up, walked across the room, and opened an inside door to a windowless drying shed that had been built as an add-on to the main log cabin. The shed had a second door that exited to the outside.

Walking into the shed, Campbell could smell the numerous bears' gallbladders hanging up to dry, quite a few more than they had the last time he was here.

"Where'd all these galls come from?" he asked.

Irv Mason said, "We've got a new contact."

"What's his name?" Campbell demanded.

"Well, Boss, I sort of told him his name would never be mentioned."

"His name, Irv."

Mason took off his cap and scratched his head.

"Come on, Irv. You know our agreement."

"Okay. Okay." Mason raised his hands in surrender. "It's Bill Hereford, is what it is."

"Hereford? Bill Hereford?" Campbell shook his head thoughtfully. "I don't know the man."

"Been around here all his life. He's got a little spread out behind the Black Rooster at Humptulips. Has a breeding bull and some cows. Raises bear dogs, acts as a guide for bear hunts."

"In or out of season?" Campbell asked.

Mason shrugged. "That's his business, I guess."

"What does he think you want the galls for?"

"As far as he knows, I represent a nameless person out of the country."

"What about money for the galls?"

Mason mentioned a figure per gall that Campbell agreed was fair.

"Has to be in cash, Boss."

"No problem. Just keep your mouth shut about us, Irv."

"Ruby, he knows from nothing about our organization."

Campbell's question about the gallbladders faded into insignificance when Josh Henley shone a heavy-duty flashlight on a furry animal curled inside an open wooden crate.

"Here's our key to fame and fortune," he said.

Campbell studied the animal, which lay motionless. "Looks like a small bear to me," he said.

"It's not a bear."

Once more Campbell heard the screams from outside. So did the other men.

"Old cougar wandering around out there," Henley said.

"Don't sound like no cougar to me," Mason disagreed, then squatted down and shone his light on the small creature.

It seemed to be dead.

The animal lay unnaturally still, completely limp, its eyelids lowered but not quite closed in the vacant stare of death.

"It's playing dead," Mason said, then added in a worried voice, "hell, maybe it *is* dead."

He pulled a skinning knife out of a holder at his waist and held the flat shining surface close to the animal's nostrils. A faint layer of mist soon covered the knife.

"Little bastard's faking it," he said.

"Where'd you get this animal?" Campbell asked.

"Found it in that deadfall out back," Mason told him. "The one by the stream."

About a quarter of a mile upstream from the log warehouse the men had built an elaborate deadfall capable of trapping bear or cougar.

It was done in the old Quinault fashion, the top heavily weighted with stones placed there after the trap was set.

Bait of old meat was lashed to the horizontal trigger. In attempting to devour the bait, the animal had inadvertently pushed the bar down, releasing a vertical trigger bar.

"Did it eat any of the bait?" Campbell asked.

"No. But it got caught in the trap just the same."

"Look at those claws. How'd you get it down here without getting hurt yourselves?"

Henley replied, "The minute we shone our lights on it the damned thing went dead. Curled up like a potato bug, just like it is now. Made it a lot easier to transport. Course, we tied it up to be safe. Untied it as soon as we got it in the crate. Right about then we heard that old cougar outside start up. Guess we'd taken its supper."

"That's not a cougar," Irv Mason repeated.

"What makes you think this thing's a Bigfoot?" Campbell asked.

"Look at the hind feet. In fact, look at it all over."

Henley and Mason spread the animal out for examination. It was a female. During the handling she remained totally immobile. The only signs of life were her barely exhaled breaths on the knife's mirrorlike surface and the warmth of her body.

When Campbell stooped to inspect the animal, he saw that her body was covered by short, very thick, protective hair, dark like an elk's mantle.

She was thin with long limbs and, in spite of being a young one, looked hard and tough and carried no excess fat.

The hind feet were about three times the size that he would expect to see on a bear cub, and the small toe on each foot was set far back from the other toes.

"See that toe," Mason said. "The way that there's set means her kind does a lot of sitting, probably in the cross-legged position. Kind of rules out the possibility that these things live in trees, like some people think. But I expect they do climb a lot."

"How can you tell?" Henley asked.

"Just study the spread between the big toe and the one next to it. That tells the story."

As for the rest of the body, Campbell saw that the face was round, in some way more like a human face than that of a monkey, and the upper arms ended in what he could only call hands, four sturdy fingers plus a thumb, jointed and pinkish.

He looked at Mason. "Irv, do you really believe there is such a thing?"

"Such a thing as Bigfoot?"

Campbell nodded.

"You want to know if I believed before we found this animal here?"

"Yeah, I do."

Mason thought it over. "Well, I'll tell you how it is, Ruby. You can't work all your life in the woods and not know these things are around. Course we don't talk about it to outsiders, not even much among ourselves. A man who has to earn a living in the woods can't have people thinking he's not right in the head."

"Okay, leave it be," Campbell told the two men. "Let's go inside."

Back in the main building, Josh Henley and Irv Mason discussed the best way to announce their amazing find to the world.

"We're going to have to give it a lot of thought, Ruby," Mason said. "For years now teams of scientists and those who call themselves scientists have been snooping around the woods looking for proof that these things exist."

"Yeah, and they've already found huge footprints," Henley said earnestly.

"Put there, I suspect, by loggers with a sense of humor," Campbell said.

"Some were phony but most of them were the real thing," Henley replied.

The men fell silent, thinking things over.

"It sure feels good," Mason said suddenly with what was for him enthusiasm.

Both Campbell and Henley turned toward the other man. Irv Mason was normally a calm man who kept his feelings to himself.

Campbell remembered being surprised that the man had children, surprised that Irv could work up enough excitement to do what needed to be done to spawn them.

"What feels good?" Henley asked carefully.

"Fame, that's what. Can't you feel it creeping up on you? I guess you haven't thought about it but that's what we're going to be, Josh. You and me. And you, too, Ruby. We're all going to be famous. Famous as hell. We'll be on television, in the movies, high mucky mucks will ask our opinions."

"Our opinions about what?" Campbell wanted to know.

"Everything. We're discoverers, important people. Like the guy who first climbed Everest. Or the guys who went to the moon. Everywhere we go people will want our autographs. Maybe we can charge for them, like the ball players do. Just you wait. You'll see."

"I don't know—" Henley said uncertainly.

"Josh, listen to me. We found this animal in our trap. We *own* this animal—"

Campbell found himself doubting that anyone could truly own a wild animal. He thought that would be like saying you owned the wind. Sure, you could keep a wild animal caged but that wasn't exactly owning.

"—and it belongs to us. Scientists will want a crack at examining it. News programs will want to show it and us. Probably even Tom Brokaw. And talk shows. We'll have to be damn careful because all kinds of people will want to steal it."

Mason turned to Campbell. "Isn't that right, Ruby? You understand what I'm talking about, don't you?"

"Oh, I understand, all right. It could be proof that Bigfoot exists," Campbell agreed. "Or not, as the case may be."

He still didn't know if he believed in the existence of Bigfoot, but he'd heard things in the woods that he could not account for.

New life-forms were frequently being discovered. New? he asked himself. They were probably life-forms that man had forgotten or never known about before—which certainly did not mean they were new.

And that animal in the drying shed sure didn't look like a bear, in spite of what he'd said earlier.

Campbell went on, "The scientists you were talking about would have the final say on that. And they'd probably argue about it until we were all in our graves."

"So what? We'd still make tons of money."

"I think there's one thing you haven't thought about, Irv."

"What?" The question cracked like a rifle shot.

"Explaining to people like Tom Brokaw, not to mention Fish and Wildlife, and the world, how you got the young Bigfoot."

"That's simple," Mason replied. "We found it in the forest."

"You found it caught in an illegal trap that you built on national park land, land that's been designated a world heritage site as well as a biosphere reserve by the United Nations. That alone is a federal offense. Then our whole organization would come to light and we'd probably all end up in the slammer for God knows how long."

"You're as guilty of that as we are, Ruby," Henley said quickly.

"I know that."

"What are we going to do?" Mason wanted to know.

"I think we should all go home," Campbell said.

"But we can't leave that animal here—" Henley burst out.

"Now, just listen to reason," Campbell said. "You can't take her to your homes, can you?"

They each replied that they could not. Not yet, at least.

"Okay, we need a plan. One that works. I suggest we all go home, sleep on it tonight. We'll get together tomorrow, lay our cards on the table, and figure out what to do with our little friend in there and how to do it for her best good and ours. You men have any objection to that?"

Henley and Mason thought it over, looked at each other, then both indicated to Campbell that they were in agreement.

"I'm just worried about leaving it here overnight," Henley said.

"Why?" Campbell asked. "She's safe in there. Nobody can get inside. We probably should put some water in that box. As for food, I don't know what to give her. I don't know what she eats."

"It might escape," Mason said.

"How?" Campbell asked.

Mason shrugged.

Campbell said, "Not unless she has a chain saw to cut through the walls she won't."

Suddenly all three heard a long, catlike snarl, low and vicious, coming from outside and very close to the building.

"That there's a wolverine," Mason said with certainty. "I hate those damn things. They're mean as hell." He reached for his rifle. "I'm going out and take care of it."

Campbell held him back. "Leave it be, Irv. No need to shoot anything tonight."

"The books say there's never been any wolverines on the peninsula," Henley said with an odd expression on his face. "But I've lived here all my life and by God I've seen them. And I've heard the old Indians say that wolverines always travel with the Seatco."

"What's a Seatco?" Campbell asked.

"It's what the Indians around here call Bigfoot," Henley told him. "Same thing that we've got in the back room."

"You mean in myth?"

"Hell, no. I mean for real. Oh, probably in their myths, too. I don't know about that."

"What's one thing got to do with the other? Why should a wolverine travel with a Bigfoot?" Campbell asked.

"Beats me, but some of the old Indians told me they always have. Supposed to keep the Seatco informed about what's going on. The wolverines talk to the tree people."

"And who are the tree people, Josh?"

"Well, it seems that a hell of a long time ago the Indians buried the worst of their criminals alive under young cedar trees. The trees grew on top of the guys and trapped their spirits. But they could still talk from inside the trees."

"Have you heard any dead people talking to you from trees lately, Josh?" Campbell asked.

Henley looked down at the floor. "I wouldn't say exactly that but I have heard some mighty peculiar things out there in the woods."

"Me, too," Mason agreed.

Campbell had, too. He knew that the forest was a mysterious place, full of sights and sounds upon which the imaginative could place many interpretations. And even the unimaginative.

Ruby did not consider himself at all imaginative but he had heard trees whisper, sigh, murmur, and roar. He had even heard them scream.

There was a certain way one tree could fall against another, either from natural causes such as a lightning strike or a heavy wind, or at the hands of an unskilled faller, that caused the most bloodcurdling shrieks he had ever heard, including during the war.

In addition, there were sounds from all the other lives that existed in a state of jeopardy out there, from black bear and cougar to banana slugs, moving about, doing whatever their genes demanded of them. And from other things that were still unidentified.

But he didn't know whether such a creature as a Bigfoot existed.

"Okay, guys, we're in agreement then?"

They both nodded.

"Then go on home."

"What about you?" Mason asked.

"Me? I'll hang around for a little while, give the animal some water, make sure everything's secure."

"Okay, Ruby, we'll be in touch," Mason said, giving

Campbell a brief salute as he walked out. Josh Henley followed on his heels.

When Campbell was certain the two men had gone, he placed a container of water in the wooden crate with the small animal.

He wasn't certain if it was young enough to still need the warmth of its mother so he gathered up an old sleeping bag one of the men had left and wrapped it around the little animal. When he placed his hand on its head, it stirred, opened its eyes, and looked up at him.

"I don't think you belong here," he said.

It tried to nurse his thumb.

"Don't worry," he said, covering it carefully with the sleeping bag.

He went into the main room, closed the inner door behind him, sat down at the wooden table, and waited. There was no sound from the drying shed.

It wasn't long before a tall, gaunt man wearing a ski mask drifted into the room.

"Thought you were never coming," Campbell said.

"And I thought those guys of yours were never leaving. Wanted to make sure they were gone for good before I stuck my nose in," the man said, pushing up his ski mask, exposing his sharp profile.

"Ready to get to work?" Campbell asked.

"I've been ready for a couple of hours."

They both laughed quietly, then walked into the drying shed where the stranger, using a point-and-shoot camera with attached flash, began taking pictures of the galls. Then, working together, they took inventory.

"I'm going to take a couple of these dried galls with me," the stranger said.

Campbell nodded.

The small animal in the crate remained absolutely still and hidden under the sleeping bag.

When the two men were finished, they went back into the

main room, the stranger shook hands with Campbell, they set a date for their next meeting, and the stranger disappeared as silently as he had appeared.

Campbell sat for a while in deep thought.

After his decision was made, he walked outside and around the building to the drying shed—it was still pouring down rain—and with several determined kicks broke down the door.

He spread some of the small animal's scent on the outside of the door.

Then he went back around the outside of the building, walked inside through the main door, and into the drying shed where he picked up the broken door from the floor and propped it against the doorway.

"This way a cougar can't walk in and get you," he told the animal in the crate. "But if you have a relative out looking for you, one with hands like yours, it can get in and out of here."

He squatted down by the crate and pulled a corner of the sleeping bag off the small face. The little animal scrambled up and tried to suck his finger again.

"Good-bye now," Campbell said. "I hope I don't see you again."

Then he left, locking the main door carefully behind him. He got in his truck and, in spite of the heavy, sheeting rain, opened the window on the passenger side, and drove slowly away, listening.

When he heard that strange hoarse scream that wasn't exactly like the voice of a cougar, he smiled. He had suspected all along that what he'd heard before was not a cougar, that it was something entirely different. But he wasn't exactly sure what.

"If they're really out there," he said to himself, "I say leave them the hell alone. They'll be discovered soon enough."

Then his thoughts turned to Ole Olson and what to do about him. He decided he'd give the man a chance, but also a warning.

When Campbell got back home, he looked at his watch. It was two in the morning. He went inside his house quietly and walked into his study where he looked up Ole Olson's telephone number.

Knowing a call at two in the morning would make anybody sit up and take notice, he dialed the number. After several rings, the phone on the other end was picked up and a sleepy male voice said, "Yeah? Who's this?"

"It's the Holy Ghost, Olson, and I've got a message from God."

"What the hell—"

"Yard all those stolen logs in your hot deck back where you got them and the devil won't get you."

"Stolen logs? I don't steal logs."

"Just do it, Ole, or you'll be in a pisspot of trouble." Campbell slammed the phone down.

He knew Olson hadn't recognized his voice. What hardworking person recognizes anything when pulled from a deep sleep in the middle of the night?

He also knew that if the man had a lick of sense he'd move those stolen logs fast. Of course, it would cost him in time and labor, but that would be better than time in jail and paying a horrendous fine.

The people those logs belonged to were going to be logging their patch very soon. They wouldn't mind having a bunch of their logs already mysteriously cut, ready for their trucks.

4 The next morning Ruby Campbell's telephone rang early.

"It's gone," Irv Mason told him, rage boiling under his normally quite voice. "Stolen. We were followed last night. Must have been. The door to the drying shed was broken from the outside."

"I suspect you were," Campbell said, yawning.

"What'll we do about it?"

"Nothing. It's like fame and fortune, Irv. Easy come, easy go."

There was silence on the line, then Mason's voice, sharp with the edge of suspicion. "Sure you don't know anything about that Bigfoot, Ruby?"

"Say what you mean, Irv. Spit it out."

"Did you take that animal?"

"I did not. If you have to ask a question like that we'd better part company right here and now."

"Ah, come on now, Ruby. I didn't mean it that way. Let's just forget it?"

"Okay, Irv, we'll forget it, but I don't want to hear anything like that from you again."

That eagle's fate and mine are one,
Which on the shaft that made him die
Espied a feather of his own,
Wherewith he wont to soar so high.
—EDMUND WALLER (1605–1687)
To a Lady Singing a Song of His Composing

Chapter 19

1 Paul Prefontaine managed to do something few people thought possible. He had trained a bald eagle to accept him as master and to hunt upon his command.

When he'd found an injured eaglet missing a leg, one whose parents had obviously been taken by poachers, he received permission from the U.S. Fish and Wildlife people to care for the orphan, try to save its life.

He rigged up a false eagle's head inside of a cage and fed her through the beak, trying to get her to eat by pretending to be her mother. The deception worked, but he sometimes wondered if she didn't know very well that it was a man feeding her behind the mask of an eagle.

Prefontaine had watched enough bald eagles in the wild, and consulted with experts, to know that eaglets must be taught to fly, as well as to hunt and kill, by repeated demonstrations on the part of their parents.

Eaglets were not born knowing this. The knowledge was transmitted by learning, by the culture of their kind; in that sense their behavior was both natural and learned.

For the first few weeks the eaglet lived in a jury-rigged cage inside Prefontaine's house on Cape Elizabeth with its wide front porch and the ocean beating on the cliffs below. Prefontaine spent as much time with her as he could. When she grew older he moved her outside.

She stayed close, roosting in the fork of a small dead cedar blowdown Prefontaine had dragged onto his porch.

Since she did not know how to fly, her method of locomotion evolved into a bizarre walk using her one leg to jump along with the opposite wing held at an angle for balance.

"You and the eaglet are very similar," Jordan said one day when she and Tleyuk were visiting Prefontaine.

"How's that?"

"Well, you're both fierce and independent as hell. But you're also both sensible enough to exercise control. And you're both crippled."

"Crippled? There's nothing crippled about me."

"Yes there is. The eaglet has lost a leg."

"And me? I haven't lost a damn thing."

"You've lost your heart to an unattainable woman."

At Jordan's reference to Hannah McTavish, Prefontaine turned away and busied himself with preparing food for his eaglet.

As soon as possible he began training the young eagle to fly. But it was very difficult.

Because the eaglet looked on Prefontaine as her parent, she apparently could not understand what he wanted her to do since he could not set an example by doing it himself.

After much thought, Prefontaine borrowed a glider from a friend and, with the eaglet strapped to his body, her sharply lethal beak wrapped to prevent assaults upon his body, sailed off a series of high sand dunes, graduating eventually to the sea cliffs in front of his house. This activity could be practiced only when the tide was out, because when it was high, the sea washed against the bottom of the cliffs and there was very little beach.

Following a month of such gliding practiced three or four times a week, Prefontaine left the eaglet on top of the cliff while he sailed off without her.

As he descended, he yelled out the cries with which he had communicated to her from the beginning of their relationship.

She shrieked back but stayed where she was. He was discouraged, fearing his idea to teach her to fly was not going to work.

But when he took off on the fourth attempt, calling out for her to follow, she lifted her unsure wings as if finally getting the idea and shakily followed him.

Although it was not a star performance, she did manage to get from the top of the cliff to the shore below without injury to herself.

After several weeks of practice, the next step in the eaglet's training was teaching her to hunt, then kill and eat her prey.

Prefontaine studied this problem for some time, eventually deciding upon the method he would use.

To begin, he did not feed the eaglet for twenty-four hours. Hungry, she grew angry and slashed at him with her beak whenever he approached her without food.

He tied a live mallard duck to a stake on the sand below the cliff, loose enough so that the duck could move about. Then he sailed off the cliff, calling out to the eaglet as he went, landed, and waited for her arrival.

After she flew off the cliff and coasted to his side, and he was certain she was watching his every move, he wrung the duck's neck, slit open its belly, and waited until she went to the steaming carcass. She immediately got busy with beak and talons.

"You're a quick study, darling," he said, smiling at her. Her fiercely intent eyes stared back at him implacably.

After several days and several ducks, he did not kill the duck. He waited for the eaglet to do so, must do so, because she would not always have him to do her slaughtering for her.

He was pleased to see she had the idea down perfectly. She understood that ducks were food and they had to be immobilized to be eaten.

Soon the young eaglet was in her own element at last, riding the thermals, ascending higher and higher until Prefontaine, his heart in his throat, sometimes worried that she might never come back to him.

Now he needed to see if she was skillful enough to catch and kill her own food.

After Old Man Ahcleet had watched Prefontaine working with the young eagle for many long hours, he soon understood the high quality of her intelligence and courage.

Aware of the strong spiritual bond forming between the bird of prey and his great-grandson, Kla'xeqlax, the hunter, the old man came to believe she embodied the spirit of an eagle of legend that had belonged to Ahcleet's own great-grandfather.

Because Ahcleet felt she was indeed worthy, he asked and received Prefontaine's permission to name her Gwaxo, meaning "eagle" in the old language, which had been the name of the fabled eagle of the past.

Edward Eagleton, the cryptozoologist Prefontaine had met at Hannah's book party several months before, the man who, with his coloring and sharp profile, looked like an eagle himself, heard about the Quinault chief of police and his bird.

He called Prefontaine at headquarters with questions and received a polite invitation to come see for himself. By now Gwaxo was flying well.

So it was that on a very early morning in August that Paul, Jordan, who had come over for the occasion, Gwaxo, and Eagleton drove away in Prefontaine's truck, headed for a swampy meadow near Lake Quinault.

Today was to be Gwaxo's big test, the first time Prefontaine would set her against prey larger than herself. Serious business, indeed.

Visiting as they drove, Jordan told them about an eight-hundred-pound Roosevelt elk with calf that had recently treed a fisherman up in the Hoh rain forest.

"She chased people into their recreational vehicles and forced park rangers to temporarily close the campground," Jordan said.

"What was wrong with her?" Eagleton asked.

"Nothing was wrong with her. She was being a good mother," Jordan replied. "She gave birth to a calf about ten days ago in the campground. Rangers closed that section of it, but the elk cow and calf moved into other parts of the campground."

"It's her land," Prefontaine said.

"Actually, a cougar was spotted in the campground day before yesterday, possibly hunting the elk, so they decided to close the whole thing. With a cougar prowling around, the rangers didn't want the mother to waste energy chasing people and become weakened."

"You mean they didn't care about people getting hurt?" Eagleton asked.

Prefontaine and Jordan looked at each other. Neither of them replied.

The three humans drove in silence for a time, thinking about elk and cougars, while Gwaxo dozed or thought her own thoughts.

After a while, Prefontaine asked, "Mr. Eagleton, how are you coming with your research for hidden animals? Found anything yet?"

Eagleton gave an enigmatic smile. "Like most worthwhile searches, it is still ongoing. Thank you for your interest, Chief Prefontaine."

When they reached their destination, they saw that a V-shaped flight of geese was flying far out across the meadow in a leisurely descending circle, then coming back low, flying into the sun.

"It's perfect," Prefontaine told Jordan and Eagleton. "She'll have the sun behind her when she towers."

After they got out of the truck, all three admired Gwaxo's dignity as Prefontaine slipped the soft leather hood off her head, not yet white because of her youth.

Her large yellow eyes slowly opened like small suns and swiftly focused on Prefontaine.

She shook out her feathers, swelled in size, puffed out her breast, then stretched the toes on her one taloned foot without lifting her leg.

When Gwaxo looked up into the heavens and saw the thick black skein of geese against the sky, fully lighted by the sun, her body began to vibrate as if filling too fast with energy.

"Hunt!" Prefontaine cried and launched her, throwing her clear of the brush and tall meadow grass surrounding them.

She ascended like a shot arrow, towering for the sun and the geese.

When the geese saw her, they stalled back on wings that were suddenly ungainly with shock.

Their tight V-shaped formation broke up as each bird turned away, two of them rising, driving hard for height.

A third bird swung east again going for the river, dropped height steeply to pick up speed he had lost in the initial stall, then leveled out low and winged hard, neck outstretched, webbed feet tucked up under his tail.

Meanwhile, Gwaxo was still towering, ascending up and up and up on wings that blurred with speed.

Prefontaine pointed out how Gwaxo was moving like the instinctive killer she was, striving for every inch of height that she could achieve, knowing even in her youth and inexperience that she desperately needed to exchange height for speed when she began her stoop.

Because she was still young and smaller than she would be after she was full grown, her body weight was lighter than the huge birds she was hunting. She seemed to realize that she must kill with shock and speed.

Even as she went up her head was twisted to the side, watching, judging, as the game scattered below her.

Geese were not her natural prey, although ducks were. And nature had not yet equipped her for the shock of binding to something so massive. The difference in size between hunter and hunted was emphasized as still she climbed.

Abruptly Gwaxo reached the height she judged sufficient. She hovered, literally standing in the air for twelve beats of Prefontaine's own heart as he watched her.

Suddenly she screamed the terrible death cry of the great bald eagle, high and shrill and fierce, folded her wings, and dropped into her stoop.

She had selected the goose that had dropped closest to earth and was even now crossing her front view at an acute angle.

She fell out of the blue heavens like a meteor plunging from the night sky. They could hear the wind hissing through her half-cocked wings, see the infinitesimal movements of her tip feathers with which she controlled the awful headlong plunge.

Meanwhile, the targeted goose flogged the air, heavy, massive, attempting to flee, its panic evident in each beat of its frantic wings.

The speed with which Gwaxo closed was chilling.

As the young eagle approached her prey, she reached forward with the steel-like talons on her one leg.

Watching, Prefontaine felt the hair on the nape of his neck

come erect as though an icy wind had touched him. This was the moment for which he and Gwaxo had worked and trained so long.

The supreme moment of the kill.

As Gwaxo bound to the goose, the sound of the hit was like a single beat of a great bass cello, which shook the very air about their heads.

Prefontaine's eyes filled with tears. An involuntary cry burst from Jordan's throat and Eagleton stared upward as if transfixed.

The spread wings of the doomed goose spun like the spokes of a wheel, and a burst of feathers filled the air as though a shrapnel shell had been fired from a cannon.

The goose's body collapsed under the shock, one wing broke off and trailed down the sky as it fell, the long serpentine goose neck arching back in the death convulsions.

Gwaxo remained bound to the goose, her talons locked deep into the still frantically beating heart. The impetus of Gwaxo's swoop had shattered bone in the big goose body and burst the pulsing blood vessels around its heart.

Now Prefontaine began to worry.

For at this point Gwaxo should break and let the goose fall, but she did not. She was still locked in.

He feared that she herself had broken bone or been otherwise injured by the force of impact.

Then, to his great relief, Gwaxo lunged, unbinding, breaking loose from her kill, hovering, letting the goose go on to thud into the swampy earth of the meadow, only then sinking, with grace and poise, to settle upon the humped carcass.

Gwaxo began to feed.

"Hell of a bird," Eagleton said, obviously impressed. "You've done a great job with her, Chief Prefontaine. It's the spirit that counts, you know."

Prefontaine was looking in the other direction.

"Whose spirit?" Jordan asked. "Gwaxo's or Paul's?"

He studied her, then said, "Both, of course. Now if you'll

excuse me while Gwaxo dines, I'm going to take a walk around."

He sauntered off through the underbrush.

"I love that damn bird," Prefontaine said as he turned back to Jordan, unashamedly wiping the tear tracks from his face. "Too young to do what she just did and crippled besides."

"I'm beginning to love her, too."

Prefontaine looked at Jordan and smiled, pleased at the rapport his sister obviously felt with the young eagle.

After Eagleton was out of earshot, Prefontaine said quietly, "What do you think of that guy?"

"I don't think he is what he claims to be."

"Neither do I. What makes you feel that way?"

"Lots of things. Most recently, the way he asked what was wrong with the mother elk. If he's really looking for so-called hidden animals, he should at least know the basics about the ones out in the open he *can* see."

"Who do you think he is?"

"I'm not sure, Paul. Right now, my mind is so full of Gwaxo I can hardly think of anything else. When she was up there in the sky, standing on air, it seemed that I could see through her eyes. Thank you for bringing me with you, for letting me have this experience."

"I thought a little outing might be a good thing right about now. For all of us, you and me and Gwaxo."

They sat cross-legged on the ground, waiting for Gwaxo to finish her meal

The rain forest semicircled around them, here and there sending exploratory fingers down into the meadow where in the old days Quinault women came to dig for the starchy roots of camas, plants with brilliant blue flowers.

Summer was at full tide and the air was vibrant with the scent of growing things. The trees rustled and sang their summer songs. Pitch glowed in the fir cones.

In the floods of fragrance, both Prefontaine and Jordan could distinguish the sweet perfumes of the cedar trees, the sharp, clean tang of firs, the resiny smell of spruce, the cold freshness of hemlocks.

And as an undertone, the aroma of the thousand and more species of plants that flourished here; all the new life continually springing from old and cushioning every square inch.

For a long while neither of them spoke, but that was not strange. Frequently there was no need for words between them.

Since before their births, while still entwined in the womb, they had both drawn spiritual and physical sustenance from the great trees breathing all around their mother, and from the great sea sending up its mists to nourish her.

Prefontaine finally spoke, his voice touched with humor. "Remember what Grandfather has always told us about that white fungi growing over there on some of the big trees?"

"The *t'owok*? Sure I do. He says echoes are caused by sound striking the fungi which, being shaped like ears, send the sound back."

Their gentle laughter expressed their deep love for the old man who had raised and cared for them, spiritually as well as physically.

After another comfortable silence, he said, "Nothing new on the murders?"

What he really wanted to ask Jordan about was her love life but there was something about her today that made him suspect that now was not the time.

Jordan shook her head. "It's as if witches came in the night, did their evil deeds, and vanished."

"Those witches have human faces, Sis."

"I know that, Paul. The girl's murder was bad enough, God knows, but there's something about the boy's killing that bothers me even more, if that's possible. It's just too weird. I mean the way his face was mutilated."

"Too tribal, you mean?"

"Yes, like stories from the old days. When people believed animals could lift up their muzzles and become human."

"And pull them down and become animals again. Sis, do you really think an Indian did it?"

"Do you?"

"I don't know what to believe. Why not take another look around the murder scene?"

"The FBI's been over everything. You know how thorough they are."

"Don't forget that you have a different perspective."

Head in hands, elbows on knees, chewing on a sweet August weed and gazing into the distance, Jordan nodded. What Paul had said was true.

With her special talents as a woman and a shaman, along with being one of The People, perhaps she could find something, anything, that would have been meaningless by itself to the other investigators.

"The FBI vacuumed up everything and put it through a sieve," she said morosely. "But I'll go."

With a smile in his voice, Prefontaine asked her if she'd like him to come along.

"Yes, I would, Paul. I always feel better when you're around."

To his surprise, he saw that she was serious.

Encouraged to boldness by her response, he said, "How's your love life? Anything work out with that guy from Chile?"

She replied slowly, "I've never felt like this about anybody in my life."

"Not even, if you'll pardon the expression, Roc Tidewater?"

She shrugged. "He was a young girl's aberration."

Wisely, Prefontaine did not remind her that he had tried to tell her so at the time but she would not listen to him. Instead, he said, "You're in love is all."

"That's what I thought at first. But it's more than that. Or less."

"You mean sex?"

"Not altogether. It's a connection of some sort that I can't leave alone. And there is a lot about him that I simply admire."

"His foreignness, maybe. I would say that he's an international man."

"I sense something else, almost a darkness, and that rouses my curiosity. What kind of darkness is it? The darkness of unknown, to me, at least, spiritual beliefs? When I question myself, my reason tells me that Lima Clemente is what he is, a different kind of man from a different place, almost a different time."

"Are you afraid of him, Sis?"

Her face a sudden mask of misery, she said, "What I'm afraid of is that because of my fascination with him I'll neglect my work or make the wrong decisions. Something that could hurt Tleyuk or Grandfather or you. Or myself. That I'll lose my sense of place."

"La'qewamax."

To underline the seriousness of their discussion Prefontaine used Jordan's real name, the name Old Man Ahcleet had given her at birth.

"You are a very strong-minded and spiritually powerful woman. I cannot imagine that any physical passion could sway you from what you know is your place."

"That's the problem. It's far more than physical. I feel as if I'm losing control, that my foundations are crumbling."

"What does your guardian spirit tell you?"

"It remains silent."

"And the rituals?"

She shook her head.

"Why not?"

"I haven't tried. And I know why."

"Tell me, honey."

"It's because I can't concentrate. My mind is filled with him. And that's terrifying. I need to observe the Klokwalle ceremony, but I fear that nothing would come when I called."

"Klokwalle. The spirit that inspires courage." Prefontaine whistled. "That's a rough one, Sis, but it sounds to me like you've got to do it. For what it's worth, count me in. And about this Mr. Lima Clemente. Why don't I just simplify the whole thing and run him off?"

"On what grounds?"

"I could probably dig around and find something."

"I already have. The FBI, Interpol. There's nothing." She looked off at Gwaxo, still busy with her food. "We've been talking about my love life. What about yours?"

"What love life?"

"Hannah McTavish, of course."

"She's married and her husband is a good guy who isn't dead anymore."

"I know that, Paul. Do you sometimes wish we hadn't found and rescued him?"

And that was a question that could only be asked and answered by two people as close to each other as Paul and Jordan were; a truthful answer required painful, unflattering honesty.

"Sometimes I feel that way. Yes. It's good to be able to say it out loud."

"No question of you two meeting each other on the side?"

"Me?" Prefontaine looked surprised. "Of course not. I'm not the type to sneak around strange motel rooms. Not Hannah either."

"Actually, I already knew that. But are you going to pine away for Hannah until you're too old to move?"

"I won't settle for second best, Sis. If someone comes along that I feel as strongly about as I feel about Hannah, then we'll see."

She sighed. "You know something, Paul," she said. "You're as crazy as I am."

He put his arm around his sister and held her quietly, remembering the youthful first love he had felt for his wife, how her subsequent unfaithfulness had made him physically sick, how deeply her death had grieved him.

And he thought about the consuming mature love he felt for Hannah McTavish, how it seemed she was part of him although he had never even made love to her.

"Sometimes I think love is a sickness, Sis," he said. "All I can do is hope you get over it."

"I hope we both do."

When they saw that Gwaxo had finished her meal and Edward Eagleton was returning from his ramble, they stood up and moved toward the truck.

The goal of life is living in agreement with nature.
—ZENO, ancient philosopher (335–263 B.C.)
Diogenes Laertius, Lives of Eminent Philosophers

𝕄

Chapter 20

1 After they returned to Cape Elizabeth, Edward Eagleton thanked Prefontaine for the privilege of watching his eagle at work and departed, promising that he would notify them both when he found signs of Bigfoot or, as the Quinault Indians called them, Seatco.

Gwaxo settled down on her special cedar branch on the front porch and closed her eyes, as if mentally rising above all matters human.

Prefontaine and Jordan both had glasses of iced lemonade after which Paul looked at his sister and said, "Now?"

"Why not?" she replied.

* * *

They took off in her power wagon, headed for the place in the forest where a little boy had met a terrible death.

Jordan saw that everything looked about the same as it had in April, except that now, in late August, there was even more foliage.

The trees and underbrush were just a little dryer but still intensely green. Douglas firs, loaded with seeds, fired off intermittent fusillades of ripe brown cones.

Ripening huckleberries, those wonderfully delicious small lipstick-red ones, grew everywhere, out of the tops of tree stumps and from the base of trees.

It was a good year. The bushes were loaded with berries. No bear had found this patch as yet.

The bloodstains on the ground were gone but those inside the boulder were still there, although faded.

Jordan shivered at the memory of what she had seen here before and at the thought of the unknown person or persons who had created violent death, residues of which were in the air all around her.

Would she ever see the killer's face?

She suspected that the face of murder looked perfectly normal in everyday life. Was it possible she had already seen that face behind the mask of professional duty or friendship?

"Who did this thing?" she asked aloud. "Why was it done?"

"Not a sex nut," Prefontaine replied. "The boy wasn't molested in that way."

She stood, chin in hand, studying the area. "The murderer's style doesn't fit anything in the FBI records."

"I hate to say this, Sis, but the more I think about it the more I'm afraid it's got to be some crazy Indian. But who?"

"All the agencies are working very hard on this case. So far there's nothing. Nothing but the remains of a child as yet unburied."

* * *

"Center yourself, La'qewamax," Prefontaine said softly.

Jordan stood very still, arms upraised, and after several moments shouted a Calling-on-Guardians prayer.

Inhaling deeply, she soon felt reassuring power flowing from the center of her being down to her feet and up through the top of her head and back, again and again, until she was the center of a shield of power.

"I am ready," she told Prefontaine quietly.

They began the search by sifting through forest debris with their bare hands, getting slivers (the worst kind being the infinitesimal ones they could not see), whispering small curses, pulling the slivers out with the tweezers from Jordan's Swiss army knife, touching the granite boulder inside and out with sore, sensitive, inquisitive fingers, hearing the fir cones banging down all around them, occasionally getting hit themselves.

"A small boy died here in a terrible way," Jordan said, as if their purpose needed to be stated clearly in out-loud words. "We need to find out who killed him."

"Have you any sense at all of the cast of characters?" Prefontaine asked.

Jordan shook her head, remembering the welter of feelings when she'd held the boy's cold, turgid head in her gloved hands.

"Only feelings from the boy himself."

They began to search again.

When they were losing the light, they sat down to rest for a few minutes before leaving.

One fir cone, executing a Parthian shot, thudded down between Jordan's outstretched legs. She looked up and saw Raven sitting on a branch above her. He cocked his head at Jordan, then flew off.

She picked up the cone.

"Careful," Prefontaine warned. "Those things are full of pitch."

"I know."

She turned the fir cone around and around in her hands,

ignoring the pitch, getting it all over her hands, peering at the cone from all possible angles.

She was drawn by something.

Something . . .

She took the Swiss army knife from her pocket once more, selected the tweezers, and pried at the cone until a tiny object fell into her hand.

"What's that?" Prefontaine asked, moving closer.

She showed it to him, cupped in the palm of her hand.

"Looks to me like a small link of some kind. Brass, I suspect." He studied the object, then said, "But stuffed in a fir cone?"

"Maybe it wasn't stuffed, Paul."

He looked at her questioningly.

"Maybe it flew. You know, out of or from something being done here on the ground."

"I wonder what the FBI found."

"Come on. Let's get back. I'll give Hunter a call."

Prefontaine helped her put the link and the fir cone in two separate plastic bags, then Jordan held her hands up all the way back to her brother's house on Cape Elizabeth where she could get some mechanics' soap and scrub the pitch off.

2 When they arrived at the Enforcement Center in Taholah Jordan and Prefontaine went directly to Paul's office where, because of the lateness of the hour, Jordan called Hunter Kleoh at his home.

"Get on the other phone," she told her brother when the connection had been made.

"Hunter, this is Jordan," she began, quickly adding that the chief of police of Taholah was on the line.

"Hi, there, Jordan, Paul. What can I do for you folks?"

"We'd like to know what your investigators found up on the site of the boy's murder," Jordan replied.

"You never got a copy of that list?"

"Never even saw one."

"I'll be damned. That must have been an oversight. It's in the office, of course, but I also have a copy in my files at home. So what do you want me to do? If it's urgent I'll be happy to run a copy up there tonight."

"Thanks, Hunter, but I don't think that's necessary." She thought for a moment. "Is it possible you could read the list to us on the phone?"

"Now?"

"I know it's a lot to ask, interfering with your evening, but we would both deeply appreciate the accommodation, Hunter."

Kleoh laughed. "Don't worry about *my* evening. There's nothing but garbage on television and I'm out of beer. Only thing is, that list will really bend your ears. It's a hell of a long one. I think they saved every speck of dirt."

"That's okay, Hunter," Prefontaine said.

"Sure, then, hang on a minute."

Soon he was back. "Ready?"

"Shoot," Jordan said.

Kleoh read off a seemingly endless list ranging from a count of fir and spruce needles, including the number of needles that were bloodstained and those that were not, to leaves, bits of sticks, rocks, and pebbles.

Jordan and Paul wondered about one item described as an eight-inch piece of wood, evenly cut at each end, smooth, no bark, and one inch in diameter for its entire length.

Another item caught their attention: a two-inch piece of brass chain made up of small links, each link measuring one eighth of an inch in length.

"I've got photographs of everything on this list," Kleoh said.

Jordan looked at Paul. "I'll be down first thing in the morning," she told Kleoh.

"Great, how about breakfast on me?"

On him? Jordan quickly banished the visual of a bare

belly that had flown into her mind and replied, "I will already have eaten, but thanks anyway."

"Lunch, then?"

"Let's see how our time goes. Okay?"

"Sure, Jordan. Say, about that all-agency meeting in Seattle, you are going, I assume?"

"Of course."

"How about we go in my car, save you the trouble of driving?"

"That would be fine, Hunter. Paul will be coming, too. And thanks again for everything."

After she hung up, she looked at Prefontaine, whose eyebrows had risen into dark half-moons.

"I am?" he asked.

"You are what?"

"Going with you to Seattle."

"Yes, as chief of police it's your duty."

"Dare I ask when this is happening?"

"Day after tomorrow."

"Do you really want me there or is it just to dilute things between you and our FBI man?"

"A little of both, actually."

"Well, Sis, it's a good thing I'm your brother or I might be pissed."

"About what?"

"About being moved around like a chess piece." He stood up, reached over, and ruffled her crisp, black curls. "Although it will be a good chance to see Roy, if he's home."

Royal Mercer was a learned and famous anthropologist whose father and grandfather had been close personal friends of Old Man Ahcleet. As far back as Jordan and Paul could remember, Royal, although he was white, had seemed a member of their family, had, in fact, been adopted into the Quinault Nation.

Nowadays Mercer traveled the world speaking to various scientific organizations: consequently no one was ever certain when he could be found at his Seattle home.

"He's home. I checked," she assured him. "Want to go with me tomorrow to see Hunter's pictures?"

"I wouldn't miss it for the world."

In Hunter Kleoh's office the next morning Jordan and Paul checked over the photographs that accompanied the extensive list of items taken from the murder scene of the dismembered boy.

When they came to the photo of the two-inch length of brass chain made up of small links, Jordan showed Kleoh the glassine envelope containing one small link. It seemed to match the FBI photograph.

"Where did you get this?" Kleoh asked.

"From inside this fir cone, oozing pitch, that happened to fall between my legs," she replied, showing him the second plastic bag. "Probably has nothing to do with the case but we never know, do we?"

She left both possible evidential items with him to be turned over to the lab for detailed inspection.

3   That night Jordan received a call from Lima Clemente who was in Seattle and would be leaving for Vancouver, B.C., early the following morning.

He was to be interviewed for a feature article in an international construction industry magazine regarding the building of roads into the coming Chilean logging shows. While in Vancouver he said he would also inspect the lines of several machinery manufacturers.

"I have just returned to my hotel from seeing Xavier off at SeaTac," he said.

"Where's he going?"

"Back to Santiago. There is much preparation to be started for our logging convention next year."

"I suppose you'll be leaving soon, too." There was sadness in Jordan's voice.

"Not until absolutely necessary, darling. And I will be back. Listen now. I have something important to tell you."

"What is it, Lima?"

"Tonight the moon is full."

"Yes."

"Remember what I told you about the moonstone? How one of its powers is to foretell the future?"

"I remember."

"Before telephoning you, I stood under the full moon with the moonstone in my mouth. It told me that I will go back to Chile from time to time but never again to stay. That I will never truly leave you and your beautiful edge of the world. My new home will be there by the sea and the forest with you."

Later Jordan called Hunter Kleoh to tell him she and Paul would take her car as Old Man Ahcleet was coming with them. Kleoh tried to keep the disappointment out of his voice.

4   There were twenty people present in the conference room, each of whom represented federal, state, county, or Quinault Nation law enforcement agencies.

Eli Raptor, agent in charge of the Seattle office of the FBI, opened the meeting by asking for general comments regarding the two unsolved murders on the peninsula.

Jasper Wright spoke about the Adams girl, saying that his officers had found no evidence that she or her family were known by anyone living in the area of the crime.

"To my way of thinking, it had to be one of those hit-and-run killings," he concluded. "Some wacko staying at the lodge at the same time as the family and long gone by now. Or a hiker she encountered on one of the trails, also equally gone."

Hunter Kleoh shook his head. "It wasn't just a onetime encounter, Jasper. Couldn't have been. Whoever had that little girl abused her for a long time, considering the amount of semen from the same excretor found on and in her body."

"The bastard didn't miss a trick," one of the state detectives said. "Sodomy, sexual penetration with a foreign object, rape, mutilation."

"Mutilation?" Jasper Wright asked.

"Sure. Bastard cut off her nipples and her clitoris."

"Had a guy like that down in Oregon a couple of years ago," Raptor commented. "About forty, leading businessman, well groomed, lived in the same town of thirty-five hundred his whole life, active in his church, a model citizen, you know the type. Had lots of invitations to Sunday dinners from mothers with marriageable daughters.

"But what nobody knew was that this guy's real business was killing prostitutes, which was bad enough, but the law enforcement people in Oregon suspected he was also going after the young boys in his church. He was always inviting one or two on overnight fishing and camping trips.

"Well, the Oregon cops set up a sting operation, couple of them, as a matter of fact. Planted two real young-looking state troopers in the church youth group, and sure enough within a couple of weeks the newcomers had an invitation to go fishing. Bastard got caught with his pants down and everything out and ready for business.

"While those charges were pending, a couple of women deputy sheriffs volunteered to play prostitutes for a few nights and they got him cold, too.

"About this time the confessions began rolling out of the suspect like sweat. And there turned out to be a ton of physical evidence. To make a long story short, Romeo is in the Oregon state pen for life. He'd killed thirty-six women that the cops could find. Claimed to have killed more."

Eli Raptor paused, then sighed. "I got a funny feeling about your guy, though. I don't think he's going to be that simple."

"Eli, we've checked the backgrounds on most of the lodge guests who were there at the same time period as the Adams family," Kleoh said. "They're all clean."

"Most?" Raptor asked.

"You've got to remember that some of those foreigners who came up for the logging congress arrived a few days early. You know, to explore, take pictures, just generally look around," Kleoh replied. "Don't forget there were Russians and Japanese there, also. It takes longer to check foreigners out but we're working on it."

"Any of them still around?" Raptor asked.

The members of the group looked at each other questioningly. Prefontaine spoke up.

"A couple of men, business partners from Santiago, are still in the area. Matter of fact, they've taken a six-month lease on a house on North Shore Road."

"What for?"

"They're looking into American-made logging equipment to be shipped down to their business in Chile. Buying heavily, I understand. Salesmen are grinning from ear to ear. Towers, loaders, skidders, cable, chain saws, the works. That kind of thing takes time. When they're through around here I understand they're going to the Midwest to look into logging trucks and trailers."

"All of that stuff going to Chile?"

"Yep. Middle of next year they're planning a big logging convention in Santiago. The Chilean government is letting several hundred huge contracts for logging national timber lands."

"Do we know anything about these two guys?"

Jordan considered telling them that Xavier Escoro had already departed the area but decided she did not want anyone in the group to suspect her close relationship with Lima Clemente.

"I checked them out through Interpol and the FBI," she said. "They're exactly what they seem. Two business partners who are already rich and planning on getting much richer. Internationally their credit is triple A, as are their reputations."

After a coffee break, Jordan talked about the unusual mutilations in the murder of the young boy. She told the group about the ancient Native American belief that animals could become people and people become animals at will.

"Considering what people are doing these days that's putting a bad rap on animals," Raptor said, studying her. "You're inclined to think the boy's murder could have been done by an Indian. Am I right?"

"It's a possibility to be considered."

"Do you have any leads in that direction?"

"I have suspicions but nothing I can lay on the table. Not yet."

"Of course you realize that we are in charge of the investigation but anything you can find out will certainly help us. And we would be most appreciative. I think you know me well enough to believe what I am saying," Raptor said.

"I know that, Eli."

Raptor leaned back in his chair, hands behind his head. "We've not been able to match those fingerprints you found at the scene, Jordan," he said.

"There were a lot of strangers around," she replied.

"One hell of a lot. Russians, Japanese, and especially Central and South Americans. But we're not finished. Not by a long shot. We're still checking the prints."

Jordan told the group about the colorful woven wool ribbon she had found on the beach, how its threads matched the threads taken from the boy's beheaded body.

She did not mention the damaged gold medallion and she did not know exactly why not, except that whenever she thought of talking about it she felt her guardian spirit very close, as if in warning.

Hunter Kleoh presented a report on the tiny brass link Jordan had found in a fallen fir cone, adding that it had gone to the lab for identification, to see if it belonged to the length of brass chain found at the boy's murder scene.

"So for the moment what we have in the way of evidence are some as yet unidentified fingerprints, a couple of threads, and maybe a small link from a brass chain. Am I correct?" Raptor said.

"Looks like that's about it," Kleoh said.

Raptor steepled his hands. "We all know that in police work most felonies get solved one of three ways. You get a tip from an informant. Circumstantial evidence leads you to the perp or the bad guy makes a mistake and gets caught red-handed. Or he simply confesses."

"There is another way, Eli," Jordan said quietly.

"So I understand."

The meeting adjourned soon after and Eli Raptor asked Jordan to stay on. She agreed and told Prefontaine she'd meet him back at the hotel.

"Jordan, I want to talk with you about what you called 'the other way' to solve a crime," Raptor said.

"That's what I suspected," she replied, smiling.

"We're talking about psychic stuff, aren't we?"

"You could call it that, I guess."

"I've heard that you've become a shaman."

She looked at him steadily, then nodded.

"I remember that case a couple of years ago out your way where some crazy Indian was burying living people under totem poles. You nailed that guy, as I recall."

"His name was Tuco Peters. He was a very sick young man."

"You mean crazy? What was wrong with him?"

"I suppose the white world would call him crazy. But he was sick. Sick with frustration and envy."

"Do you think our doctors would have given such a diagnosis?"

"They would be wrong if they did not."

"What was he so frustrated and envious about?"

"All of his life he had wanted to be a shaman."

"So why didn't he just study or do whatever he had to do to become one?"

"It wasn't possible for him."

"Wasn't he smart enough?"

"Oh, he was plenty smart."

"Then what was the problem? If you don't mind telling me, that is."

"The problem was that he was descended from slaves. In his culture that made it impossible for him to ever become a shaman."

"In this day and age?"

"Yes, Eli. Not everyone is Presbyterian or Catholic or Lutheran."

Eli Raptor rubbed a hand over his face. "Talk about xenophobic. Anyway, sick or crazy or whatever, I don't recall that case ever coming to trial."

"It didn't. Tuco Peters died trying to run away."

"That certainly simplified things, didn't it?"

"Nobody shot him, Eli. He died falling from a cliff. As far as we know he was alone when it happened."

"All right, Jordan. Tell me this. How did you personally know that this Tuco Peters was the guilty party?"

"I'd suspected him for some time because I was aware of his cultural background, of his one great desire in life, of his frustrations.

"Late one afternoon during a terrible storm I watched the wind and water washing away much of the ground at the base of a totem pole on the shore at Lake Quinault, leaving quite beautiful patterns in the sand. I began thinking of patterns of life. Tuco Peters's life.

"And I heard a voice telling me to search for things of the spirit with my spirit."

"Where did the voice come from? Inside your own head?"

"You might say it came from Raven, Bear, Salmon, and Eagle."

"I don't understand. That sounds like a chorus. Where were these animals?"

"They were carved on the totem pole. Their spirits, the Listening Ones, spoke to me."

"Fascinating stuff, Jordan. But you couldn't take that to court."

"No. But very soon I found the physical evidence to prove Tuco Peters's guilt. Had he not died trying to escape you would have had an airtight case for the U.S. attorney."

"I believe all you've been telling me, Jordan, and I appreciate your frankness. I don't understand it but I would like to. Is this thing that you do called psychic perception?"

"Partly. Perception itself is creative. Like all other forms of creation, it yields results in proportion to effort. We humans determine our own energy level. We decide what is boring and what is exciting. Most of us have plenty of reserve energy, plenty of reason for being glad to be alive."

"Then why are so many people just dragging themselves along?"

"They've simply allowed themselves to lose sight of the joy of living through excessive preoccupation with trivialities."

"Is there a course of study I could take to understand all of this?"

"There are those who give courses but I'm not sure I'd recommend any of them." Jordan's answer was based on her knowledge of her ex-husband, Roc Tidewater, the mushroom guru.

"I can recommend one or two books," she went on. "But most important would be a long period of time by yourself, with no radio or television or close neighbors, out in the forest, where you give yourself over to your innermost thoughts, the ones you don't even know you have. Give yourself time for what's deep inside to come to the surface. You might not like what comes at first but that's beside the point. And it's only the first step."

"What happens next?"

Jordan did not answer directly. Instead, she said, "Eli, a

human being generates a lot of energy. Different people generate different kinds of electromagnetic energy. Haven't you met people whom you know at first sight are just plain bad?"

Raptor laughed. "In our line of work? A hell of a lot."

"I knew Tuco Peters was wrong, sick, but I had to wait and watch for the evidence that could convict him in a court of law."

Studying Raptor, Jordan wondered if this man could ever believe in or even try to understand the power and meaning of mystical experience.

By necessity he was pragmatic, excellently trained in his field, a man of charts, graphs, percentages, recidivism rates, things that could be entered into computers, put down in black and white columns.

But the ways of the human animal were not black and white. They were many-colored, many-faceted, springing from past experience, from genetic demands, from character and personality.

Search for things of the spirit with your spirit.

She remembered the words all right.

Search, Shaman, search . . .

And she had.

She had searched and she had found.

The ability was in her lineages, her genetic code.

But it was nothing she could truly explain to a man like Eli Raptor, although he obviously wanted the knowledge and his desire to learn seemed more than idle curiosity.

She decided to give him words he could think about after she had gone. He could do with the words whatever he wished. Perhaps he would want deeper knowledge. Perhaps she would reveal more to him.

Later.

"Some researchers say that psychic perception, like our familiar sense of sight, smell, hearing, may depend upon a sense organ adapted to its own sensory field," she said.

"What organ is that?"

"The temporal lobes of the brain. They may function as a sense organ for psi. Until recently no sensory field was known that this hypothetical sense organ might respond to.

"But with the recent verification of the existence of gravitational waves, the medium through which they travel, space-time has also been verified.

"Apparently the temporal lobes are well adapted to this field because of their orientation to the past. While the familiar senses place the body in space, the temporal lobes place it in time. Space-time may also be the medium for psi interactions."

Raptor was following her with intense interest. "What prevents one brain, through enhanced temporal lobes or some other variation, from perceiving more than another brain?" he asked.

"I don't know, Eli. But remember that the other senses in humans vary. Some of us have stronger senses of smell, keener senses of taste and touch, stronger vision and hearing."

"That's true enough," Raptor said. "I, for example, cannot smell my wife's perfume, which she tells me is very expensive. It really pisses her off."

"I can imagine that it does," Jordan replied with a smile. "It's strange, but among all animals the degree of sensory development is even more diverse.

"Dogs can hear sounds we cannot," she went on, "but because we don't hear them do the sounds not exist? A cat's eye requires only a fraction of the light needed by the human eye to see an object."

"You've really piqued my interest, Jordan. I'd like to go into this more completely." He checked his desk calendar. "Is it possible we could continue this discussion at dinner tonight?"

She realized that Raptor was not trying to hit on her. He was deadly serious.

"I would like that, Eli, but I have another engagement."

He nodded. "Maybe some other time."

She agreed pleasantly, stood, and shook hands with him.

"Since I've kept you, let me run you back to your hotel," he said.

She politely gave the standard refusal.

"I'll not hear another word. I'm going out anyway. Come along now."

They left the offices of the FBI together.

Before she got out of the car at her hotel, she said, "Eli, I've got an idea. My dinner date tonight is with my brother, my great-grandfather, and Royal Mercer. You may have heard of him."

"The anthropologist? Who hasn't?"

"Why don't you join us? I would like that very much and so would the others in the group."

"I'm flattered. Tell me the time and place and I'll be there with bells on."

On the way back to his office, Eli Raptor thought about how much more there was to Jordan Tidewater than met the eye.

She was a beautiful woman. A blind man could see that. But that was the least of her qualities. She was an excellent police officer. Her work proved it.

It was just too damned bad they hadn't gotten her in their ranks. Couple of years ago she was all set to go back to Quantico and then something happened on the reservation, he never knew what, and she changed her mind.

He wondered if whatever had happened had something do with her becoming a shaman.

He wanted to get to know her better. He suspected that in some way he did not yet understand she had a lot to offer law enforcement.

He personally had always operated on the belief that human beings were just skin bags of chemicals and electrical impulses. But who knew?

Hell, before meteorites were seen to fall in 1803 by the experts themselves, scientists thought that reports of stones falling from the sky were legends, fables told by crazies.

*There is one area, at least, where I find that peoples of tradition are
more advanced than we: the powers of the mind. As Westerners, we
have come to accept the tenets of science: that whatever cannot be
experimentally proven must be false; that whatever cannot be explained
rationally must be fake; that whatever cannot be duplicated in a
laboratory must be sheer fraud.*

*Yet I have experienced a mystical and often frightening world, in
which human beings seemingly involve the powers of the spirits. I have
met people who have chosen to use their powers not for economic or
technological advancement, but for cultural and spiritual survival. . . .
These powers come from the repetition of age-old ceremonies, and their
effectiveness has insured the survival of different societies
for many centuries.*

—DOUCHAN GERSI,
Faces in the Smoke

Chapter 21

1   Jordan, Paul, and Old Man Ahcleet were enjoying
a late dinner that night with Royal Mercer in Seattle.
When Eli Raptor of the FBI arrived, without the bells he
had promised but with a big friendly smile, Jordan introduced him to Old Man Ahcleet and Royal Mercer, each of
whom gave him a warm welcome.

The restaurant, in business over one hundred years in the
same location, sat on ancient pilings sunk deep in Puget
Sound.

The tablecloths were white linen, the napkins white
damask, the servers swift and courteous, the food superb.

Most of the interior lighting came from numerous candles

that served to draw diners' attention to the dramatic view through nine large plate-glass windows.

Outside flamed a furious sunset, seeming to gush its colors volcanically onto the gray-green surface of the Sound, whose deep waters they could feel surging against unseen pilings beneath their feet.

Lighted ferries, coming and going, moved like twinkling fireflies between the Seattle docks and the San Juan Islands.

Royal Mercer was one of those fortunate men who grow better looking with age. His thick, graying hair fell in waves to his shoulders; his precisely trimmed goatee lent a certain sinister charm to his otherwise round friendly American face. Looking at him, Jordan decided that every man needed a touch of the devil about him somewhere.

Jordan, Mercer, and Prefontaine ordered razor clams while Eli Raptor said he'd have the prime rib, bloody; better yet, still bellowing if at all possible.

Prefontaine quietly suggested scallops to his great-grandfather.

"Why?" Old Man Ahcleet asked.

Dropping his voice yet lower, Prefontaine said, "They'd be easier for you to eat, Grandfather. Because of your teeth."

"That's all right," Old Man Ahcleet responded. "I've always liked scallops. They taste like *wi'qectq,* you know."

Nonplussed, hoping the rest of the party had not overheard or understood their conversation, Prefontaine said even more quietly, "And how long has it been, Grandfather, since you've tasted *wi'qectq?*"

Ahcleet looked at his great-grandson with hauteur. "Not so long as you might think."

Prefontaine was not clear if Old Man Ahcleet was still talking about scallops or women and he certainly did not want to explore the issue.

"This is one of my favorite restaurants," Jordan said loudly, sensing the conversation at her great-grandfather's end of the table was getting out of control. "They really know how to prepare razor clams."

"Just a skid into sizzling butter for a second or two on each side, then a small drift of garlic salt and they're done," Prefontaine added.

"Prepared correctly there's no food quite as good other than freshly caught blueback," Old Man Ahcleet pronounced, his expression brooking no disagreement. Then he smiled and added, "Except maybe scallops."

Dismayed expressions were exchanged by Jordan and Prefontaine.

Eli Raptor drank some water, quickly swallowing a smile. Dinner tonight was going to be memorable, and not necessarily for the food. He did not understand what had just gone on conversationally with the three Quinault but he promised himself that sooner or later he'd find out.

"I've always loved Puget Sound," Mercer said, gazing out the window. He turned to Eli Raptor and said, "I understand you're not a native Washingtonian."

"I came here from Minnesota and immediately fell in love with the place," Raptor said. "Even if it meant leaving the FBI I'll never move away."

Mercer touched Raptor on the arm. "If that's the way you feel, Mr. Raptor, welcome. You're one of us. Look outside again. Those marvelous sunset colors reflected in the snow-capped Olympics. I had a logger friend once who said the peaks reminded him of the teeth of a chain saw."

He went on, "Out there in the Sound freshwater from the mountains flows directly into a salty sea. Actually it's a vast estuary fed by thousands of streams and rivers."

Suddenly Mercer changed the subject. "Jordan, I have a feeling there's something we need to talk about. Am I right?"

"Yes."

"Then let us begin."

Jordan started from the beginning, giving a detailed report

on the murders of the two children and the inability of the
investigative agencies to find any clues—except for the fingerprints inside the boulder and, possibly, the small brass
chain link. With the little girl, there was also the semen of
the secretor, for which no match had been found.

"I do not believe the two murders are connected in any
way at all," she concluded.

Eli Raptor studied Jordan, listening attentively, neither
nodding in agreement nor shaking his head in disagreement.

Mercer did not interrupt Jordan with questions, and
when she was through talking he remained silent for a
time.

Then he said, "At present I have no thoughts at all about
the young girl's killing, although there's obviously a lot of
symbolism involved in it."

"As well as pathological sexual activity," Raptor said.

"All part of the same thing," Mercer said.

"Someone very sick," Prefontaine commented.

"Without a doubt," Mercer agreed, then fell silent again,
deep in thought.

Into the silence Eli Raptor spoke. "What strikes me is that
there's no neatness to the girl's killing, no pattern," he said.
"But it seems to me that there is some reason, a plan if you
will, no matter how ghastly or far out it is, for the boy's murder."

Jordan looked at Raptor, surprised that his thoughts
seemed to be following hers. Perhaps he *could* become a
serious student of the old Indian ways of approaching problems.

"I can suggest something that would provide a pattern for
the young boy's killing," Mercer said.

"What is that, Professor?" Raptor asked.

"Human sacrifice."

Human sacrifice?

Raptor stared at Royal Mercer, the FBI man's green eyes
seeming to flare open with thirst for information like dry
pools welcoming the rain.

Old Man Ahcleet remained silent, showing neither astonishment, fear, nor disbelief.

Although Mercer had spoken quietly, the two terrible words seemed to thunder through the large candlelit restaurant.

Human sacrifice.

Jordan looked quickly around, expecting to see horrified expressions on the faces of the other diners. But they remained calmly eating or softly laughing.

"Nowadays?" she asked.

"Yes," Mercer replied.

"Ancient evil from the bad old times?"

Mercer brightened as his professorial role fell on him like a soft mantle.

"Well, now, Jordan, that depends on what you think of as evil. Let me go back in history for a moment or two. The Aztecs, the Mayas, and other Indians in South America believed in human sacrifice.

"It was a major part of their religion. They sacrificed thousands of people. The stench of their bloodstained altars, like those of the Carthaginians, could not be overcome even by enormous quantities of incense burning night and day.

"Ask yourselves this: Did those people think of human sacrifice as evil? They did not. To them it was an all-important religious rite, a holy ritual, something that must be done to sustain their own lives physically as well as spiritually."

Prefontaine spoke up, his expression skeptical. "Come on now, Uncle Roy, human sacrifice in this day and age? I'm not sure I can buy that."

"It's still going on all over the world," was Mercer's calm reply.

Eli Raptor listened to the conversation with obvious fascination.

"That could explain the weirdness, or lack of it, that I felt when I first examined the crime scene," Jordan said thoughtfully.

"Which one?" Mercer asked.

"The little boy's."

"Tell me what you felt," Mercer said.

"When I first realized the awfulness of what had been done to that little boy I got sick and vomited."

"Understandably."

"After I got myself together, I could not sense hatred or evil. There was none of that special smell, a stink, really, that I pick up on around sexual deviation. I was almost overwhelmed with it when the girl's body was discovered."

"You mean it's an actual stench?" Raptor asked.

"I don't think anybody else can smell it, Mr. Raptor. It's one of Jordan's special abilities," Prefontaine tried to explain.

"Maybe the killing was an act of love," Mercer said quietly.

"Love?" Prefontaine exclaimed, so surprised that he choked on a mouthful of food.

Raptor studied Mercer intently.

Prefontaine, recovered, said that was hard to believe.

Old Man Ahcleet crossed his arms, his face impassive.

"It is to us, I admit," Mercer said. "But cultures are different. Anthropologists and archaeologists are only now beginning to recognize that the ritual power to kill stands at the heart of many ancient societies as well as of much of our own cultural heritage."

He looked around the table. "Or more correctly, I should say of my cultural heritage and that of our FBI guest. I assume you are of the Protestant faith, Mr. Raptor?"

Eli Raptor nodded.

Mercer's audience listened spellbound.

"For example, human sacrifice is the mystery that unlocks the enigma of Stonehenge. Also the complex chain of high-altitude Incan shrines as well as Abraham's thwarted sacrifice of Isaac, and even the crucifixion of Jesus.

"Incidentally, as a footnote, many biblical scholars

believe that Abraham actually sacrificed Isaac but that the story was cleaned up in subsequent translations."

Mercer had the small group's fixed attention.

"Stonehenge, for example. Most visitors think the standing stones belonged to an ancient astronomical observatory. Certain archaeoastronomers popularized the notion that Europe's megalith builders were genius stargazers who used stone circles as giant calculators."

"Are you saying you don't think so?" Raptor asked.

Mercer smiled and shrugged his shoulders. "I would like to because it's a lovely idea but other evidence lies close at hand, as well as underfoot."

When he paused to take a sip of wine and chew on a bread stick, Jordan looked around once more, thinking that the background noises of the restaurant, including an occasional shrill laugh from the bar, served as a commonplace divertissement to this exotic conversation.

"A man shot to death by arrows lies buried at the main entrance to Stonehenge," Mercer continued. "The Greek geographer Strabo wrote that the Druids performed human sacrifice by arrow shooting.

"And within two miles of Stonehenge there is another circle, built of wooden posts, called Woodhenge. In the center of Woodhenge excavators found a three-and-a-half-year-old girl whose skull had been split by an ax before burial.

"She was killed four thousand years ago, about the same time the giant standing stones at Stonehenge were erected. Apparently she served as a foundation sacrifice for Woodhenge, making her the guardian spirit of the place.

"At another spot just a mile from Stonehenge there is a hundred-foot-deep pit, known as the Wilsford Shaft, which contained an ox skull, pottery, and organic remains suggestive of votive pits known elsewhere. Sacrificial pits such as this, with a human being lashed to the post, are known on the continent.

"One of the most common features of British stone circles, including Stonehenge, is the presence of cremated human bones. Forensic analysis of bones at fifty Scottish stone circles revealed that there were too few individuals for family burials, and that a disproportionate number were children.

"Folk tales about children being burned to death inside those stone circles have survived until modern times, along with the custom of having kids leap over bonfires at the harvest. That's a rite linked to real sacrifices in antiquity.

"In his 1987 book *The Stonehenge People* Aubrey Burl says that Stonehenge was not an academy for research into the stars and the nature of the universe.

"It was a place of death, built by people whose needs and fears were very different from our own. Now, let me see, where was I going with this—"

The waiter deftly served the first course, a chowder made with rich milk, butter, cut-up potatoes, diced fresh razor clams, a breath of baked garlic, and a hint of chives.

Mercer held up his hand. "Eat while it's hot and we'll finish this discussion after dinner."

But he was too engrossed in his subject to leave it alone until after dinner. Just as they started on the main course he began his impromptu lecture once more.

"For fifty years the mathematician Maria Reiche studied the Nazca Lines that Peruvian Indians made by displacing shiny desert rocks to create the world's most enormous designs.

"Her conclusion? That the figures and lines are storehouses of calendrical data. Although widely accepted, this view has now been refuted by computer analysis, which found only chance relations between the lines and heavenly bodies.

"But there is a wealth of historical, ethnographic, and archaeological data that links the lines to Andean water and fertility cults.

"Decapitated heads, used in fertility rites, have been found near the lines and many pottery shards show trophy heads, some of them drawn to appear dripping with blood.

"The Maya were also supposed to be happy stargazers working from pyramid observatories. But researchers have found that the Maya possessed an almost aesthetic passion for human sacrifice, with their art portrayed in all its ghastly, gorgeous variety.

"Although Maya warfare fulfilled several needs, the primary ritual role was to provide the state with sacrificial victims, whose blood was then drawn and offered to their gods.

"With increasing knowledge, the old fairy tales have been thrown out and a grimmer, more realistic appreciation of our ancestors is replacing them."

"Why has it taken so long for scientists to come to these conclusions?" Eli Raptor asked.

"Some of the evidence on the Maya, Nazca Lines, and British stone circles is new, but much of the data has been available for decades.

"And you may well ask: Why do archaeologists arouse more enthusiasm among peers by finding ancient scholar-scientists like themselves than by investigating leaders who buried children alive?"

Mercer took a bite of perfectly cooked razor clam, masticated slowly, then continued.

"It's understandable when you think about it. Scholars tend to see their own specializations mirrored in the past. Archaeoastronomers see stars everywhere. Others see data-retrieval systems where head-hunting was the real business.

"Archaeologists have appeared too rational to accept the irrational tendencies of our human past. Mary Ellen Miller at Yale noted that scholars seemed to blind themselves to the evidence of ritual killing in Mayan culture.

"Perhaps we're all really trying to protect ourselves from the unpleasant truth about our ancestors. Every culture develops distancing devices to hide the facts about its bloody past."

"Our own ancestors were headhunters," Old Man Ahcleet said.

Jordan and Prefontaine nodded.

"What was the purpose in taking the heads?" Raptor asked.

Old Man Ahcleet said, "The spirit of the man resides in the head. Take his head and you own his spirit. Especially if he is strong, brave, or highly intelligent."

"Uncle Roy, have you ever witnessed a sacrifice?" Jordan asked.

"Not a human sacrifice," Mercer replied. "I have seen animal sacrifices. I found it unpleasant and frightening. It was more than frightening. It moved me in a way I still cannot come to terms with."

"Could you explain?"

Mercer stroked his goatee, deep in thought. "The essence of sacrifice is surrender, losing control in the excitement and fear of ultimate risk. Blood sacrifice throws out the structure of our everyday thoughts and inhibitions, threatening to swallow up the safety of normal life."

"What's it really like?" Eli Raptor asked.

"As I said, it's about throwing out our inhibitions. I've felt this in the frenzied screaming surrounding animal sacrifice. If you can believe it, and I assure you it is true, I found myself screaming along with the natives.

"And when the shamans had finished the kill, I felt the double sensations I knew the others were feeling."

"And what were those?" Raptor asked.

"Relief and guilt. It's very peculiar, but in this mingled guilt and relief a pleasurable sense of incorporation takes place.

"The victim becomes one with his killers, or perhaps more correctly the killers become one with their victim.

"It is a heartfelt emotion that embraces all of the participants. It seems like an intimation of immortality, as if the killers are saying 'Someday I will witness my own death and yet live because I have witnessed yours and yet I live.' Yes, that is true. I felt it myself.

"The shamans around Lake Titicaca, for example, regard

human sacrifice as the most auspicious ritual. The sacrifices are performed to obtain wealth and immortality, to fulfill vows, and to lay the foundations of buildings.

"These Andean seers do not flinch at killing men. The victim, in the case of a human, becomes a god, so to their way of thinking he or she is being done a great favor."

"But our murdered little boy was an Indian," Eli Raptor said.

"Many Central and South Americans are Indians," Mercer reminded him. "Perhaps you've been looking for Indians on the wrong continent."

Jordan, Paul, and Eli Raptor exchanged glances with a new, disquieting awareness.

"There were an awful lot of Central and South Americans attending the logging congress," Prefontaine said.

"And many of them were undoubtedly Indians," Mercer added.

Unspoken were the words: *How will we ever find the guilty party?*

"What you absolutely must consider about present-day human sacrifice—don't fool yourselves, it's still going on— is that in many cases, not necessarily those of the drug lords, the sacrificed must be someone the sacrificer loves.

"Surely Abraham really loved Isaac. And just as surely Abraham really sacrificed Isaac. As I said before, like so much in the Bible, those with tender sensibilities changed the meaning in various translations."

"All right, let's say that a Central or South American sacrificed that little boy in our forest. Why here? Why not do the sacrifice in the land where they came from?"

No one at the table had an answer to that, not even a wild guess.

"I wonder how South American law enforcement views such sacrifices?" Eli Raptor asked. "Surely they must know about them."

"Oh, they know very well," Mercer replied. "Officially, of course, they know nothing."

He ate the last piece of razor clam on his plate, then continued. "Although, to be fair, I do know of a case in which police prevented the sacrifice of a child to the local mountain deity who the natives thought was angered at the construction of a new road through his territory."

As they left the restaurant, Eli Raptor departed the group after shaking hands all around, and thanking them for including him in the dinner. He told Jordan he would be in touch with her.

Mercer suggested that Prefontaine get the professor's car from the parking lot, handing him the keys to the restored 1965 silver-gray Chrysler Imperial as if conferring the keys to the kingdom upon him.

Jordan, Old Man Ahcleet, and Mercer, leaning on his cane, waited at the restaurant entrance.

"I'm going down to Santiago in a couple of weeks," Mercer told them, his eyes on Jordan.

"To do what?" Old Man Ahcleet asked.

"The usual. I'm one of the speakers at an international anthropological conference." He smiled at them both. "Interestingly enough, this time I'll be talking about contemporary human sacrifice."

Old Man Ahcleet and Jordan raised their eyebrows at each other.

Mercer touched Jordan's arm. "Do you have any vacation time coming?"

"Yes," she said slowly. "Actually, I've got quite a bit saved up."

"With the murder investigations going on could you get away?"

"They're really not my investigations, Uncle Roy. Being felonies, federal crimes, the FBI is in charge."

"If you come with me it'll be my treat."

Jordan asked if there would be an opportunity to visit a certain place, naming Lima Clemente's village.

"I don't see why not," Mercer replied.

She turned to Ahcleet. "Grandfather, do you think I should go with Uncle Roy?"

Ahcleet replied that he'd have to check and see if such a thing would be a good thing.

Jordan leaned over and kissed him. She knew very well with whom he'd check: his feelings, his premonitions, his fears, his guardian spirit.

As Jordan thought about Mercer's invitation, she realized such a trip would cause her to be parted from Lima Clemente, which she was now anyway. The trip would provide her with an opportunity to think clearly about their relationship.

They would visit Lima's village, his spiritual headwaters. If so, perhaps she'd have a clearer understanding of his foreignness.

Prefontaine arrived at the restaurant entrance driving, with the appropriate stateliness, Mercer's treasured car.

"Since you have driven safely so far why don't you remain at the wheel and chauffeur us home?" Mercer suggested to Prefontaine.

Prefontaine replied seriously, "My pleasure and honor, sir."

They were spending the night at Mercer's old family home on Alki Point, and would leave for Taholah the next morning.

2 Mercer's longtime housekeeper, Miss Eugenia McConahan, prepared breakfast for them; light-as-air Swedish crepes with lingonberry sauce and invigorating freshly brewed Starbucks coffee.

Old Man Ahcleet announced that he hadn't slept all night. But he looked bright and alert.

Concerned, Mercer asked, "Were you sick?"

"No. My mind was boiling over like the winter sea when it rushes into the caves at Cape Elizabeth.

"Last evening's dinner talk stimulated me. I spent the

night thinking of things I have not thought of for a long, long time. Good things. All night I felt young, vigorous, ready for the whale." He smiled. "And for what came after the successful hunt."

Except for Mercer's housekeeper, they all understood what Old Man Ahcleet was talking about: the anticipated danger of the hunt when sometimes no one came home, neither whale nor hunting crew, the joyous celebration when the hunt was successful, the age-old devotions, the arms of ardent wives who had too long slept apart from their husbands as the rituals required.

Ahcleet downed a great gulp of Miss Eugenia's coffee. He looked at Jordan. "Last night my guardian spirit advised me that you should accompany Royal on his trip to the other end of the world."

Taking an elegant sip from his shot glass of Jack Daniel's, he added, "But take care. Their spirits are much different than ours."

3   When Royal Mercer and Jordan arrived in Santiago two weeks later, Jordan was exhausted from the long air trip and disoriented from the time difference.

Sitting in on Royal Mercer's part of the conference the next day, she found it hard to understand how the professor could look so fresh and alert up there on the podium as he addressed delegates from nearly every country on earth.

But, she considered, he had been a lecturer for many years and was truly a citizen of the world, accustomed to travel and addressing professional groups.

An equal source of amazement for Jordan was what she learned about human sacrifice during the conference, especially that it was still going on in many places in the world. Royal Mercer told the audience that human sacrifice remains a powerful social force in Andean society, with important consequences in rank, status, and wealth.

"Human sacrifice creates three types of demigods," Mercer said. "The first is the victim. After his death he becomes a deity, a focus of magical power.

"The second deity created by human sacrifice," he went on, "is the patron, the person who arranges for the sacrifice of a child he loves. He acquires immense prestige and people are intensely afraid of men like these. They are considered invincible because of the powers they get from their human-sacrifice pacts.

"The third supernatural produced by human sacrifice is the sacrificer himself, the shaman who presides over the offering. He is feared. He holds the keys to wealth and success.

"In the past the victims were sons and daughters of Incan nobility who were carefully prepared for their role. Today, mostly they are poor people betrayed by unscrupulous shamans."

Jordan sat through all of Mercer's speech, her mind on the little butchered Indian boy she'd found in her rain forest at home.

After the conclusion of the three-day conference, making arrangements to go up the mountains to Lima Clemente's village required all of the next two days.

First she and Royal Mercer visited the American embassy in Santiago where they were officially greeted and invited to a lengthy formal luncheon.

The sum of what they were told was that it was probably impossible to get where they wanted to go from here, and even if they could, by some miracle, find transportation, the trip was far too dangerous.

"The roads hardly exist and there are bandits behind every boulder," the ambassador's aide informed them.

After much conversation in various languages it developed that the embassy chef had a nephew who owned a taxi, spoke English, and was willing to make the perilous trip.

Eventually the nephew himself, whose name was Narcissus, arrived at the embassy to be interviewed.

He was a young and good-looking man, neatly dressed, whose dark eyes flamed whenever he looked at Jordan. She could not decide if the flaming eyes indicated suppressed passion or a simple hangover.

Narcissus proclaimed himself to be very brave; a man who made exotic journeys, and was ready and willing to go to hell itself for them if that was their requirement.

"Would you bring us back?" asked Royal Mercer, half in jest.

"From hell, Professor?" Narcissus looked puzzled.

"Of course not," Mercer said impatiently. "From the village we're hoping to visit."

"Certainly I bring you back," Narcissus replied with an operatic gesture. "All in one piece. Or since there are two of you, I should say in two pieces."

"I'm not sure that's any comfort," Jordan murmured.

"Let's talk price." Mercer's voice was all business.

"One thousand American dollars," came the prompt reply. Mercer neither reacted nor replied.

"For each. Two thousand American dollars total."

Mercer turned as if to walk away down an elegantly carpeted walkway that led directly to the outer doors of the embassy.

"All right, I'm a businessman. I compromise. One thousand American dollars total for both you and the lady."

Mercer started to walk away.

"Five hundred American dollars each."

Mercer was growing dimmer down that long red carpet.

Narcissus hurried after him, lowering his fee again. "Two hundred fifty American dollars for the whole package. What a deal you are getting. My luxurious taxi service for only one hundred and twenty-five American dollars for each of you."

Mercer halted. "Both ways?" he asked, addressing the front doors of the embassy. "From our hotel to the village and from the village to our hotel?"

"Yes, Professor."

Mercer turned about-face and began walking back down the red carpet, Narcissus at his heels.

"Then we are agreed. For two hundred and fifty American dollars total, you will drive both myself and my colleague to the village and back again to our Santiago hotel, staying with us for two nights in the village."

Narcissus nodded. "Of course."

"You will receive half your pay when we start out in the morning and the remaining half when we are returned safely to our hotel."

"And I will be personally checking that Professor Mercer and Ms. Tidewater have arrived safely back," the ambassador's aide said sternly.

Mercer asked for a pen and paper, which were promptly handed to him by a member of the staff.

He sat at an ornate desk and penned the agreement, signed his name, then demanded that Narcissus do likewise. One look at Mercer's face and the taxi driver quickly complied.

"At that insignificant price you must supply the gasoline," Narcissus said.

For the first time in Jordan's life she saw Royal Mercer lose his temper and found both the sight and the accompanying sounds to be awesome.

Using terms in various foreign languages that Jordan could not understand but knew by Mercer's expression were serious cuss words of various provenance, the issue of gasoline was dropped, after Mercer added the point in writing to both copies of the agreement.

"We will start at four in the morning," Narcissus said. "I will pick you up at your hotel. I ask that you be ready."

Four in the morning. Jordan groaned.

The next day Narcissus and his taxi arrived at the hotel promptly at four A.M. Jordan noted that he was wearing dark pants, a faded red T-shirt under a dark suit coat, and an Andean wool cap.

She and Mercer had clad themselves in clothing that could be removed layer by layer if it got hot. Their bags were packed with additional layers that could be put on if it got cold.

The people at the embassy had warned them about the changes of climate. Jordan and Mercer were told that as they ascended into the mountains, the colder the weather would be, but in between the mountains were valleys that at times were blistering with heat.

The people at the hotel, equally helpful, insisted on serving them a hot tea made from coca leaves that they said would ease the pain of the high altitude to which they would be ascending and to which they were unaccustomed.

They left Santiago driving down a wide, clean, tree-lined boulevard and Jordan anticipated a nice ride in the country.

"These roads are better than ours," she told Mercer.

"Just wait," he said.

They drove miles on good roads through farmland and vineyards. But finally all Jordan could see was sand and dirt.

"The road's gone," she told Narcissus.

"It may seem so to you, Ms. Tidewater. But fortunately for you I know where we're going and how to get there and that *is* important."

He directed a large white smile and sparkling glances from his dark eyes her way as he took off.

They drove upward, every so often on what seemed to be a donkey track that periodically disappeared among terraces of green fields beneath the lead-colored ocher of the mountains.

Up to the cold barrens, then down into hot valleys, then ascending and descending again until they reached the three-thousand-foot elevation point. Here Narcissus stopped near a spot marked by a mound of stones.

"We shall alight here," he said, getting out of the taxi.

Jordan and Mercer did likewise. They walked around, stretching their legs, and watched as Narcissus added a rock to the pile, sprinkled coca leaves and splashed alcohol over the rocks, after which he took a good swig from the bottle himself. Then he uttered a series of what seemed to be prayers.

He insisted that Jordan and Mercer do the same. If they did not, he warned, their trip would be doomed.

"To whom are we making offerings?" asked Mercer.

"To the mountain gods," Narcissus said. "And to Pacha Mama, the Earth Goddess, and to our ancestral spirits."

"We have no alcohol with which to make an offering," Mercer said.

Narcissus handed Mercer his bottle and several coca leaves. "You may use these. Just a drop or two will do."

He found each of them a stone that he considered suitable for offering.

When Jordan and Mercer had each placed a stone on the pile of rocks, dropped the leaves that immediately blew away, and poured a small amount of alcohol, Narcissus said, "You have made offerings. Although our gods are not your gods, they will find your gestures good. But you do not need to say the prayers."

"Why not?" Jordan asked, beginning to grow a little fearful after all she'd been hearing about human sacrifice. Were their lives to be so short that the full ceremony was not necessary?

"Because you are strangers to us and our people. What you just did was show respect to our gods. That is good."

"What do these piles of stones represent?" Mercer asked.

"They are the mountains," Narcissus said.

Jordan realized that the stone mounds modeled the great bare mountains all about them like miniature pyramids.

Taking advantage of the stop, Narcissus built a small fire and brewed tea from coca leaves. They each drank a cup of the steaming liquid.

"If you do not drink this," he said, "you will not arrive where you want to go. Your lowland systems cannot withstand the heights."

Jordan and Royal Mercer drank without argument.

At fifteen thousand feet a storm of hail roared in like a deathly rain of pebbles.

"In half an hour a storm like this kills crops and stones baby llamas to death," Narcissus told them.

Under Narcissus's direction they got out of the car and hurried into a small cave formed by an overhanging rock. He placed a woolen blanket on the dirt floor and told them to sit on it.

He ran back to his taxi and got a huge black umbrella that after all three of them were huddled together on the blanket in the cave, he opened and held in front of them.

Trying desperately not to laugh, Jordan thought Narcissus looked like an inexperienced bullfighter trying to fend off a charging bull by sitting on his backside.

Narcissus's technique worked, for while the storm of blowing hail raged beyond the umbrella, they all stayed dry.

The hail storm blew away after fifteen minutes or so and they were on their way again.

At seventeen thousand feet they were on the altiplano. Jordan pointed out to Mercer surprising displays of lupines growing in clumps between rocks and in apparently infertile ground.

"They're not like our lupines," she said. "With ours, all the flowers in one plant are the same color. With these lupines, each blossom of the plant is a different and very brilliant color."

"It certainly is a sight," Mercer commented.

Soon Narcissus stopped and asked them to get out. When they did, he pointed to the nearest hillside that was covered with pictures of llamas. They all stayed close to the car.

"Those are geoglyphs," Mercer said. "Beautifully done. Amazingly lifelike. See how they're formed by incising the animals' forms into the hillside's earthen surface."

"They were made over twenty-five hundred years ago, Professor. The ancient Incas believed that llamas and vicu-

nas were gifts to them from the sun," Narcissus told them.
"Only royalty could wear vicuna cloth. Anyone else caught
wearing it was executed."

"What a car you've got," Jordan said with admiration as they
chugged along, always upward, over snow-and-hail-covered
areas. There were no roads that she could see in any direction. "What make is it?"

Narcissus lifted his head and said proudly, "Make? She is
my make. I build her from pieces of other cars. Part is
Chevrolet, part is Cadillac, part is Ford, part is Packard. To
tell the truth, I've forgotten all the parts I used to build her.
Not to brag, but she is wonderful, is she not?"

"Very wonderful," Mercer said admiringly.

"Does she have a name?" Jordan wanted to know.

"Her name is Magnificent Obsession."

Jordan looked into the man's burning eyes and replied,
"Of course. What else could it be?"

And still they drove on and on, Jordan mystified because she
never did see a road or even remnants of one. But evidently
Narcissus could and she was thankful for that.

Finally he stopped, announcing it was time for calls of
nature to be answered. He advised both Jordan and Mercer
to stay within sight of the car.

"Do not worry, Ms. Tidewater. I am not a voyeur, I will
turn my eyes," he said, reaching under his seat and pulling
out a weapon. "But I and my gun will be very near you.
There are bandits all around us."

"Here? In this wilderness?"

For that is what it was. All around were sharply peaked
bare stone mountains, with not a tree in sight. She saw that
still higher mountains in the distance were snowcapped.

"Oh, yes, I assure you it is so. You cannot see them. They
build houses by piling up boulders, as if nature had done it,
and live inside the rock structures."

"I wish I had my gun," she said.

"I have mine. More important, the bandits know I have it. They respect people who go armed," Narcissus replied.

Jordan didn't get out of the taxi. "I don't have to go anymore," she announced.

"Neither do I," said Mercer.

"You may be sorry. We have some very rough country coming up and worse conditions as far as robbers go. This is just the beginning of bandit country."

Jordan and Mercer looked at each other. *How much rougher could it get?* was the unspoken question. They both got out of the car, took care of personal business, and rushed back to the vehicle, slamming the doors behind them.

They were on their way once more.

Some time later, Narcissus asked Mercer, "Do you know where we are, Professor?"

"No, I don't. But I certainly hope you do."

"We approach the most powerful mountain in the world. It is the highest mountain in North or South America."

"How much farther to our destination?" Jordan asked slowly through lips stiff with cold. She was finding it difficult to draw breath into her lungs.

Narcissus looked over at her with those burning eyes. "If all goes well, I would say about two hours. And please do not think me impolite, but if you would move closer to me, my body warmth would warm you."

Jordan, sick and dizzy from the height in spite of the coca tea she had taken, said, "Thanks," but did not have the energy required to move.

Royal Mercer cleared his throat in the backseat. Letting her know he was there to protect her? Letting her know that he was still alive?

Jordan didn't know if she was. And didn't much care. Was it true that after death the spirit hovers around its body for a long time?

She fell asleep on that thought and dreamed of being warm and floating among the stars that she discovered actually were, as The People once believed, campfires of ancient warriors.

When they arrived at the village of their destination, it was still light at this twenty-thousand-foot elevation.

Jordan's and Mercer's lips were purple and the skin on their faces was beginning to crack from the cold. Jordan was either in a deep sleep or unconscious, for they could not wake her.

Before Narcissus had turned off the ignition of his miraculously still-running Magnificent Obsession, a tall, gawky man wearing long, black robes emerged from a house of clay blocks and hurried toward them.

He introduced himself as Father Lavate, the local Catholic priest, and an Englishman.

Next door to the clay blockhouse stood an unusually beautiful church, small but built of fine woods with a golden cross on top.

As Mercer and Narcissus got out of the car, the priest invited them into his house, then he and Narcissus carried Jordan inside and placed her on a sofa that stood in front of a roaring stove.

Father Lavate's housekeeper, a beautiful young woman whom the priest introduced as Leucaria, came from the back of the house with sheets of warmed wool that she carefully placed around Jordan after undressing her except for her underthings.

When they were certain that Jordan was coming to and not too much worse for her chilling experience, Narcissus effusively excused himself, saying one of his relatives lived in this village and he must see this person immediately or a family schism would occur.

"Ah, that Narcissus," Father Lavate said. "So thoughtful, knowing that I desire to speak with my guests privately."

But Jordan had seen the wink he'd given her as he left and wondered if the person who must be seen so quickly was female and definitely not a relative.

Father Lavate invited Mercer to sit in one of the stove-side chairs while he sat in the other. He advised Jordan to remain lying on the sofa and remain warmly wrapped.

Leucaria, who had disappeared, came back into the room bearing a tray containing a teapot, three mugs, and a small pitcher of milk.

"Cream from the vicuna," commented Father Lavate. "The best in the world."

By this time Jordan was nearly herself.

"Do you have oxygen in your village?" she asked, fearing another attack of the terrifying breathlessness.

The priest shook his head. "Unfortunately, no. Our medicine man has cures for many ailments, but he does not possess the oxygen that comes in a tank. You were suffering from altitude sickness but since you recovered so quickly I am sure that if you move slowly you will have no more problems."

As Father Lavate sat visiting with them, Jordan noticed that behind the priest hung a Christian poster showing a blue-and-white-robed Christ hovering over the right shoulder of a young man who looked a great deal like Narcissus.

Over the young man's left shoulder stooped a black devil with sharp horns.

"What does that caption read, Father?" Jordan asked.

"In English it poses the question: Will you serve God or the Devil?"

Pretty clear choice, Jordan thought. So Lima Clemente had been brought up in the Catholic faith. That explained the crucifix he wore around his neck.

"Is there a hotel or guest house in your village?" Mercer asked.

"You are in it, now," Father Lavate replied with a smile. "You will be my guests for the night, or as many nights as you would like to stay.

"Receiving travelers is an unusual occurrence. My rooms are spartan. But they are clean and my housekeeper at the moment is putting fresh sheets and blankets on the beds. You will of course take supper with me and breakfast, also, for as long as you wish to stay."

They thanked him and asked if there was a place to wash.

He told them that all water came from the village pump. Looking out one of the tiny windows, Jordan and Mercer saw villagers already gathering, the crowd growing larger by the minute.

"How am I going to take my clothes off with that crowd staring at me?" Jordan muttered to Mercer.

"If you're wearing panties and a bra leave them on. As for me, I'm so hot from the priest's fire as well as tired and dirty from the trip I don't give a damn.

"They can look all they want," Mercer went on. "Lots of native peoples all around the world have seen me naked. So far not a one of them has fainted from the sight or been hopelessly overcome by raging lust. To people of tradition, the matter is very simple. One is either a man or a woman. If a man, there are certain appendages. If a woman, certain different appendages."

"Ignore the people at the pump," Father Lavate said as his housekeeper brought in a large tin tub. "Most of them wash themselves at the pump and I'm sure they were hoping to see you folks without your clothes to make sure you don't have anything unusual growing from your bodies. Such as tails from the end of your spines, which of course would prove to them that you are devils and must be avoided."

Jordan laughed hysterically. Mercer gave her a worried look.

The housekeeper began filling the tub with hot water from a faucet protruding from an odd arrangement of pipes that threaded through the stove.

"Whenever I have a fire in the stove I have hot water. Lots of it. Probably enough for the entire village to bathe."

"Have you ever invited them to come in and take baths?" Jordan asked.

"Many times. But all to no avail. They're afraid."

"But you're their priest. What do they fear?"

"That if they got in my tub I'd boil them down until I could skim off their human fat."

Now Father Lavate was adding cold water to the tub to even out the temperature.

"Some of the families have what is called a *liquichiri* tradition," he went on. "Supposedly they have many uses for human fat so you can see that taking a hot bath in the house of the priest is a touchy subject."

"And you say they're Christians?" Jordan asked.

"They are Christians, according to their lights," Father Lavate replied.

"I don't understand," Jordan said.

"In ancient traditional places like this, the natives' old religion blends with the Catholic faith. It must be this way or we would have no converts at all. It is a very hard thing for others to understand. Especially Rome." He shook his head ruefully, then added cheerfully, "The first bath is for the lady, don't you agree, Professor Mercer?"

"Most assuredly."

While Jordan bathed, Leucaria handed her a rough soap, giggled, then gently washed her back.

Mercer and Father Lavate stepped outside the priest's house and walked over to the group of people gathered around the pump, most of whom seemed shy. But as they were introduced to the professor they looked at Mercer sideways and most of them smiled.

After the baths were finished, Jordan and Mercer were provided with native costume while an apparent underling of the housekeeper's washed and dried their own filthy clothes, then hung them over a line stretched from wall to wall in front of the stove.

Father Lavate invited them to be seated around a table set for four. After a prayer, Leucaria served a dinner of breaded steak with fried eggs, fried potatoes, and white rice along with a dark beer.

When everyone was served, she sat down at the fourth place at the table and began to eat.

In the morning both Jordan and Mercer rose early and went outside. Father Lavate found them there, dressed in their own clothes, clean but stiff with the local soap. They were watching the condors drifting on the airstreams overhead.

"The condors are as important to the Andean culture as are the mountains," Father Lavate said. "In some villages during the fiesta for their particular patron saint, certain brave men capture condors alive and tie them to the backs of bulls so that the birds can tear at the animals' flesh with their beaks while the *serruchos* fight the bulls."

"That is cruel and unfair," Jordan said.

"My dear lady, that is exactly what life is," the priest replied. "Especially for people of the altiplano."

After breakfast Father Lavate showed them the families of vicuna that were being herded into pens by the villagers.

"Beautiful animals," Mercer commented. "But small. Are they full grown?"

"Yes. They stand about three feet at the shoulder," the priest replied. "They are the mainstays of our lives. They give us milk and meat and wool to make our beautiful fabrics."

"How do they stay alive in this bleak land?" Jordan wanted to know.

"God in his goodness has caused their hearts and lungs to be enlarged so they can handle heights that would leave other animals gasping and dying. Just as He has given the people here extra capillaries in their fingers and toes to bring extra blood to their extremities."

"Is that a medical fact? About the extra capillaries?" Jordan asked.

"Yes, it is true. Regarding the vicuna, they live on the low shrubs and grasses you see growing here and there and eat the mosses found in boggy areas. They must have water every day, which they get from the bogs.

"They are very territorial animals. Each family group occupies a hundred-acre area and marks the extent of their areas by piles of dung where every member of the group defecates. Only there and no place else. If a member of a different family tries to step over the dung line, he is swiftly driven off."

"Why are they being herded in?" Mercer asked.

"You have arrived at the time of an ancient ceremonial in honor of the vicuna," the priest said. "Once a year our people clean and comb the animals. You can see how dusty they are because they take dust baths every day. Then they decorate the animals with strips of colored wool."

Father Lavate had business in the church so he invited Jordan and Mercer to watch the preparation of the vicuna.

First, each vicuna was subjected by the village men to a thorough brushing and combing until all dust and burrs were gone and their fur shone.

Then the native women took over, tying beautifully fashioned pieces of wool all over the animals' coats.

Jordan had brought her camera and she took photographs of the preparations. The women were welcoming, some showing her how to tie the decorative woolen bows. Everybody was happy and joyous.

The vicuna themselves were friendly. When she bent to look in their eyes and touch their lovely faces, the small animals gently blew their breaths into her nostrils.

The preparations took all day. Upon invitation, Jordan and Mercer ate lunch outside with the villagers, a delicious stew from a large pot steaming over an open fire. Narcissus joined the group and introduced them to people Jordan assumed were relatives of his.

In the distance she saw seemingly endless rows of dry, smooth mountains. Toward the south, the flat plain suddenly crumpled and threw up barren hills, which hung from the sky like the folds of a closed velvet stage curtain.

She tried to imagine growing up in a high, cold, barren place like this, where cruel winds shrieked constantly, where nothing was green, where one could never hear the voice of the sea, where the only water was in an occasional marshy bog.

No wonder Lima Clemente said he was lonely. Jordan imagined that growing up here would form a lifelong loneliness of the spirit, especially for someone who had escaped into the world of exciting international business.

That evening father Lavate told them they would all remain in his house.

"The festivities tonight are for the villagers only, for people of the blood, and none of us would be welcome at an ancient ritual that predates Christianity by unknown centuries."

When they arrived at the priest's house, they found ten young girls between about twelve and fifteen years of age, and three small boys, all of whom seemed to be under the supervision of Leucaria.

After dinner Leucaria and her charges disappeared into the back of the house. Occasionally a giggle was heard.

"Tonight is the one night of the year when I lock all the doors and windows of my house," the priest said. "Excuse me while I take care of that now."

When he returned he counseled them not to open a window or go outside for any reason whatsoever until the sun had risen the next morning.

"The virgins?" Mercer asked cryptically. "And the orphans?"

The priest nodded. "There's no point in taking any chances," he replied.

Nothing more was said on the subject.

Jordan, Mercer, and Father Lavate sat by the stove. Mercer told the priest some of the practices he had seen in various spots in the world, and how, although they differed greatly in details, they all, with the exception of some of the Indians in North America such as the Quinault, seemed to have one

thing in common: worship of higher beings, gods whose
goodwill they prayed for, sacrificed to, whose ill temper
they feared and attempted to placate. He added that Jordan
was Quinault and that he had been adopted by the Quinault
people.

"In my studies and travels I have found that man is never
good enough for his gods," Mercer commented. "It seems to
be a fault in man."

"Tell me about these Quinault," Father Lavate said.

"In ancient days, as well as some today, the Quinault
believed in a good and omnipotent creator called Kwantee,
not terrorizing beings before whom they must bow and
make sacrifice."

After an hour or two of conversation, when Father Lavate
seemed relaxed and at ease, Mercer told him about the gathering of anthropologists in Santiago at which Mercer had
spoken about current human sacrifice.

"Human sacrifice," Father Lavate said musingly, staring
through the isinglass door of the stove at the flames within.
"I've always considered it a fascinating subject. There are
many documents on the subject in the library at Rome. I've
been fortunate to have read most of them but some are
sealed, even to the priesthood."

Mercer said, "What seems peculiar and definitely
unchristian to most modern people is the belief that someone else's life can be saved by murdering a child. Or for-
tunes gained. I know that child sacrifice is used extensively
in the cocaine trade, to make the drug lords even richer than
they already are."

"I am aware of that," the priest said, pausing to light a
corncob pipe.

After the pipe was burning to his satisfaction, he said,
"You know, when one really examines the subject with a
clear mind free of any sort of religious prejudice or dogma,
the practice is not really so peculiar or unchristian."

"Please explain," Jordan asked.

"The core of human-sacrifice ideology is that a surrogate

victim saves another or contributes to the welfare of another by his or her death.

"We Christians believe and teach others like our natives here in this village that we are all saved by the blood of a sacrificed Jesus.

"If God the Father sacrificed His own Son by allowing nails to be driven through him to save humanity from the power of Satan, many unsophisticated people see no difference in driving a stake through their own sons or nephews to save a beloved father or mother or other child, at the same time vanquishing the demonic powers that threaten the family."

Jordan wondered what such an obviously well-educated man was doing in this remote part of the world but she said nothing.

"I have had similar discussions many times with the leaders of this village," the priest went on. "They smile and are very polite but at the same time point out recent cases in other villages where earthquakes or avalanches were stopped by the ritual killing of a child."

"But the cruelty, the horror—" Jordan began.

The priest shrugged, interrupting her. "They also believe that the person sacrificed becomes a god. Actually many Andeans feel they have a 'purer understanding of the Bible than the missionaries who gave them the book in the first place.' And that's a direct quote."

"In the Holy Land," Mercer said, "the tradition of child sacrifice was an ancient necessity that followed carefully prescribed patterns.

"The Pontical Museum of Jerusalem contains the skeleton of an infant whose head was violently severed from its body some five thousand years ago, before it was buried in a jar underneath a house near the Dead Sea. There's another infant in a similar jar right next to the first.

"The caption below the jars reads that the necropolis at Ghassul has not yet been excavated, but a few dozen infant burials such as the first two have been found in the town area, adding that they were always under house floors and were undoubtedly foundation sacrifices, same as encountered elsewhere in the ancient Near East."

The priest carefully placed more wood in the stove, then sat down. "The peasants around Lake Titicaca distrust the new bridge recently built over the Ilave River because no infants were buried in the pillars. If at all possible they try not to use it. I would say that's a modern-day conviction common to your ancient people of Ghassul, would you not?"

"Of course," Mercer replied.

"Not long ago a group of researchers discovered an eight- or nine-year-old boy on one of the peaks who had been sacrificed long ago. After five hundred years his body was still flexible.

"The Incas used several methods of sacrifice including strangling, garroting, breaking the cervical vertebrae with a stone, tearing out the heart, and burying alive.

"Freezing to death at a high altitude as this young Incan boy did was probably the least painful. It's easy to lose consciousness at eighteen thousand feet above sea level. Never forget that from the Incans' point of view they were doing the children a favor since the victims were transformed into deities after death."

Jordan could see by the expression in Mercer's eyes that he was set to stay up all night talking with Father Lavate, even though they were to leave the next day. She excused herself and went to bed.

The next morning Father Lavate found Jordan and Mercer outside watching condors drift on the air streams overhead.

"I must show you our place of worship before you leave," the priest said, leading them inside the church. "We are very proud of it."

"And well you should be. It is a gem," Mercer said, looking at the beautiful design, the specialty woods used in its construction, the altar made of gold.

"This is something one might expect to see in Rome. Forgive my question, Father," Mercer said. "And please believe that I mean no disrespect."

"But you want to know how a poor village like this can afford such an expensive place of worship."

"That is true, Father."

"Several of our citizens left the village for the city and became very rich businessmen. They have not forgotten their place of origin. Our beautiful church was provided by them. Also funds come every year for various things that the villagers need. And they are beginning to open worldwide markets for our precious vicuna materials."

"You are very fortunate," Mercer said.

"I thank God every day for those good people."

Father Lavate led them into a small side chapel where another altar was covered with burning candles.

"Talking about good people Father, I wonder if you know a man by the name of Lima Clemente? And another man, quite a bit older, whose name is Xavier Escoro?"

Father Lavate looked at her. "Do you know Señor Clemente and Señor Escoro?"

"Yes, I met both of them at a logging congress held at Lake Quinault recently."

"Wonderful men, both of them. They are of our people but they both left this small village long ago. They have been phenomenally successful in business and have not forgotten their roots."

Father Lavate led them into a small side chapel where one of the altars was covered with burning candles.

"These are kept lighted day and night in remembrance of our beloved dead," the priest said.

Jordan noticed that occasionally a photograph of the dead person stood behind a burning candle. Toward the front of the altar she saw a photograph with something partially draped over the frame.

She stepped closer. Her heart seemed to rise in her throat when she saw that it was the other half of the gold medal she had found on her beach at Taholah. A torn woven ribbon was fastened to the medal.

"Father Lavate," she asked, her pulses racing. "Who is this little boy?"

The priest bowed his head sadly. "That is little Antonio Salinas. A beautiful boy, is he not? So sad, his death. The man and woman on either side of him are his parents."

"They look so young."

"Oh, they were. Just young people starting out. Struck down by a fever. But it was God's will."

"There's something very familiar about this half of a gold medal," she said, fingering the torn woven ribbon attached to it and absolutely certain she had the other half at home.

"Can you tell me something about this little boy?" she asked.

"I can tell you he was much loved. And sorely missed."

"I would like to go to the cemetery and place a remembrance on their graves," she said.

"We have no graveyard," the priest replied. "Our people follow the ancient practice of giving the dead to the condors. They believe it is the wish of the gods."

"I've never read that anywhere in the Bible," she said.

"Well, my dear, the gods involved in this matter are far older than the Old Testament."

"Haven't your people ever heard of cemeteries?"

"Yes. But they think the idea of putting a loved one in the ground to rot is disgusting."

"Do they believe the dead live on in the bodies of the condors that eat them?" Mercer asked.

"They believe the spirit of the dead loved ones lives on in the birds for a while," the priest replied. "And when the bird falls and dies, returning to Pacha Mama, or Lady Earth, the spirit simply enters another condor."

When Father Lavate and Royal Mercer walked slowly back into the main part of the church, Jordan took her point-

and-shoot camera from her shoulder pack and quickly got several shots of the young boy whose name was Antonio Salinas.

They left shortly thereafter, with the entire village turning out to bid them farewell. One of the men who seemed to be a leader of the village shook hands with Jordan and Mercer, saying to both of them, "May you run like a vicuna."

"That is the finest expression of goodwill in these parts," the priest whispered to Mercer.

Mercer heartily shook a number of outstretched male hands, repeating the farewell and receiving wide smiles and back slaps in return.

Some of the women presented Jordan with intricately woven lengths of yardage and ribbons made from vicuna wool. She thanked them graciously, hugging each one.

On the plane back home, Jordan asked Mercer how a man of Father Lavate's obvious education and intelligence could stay in such a primitive place.

"He is punishing himself and also performing an act of love," Mercer said.

Jordan looked puzzled.

"Leucaria is his daughter, conceived after Father Lavate became a priest and gave himself and his virginity to God."

"Is it a secret?"

"I wouldn't say so. The whole village knows about it. They respect him more for what they consider his responsible action."

"What about the girl's mother?"

"She lives in the village and is happily married. She and her husband treat Leucaria with love and kindness, Father Lavate told me, as if she were their niece."

"I want to go home," Jordan said.

"We are, my dear, we are on our way."

On the plane Jordan turned the puzzle over and over in her mind.

Father Lavate said the little boy named Antonio Salinas

was dead, *knew* he was dead. Dead by a fever that had also killed his parents, all of whom had been eaten by condors.

Fine. That was their way.

But that wasn't exactly what the priest had said. He'd said the young parents had been stricken down by a fever. He did not say how the boy had died.

She had the other half of the gold medal and woven ribbon she'd found hanging over Antonio Salinas's memorial photograph in the chapel.

How did it get thousands of miles to her coastline in such a comparatively short time? What other Indian boy would be wearing a portion of a gold medal that belonged to Antonio? Could Antonio himself be the little Indian boy, parts of whom were still in the morgue in the state of Washington?

And if he were Antonio Salinas, how would the priest have known about the boy's death in a distant country?

If he did know, why had he said nothing about it?

She could wait no longer. She must seek the Klokwalle's help.

4   After Jordan and Royal Mercer returned home, she immediately delivered the roll of film she'd taken in the high Andean village to Hunter Kleoh.

Kleoh, in turn, sent the film to the state lab, where it would be developed and printed.

Scientists began working to rebuild the dead boy's scalped face, to see if he could possibly be Antonio Salinas, who was supposed to have died in the altiplano of southern Chile and been devoured by condors.

*The wider more knowledge became the more I realized my ignorance.
It is only the ignorant who can be positive, only the ignorant who can
become fanatics, for the more I learned the more I became aware that
there are shadings and relationships in all things.*
—LOUIS L'AMOUR,
The Walking Drum

Chapter 22

1   Back home in Taholah, Jordan feared that obtaining the Klokwalle's help at this time of year when it was only August—actually the ceremony would be a month from now in September—would be impossible.

She knew that the great spirits, the Listening Ones, began to arrive in late November, the winter dance time, and left during March.

But now was when she desperately needed spiritual guidance. She consulted Old Man Ahcleet.

"Is it absolutely necessary that you do this thing now?" he asked.

"Yes, Grandfather."

He looked off into space. "For the first thirty days you must do your cleansing. That would take you into September."

"Yes."

Ahcleet remained silent, then he said musingly, "The Klokwalle dances were held only during the three moons following the winter solstice. There is no one alive now who participated in these dances.

"I remember my father telling me about one of The People, a woman, who frequently dreamed of the Klokwalle spirit. In her dreams she'd see a big canoe rounding Cape Elizabeth and hear the people in it faintly singing Klokwalle songs, which grew louder as the canoe approached."

Ahcleet was quiet for a time, then asked Jordan again, "Are you certain you cannot wait until after the geese fly?"

"I cannot, Grandfather. Is there a way?"

The old man thought for a time before he spoke. Then he asked, "Did you not see the Klokwalle yourself at the time of *Pangwuh?am Huhnsha?ha*?"

Pangwuh?am Huhnsha?ha. That evening in mid-April when there were small drying *valella* bodies blowing all over the sand. When Raven brought her the woven ribbon and the broken gold medal. How could she ever forget?

All of her life she would remember the humped figure wearing a long black robe piloting a black canoe with no markings through tumultuous breakers, emerging and disappearing into the fog, but leaving clear footprints for her to see.

"Yes, Grandfather, and I've seen him again."

Ahcleet raised his eyebrows.

Jordan told him about the day she'd been involved in finding the body of the murdered girl tied in an abandoned eagle's nest, attended the autopsy, and arrived home exhausted to find Old Man Ahcleet's house by the sea filled with thousands of Autumn Damask roses. About leaving the sweat bath that night and seeing the Klokwalle again.

Fleetingly seen, instantly gone.

And she had seen him once again, up on the palisades of the island she now owned. But she did not mention that.

Whenever she'd seen the Klokwalle it had been twilight or dark night and there had been fog, when the supernaturals come.

"The fact that the Klokwalle has shown himself to you before the time of winter is very significant," he observed.

Jordan waited for her great-grandfather to continue his thought.

"I believe it means that he knows of your need and is waiting to help you. Provided you observe the proper rituals."

2   August ended and September began. Lima Clemente called Jordan frequently. He was still traveling around the United States on his buying trip. He longed to see her.

3   As he frequently did when he wanted to getaway from the demands of his professional commitments and refresh himself, Royal Mercer stayed with Old Man Ahcleet in his house by the sea.

One evening Ahcleet and Mercer sat in the seat of the shamans on the beach. Jordan was gone and Tleyuk was playing with a group of kids down the street.

For a time they sat watching the sky turn from blue to multicolored to that hard black that presages the sight of billions of stars, layer upon layer upon layer, looking as if someone with enough patience could see through the stars to the very edge of the universe.

Mercer said, "The spirits have always fascinated me,

Ahcleet. I believe in them. I, who was reared in the Lutheran faith and whose origins are English and German. Have you ever found that strange?"

Old Man Ahcleet smiled. "When your grandfather first brought you here as a small boy to visit, I knew instantly that the Listening Ones saw you, that given the chance, you would become one of us in your heart."

"How did my grandfather feel about that?"

"Oh, he never knew my thoughts on those matters. He was a priest in his church and carried the Book of Common Prayer with him at all times. Even when we were making deals for timber."

Mercer nodded. "Imagine an Episcopalian taking part in the Klokwalle ceremony."

"It will happen soon. I don't imagine there is anything in your white church as demanding or as painful as the Klokwalle ceremony. When you have your communion services, do you not just sip a little wine or grape juice and nibble on a cracker?"

"Yes. It's symbolic of eating Christ's flesh and drinking His blood."

Ahcleet made no direct reply. Instead, he said, "Most of our spirits, as you well know, are ageless, sexless, sometimes cruel. And they never die. They partake of the nature of both men and animals. They are the reality of the world. In the old days, and still today for those with the wisdom to see, they arrive in the form of animals, yet look like men."

"I understand," Mercer replied. "Remember that I, too, have seen them."

Ahcleet went on, "After my first spirits came to me following my Vision Quest, they've stayed close throughout my life. I catch sight of them near my carved rattles which as you know are their symbols. Sometimes I see them in the corners of my house." The old man slid his eyes to his friend. "I suppose you've had the same experience?"

"Yes," Mercer replied. Then he laughed. "Not long ago

our bishop, who for decades has been a personal friend of mine, came to my house for dinner.

"At one point in the evening he excused himself to go to the bathroom and, having had a little too much port, opened a closet door rather than the bathroom door.

"That particular closet, which is always locked, and I still don't know why it was not locked that night, is where I keep my Quinault ritualistic material. It is also where my guardian spirit likes to stay when he's in my part of the world, which he was that night.

"Now I'm not sure what the bishop saw when he opened that door but by his reaction I thought he was having a heart attack."

"Probably thought he was seeing the Satan of his faith," Ahcleet replied.

Mercer went on. "Of course I instantly called 911, and when the bishop's cardiologist arrived at the hospital he assured poor old John that hallucinations are not unusual when an attack is coming on."

"So he *was* having a heart attack?"

"Not at all. Something just scared the shit out of him. Which, incidentally, he has never spoken about to this day."

"There are many things so-called educated people do not wish to know or see," Ahcleet commented.

Mercer sighed. "I'm afraid I've lost John as a friend. It seems that he never has time to get together anymore."

The two men relaxed and listened to the thunder of the sea. Finally Mercer spoke. "Will you be able to find enough believers for the Klokwalle ceremony to take place?"

"I've been thinking on that. There are Jordan and Paul, you and me, and three senior ritualists."

"What about Crazy Lady?"

"She's spent the summer over on Hood Canal doing some work. But I've been thinking about her so I expect she'll turn up any day now."

Mercer understood that many of the Old Ones were like that. They knew who was coming and when they were coming. They could mentally call for each other when needed. He believed it was an ability that the entire human race had once possessed until modern methods of communication wiped it out.

Ahcleet said, "She owns a lot of power and being close to my age she is old enough to remember what her mother and grandmother told her about the Klokwalle observance."

"Do you plan to bring Tleyuk to the ceremony?" Mercer asked.

"No. I think he is too young for this particular ritual. He would be frightened. He must put in several years of study first. Our rituals of religious power are seen most forcefully in the Klokwalle observance."

"The Black Tamanois Society," Mercer said.

"Yes. A man or a woman must be old enough to understand the meanings behind what at first appears fearsome."

Dizzy from looking at the stars and their conversation, the two men got up off the seat of the shamans and made their way back to Ahcleet's house.

When they got there they found Crazy Lady inside sitting in Old Man Ahcleet's favorite leather chair watching television, her old gladstone bag at her feet.

"Thought you'd never get here," she said, looking at Ahcleet with a scowl on her face.

There was someone else in the room.

He introduced himself. "Pardon me if this is an intrusion. This lady"—he indicated Crazy Lady—"was here and invited me in. I am Lima Clemente. Will Jordan be home soon?"

"Not for some time," Ahcleet said. "She is away."

He did not explain the nature of Jordan's business; seeking a new closeness with her guardian spirit in the vastness of the ancient forest.

He could not wait, Lima Clemente said, handing Ahcleet a letter for Jordan that, he said, would reveal to her his itinerary.

Then he politely took his leave.

4   There followed a swift passage of days during which those involved were extremely busy getting themselves ready for the Klokwalle ceremony, the most powerful ritual of *tamanois* in the Quinault culture.

After much serious contemplation and thumbing back through his memories of old knowledge and ancient rituals, Old Man Ahcleet calculated when the Klokwalle ceremony should be conducted.

The dark of the new moon would fall on September 12, the autumn equinox at six P.M. on September 22. The full moon would rise on September 27.

Ahcleet worked over his calculations again and again. Each time they proved that the most effective date for the Klokwalle ritual was September 27, expected to be a very bright night unless the weather changed and rain came.

Traditionally, all ceremonials were conducted during the dark of the moon to avoid confrontations with the *mala'h,* the Shadow People.

He consulted with Crazy Lady, who agreed that the participants should be told in detail what was involved in the Klokwalle ceremony as remembered by her ancestors and his.

"Warn them about the *mala'h* first," she advised.

Old Man Ahcleet called the group together.

"Sare and I will speak to you about the Klokwalle ceremony so that you will know what you are getting into," he began. "Anyone who wants to withdraw is free to go and with no hard feelings on anybody's part."

Ahcleet had everybody's attention.

"Most of The People have forgotten what I am about to tell you or think it's foolishness," he went on, "but I tell you it is true.

"When the moon is full or nearing full, the *mala'h,* the Shadow People, come. They are visible only as shadows in the daytime, but they become real people on bright nights."

"Are they dangerous?" Mercer asked.

"They can be very dangerous," Ahcleet replied.

"Why?"

"They are malcontents from the Land of the Dead. Years ago the Land of the Dead was spoken of as the Mala'h Village.

"As for now, they may have nothing against any one of us personally, but perhaps one of us has an ancestor who feuded with a Shadow Person long ago.

"Or maybe a Shadow Person was jealous of one of our ancestors. Or a person from the Land of the Dead is simply lonely and returns to try to get one of his loved ones or friends to return with him.

"That Shadow Person could cause us a lot of trouble when he becomes real in the light of the moon. I've known cases where friends of mine have been killed by the Shadow People."

The members of the group exchanged worried glances.

Mercer asked, "How will we know when they're around?"

"Usually they appear as drifting fog in the form of a human being," Ahcleet replied. "But when they see us out in the bright moonlight they will become as real as we are.

"I will tell you the warning signs. A Shadow Person might come alongside you in the form of a real person and start doing what you are doing. One of them appeared at the mouth of the river and drift netted for salmon alongside one of my friends.

"Another friend once heard voices near the graveyard but could not understand what was being said. But soon he smelled an odor of mold and knew they were ghosts.

"Also you might hear the language of the dead being spoken, which sounds to us like *ku ku ku ku*. Or they might make a sharp sound like that made by pursing the lips and drawing in air."

"Do we have any defense against them?" Jordan asked.

"The best I know is to appear unafraid, show a fierce face, and shout in a stern voice: 'Go on your way and don't bother me.'

"Above all, do not whistle after dark for that calls the Shadow People to you." Old Man Ahcleet, who had been standing, sat down. "Of course, a storm could come up," he added as a hopeful afterthought.

"Tell them about the ceremony," Crazy Lady said.

Old Man Ahcleet nodded and went on. "Both of our grandfathers and great-grandfathers were members of the secret society of the Klokwalle. We both remember hearing the stories as if we had been present at the time.

"The Klokwalle dances were held only during the three months following the *Xa'ltaanem,* the winter solstice, as I have explained before. This is the way it was.

"The members met at night in the village potlatch house. Here novices were instructed in the rituals and songs. The novitiate usually lasted five days and nights.

"During this time the novices were kept in a dark room. Nonmembers heard continuous drumming and singing and believed that the spirit entered the candidates at this time.

"The members made no claim that the novices were dead and were to be brought to life, as some of the tribes did. In the ceremonies that followed, the ones that were open to the public, there was no death and resurrection rite nor did blood appear on the mouth of the novice.

"Now if an outsider stumbled in on them he was sworn to secrecy, hit about the arms, shown how to thrust bones through the flesh of arms and lips, and forced to join the society.

"The leaders of the nation, the rich men, wore masks representing their own individual guardian spirits. They never wore masks representing the Klokwalle spirit.

"This was the only rite where The People used masks. The ordinary members wore no masks. All the dancers wore headdresses of twisted cedar bark dyed red in which they had placed undyed eagle and seagull feathers.

"Usually the public was invited to witness the rehearsed dances of the society. While the audience waited, the members retired to a secret room, or behind a screen, or to another house and made the necessary preparations—painting their bodies and wearing the correct costumes.

"The spectators were silent. Sare's grandfather told her that if one of the audience smiled or laughed, two members of the society would seize him while a third inserted his fingers into the laugher's mouth and stretched his lips painfully. Or they might gash his arms or put skewers through them.

"The laugher's face would then be painted black and he would be dragged around the fire by the hair of his head and later be forced to join the society."

Crazy Lady spoke up. "I know other things about the Klokwalle society. Now I can't swear that what I'm about to tell you is true, nor could my father swear, but it was said that in a performance at Skokomish a girl was killed because she entered the secret room while the members were preparing for the dance. My father swore that nonmembers were afraid of the organization and often feared to attend.

"A Makah member whose spirit was Bear dressed in the skin of a bear for the dances," Crazy Lady went on. "And one man used to stick arrows through the flesh of his cheeks and dance with them hanging from his mouth."

Mrs. Clam, Sam Olden, and Charles Seventrees, the senior ritualists, listened intently.

"Some men stuck knives or arrows through the flesh of their abdomens. Another man used to eat live coals. My very own grandfather saw a dancer seize a dog, tear it limb from limb, and devour the dripping flesh."

"A small dog, I presume," Jordan said.

"That I don't know. But I can tell you this. The Klokwalle members had reputations. Everybody was scared to death of them. Some of them killed and ate people during their secret rites, or so it was said."

"Don't start eating on me," Jordan said dryly. "I'll give you heartburn."

"Course not. Don't be foolish. Just want you to know what you might be getting into. That Klokwalle, he's powerful strange. If he's still around, that is. If he hasn't been killed off by them *hoquats* with their A-bombs and H-bombs. Probably got theirselves a Z-bomb by now."

Old Man Ahcleet paused and looked around the group. "That is what we can tell you. Each of you must make your own decision."

Ahcleet fell silent, Crazy Lady at his side, while the others in the group talked among themselves.

Within a short time the others agreed unanimously that they had the courage to go through with the ritual, Shadow People or no Shadow People, skewers regardless.

They *would* assist Jordan in seeking the Klokwalle's help on September 27, unfortunately a night of light. Unless an unexpected storm came.

"Fine," Old Man Ahcleet said briskly. "Now is the time to discuss the masks.

"In the past our leaders, the rich men, wore masks representing their own individual animal spirits, the Listening Ones.

"During part of the ceremony we, too, will be masked. Each of us will wear the mask of his or her animal spirit.

"The Black Tamanois was the only rite during which any of The People wore masks," he added. "No one ever wore a mask representing the Klokwalle for he is neither guardian spirit nor animal spirit. He is something beyond human description or understanding. He simply *is* and always has been.

"I, of course, will wear the mask of Thunderbird," he went on, "the great creature that causes lightning by flapping his wings. His home is in the high country. As you know, no human has ever seen him.

"Rain is his urine, hail is what he urinates when he's angry. He always urinates just before or after he flaps his wings. In the past most whale hunters received at least some of their power from Thunderbird. From him I received a great deal of power." Ahcleet touched the jagged white scar on the bridge of his nose.

Jordan said, "I will wear the mask of Cougar, whose spirit

imparts strong medicine power and high skill in fishing, hunting, tracking, and stalking."

Old Man Ahcleet nodded.

"My mask is Frog," Crazy Lady said. "Until the beginning of the twentieth century The People used to see a living frog over thirty inches long jumping around here. That there frog had five dentalium shells of different sizes on his back.

"Now in the old days the person seeing that there frog was supposed to take a stick and lightly touch the smallest shell, then turn his back real fast. And when he turned around again, the frog would be gone but he would have left the shell that had been touched. This shell then multiplied until that person grew rich.

"One man I heard about made the greedy mistake of touching the largest shell, which he put in a box. That there shell multiplied all right, multiplied until the box broke and a monster came out and killed everyone in the house."

Charles Seventrees told the group that his mask represented both Wolf and Porpoise, "because when there were still wolves here, before they'd all been killed off, they hunted the beaches at night when food became scarce.

"If they found no game or dead animals," Seventrees went on, "the leader of the pack started running in a circle, soon followed by the others.

"At last the bravest led the way into the surf and the other wolves followed, swimming out to ever deeper water, then diving and coming to the surface as porpoises. The alpha animal remained on shore to remind them what they were when they returned to land, wolves and not porpoises.

"When as porpoises they had killed as many sea creatures as the pack needed for food, they swam back to the alpha wolf, turning back into wolves the moment each met the alpha wolf's eyes."

Sam Olden would wear the mask of Elk, "the father of all elk," a creature larger than any others of its kind.

He said, "Once upon a time a hunter killed a huge black elk and, upon butchering, found that its heart was covered with hair. He realized with remorse that he had killed the father of all elk, a creature which was mystical as well as real, and the man spent the rest of his life trying to make amends."

Mrs. Clam's mask was that of Bear. Women endowed with that spirit were industrious, skilled housekeepers, fine cooks, good mothers. Mrs. Clam's smile revealed her awareness that she was all of those things.

"I'll wear the Bear mask, too," Prefontaine said. "And I'll also wear the entire bearskin. In a man, the spirit of Bear instills strength, skill, and daring."

Royal Mercer said that he of course would wear the mask presented to him by Old Man Ahcleet when The People adopted him.

"If you folks remember, it was that of the highly respected Eagle, symbolizing authority, knowledge, and power as well as kindness and honesty. Since my adoption I've tried very hard to live up to those attributes."

"You already had," Old Man Ahcleet said, placing a hand on the professor's shoulder. "That's one of the reasons we adopted you."

5   Before the black Tamanois, Jordan must first ritually cleanse herself to obtain the full power of her guardian spirit.

To do so, she took the required four baths a day, underwent sweat baths, fasted by eating only dried foods, and remained continent, which was not difficult since her lover was gone.

Lima Clemente was now in Kansas City. He telephoned her almost every day. Many of the calls she missed because she was on patrol. When this happened, Old Man Ahcleet informed her that her foreign friend had called.

"Did he leave any message?" she asked.

"Only that he would call again."

Just before she left to seek her guardian spirit, Lima Clemente called once more. She told him about the weather, about her great-grandfather, about her young son, that she missed him.

She did not tell him about her coming journey to petition her guardian spirit or the Klokwalle ceremony. Those were matters rarely spoken of even to fellow believers. And the identity of one's guardian spirit was usually never mentioned, not even to one's closest relative.

As their conversation ended, Lima Clemente's last words were, "Dearest Jordan, I am discouraged."

"Why?"

He sighed. "It is difficult to explain. I know that you are my love. Sometimes I have the feeling that you are also my death."

6   As Jordan drove to Graves Creek at the end of South Shore Road, she thought about how she had first sought her guardian spirit as an adult. That ritual had taken fourteen days and when she was through she looked like a woman who had suffered. She had.

Sta'dox!wa, the most powerful of shamanistic supernaturals, had given himself to her and helped her find her song.

The People did not believe in taking hallucinatory drugs of any kind in their efforts to achieve supernatural experiences.

They had always done it the hard way by putting their bodies through great physical efforts.

If they were successful, their minds were masters of their bodies, their bodies were not masters of their minds. And they owned the most powerful spirits in the world.

She knew that modern psychiatrists specializing in shamanic ceremonialism as it is practiced today named these ancient exercises "somatopsychological factors in the learning of spontaneous dissociative states."

They include extended sleep deprivation; hypoglycemia caused by lengthy fasting; dehydration from thirst, forced vomiting, purgation, and intensive sweating; hypoxemia, or reduced oxygenation of the blood caused by hypoventilation, exposure to temperature extremes, and the stimuli of self-inflicted pain.

She had been through it all before. Since her ordeal of mental and physical anguish Jordan had been triumphant. She now owned *Sta'dox!wa*.

But as with any loved one or dear friend, she needed to keep in contact. A one-sided friendship is no friendship at all. Neither can the ownership of a powerful supernatural be one-sided.

A neglected supernatural can become an enemy. She prayed that had not happened with *Sta'dox!wa*.

To show her faith and illustrate her need she would have to go through all the torture again.

Arriving at her destination, Jordan parked and locked her power wagon, then hiked thirteen miles into Enchanted Valley.

As before, she took nothing with her but the clothes she was wearing, a mussel-shell knife, and a small drum.

She hiked another ten miles north of an emerald-green ice cave, where she found the same place where she had undergone the rigors of her first Vision Quest as an adult.

Here, far from any trails, was the glacial stream tumbling down a series of waterfalls into a pool fringed by maidenhair ferns and surrounded by ancient cedars.

On one side was the small, natural cave sheltered by vine maple, a few leaves just beginning to turn into the scarlet glory of fall.

Jordan knew this was one of the sacred spots in the forest: in fact, it was her own sacred space. She wondered how many others had sought and found their guardian spirits here in past centuries.

There had been sacred spots throughout the forest, places that still retained their purity and solitude, unspoiled by intrusive hikers. Unfortunately, logging was destroying most of them.

The small rock wall she had built before to reflect the heat of a fire back into the cave was still standing, as was the sweat lodge; seven feet long, six feet wide, and four feet high and covered with twigs, brush, and sweet-smelling mulch she had gathered from the forest floor.

She saw that the mat of reeds she'd woven as a covering for the door opening was hanging in tatters, the missing parts put to use by creatures of the forest.

She entered the small cave gingerly. Inside, her stones still lined the slight depression she had made in the ground for her fires.

Her bed of needles and hemlock branches had dried out, so she needed to make herself a fresh one.

She dragged the old bed out and carried it a distance away from the cave, then returned carrying hemlock branches and made herself a fresh bed.

Once more she left and came back, this time with a large sheet of moss that she carefully fastened over the doorway, then rolled up carefully.

Inside the cave again, she looked for spiders but there were none, only many empty webs.

Realizing that these small creatures had known she was coming and had departed for her comfort, she whispered, "Thank you for your courtesy, Spider People."

She removed her clothing and placed it inside the cave.

Jordan built a fire outside between the small rock wall and the doorway to her cave, took the rocks from the cave, heated them in the fire, rolled them back inside, sprinkled them with water, then lowered the moss door covering, alone inside with the steam.

After the sweat bath, she emerged from the cave, rosy and damp all over, and dived into the ice-cold water of the pool.

Standing upright in the pool, water dripping from her like

molten silver, she stretched her arms upward and cried aloud:

> "Sta'dox!wa, most powerful of guardian spirits,
> I command you!
> I am La'qewamax. I am of Musqueem's lineage.
> I am Old Man Ahcleet's great-granddaughter.
> My ancestors won their strength from you.
> You showed yourself to me on my Vision Quest.
> You are so strong you speak with the earth as an
>   equal,
> Yet you allowed me to own you.
> Sta'dox!wa, it is your daughter who commands you.
> Come to me now!"

Expecting to begin her hard work the next day, Jordan decided to rest up tonight.

During the unusually noisy twilight, she sat next to the pool with her feet in the water, listening to the songs of the trees, of the eagles shrieking on their way to their nests, of the osprey calling, to the elk talk as they bedded down.

In a moment everything instantly hushed as if something of immense spiritual power was suddenly present. No frog croaked, no elk muttered, no bear grunted, no spotted owl barked. Even Raven was silent.

Jordan watched as a great radiance slowly filled the deepening twilight.

She arose from the bank of the pool and found standing before her under the cedars a smiling man made of sparking electricity.

No, she decided, it was not electricity.

Diamonds, perhaps, thousands of them, because although diamonds were colorless themselves, they sparkled with all the colors of the rainbow as did he; the red of rubies, the sea-green of emeralds, the blue of sapphires, the purple of amethysts, the gold of sun topaz, the iris of opals.

Although he stood motionless, the colors forming the

man moved about continually, drawn by unknown magnetic forces so that he appeared to be continually flashing.

She felt that same great surge of vigor throughout her body that she had felt before and knew with a stabbing thrill that she still owned *Sta'dox!wa,* that most powerful of shamanistic supernaturals, and he had answered her call.

She wanted to run to him, to become absorbed by him, to glory in his glory, but the luminous man put up his right hand, palm out in a gesture for her to halt.

She realized that he was the source of light, that the incandescence came from him. And almost immediately she wondered if he was the origin of the old stories about The People of ancient times mating with stars.

He continued to smile benevolently even as his radiance faded into the fire surrounding him.

With his going, the forest darkened and with the darkening, the great trees and the creatures of the woods began to whisper and move.

Jordan's heart overflowed with joy.

Sta'dox!wa, the most powerful of shamanistic supernaturals, her own guardian spirit, had come to her once more, and by his presence assured her of his help in summoning the Klokwalle. And she did not have to go through all of the ritual for him to come to her.

Part Four

And I have felt
A presence that disturbs me with joy
Of elevated thoughts; a sense sublime
Of something far more deeply interfused,
Whose dwelling is the light of setting suns,
And the round ocean and the living air,
And the blue sky, and in the mind of man;
A motion and a spirit, that impels
All thinking things, all objects of thought,
And rolls through all things.

—WILLIAM WORDSWORTH,
"Lines Composed a Few Miles Above
Tintern Abbey," July 13, 1798

Chapter 23

1 The sun moved toward the western reaches of the North Pacific reluctantly, it seemed to Jordan, as if into the arms of a gray and infirm lover.

Proving its virility, the sea rampaged onto the shore with a force of two tons per square inch of land, stealing back with each ebb a part of the earth.

Breaker after breaker they surged in, twelve breakers deep, sometimes fifteen, one crowding upon the watery heels of the other with a roar that deafened.

Mare's tails streamed a quarter of a mile back over the sea. The air was full of invigorating sea salt. Jordan inhaled deeply.

The mists of exploding breakers, intermingling with rays from the westering sun, created thousands of small rainbows. Soon, seawater and rainbows began filling the numerous bowl-shaped tidal pools.

On and on the breakers raced, heaving up into the western shore of the Olympic Peninsula, on the beach below a steep basaltic headland at the mouth of the Quinault River, the edge of the world.

It was September 27, the night of the full moon.

Despite the foretold brightness of the night to come, and the feared appearance of the *mala'h,* those dangerous Shadow People, it was the time when Jordan must try to summon the Klokwalle.

She knew that in the old days the Klokwalle ceremony would have been performed in the potlatch house and attended by all of The People who were not afraid to do so. Now, most of them felt such ancient ceremonies to have no place in their modern lives.

In fact, Paul Prefontaine had posted several tribal police at strategic points just in case any ardent disapprovers decided to interfere.

The only true believers left in the old Smokehouse Religion were Old Man Ahcleet, Jordan, Prefontaine, Crazy Lady, Royal Mercer, and the three ritualists: Mrs. Clam, Sam Olden, and Charles Seventrees.

All were gathered here to help Jordan by performing the Black Tamanois, a ceremony whose ancient mysteries none living had ever witnessed or attempted.

Each had gone through his or her own personal spiritual and physical exercises to prepare for this long-outlawed ritual. One that, if they were successful, would be charged with fearsome power.

2   Prefontaine, assisted by Royal Mercer, gathered drift-
       wood and, with difficulty because a strong west
wind had begun to blow, managed to build a large fire on the
beach, feeding and nursing the flames until the blaze was
strong enough to withstand the wind.

The rest of the group gathered behind a great pile of
whitened driftwood to prepare themselves for the dance.

When they walked onto the beach, one following the
other, each wore his or her regular clothing and a headdress
of twisted cedar bark dyed red.

Except for Jordan, who came first, looking majestic,
attired in a princely shaman's costume of antique beauty and
inestimable value.

The costume had been in her family for many generations. Upon entering her shamanhood two years before, Old
Man Ahcleet gave her the costume with the words, "It is
yours for you are the next shaman."

When the white man's church and the United States
government outlawed spirit dancing in 1871, Ahcleet's
grandfather, forewarned by a white friend, carefully hid
all of his shamanistic materials in a hollow tree out in the
forest.

Even though representatives of the government and the
church searched his house carefully, actually tearing it apart
in their zeal, they found nothing to incriminate him as
belonging to the Smokehouse Religion or having artifacts or
ceremonial articles.

Nevertheless, the man was publicly whipped, fined, and
sentenced to years of hard labor for being known as a shaman.

It was Jordan's shaman's costume now, invaluable, made
holy by time, human faith, and suffering.

It included a flowing cape with matching dance apron,
both pieces fashioned of the silky-soft inner bark of
cedar.

When first designed several hundred years before, the
cedar had been bleached ivory, then interwoven with rich,
dark otter skins.

Sewn along the seams and interspersed with three-inch dentalium shells were tiny hard-carved ivory and bone charms representing various spirit helpers.

Rattles made of deer hooves strung on beaded ankle bands completed the outfit.

When the group came into view, Prefontaine and Royal Mercer retreated from the fire, walked behind the great pile of whitened driftwood, and returned wearing the same type of headdress as the others.

Old Man Ahcleet appeared last, also wearing a twisted cedar headdress dyed red. But in his headdress there were undyed eagle and seagull feathers. He carried a drum.

At his signal, the group circled and faced the fire.

The drum began to talk, so quietly at first that it could not be heard above the roar of the breakers.

The drum's voice grew louder, ever louder, until it seemed to outshout the sea, summoning the participants to begin the dance.

They obeyed, moving in a clockwise direction, their upper arms held horizontally, their lower arms vertically, while their hands moved slightly, keeping time to the beating of his drum.

Ahcleet started to sing:

> *"Nolamen nolamen Tsis e lokallie . . .*
> *Nolamen nolamen Tsis e lokallie . . ."*

He sang the words over and over again, changing the emphasis from word to word so that it seemed to the listeners a very long song.

The group danced and danced while Ahcleet sang and beat his drum, even the oldest among them showing no signs of exhaustion as the dance went on.

As she danced, Jordan saw that the sun had yielded to a bloodred sea. After a lengthy twilight, night would fall.

When Old Man Ahcleet's singing and drumming faded

away, the dancers all stopped dancing and moved back behind the piled driftwood, leaving the beach to gathering mists and rampaging breakers.

On the horizon, black storm clouds were gathering.

3   Jordan walked back onto the windswept beach first, wearing the mask of Cougar. On her body she wore only paint. She felt the sea winds growing stronger.

Old Man Ahcleet, appearing next, wore the mask of Thunderbird, a great creature no human had ever seen, the one that caused lightning by the flapping of his wings.

Crazy Lady walked toward them, wearing the mask of Frog, symbolizing the frog that married the moon. On the back of Sare's frog mask were five dentalium shells of various sizes, just as had been on the original living frog.

Charles Seventrees wore his mask representing both Wolf and Porpoise, illustrating the duality of nature, the link that binds all living creatures, animal and human.

Sam Olden wore the mask of Elk, representing "the father of all elk," a creature larger than any others of its kind.

Mrs. Clam proudly wore her Bear mask.

Prefontaine also wore the Bear mask. In addition he wore the entire bearskin, which was heavy even for a man of his strength.

Royal Mercer wore the Eagle mask presented to him by Old Man Ahcleet when the The People adopted him.

All of the participants were naked except for their masks and the appropriate body paint.

Jordan did not feel the deepening chill of the sea winds, only excitement and a feverish fear.

Although she had seen the Klokwalle before, she had really only glimpsed him. She had never seen him face-to-face.

He was from the ancient pantheon of spirits, long neglected; cursed, even, by many who now believed that if he had ever existed at all he must have been one of the manifestations of Satan.

But she realized that the world was very, very old. The religion of Christianity, from which the concept of Satan had sprung, was comparatively young.

And in spite of Ahcleet's analysis that the Klokwalle had allowed Jordan glimpses of himself because he was willing to help her, she could not banish her doubts.

Was she bringing death and destruction on her friends as well as herself by this act? She simply did not know.

What she did know was that she was afraid, terrified, actually. And, should anyone ask, she wasn't too proud to admit it.

Now the dance began again, different this time, Old Man Ahcleet dancing with the others to the sound and rhythm of the sea; all singing, all with arms folded, all with hands concealed.

As the sea raged, the dancing and singing grew more and more frenzied. Old Man Ahcleet slashed his arms, as did Jordan, both of whom were bleeding as they danced, the blood running down their bodies and into the sand.

One by one, each of the other dancers injured himself in some way with mussel-shell knives so that blood was running from all of them.

The pearly twilight, the roar of the sea, the strengthening winds, the flames of the fire, the wild singing, the pain of running blood, all helped to disconnect each human consciousness into the spirit of the mask each dancer wore and the animal it represented.

In so doing, each became, in a very small way, a part of the congregation of Listening Ones.

A shadow moved swiftly along the beach.

Jordan shivered. The *mala'h* were coming.

But when she looked up, Jordan saw that it was only Gwaxo, the eagle who lived with her twin brother.

Her spirit rose to meet that of the bird of prey. Within moments she was seeing through the eagle's eyes, looking down upon the beach.

Watching, she saw herself drop to all fours and step softly around the fire like a cougar, stopping every so often to sniff the winds, stretching her body, making soft chirrups, smiling her cougar smile.

From above, she saw that her cougar self stopped in midstep and looked around at the other dancers through unusual blue cougar eyes. Suddenly she heard herself utter shrill screams, over and over again, the ritual calling for a mate.

Nothing answered.

Through the eagle's eyes she watched Old Man Ahcleet thrust skewers through the flesh of his upper arms.

Bleeding, he flapped his arms like the wings of Thunderbird, urinating before and after each flapping motion.

Crazy Lady squatted down, hopping like a frog, as she slashed her thighs with a mussel-shell knife.

Charles Seventrees imitated the movements first of Wolf, then of Porpoise, running into the water, seeing in his mind's eye the great alpha wolf calling him back from the sea.

Sam Olden became Elk, body poised and listening, the antlers of his mask held high, leaping now and then as if charging an opponent during the rut.

Mrs. Clam, wearing the mask of Bear, produced a small broom from under her folded arms and swept the beach with great zeal.

Prefontaine, who wore the entire bear head and hide, lumbered about on all fours, growling and grumbling, finally picking up a huge beach boulder that in his normal state he would not have been able to move even slightly.

Mercer, meanwhile, slashed the palms of his hands, then lifted his feathered arms, swooping and stooping, a man with the heart of an eagle.

There were no shadows except that of the Gwaxo soaring back and forth, Jordan looking out from the eagle's eyes.

No *mala'h* appeared. At least, none that she could see.

4   While the dancers danced, the full moon wandered
     into the twilight sky at a spot exactly opposite the
sun.

Mere days after the autumn equinox, it was a time when
earth's million-mile-long shadow stretched way beyond the
quarter-million-mile distant moon.

Normally the full moon was the sky gazer's disappointment, the least interesting phase, because craters and other
topographic features were whitewashed into oblivion.

But an eclipse changes everything.

Now a normally dull full moon underwent an hour-long
series of peculiar patterns, displaying eclipse-induced
slices unlike anything seen throughout the normal lunar
month.

5   With the first flood of moonlight, the dancers gazed
     upward with their animal faces, then quickly back
down with fear because now they knew the *mala'h* must
come . . .

Jordan's shrill screams continued, sounding like those of
Cougar when seeking a mate and were heard by Jordan's
spirit in Gwaxo.

She watched herself straddle a whitened beach log without bark and, resting her forearms with her hindquarters
raised, plow her neck alongside the log, rubbing it repeatedly in imitation of female cougars that do the same thing
until a moist, viscous fluid is secreted from a gland in their
necks.

She lifted her head and screamed again.

This time her call was answered.

A young male approached the scent log.

In an attempt to smell the female's odor he lowered his
head as if to sniff the secretion, then raised his nose, allowing air to pass into his pharynx.

Curling his lip, he grimaced as if displeased but his behavior caused the smell to pass over a sensory gland in the roof of his mouth, allowing him to taste her scent.

He attempted to copulate. Jordan saw herself turn and swat him in the face. He withdrew, abashed.

In the way of female cougars, she persisted in tormenting him, flicking her imaginary tail to one side and pressing her hindquarters to his nose, or crouching seductively in front of him, then swirling around to tear at his face with her claws.

At that moment Jordan's spirit sped down from the eagle and settled into her own human body. She pushed the cougar mask up on top of her head.

And found that she was looking at Roc Tidewater, her ex-husband.

Disconnecting totally from the cougar consciousness, returning entirely to her human self, Jordan became aware that Roc Tidewater had died and gone to the Land of the Dead, and had now returned as a *mala'h* in an attempt to take her back with him.

She remembered her great-grandfather's words of advice regarding the *mala'h*. She followed them now.

Frowning her fiercest frown at her ex-husband, she shouted, "Go away, Roc Tidewater. Do not bother me or mine. Go away. Leave this place."

A man now, seeming to be as real as herself, he stared at her longingly and reached out his hand.

"Now!" she shouted.

As he dissolved into mist and disappeared into the sea winds, tears fell down her cheeks.

Jordan saw that now the *mala'h* were all around, tormenting the dancers, breaking up the dance.

Each participant except Royal Mercer had one or more *mala'h* pulling at him or trying to strike out.

One *mala'h* belabored Crazy Lady with a length of driftwood in the shape of an ancient slave killer tool.

All the *mala'h* wore the dress of long ago, so Jordan knew that her friends were being punished for hurts, real or imagined, that their ancestors had inflicted upon others.

Only Roc Tidewater had been from the modern age and was dressed accordingly.

With a sense of pity and a certain grief because she loved him once, Jordan wondered how and when Tleyuk's father had died.

6   Jordan ran to Mercer's side who, unafflicted by *mala'h*, was looking up at the full moon.

"It'll turn red any minute now," Mercer said.

"Why red?"

"It's a lunar eclipse. You and I may cast a dark shadow, but earth's is coppery red. That's because all our planet's sunrises and sunsets refract their ruddy light into the shadow. And any cloud cover or volcanic dust over parts of earth will give an artistic variety to the moon's eclipsed appearance."

But something strange happened.

Under the roar of the sea, they heard another roar, a great roar, faint from distance, but approaching nevertheless.

"Did you hear that?" Jordan asked Mercer.

"Yes."

"Is it another earthquake?"

"I don't know yet, Jordan."

The moon disappeared from their sight.

Entirely and literally, as if some heavenly presence had snatched it out of the sky.

There was no moon at all.

Nor were there any *mala'h*. They, too, had vanished with the light of the moon.

"The moon has left us!" Crazy Lady shrieked.

All of the group, released now from vengeful *mala'h*, gathered around Mercer.

"It's not gone," Mercer told them. "It's turned black. Happens sometimes, but not often."

"Why?"

"Because we're seeing a lunar eclipse, the last one of this century."

"In the old days we danced to bring back the sun and the moon when they went away," Ahcleet said. "They always returned. I wonder if the moon will return this time."

"It's left us, I tell you, it's gone," Crazy Lady cried, fear making her voice tremble. "We're being punished for trying to summon that there Klokwalle."

"What we're seeing is the greatest *mala'h* of all," Mercer said. "Mala'h Earth has eaten the moon."

Crazy Lady howled.

"Sare," Jordan began. "Don't be upset. This is a perfectly natural event."

"Next we'll all disappear. *Anananana!*"

Jordan reached out in an effort to comfort the old woman.

"Leave her be," Old Man Ahcleet said. "Sare needs her dramatic moments." But he, too, looked worried.

Crazy Lady ran back behind the pile of driftwood to rummage, Jordan suspected, in the old gladstone bag Sare carried with her wherever she went.

When the old woman returned Jordan could tell by the smell that Sare had rubbed herself with some special ointment or herb.

With the moon gone, the night was black, the sky encrusted with stars.

7   Cougar, Thunderbird, Frog, Wolf and Porpoise, Elk, and the two Bears, their heads animal, their bodies human, stood facing the vastest ocean on earth, enveloped by its breath, shrouded by its mists.

Then, oddly enough and as sometimes happens, the sea fell silent and drew back. The winds fled westward as if urgently called.

By starshine Jordan saw in the far distance an impossibility: the waters seemed to be gathering themselves together.

Wrapped in clouds, a great waterspout arose from the sea, growing higher and ever higher, becoming a great circular storm with the magnitude and power of a tropical typhoon and a shape similar to that of a coiled snake.

Then came a sound as if all the roars ever uttered upon the earth by man or beast or by the planet itself were combined into one.

The typhoon was racing toward them.

As was the sea, assaulting the shore once more like liquid thunder. A voice seemed to cry, *I am coming, I am coming.*

"Now is the time to be strong," Old Man Ahcleet said quietly.

The typhoon advanced, hurling jagged shards of lightning from all surfaces of its coiled self.

Jordan watched in terror as a black figure outlined in phosphorescence belched forth and rushed toward her, the typhoon racing behind it.

Old Man Ahcleet and the rest of the group fled. She heard him shout, "Come back to the fire! Now we must dance as we've never danced before! Our lives and Jordan's depend upon it!"

The dance began once more.

Jordan remained where she was, frozen in position, staring into the terror approaching from the sea.

As the blackness within the typhoon drew even closer, Jordan saw that it was a tall humped figure, hooded, standing upright in a large black canoe.

It was the humped figure she had seen before. This time he was guiding the vessel through raging breakers with the authority of total command.

By his proud stance and in spite of the hump on his back, the sea was his, the land was his, the sky above, also.

Fear seized her by the throat. When she came face-to-face with this being, what would she see? A monster with the crippled body of a man? A creature too terrible for a human to look upon?

But Old Man Ahcleet said that this was the spirit that inspired courage. Could that mean that if she survived looking at the surely awful approaching face she could survive anything?

And then he was upon her, the Klokwalle. The whirling, roaring lightning-laced typhoon remained in position behind the black canoe as he jumped out, dragged it farther up the beach out of reach of the sea, and strode toward Jordan.

Trembling but not moving an inch, Jordan felt her naked spray-soaked body break out in a sweat of hot fear.

Gathering her courage, she gazed into the blackness beneath the hood, having to look up even though she herself was six feet tall. She saw no face, simply a roiling mix of human feelings: hatred, jealousy, chaos, and disillusion.

A stray thought sprinted through her mind. She'd sometimes wondered about the color of negative feelings.

Now she knew. Jealousy was a sickly yellow; hatred, the color of old blood. Chaos was pustulant green; disillusion, a bruised purple.

She feared that this spirit, whatever he was, would demand fresh blood. Blood in exchange for courage. Would it be hers? Or the blood of her great-grandfather? Or the blood of her friends?

The winds had returned with the Klokwalle's approach. Now they were so strong it was difficult to stand. Sand, leaves, small rocks, as well as some not so small, were being hurled up and down the beach.

She feared for the lives of Old Man Ahcleet and her friends. She had brought them here. What should she do? Mentally she called upon her guardian spirit.

As the Klokwalle drew ever closer to Jordan, a flame of tiny moving lights, as if from thousands of electrified dia-

monds, poured themselves into the air between herself and
the arrival from the sea.

Her heart lifted and she knew that Sta'dox!wa, the most
powerful of shamanistic supernaturals and her own guardian
spirit, was announcing his presence both to her and to the
newcomer.

Abruptly the humped figure stopped at the waterfall of
blazing diamonds as if at an impenetrable wall.

He spoke; more correctly, Jordan's mind felt his words,
becoming aware of them without actually hearing a voice.

They were expressed in the most ancient form of the
Quinault language, which she had studied and most of
which she understood.

"I see you, Sta'dox!wa, and I greet you. I have not been
called for long ages. Who dares to call me now?"

The diamondlike mist comprised of the red of rubies, the
sea-green of emeralds, the blue of sapphires, the purple of
amethysts, the gold of sun topaz, the iris of opals, all in
constant electric movement, entered into the blackness that
was Klokwalle and they seemed to dance together for a
time.

The light of sparkling jewels coalesced and Jordan saw
once more, for an instant only, her guardian spirit in the
form of a man before he disappeared in a mist of diamonds.

The humped figure turned toward Jordan and threw back
the hood covering his head. Once again she looked up into
the face of the Klokwalle.

Now, after his interchange with her guardian spirit, he
possessed a face of inexpressible beauty, black as the black
moon, so black she was surprised she could make out his
features.

"You called me," his mind said to hers. "I answer."

The pupils of his eyes shone like black shale, while the
whites were emerald-green. His full lips were black with
phosphorescence playing around them as it did the outline
of his figure.

When he smiled she saw that his teeth flashed ivory.

He had a head of sable curls that fell to his shoulders. Were it not for the hump on his back he would have been exquisite in appearance.

The Klokwalle's mind said to hers. "You seek courage, La'qewamax. That is strange because courage you already possess."

Aware of her guardian spirit's presence by the mist of diamonds moving about in the air, and of the small group headed by Ahcleet dancing madly around the fire, all the while slashing at their arms and legs, Jordan moved closer to the supernatural and stood, absolutely still.

He reached out and enfolded her in his arms. As he did so, Jordan entered a realm of darkness in which she saw a future.

She saw Tleyuk, her son, threatened by an unknown danger she could not bear to look at; she saw Old Man Ahcleet and her twin brother in great distress, again a danger she refused to view.

Quickly she drew back and he let her go.

"Remove the hump from my back," the Klokwalle commanded.

Remove the hump from his back?

"Remove the hump from my back."

Still she hesitated. How could she remove a supernatural hump from a supernatural body?

"Remove the hump from my back!" Now his voice was a roar.

She reached up under his black robe. What seemed to be a hump was actually a separate container of some kind. She lifted it down, placed it on the sand, and saw an ancient valise made of bone and elk hide.

"Open it," came the voiceless command.

Obeying, she found a living bald eagle roosting within. The eagle glared up at her from burning yellow eyes.

"Pick it up."

A fully matured bald eagle, which this was, was nothing to be trifled with. Trembling, she reached down to follow the Klokwalle's command. Lifting the eagle, she felt it slash her arm with its sharp, curved beak, right between two slashes she had already made herself with a mussel-shell knife.

Wincing from pain, she nevertheless held the eagle at eye level, staring into its fierce eyes. It did not attack her again, only stared back. She felt something pass from the eagle into herself.

Gwaxo screamed from aloft.

The eagle in Jordan's arms flapped its great wings once, screamed, flexed its talons, tearing them into her arm as it did so, then made the little jump eagles make before they take off.

Then the eagle slowly lifted itself aloft with great, slow sweeps of its wings, gathering speed as it rose.

Watching its ascent, she saw the supernatural eagle join Gwaxo.

She walked back into the Klokwalle's arms, determined now to see what she had been afraid to face before.

For a brief moment she saw.

She saw them all.

Her small son, her great-grandfather, her twin brother.

All of them dead.

Mutilated and dead, leaving her alone except for her depthless grief. Above the scene of carnage she heard Lima Clemente calling out to her.

Shaken, Jordan looked up into the sky as the two eagles ascended together until they were out of her sight.

Bloody and disheveled, she knew what she had to do. Something heartbreaking.

The storm had stopped. Simply vanished as had the moon, earlier. Old Man Ahcleet and her friends were still dancing around the fire.

She turned and the Klokwalle was gone.

Looking out to sea she saw a man standing upright in a black canoe heading westward through the breakers, his back to her.

Overhead, earth's great shadow had passed and the full moon shone with a benevolent light. Jordan was certain no more Shadow People would appear tonight.

She had passed through her travail.

The moon had been released from earth's shadow just as she had been released from the shadow of a dark love.

8   Exhausted, bloody, triumphant, they all returned to Old Man Ahcleet's house, where Crazy Lady administered a liquid solution of arnica and calendula to all those with open wounds, including herself. Then, with Jordan's help, she applied poultices of fresh comfrey leaves.

After being treated, Mrs. Clam, Sam Olden, and Charles Seventrees each went to their own homes. The others went to bed in Ahcleet's house.

After everyone who was leaving had left, and the others had retired, Jordan went to bed, physically exhausted but filled with so much mental energy, such clarity of thought, she could not sleep.

Memories—and questions—flooded her mind, as if her guardian spirit whispered to her all during what was left of the night. Remember that? Remember this?

Most intriguing of all, why had she seen the other half of a gold medal and a torn woven vicuna wool ribbon hanging from a framed photograph in the Catholic church in the Chilean village that was Lima Clemente's home?

And she especially remembered the harshness of Lima Clemente's words, the ones he had spoken upon their discovery of the dismembered little Indian boy in the hollow of the granite boulder.

"Stay away, Jordan! Do not look at that! It is not for your eyes!"

Why had he said that? Whose business was a murder on Quinault lands if not that of the tribal sheriff?

But he had spoken those words *before* she had fully realized what was in the hollow of the boulder. He had rushed past her and ordered her not to come any closer.

He had known what was there.

Still the words sounded again and again in her mind, as if on an endlessly playing tape. She could not turn them off.

Raven is a loyal and eternal friend of human beings, although he sometimes does not mind punishing them when their disobedience or mockery angers him.
—FATHER ANATOLII KAMENSKII,
Tlingit Indians of Alaska, 1906

Chapter 24

1   The next morning Jordan got up at seven and called New York, leaving a message for Lima Clemente with the Plaza Hotel. She asked that he call her back around eight o'clock that night, Pacific daylight time.

Considering the time difference, she had not expected to find him in his room because she knew that for several days he would be in discussions with bankers and the Chilean ambassador.

No one else in the house was up except for Tleyuk, who was eating breakfast. Jordan kissed him, then ground beans and made fresh coffee. She sat down at the kitchen table and ate a toasted English muffin spread with butter and clover honey.

Wide-eyed, Tleyuk asked, "Mom, what happened to your arms?"

"Nothing serious, honey."

"But they're all bandaged."

"It's okay, Tleyuk."

"Is it something to do with what I'll be learning in my training?"

"Yes, it is." She looked at the clock. "You'd better run, honey. It's late."

He kissed her and was out the door before she could kiss him back.

At ten minutes after eight Jordan called the FBI office in Aberdeen and asked for Hunter Kleoh.

"Top of the morning to you, Jordan," Kleoh said cheerfully when he came on the line.

"Hunter, what's the progress on the Indian boy's face?"

"Let me check." She could hear him shuffling papers. "According to the latest report, the beetles have done their job and the experts have started the actual rebuilding."

"Okay. Fine. I'd like to make a request."

"Go ahead."

"The remains included one hand."

"Yes."

"Could you have that hand autopsied by someone who specializes in vascular surgery?"

"Why?"

"If you remember, nothing was done with it at the original autopsy."

"Well, it was only a perfunctory autopsy because the cause of death was so obvious. What would we be looking for, Jordan?"

"Blood vessels. Tell the surgeon to look for extra blood vessels."

"And what would that prove?"

"That the little boy came from a very cold place."

"There're lots of very cold places in the world."

"I realize that."

"I'm not sure I could get an authorization."

"Would you mind if I called Eli Raptor?"

"Not at all."

"I'll do that, Hunter."

"Let me know what he says, okay?"

"Of course. Bye now."

She hung up and immediately called Eli Raptor in Seattle.

"Good to hear from you, Jordan," Raptor said. "I've got some news. We've found a match on a fingerprint you took from that boulder."

"Who does it belong to?"

"A woman by the name of Machi Juana. I can't figure out how she had anything to do with the logging congress, unless she was somebody's maid or child minder. According to customs, she entered the country in early April and left a couple of weeks later. Her destination was Lake Quinault."

"Where was she from?"

"A small village in Chile," he replied, naming the village.

Jordan became speechless. It was the same village she and Royal Mercer had recently visited. What would that have to do with Lima Clemente? The village was his childhood home but he had lived for many years in Santiago.

"Jordan? Are you there?"

"Excuse me, Eli, I was lost in thought for a moment," she replied, going on to tell him what she wanted and explaining that Hunter Kleoh saw no point in doing an autopsy on the small boy's hand.

"I find myself wondering what that would prove as far as the case goes," was his comment. "Give me your views."

"The point is that if that little boy's hand does carry extra blood vessels we will know he came from a very cold place."

"I agree with Hunter. There are a lot of cold places. So what?"

"Eli, today I'm sending you a print of a photograph I took in southern Chile, in the same village, as a matter of fact, that you say Machi Juana came from."

"*What?*"

"The photograph is a shot of a framed photo in the small Catholic church in that village," she continued. "It's of a little boy who's supposed to have died of fever along with his parents and been disposed of in their way, which is that they leave the dead body in a special place outside to be devoured by condors. His name, by the way, was Antonio Salinas."

"My mind is reeling. What in God's name have you been up to? Chile, you say? Who authorized that?"

"Nobody. I had vacation time coming and I went with Royal Mercer, who was speaking at an anthropology conference in Santiago. After the conference, Uncle Roy and I went to that village, high in the Andes. It's an extremely cold place. The people who live there, according to the priest, who is not one of them, have extra blood vessels in their hands and feet."

"I'm speechless."

"So how about an autopsy on the boy's hand?"

"Whoa, there. I think the first question is how you knew about that village."

"I heard about it from a friend."

"A friend. Would you care to tell me who that friend is?"

"Not now, Eli. This all may be coincidental. I don't want to get an innocent person involved."

"Commendable."

"Now, will you authorize an autopsy on that hand, please?"

"You've got it, Jordan."

"Please remember to have it done by a board-certified vascular surgeon."

"Under those circumstances, thy wish is my command," Raptor said.

Jordan thought she heard a smile, as well as something else she couldn't quite identify, in his voice.

2   At nine o'clock all of the household except Tleyuk were still in bed. Jordan realized that she herself had not yet recovered from the ritual of the night.

Nevertheless, she left on patrol. Taholah was socked in with fog but about a quarter of a mile inland she found, as she had expected, hot, bright weather. Her wounds aching, she stopped at a small clinic for a tetanus shot. Cuts from an eagle's claws could easily become infected.

She made up her mind to see how Anson was getting along. She hadn't checked with him since the night she'd arrested Able Majors and Jack Flanagan, now safely jailed.

She thought highly of Anson. Somehow he seemed to her an emotional link to her father. Mika had liked and respected the man; so did she.

Consequently, her next stop was the hollow cedar stump in which Anson lived. When she got out of her truck, she heard the rustle of approaching autumn here in the high country. There was a different fragrance in the air and a deeper, lusher beauty to the forest: something mature, like an older woman at the very height of her beauty.

Smiling, she listened as the great trees—Douglas fir, western red cedar, hemlock, Sitka spruce—whispered together quietly.

Occasionally, one of the trees, and then another, waved its huge dark branches, as if in disagreement, while the other trees remained still, apparently listening.

As a child, Jordan had always wondered about the phenomenon of only one tree in a group of trees moving about. If a wind caused the branches to move, all of the trees would be moving, instead of just one.

But it happened. And, while no longer a child, she still wondered.

The leaves on big, sprawling maples, soon to be drenched with fall color, were still green and the trees themselves were heavy with gray-green goatsbeard moss and tiny vivid green ferns.

One dry leaf fell to the ground as Jordan got out of her

truck. She looked up. None of the other leaves that she could see were dry yet and none were coming down.

She walked around the body of the great cedar that had supplied by its falling the huge stump in which Anson lived.

By now it had metamorphosed into a nurse log with thousands of small vigorous trees growing up through the cedar's thick moss blanket.

As she knocked on the tree trunk she noticed there was no mat of fresh young branches placed on the ground for Anson to wipe his feet on.

What was there was stale, dried out. That was odd. Anson always kept a fresh mat in front of his only door.

There was no answer.

She knocked again and waited. Silence.

Perhaps he was out cutting shake blocks. She decided to knock one more time, then leave if there was no response.

There was none.

She worried about Anson. He was nearly always alone. If he got sick, really sick, how would he get word to anyone for help? Suppose he had a heart attack? Or a stroke? Suppose he was injured when hunting? Or when he was out cutting firewood?

She'd often expressed her concern about these matters to the man himself.

"Everybody's got to die sometime, Jordan," he'd said with a somber look in his eye. "There's a time to die and none of us knows when that time is."

She remembered that the last time she was here he'd talked to her about the big-time poaching he suspected—and she knew—was going on. Suppose he had run afoul of one of the poachers and had been murdered?

Just as she turned to walk away, she noticed that the door cut into the tree was ever so slightly ajar. That was peculiar.

She pushed the door slightly and it swung open. She walked inside. Anson was not present in the large circular cedar-smelling room.

She looked around. Everything was neat, the bear rugs appeared newly shaken and placed back on the floor.

Anson's trunks containing his many books were lined up and closed. The rough-hewn table was clear except for a polished kerosene lamp with a neatly trimmed wick.

There was one more thing on the table. Moving closer, she saw that it was an envelope addressed to her.

She didn't want to pick it up.

Her hand poised in midair, she wondered why she'd gotten into a line of work where there were so many things to do that she did not want to do.

She picked up the sealed envelope, went back outside, and opened it. The letter, dated a couple of weeks earlier, read:

> Jordan:
>
> I know you will be the first to read this. What I don't know is how long before you arrive on your next visit.
>
> I am sorry that I will not see you again. Yes, my dear Jordan, I am leaving my forest, I am leaving the treasured visits first from your father and more recently from yourself. I am leaving my books.
>
> Here I have found peace. I have already administered justice, if such is possible, and am going now to perhaps find an even greater peace.
>
> You will ask why. You deserve to know.
>
> I am sure you remember the photograph of the young man you remarked on during your last visit. I told you he was a young friend. He was more than that. Much more.

Jordan stopped reading and looked musingly off into the trees. Had Anson been a man who loved men? She returned to the letter.

> I am equally certain that you remember the case of the murdered girl, the one found in an eagle's nest. I understand there have been no leads as to the killer. Oh, yes, even in my isolation I hear things.
>
> I discovered that my young friend had murdered that girl. He kept her for several days at least, proba-

bly more, in the cave where I store my perishables. My root cellar.

Eventually I realized that when he said he wanted to go out for a walk in the forest by himself, he went into that cave and did what he did to her.

He'd only been here a few days when I noticed that he never permitted me to go to the cave for supplies. He'd always say, "Now, Anson, you're older than I am. Let my young legs do the work."

And God forgive me, I did. It was pleasant being waited on. He must have known that when he left and I had to go to the cave for supplies I would discover her body. I know he counted on my silence just as he had in the past.

The day came when he was gone, I don't know where; not to the cave anyway; and I went there to get potatoes for a stew, one of those slowly simmering kinds of stews, the best.

There she was, dead, horribly abused, spoiled and rotting among my foodstuffs.

I know now I should have hiked down the mountain and found a phone to call you. After all, it's only ten miles. But I did not.

I can hear you asking, "Why didn't you, Anson?"

I have no defense. When I found the girl's body I felt an awful terror and fear.

I was afraid to confront what I knew would be coming if I did—the law in its many forms and with its loud bodies, stories in the gossip rags about the hermit who was probably the murderer. And my former colleagues whispering among themselves: "Did you hear what happened to old Anson? Doesn't surprise me. Always thought he was a bit off."

Of course I knew. Hadn't I been one of the best criminal defense attorneys in the East?

What I did do was this: I picked up her naked body (she had passed beyond the first rigor) and quickly *dressed it in her clothes, which had been flung aside. I did not have time to clean her up as I would have wished.*

I knew that Michael McTavish was logging on Fire Road Six because I'd been cutting shake blocks there. I knew about the abandoned eagle's nest in the stovepipe branch of the old dead cedar, that in a few days those trees would be coming down.

I wanted her quickly found. But until she was found, her body must be kept from the animals. What better place than up in an old eagle's nest?

But I had to wait for night.

In the meantime, my young friend returned and suspected by my eyes that I knew. Neither one of us mentioned it. Until dark fell he read and I studied. I could find no defense for her killer in my law books, nor in my heart.

When it was dark he went to bed and I set out on my journey, taking my climbing gear with me. I found the eagle's nest, climbed the tree, and placed her there. Although I am not a religious man, I said a small childhood prayer for her family.

When I returned it was nearly morning. My young friend was still asleep. I stood over him for long minutes. I bent down and ran my hand through his hair, remembering tender moments in the past. My young genius. A genius with a terrible flaw.

Then I shot him through the ear, giving him the beneficence of an instant death, which he certainly had not given that poor girl. After that, I lay down beside him and held him in my arms and wept.

I have no choice in what I am about to do, Jordan. If there is a life after death I will soon be where he is and I will find him.

Tried in our courts he would undoubtedly go free as he knew a number of excellent attorneys and had the money to pay them.

He had to be punished, not by man's law, which might or might not have imprisoned him for a few years, but by a greater law which I have to find.

The few belongings that I leave are yours. The only thing of value is my library. It is yours to sell or keep, as you wish.

Farewell, Jordan. I doubt that we will meet again for when you die you will go to your Land of the Dead.

When I die I'm not sure where I will go. I know it will be the same place he went. The two of us will be together.

Down here on earth our bodies will be together as they should be. No need to look for us, Jordan. He is out in the forest mouldering in a distant spot, as I will be soon, at the bottom of a steep canyon, where no stray hiker is likely to have the unpleasant experience of stumbling upon our remains. Given time, the forest cleanses everything.

He was, after all, my only child, my son, and I killed him for what he did.

I am leaving you my social security card, a business card from the glory days when I worked in New York, and the name and address of my son's mother. I am also including his identification papers.

Jordan felt the muscles in her throat tighten and a stinging in her eyes as she folded the letter, glanced at the cards, put everything back in the envelope, and placed the envelope on the seat of her truck.

Poor Anson. She hadn't even known his last name. Until now. It was Bancroft. He had been Anson J. Bancroft, III; his son, Anson J. Bancroft, IV.

Masks, she thought. Another mask pushed up to reveal the true face beneath. She was brushed with sadness and a feeling of guilt.

Her father had always watched out for Anson. Had she failed him in some way? If she had dropped in more frequently, could she have prevented his death?

Probably not. Anson had understood better than most the publicity sure to follow such an event, especially if he were still alive to be an object of interest to the media. And he would have hated it.

Before she drove away, Jordan drank from a nearby mountain stream, numbing her mouth, and splashed the icy water on her face.

3   It was noon when she arrived at the Enforcement Center in Taholah. She told Prefontaine about Anson's death, the existence of a son, and his son's guilt in the young girl's murder. She showed him the letter Anson had left for her.

When he finished reading it, Prefontaine asked, "How do you know he killed himself, Sis? Maybe he just disappeared again."

She shook her head. "He would never have left his books."

"So somewhere in a deep, dark canyon we've got two dead bodies, is that right?"

"I believe so."

"But where? On our lands? In the national park? In the national forest?"

"I don't know, Paul."

Prefontaine picked up the telephone as it rang and listened. Then he slammed it back down.

"There's been a fire at the Scatt place. The fire chief said there's a dead body 'or something,' as he put it. I'll call Hunter Kleoh and the coroner's office and then let's go."

"Call Jasper Wright as a courtesy," Jordan suggested.

Prefontaine did so and he also called the state police.

4   They drove separate trucks to Old Woman Scatt's,
       where they found a group of volunteer firemen
standing around. Jordan noticed that the Scatt livestock—
pigs, chickens, and geese—had evidently escaped as none
were in sight.

She glanced around, looking for Old Woman Scatt's cat,
knowing how much Tleyuk loved the tattered animal, but he
was nowhere to be seen.

The fire chief, walking wide-legged because of his rolled-
down boots, came up to greet them.

"Where's the fire?" Prefontaine asked.

"It's a strange one, folks. You'd better see what's inside,"
the fire chief replied, leading the way.

As they followed him to the house Jordan smelled a
sweetly heavy odor that grew almost overpowering as they
drew closer.

"What's that smell?" she asked.

"Terrible stink, isn't it?" the fire chief replied.

Closer to the house she saw a light blue haze in the air
and when they entered through the doorway they found the
main room filled with blue smoke. There was no sign of a
blaze.

Garbage was still all over the floor. A small fire was inno-
cently burning in the cooking space, that hole chopped
through the floor and lined with rocks.

Overhead, the hole in the roof still served as an escape
route for smoke. The walls were still grimy with old smoke
and grease, but now a new odorous layer seemed to have
been added.

It was difficult to make out any details through the bil-
lowings of the strange light blue smoke, but it seemed to
Jordan that there was a blackened area of flooring over in the
corner in front of the television set, which was still playing,
although the screen was covered with what seemed to be
grease. The upholstered rocking chair Jordan had seen
before was gone.

She and Prefontaine picked their way carefully toward
that part of the room, gagging on the sickening sweet stench

in the air. What she had taken to be a black patch was actually a large hole burned clear through the vinyl flooring and underlying boards.

Several floor joists were exposed, their upper surfaces charred into curvatures. There was no active flame. But there was a mound of fine gray ash. Protruding from the ashes were the bones of what appeared to be a human foot.

"I don't know what in the hell it is," the fire chief said. "One of the boys thinks it's a case of spontaneous human combustion. Says he saw a program about it recently on television."

"I've heard about that," Prefontaine said.

"Hope you don't mind, Paul," the fire chief continued, "but I've called Norman Platt to come on over."

"Hell, I don't mind. Just as long as you realize we can't do a thing until the coroner gets here. And Hunter Kleoh's on his way."

The fire chief nodded. "That Norman Platt, he's some kind of specialist on cremation, you know. Actually, he was over at the lodge so he should be here any minute now."

Platt soon arrived, driving an elderly Volkswagen at top speed and screeching to a halt in front of the house.

A fat man with a ruddy, smiling face and bristly white hair, he squeezed himself out of the car with difficulty, waved to the volunteer firemen, and proceeded to go inside the Scatt house.

"I had to borrow a car not of my choice," he said, pointing to the Volkswagen. He sniffed, then added, "Is this what I think it is?" he asked.

"Hell, I don't know what it is, Norm," the fire chief replied. "That's why I sent for you."

The fat man's eyes quickly went to the corner where the television sat; his feet soon followed.

"Please don't touch anything until Amos Zander gets here, okay?" Prefontaine said.

Zander was the county coroner.

Platt nodded, then gingerly picked his way around the rest

of the room, humming as he went, after which they all went outside where the air was somewhat better.

Jasper Wright, the deputy county sheriff, arrived next, was shown the sight inside, then waited outside with the others. The state police soon followed. After what seemed an endless wait, the coroner, a small, thin man, arrived with his assistant.

He nodded to the group, asked Prefontaine what he had, and was led inside the house and shown the pile of ashes and the bones of a human foot.

"What's Platt doing here?" he asked.

"The fire chief called him," Prefontaine replied. "Thought he might be able to throw some light on this."

"Get him in here."

Platt was summoned inside.

"Okay, Norm, do your stuff," the coroner said.

Platt squatted on his haunches with difficulty, licked his forefinger and stuck it in the ashes, then lifted the ash-coated finger to his nose and sniffed. He nodded his head and wiped his finger with a tissue.

"Please don't touch anything," he said.

"That's my line," the coroner replied with a thin smile.

Platt waddled out to his car and returned carrying a tripod and an old but well-maintained Speed Graphic camera, four by five, with an Ektar lens and a Kalart Synchronized range finder.

He mounted the camera on the tripod and, removing the dark slide from the film pack holder, took a number of shots of the ash pile. When he was finished, he carefully inserted the dark slide back in place.

"This is sure enough the corpus, if you had any doubts," he told the coroner.

Amons Zander nodded.

"What burned her up?" Jordan asked.

"She burned herself up."

"As far as I know the woman never smoked," Prefontaine offered.

"Ever heard of spontaneous human combustion?" he asked.

"One of the guys was telling me about the TV program," the fire chief replied.

"I've heard of this for years, seen photographs of it, seen a few cases with my own eyes. I know it happens. It's the damndest thing. Sometimes living human bodies simply catch fire inside and burn up."

"It seems impossible," Jordan said. "There's not even any skeletal remains, except for that piece of foot."

"That's what makes it so peculiar. Now in our business we cremate bodies between temperatures of six hundred to nine hundred fifty degrees Celsius for on average one and a half hours and bones, not ash, always remain."

Jordan asked, "What if the cremation process was continued for several hours longer? Would that reduce the bones to powder?"

Norman Platt shook his head. "All that does is burn the bones further and turn them black. You would still end up with bones, not dust. The larger bones such as the pelvis and the thigh bones are still recognizable."

Warming to his subject, Hunt continued, "We'll take a corpse inside a wooden coffin, subject it to terrific heat at over six hundred degrees C for an hour and a half. The resulting energy literally *vaporizes* the entire wooden coffin, skin, muscles, sinew, and internal organs. And yet what remains, what could not be destroyed by the inferno, is a recognizable skeleton."

"Then what's the point in cremation?" Prefontaine asked.

"Well, we don't stop there. What the heat does is make the bones brittle. Once they're cooled, the bones are raked from the cremator and this action breaks most of them up into smaller pieces, several inches in length on an average.

"We have a final process which does reduce the bones to dust so they can be placed inside a receptacle and presented to relatives."

"What's 'the final process'?" one of the state police officers wanted to know.

"The bones are placed inside a machine called a cremulator."

"And that is what?" Jordan asked.

"It looks and works like a heavy-duty spin dryer. It's actually a drum with eight heavy iron balls inside, each weighing several pounds. When the machine is switched on the drum revolves and the bones are only then pounded into dust."

"I think we better keep this under our hats," the coroner said. "If it gets out that we've had a case of spontaneous human combustion, all the wild-assed reporters in the world will be plowing around here."

"Good idea," agreed Hunter Kleoh, who had arrived during the last part of Platt's explanation. "Does anybody know what causes this kind of thing?"

"Nobody knows for certain. Not yet, anyway," Platt replied, stroking his upper lip in thought. "As I said, I've seen several cases like this. It's one of my special interests. And I'm in correspondence with mortuaries all over the world who've run into this.

"Those of us who study this phenomenon are certain that the generated heat must come from within the body—caused by an internal fire that's hotter than those in the crematory."

"How could that be?" Kleoh asked.

"Some of us have a theory, as yet unproven."

"Care about sharing it?" the coroner asked.

"Not a bit. Think about this. Humans are between seventy and eighty percent water. What if this could spontaneously break down into hydrogen and oxygen, the gases that combine to form water molecules?

"Hydrogen itself burns extremely well—and with a blue flame. Oxygen could catalyze the reaction. And the spark could very well come from a buildup of static electricity within the body."

Kleoh announced firmly, "The report will be given out to the media that an elderly woman died in a house fire. We'll leave it at that."

At that moment Jack Scatt drove up in a battered old pickup. As he climbed out of the truck and strode toward the house, Jordan saw that he was dressed in a neat three-piece suit with a starched white shirt.

"What in the hell's going on around here?" he asked.

"Where'd you come from?" Prefontaine asked.

"Friend of mine called. Said that there was some kind of ruckus at my place."

Prefontaine pointed to the mound of ash and the skeletal foot. "There's been a peculiar fire, Jack, and I'm afraid your grandmother here is dead."

"She wasn't my grandmother. She was my great-aunt's grandmother. Since there was only the two of us left we kind of kept track of one another."

"What was the lady's full name?" the coroner asked.

Jack Scatt shrugged. "Beats me. All I ever knew her by was Old Woman Scatt."

"What'll you do now that she's gone?" Prefontaine asked.

"What'll I do? First thing is burn this whole damn place down. How anyone could live in such a mess I don't know."

"Didn't you live here with her?"

"Hell, no. Spent a lot of time around here because this is where I keep my collection of old cars, as you probably noticed. I live in a hotel in Hoquiam."

"Would you mind giving me that address?" Hunter Kleoh said.

"Nope." Surprisingly, Scatt took a business card out of his vest pocket and handed it to the FBI man who, after looking at it, glanced around at the others.

"Just what is your line of work, Mr. Scatt?" he asked.

"Can't you read? It's just what it says on the card. Computer consultant." He looked over at Prefontaine with a sarcastic smile. "What's the matter, Chief? Did you think all I did was grow pot out in the woods and steal anything I could lay my hands on? If you did, you had me figured wrong."

Jordan and her brother exchanged glances. Another mask removed.

One of the firemen walked inside looking for the fire chief. "Hey, Boss, can I speak to you for a minute?"

The fire chief went outside. Jordan watched them through a grimy window. She saw three firemen digging in Old Woman Scatt's poison garden.

"Well, if that's all, I've got to be on my way," Norman Platt said, taking his leave. Soon they heard the little Volkswagen rattle off.

Meanwhile, the coroner and his assistant had begun to carefully bag the pile of gray ashes and the skeletal foot.

"Paul, I think we should go outside," Jordan said. "All of us."

Hunter Kleoh, Jasper Wright, the three state police officers, and Jack Scatt followed Jordan and Paul outside where, in the poison garden, they all saw a skeletal finger pointing up through the riotous morning glory.

"What the hell's *that*?" Kleoh muttered.

"I'll get the coroner." Prefontaine ran back into the house.

Zander told his assistant to continue preparing the ashes for transport to the lab and followed Prefontaine into the poison garden, where he took one look then asked the fire chief to have his men continue digging.

"Carefully," he ordered. "Very carefully."

When the digging was finished, four skeletons had been exposed; two adults and one young female with a tiny skeleton curled inside what had once been her womb.

"I know who they are," Scatt announced.

Prefontaine and Jordan stared at him.

"I know when the old woman killed them."

Now he had everybody's attention.

"It was years ago. They were trying to nail that kid's pregnancy on me. Hell, I never touched her. Never even knew her. Anyway, Old Woman Scatt invited them down for lunch, as I understand it, to talk things over. Don't look so surprised. She didn't always keep the house in such a mess as it is now. Anyway, the business was done by the time I got here.

"She'd poisoned all three of them. There they were, dead

s dodos. I was the one that buried them all right. I didn't
vant to say anything about it while the old woman was alive.
he way I figured, she'd done the world a favor. They were
cum."

Jordan studied him, pondering the various levels of
umanity as perceived by Old Man Ahcleet, who himself
ooked down on the Scatts because they were the offspring
f slaves. Jack Scatt turned up his nose at the occupants of
he informal grave because he considered them "scum."

Scatt looked over at Prefontaine. "I suppose you'll want
o take me in, Chief. Go ahead, I won't fight you."

"First I want to take in what I've just heard," the police
hief replied.

When Jordan finally drove away, leaving the coroner,
Iunter Kleoh, her brother, and Jack Scatt in deep conversa-
ion, she thought about the recently dead and the longtime
ead, all found on the same day.

She wondered if Old Woman Scatt had killed them, as
ack Scatt claimed. She remembered when she'd asked him
bout the faces nailed to the north wall of the woodshed.

Animal faces. When the gray of weathered cedar planks
ooked back at her through numerous empty eye sockets. At
he time Jack Scatt said he knew nothing about it.

"That's the old woman's doing," he'd said.

As for Old Woman Scatt, she had lived a long, strange life
nd died an even stranger death.

5   When Jordan arrived home she found that all of
        their overnight guests had left, even Royal Mercer.
Things were back to normal. Only she and her great-grand-
ather and her son were home.

Eight o'clock came and went and Lima Clemente had not
alled. Nine o'clock the same.

"Grandfather, were there any calls for me today?"

He replied that no one had called her.

At ten o'clock, although Jordan knew it was one in th morning back East, she called the Plaza Hotel and was tol that Lima Clemente had checked out.

"What time?" she asked.

"Mr. Clemente checked out at noon today, madam."

"Did he leave any message for Jordan Tidewater?" sh asked.

None, she was courteously told. She thanked the Nev York voice and hung up.

Jordan walked outside, suddenly feeling too enclosed i Old Man Ahcleet's house. Glancing up, she saw Rave watching her as he sat on a black branch.

Raven the trickster. Black on black.

You learn of things only hunters know, that can't be explained but must be felt; of ancient, primal emotions intrinsic to men and wolves. You discover the peerless freedom of the hunt surging in the grip of wood and cold steel or howling in the wind of a high pass. You're introduced to basic realities of success and failure, life and death. With time, the elemental lessons of hunting grow more complicated. You discover that hunting has a side as dark as humanity itself: There is subsistence, there is sport, and there is greed. Somewhere in this tangle of ego and nature, where innocence and knowledge mingle, we define ourselves—as a species and as individuals.

—KEN MARSH,
Hindsight

Chapter 25

1 At midnight that same night the telephone in Ruby Campbell's study rang repeatedly. He did not answer it at first, hoping the caller would go away.

When the caller kept ringing without having the sense to hang up, Campbell muttered a mild curse. He was busy working on a report and did not want to be disturbed because he hated doing reports and wanted to get it over with.

Finally he picked up the phone and growled, "This better be good."

"Is that the way you always answer the phone?" the caller inquired.

Campbell recognized the distinctive voice at once. It

belonged to the tall, gaunt man who had met with him in the shack in the forest the night of the Bigfoot—when Irv Mason and Josh Henley had caught the young animal in a trap and Ruby had let it go.

Edward Eagleton, the cryptozoologist, the man who said he worked in the branch of zoology that focuses on the possibility that creatures like the Loch Ness monster, Bigfoot, and the Yeti may actually exist.

"There's something you need to know about those bear galls," Eagleton said.

"What about them?"

"Some of them don't belong to bears."

"What then?"

"They're pig galls."

"*Pig galls?*"

"Yep."

"Where in the hell did *they* come from?"

"You'd better check with your crew about that."

"They'd be the freshest ones hung up to dry," Campbell said musingly.

"I took only the freshest ones. A couple are bear, all right, but the rest came straight from pigs."

"Wait just a damn minute. I remember Irv Mason saying he'd dug up a guy who was selling us bear galls."

"Who is the guy?"

"Let me see now. His name is Hereford. Bill Hereford. I don't know the man. Lives in Humptulips." Campbell paused, then asked, "You mean bear galls and pig galls look alike?"

"You could fool most people. They both look like a baby yellow squash, you know, the kind with a bulb on one end. They're about six inches long and the bulb is about an inch and a half in diameter. They weigh twenty grams more or less and the real thing sells for a thousand dollars a gram in Korea and Hong Kong. The average bear's gall sells for twenty thousand American dollars. Local buyers, or middlemen, get a couple hundred dollars per gallbladder.

"Now a pig's gall is exactly the same in appearance. Most customers cannot tell the difference. But if the Korean or Chinese customer suspects a fraud, somebody gets killed, like the guy the other day in a New York hotel room with his throat cut.

"Pigs' galls you can buy at any slaughterhouse for fifty cents each, hang them up to dry, then sell them as the real McCoy."

"Sweet margin of profit," Campbell said. "I think I'll go see Mr. Hereford."

"Now?"

"Why not?"

"Want some company?"

"Sure, Ed. Where are you now?"

"At the lodge."

"Okay. Meet me on 101 at the intersection. Say an hour?"

"Okay, buddy, see you soon."

After Campbell hung up he immediately called his main man, Irv Mason. "I've got to get ahold of some galls right away," he said.

"Now, Ruby? In the middle of the night?" Mason protested.

"Yep. I want you to call that guy in Humptulips, tell him I'm your boss and I'll be there in an hour or so. And call me back when you get through clearing it for me."

A few minutes later Mason called back and informed Campbell that Bill Hereford had a supply of galls and would be waiting.

"How do I get there?" Campbell asked.

After Mason had given the directions, he asked if Ruby wanted him to go along.

"It's not necessary, Irv. But thanks anyway. Appreciate your help."

The intersection of the Moclips Highway and U.S. 101 was hard to distinguish in the dark unless one knew the territory.

When Campbell arrived he found Edward Eagleton wait-

ing for him. They decided to go in separate vehicles with
Campbell leading the way.

"Let me go in alone, Ed. He's expecting one man, me, and
he'll probably ask for ID."

"Okay, but I'll be sneaking around outside just in case
there's any trouble."

When they arrived in the vicinity Edward Eagleton left
his car in the parking lot of the Black Rooster, then, walking, followed Campbell, who remained in his pickup, down
what looked like an alley until they reached a sign reading
BULL SERVICE AHEAD along with the name *Hereford* and an
arrow.

Following the arrow, Campbell turned right, driving very
slowly so that Eagleton, on foot, could keep up with him,
and soon found himself on a wide gravel apron that fronted
an old house with a big porch.

The house was dark. *Strange,* Campbell thought. Irv
Mason had called Hereford and made arrangements for
this meeting. Two hoots of a small owl told Campbell that
Eagleton was right behind him, hidden in a clump of
bushes.

When Campbell got out of his pickup, he heard a chorus
of dogs barking somewhere behind the house. Using his
flashlight, Campbell walked up the steps and across the
porch to the front door. He pressed the doorbell and heard it
ring inside.

Suddenly the door was swept open. Campbell could
barely see the outline of a man who stood facing him, holding a gun aimed at his heart.

"You Hereford?" Campbell asked.

"Who wants to know?"

"Ruby Campbell wants to know. Irv Mason told you I was
coming."

"Let me see your ID."

Campbell showed Hereford his driver's license.

Hereford reached for a flashlight, apparently on a table
inside the door, and studied the license by its light. Then he

pointed the flashlight at Campbell's face, comparing his features with the photograph on the license.

"Satisfied?" Campbell asked.

"Can't be too careful. Come on in."

Inside, he went around turning on lamps. Campbell saw that all the windows were covered with pulled-down shades.

"Sit down," Hereford said.

Now Campbell got a good look at him. Mean-looking son of a bitch.

"Have a drink?"

"Thanks, no."

"You one of these guys who only drinks with his friends?"

"I just don't feel like a drink right now. Thanks anyway."

Hereford grunted.

Campbell looked around and saw two well-groomed dogs lying together in front of the fireplace.

"Strange these dogs didn't bark when I came up," he said. "I heard the ones out back."

"Sally and Old Griz there were too well trained to bark when they're in the house unless I tell them to."

"What kind are they?"

"Redbones, Mr. Campbell. Bear dogs. These two are the prize of the pack."

Campbell wondered, if things got rough, what they would do with the dogs. Certainly they'd come to their master's defense and just as certainly he did not want to hurt them.

"Understand you're in the market for some galls," Hereford said.

"Bear galls," Campbell replied.

"Sure. What else? How many can you use?"

"How many have you got?"

Hereford laughed. "Enough."

"That's pretty vague."

"Believe me, I've got enough."

"I'd like to see the merchandise."

"Sure you would. Just follow me."

Campbell got up and followed Hereford through the house onto a screened-in back porch furnished with a twenty-foot freezer and a couple of straight-backed chairs.

Hereford took a key ring thick with keys from his pants pocket and unlocked the freezer.

"Come on over and take a look," he said to Campbell.

Campbell looked.

The freezer was packed to the brim with small plastic freezer bags, each of which was bulging.

"Are those all bear galls?" Campbell asked.

"Sure are."

"Some of these look different than others," Campbell said, picking up one of the packages.

"The difference is that some of them I freeze after I've dried them and others I freeze raw."

"Well, there's no question you've got plenty." Campbell put the package back into the freezer.

"Still interested, Mr. Campbell?"

"Yes."

"Let's go back into the front of the house where it's warm and talk things over."

Campbell knew that meant "talk price."

Hereford led the way into the living room and the two men sat back down in the chairs they'd used before.

"Sure you don't want a drink?" he asked again.

"No thanks."

"By the way, Mr. Campbell, I want to thank you for the business you've already given me. What your man bought was raw but I can provide the product already dried if you'd prefer."

Ruby Campbell was silent for a few moments, staring at Hereford.

"I'm going to want that money back," he said quietly.

"What money?"

"The money we paid you for those galls."

"What? Did I hear you right? You want your money back?"

"Yes, I do. All of it."

"What in the hell for?"

"Because if I want pig galls I can go directly to the slaughterhouse and buy them for the same price you do."

Hereford stood, his face flushing. "Now wait just a damn minute. Are you accusing me of something?"

Campbell stood also; they stared at each other eye to eye, Campbell figuring that if the other man made a move he'd deck him before things got hotter.

"I'm accusing you of selling me pig galls and representing them to be bear galls. If I had actually shipped those bear galls, my people would have had me killed. And you, too, if they found out about you, which they would."

"What is this, Campbell, some kind of scam? You get the product as well as the money? Well, it won't fly, not with me it won't."

"I want what I paid for. Bears' galls."

"You got bears' galls."

"I got pigs' galls."

"Yeah, how do you know?"

"How do I know what?"

"That them things are pigs' galls. Hell, nobody can tell the difference."

"Some people can."

"Well, I ain't giving your money back and there's nothing you can do about it. You can just go piss up a rope."

"Oh, but there is."

"What?"

"I'm going to report you to the authorities and you'll be spending the next long years in the penitentiary."

Hereford laughed his derision. "I'd like to see that. You'd be in the soup just as deep as me. Hell, your operation is big-time illegal. Compared to you, I'm small potatoes."

Hereford stopped talking and stared at Campbell intently. "Unless you're queer. One of those undercover agents sneaking around. Is that it, Campbell? You a cop?"

Campbell didn't reply. He also didn't take his eyes of
Hereford, which was, he thought later, the thing that save
him.

"By gum, that's it. You're a filthy cop."

Hereford made a lightning-swift move. Campbell ducke
just as swiftly as a switchblade knife zinged by his left ea
so fast he could feel the heat of its passing. It thudded int
the mantel, its sharp point buried deep.

"Shit!" Hereford exclaimed when he realized he ha
missed his target.

Campbell held up his hand. "Cut out the horseplay. Thi
is not the way to work things out, Hereford."

"Yeah? Well, I'm going to shut you up the only way pos
sible."

Campbell realized that Hereford would not settle for hal
measures. The man was out to kill him.

Hereford began to approach him in the crouched positio
of the practiced knife thrower. And he had another knife i
his hand.

Campbell wasn't surprised. Knife throwers usually ha
several of them secreted around their bodies.

He began to move, never taking his eyes from Hereford'
hands, which kept making false throwing actions so that h
would be off guard.

But Campbell was not taken off guard. A knife had bee
one of his weapons once and although many years ha
passed he was still familiar with their use in combat.

Besides, he would not allow himself to be killed. If he di
Melisande would never forgive him.

By now the dogs were active, crying softly, surroundin
the two men, waiting for a command from their master.

Hereford ignored the dogs.

He made a sudden leap, both feet off the floor, hitting wit
the soles of his boots and knocking Campbell down with th
force of the attack.

His right hand rose, ready to plunge the knife i
Campbell's heart.

But Campbell seemed to grow liquid, rolling out from under his attacker, in one swift movement straddling Hereford's body with his legs, using his left arm in a killing chokehold around Hereford's neck.

Just as swiftly, his right hand reached inside the waistband of his pants, drew out a length of piano wire with a wooden button at one end and a flat wooden handle on the other.

Seemingly in the same movement, he released the chokehold and worked the piano wire around Hereford's throat. Using both hands, he pulled with all of his strength.

In seconds the wire had bitten into the flesh of Hereford's neck down to the bones of his spine.

The dogs whined and nudged Hereford, waiting for an order to take action, not knowing that their master would never issue a command again.

Bloodied and staggering, Campbell got off the body and walked to the front door, which he opened, then yelled, "Eagleton! Get in here!"

Eagleton came running.

Inside, he took one look and said, "Good God, Ruby, what happened?"

Campbell told him the facts, adding, "I didn't think I could still move so fast."

"Thank God you can," Eagleton said. "Is there some place we could put those damn dogs? They're giving me the creeps, nudging the body like that."

Campbell suggested the back porch. Surprisingly, the dogs went with Eagleton, heads and tails hanging down in attitudes of despair.

"I'll tell you one thing," Eagleton said when he was back in the room. "Hereford must have been awfully good to his dogs. There's not a mean bone in them."

"We've got to call the cops," Campbell said.

Eagleton shook his head. "Not you. I want you out of here now. We don't need your presence complicating things. If you talk to the police, you'll end up spending a hell of a lot

of time with them instead of doing what you're doing. Don'
forget, we've got the big fish to catch yet."

Campbell removed the wire from the corpse's neck an
washed it off in the kitchen sink and dried it on a dish towe

When he came back, he said, "You're probably right. I'
go. I'd like you to do me a favor if you can."

"Sure enough. What is it?"

"If those dogs need a home, let it be known you've go
one for them. Me."

"Sure. We'll get the humane society up here about al
those dogs out back. Say, Ruby, I've got to ask you some
thing."

"Shoot."

"How the hell did you come to be wearing piano wire?"

"I have ever since the war. In the right hands, piano wire'
a lot quicker than a knife."

"I'll be damned. Now get lost, okay?"

Ruby Campbell got lost.

*. . . if love would die along
with death,
this life wouldn't be so hard.*
—ANDREW VACHSS,
"Sacrifice"

Chapter 26

1   Jordan awoke to a cool, wet, late September morning. The pungent aroma of cedar smoke perfumed the air and a misty gray sky rested its belly atop the headland.

The tide was coming in. She could hear the age-old sound of breakers crashing onto the beach and thought, *I couldn't live where I could not hear the voice of the sea.*

She got out of bed and examined her arms. They were healing nicely.

She showered, then prepared a breakfast of smoked salmon, one of her great-grandfather's huge fluffy biscuits, and freshly brewed coffee made from freshly ground beans.

Although it was still early, Old Man Ahcleet and Tleyuk

were already gone, working on her son's training in the old
ways. She was alone in the house.

As she ate, she thought about the developments of the last
several days.

In one way she was surprised that she did not feel an ache
in her heart because of Lima Clemente's perfidy, or what she
saw as perfidy—disappearing without a word to her.

But in another way she realized that her lack of painful
grief was a gift to her from the Klokwalle.

And the great mystical spirit had given her yet another
gift, the courage to look behind the mask of love and
examine the possibility that perhaps Lima Clemente himself might in some way be involved in the death of the little boy.

But exactly what that involvement could be, she had no
idea. Naturally, she thought of human sacrifice after all
she'd heard about it, but concluded such a thing was impossible as far as he was concerned.

She knew Lima, loved him. He was a sophisticated international man, not a peasant who'd never been exposed to the
knowledge and advanced technologies of today.

Everything as yet was so ephemeral. She took a piece of
notebook paper and a pen from the "miscellany drawer" in
the kitchen that, as usual, was a wild mess and wrote down
the points she knew about, playing the devil's advocate with
each of them.

First of all, Eli Raptor had informed her that the fingerprint she'd found inside the boulder belonged to a woman
named Machi Juana who had come from, and presumably
returned to, the village of Lima's childhood.

So what? How did that involve Lima Clemente? How
many years had it been since he'd even been in the village of
his birth? His life was in Santiago.

Next, she'd seen the other half of the woven vicuna ribbon and gold medal she'd found on her beach hanging from
a framed photograph in the small Chilean chapel high in the
Andes, again in the village of Lima Clemente's birth. Again
so what?

And what about that tiny brass link she'd found in a fir cone? It must be involved, but would the involvement be significant?

Soon the scientists whose work was reconstructing faces from bones would be finished and Jordan would know if the scalped face she had found in the forest belonged to Antonio Salinas, whose photograph she'd seen in the Andean chapel.

After the small hand was autopsied by a vascular surgeon, she would know if the young stranger had come from a very cold part of the world such as that same Andean village.

What little information she had pointed to that village, not necessarily to Lima Clemente. Was he the only person to attend the logging congress whose birthplace was that village?

She thought of the large scary man she'd been introduced to when she first met Lima. What was his name?

Ah yes, Xavier Escoro. Now him she could suspect—of practically anything. What was his relationship to Lima Clemente? She remembered Michael McTavish telling her they were business partners. And Father Lavate said they'd both come from his village.

Did she still love Lima Clemente? she asked herself, adding, *Be honest.*

Yes, she did. Love like she felt for him would take a long time to wither, if it ever did. Then she wondered: Could that love turn to hate?

What was behind the face he showed the world? Anything more than seemed apparent?

Suppose she discovered that Lima Clemente *had* played an active role in the death of the little Indian boy? How would she feel then? She didn't know.

What would she do if he came back? With no hesitation whatsoever, she knew she would continue gathering evidence, even if it was blatantly against him, and hand it over to the FBI. But she hoped she wouldn't have to face that situation.

She was off duty today. She decided to go to the house
Lima Clemente had rented on North Shore Road, see if she
could get in and look around. Who knows what she might
find?

2   What she found was Binte Ferguson cleaning the
     house Lima Clemente had rented. The little old
woman let her in, showing surprise and pleasure.

"What are you doing here, Binte?" Jordan asked.

"Cleaning house for Mr. Clemente."

"I thought you worked for Hannah McTavish."

"Oh, I do. This is just a little extra. Hannah knows all
about it."

"Have you heard from Mr. Clemente?" Jordan asked.

"Yep. Got a message on my fax."

Jordan stifled laughter with difficulty. Unbidden, it welled
up in her throat and she had to swallow hard to keep it down.
She found the idea of feisty little Binte Ferguson, with her
1920 Model T automobile named Tilly, possessing such
modern-day equipment as a fax to be hilarious.

"He asked me to please straighten up his place."

"When was this?"

"Yesterday, as a matter of fact."

"Did he say when he was coming back?"

"Now that he didn't say. Wanta look around, Jordan?"

"A little. I've never been in this house before."

"Go ahead then. Be my guest." Binte said. "Or I guess I
should say 'Be Mr. Clemente's guest.'"

Jordan walked around, seeing only impersonal things, the
kind of furnishings that could be found in most higher-class
rented houses.

"Binte, does anything here belong to Mr. Clemente?"

"Not anymore. He used to have some clothes in the closet
but now the closet is empty. Oh, and that toy truck over there
on the table. That's his. Only thing around here that is."

Jordan casually glanced at the toy. Then she did a double take. It was a wooden model of a logging truck. It had wheels that turned, mud flaps on the back wheels, with small, smooth "logs" on the trailer held in place by chains made up of tiny brass links.

Brass links.

Jordan picked up the replica of a logging truck and trailer. Upon closer inspection she found that a two-inch length of chain was missing. On the bottom of the trailer the legend read: HANDMADE BY JOHN DUNCAN, giving Duncan's address in Pacific Beach.

"I'm going to use the phone," she told Binte.

"Be my guest."

Jordan got John Duncan's telephone number from directory assistance. When she called, the man himself answered.

She introduced herself, and said that she was looking at one of his marvelously made trucks at the house of a friend. He told her the price and explained various construction details.

"I love the mud flaps and the brass chains. It's all so realistic."

"I'm a man who believes in taking care of the details," Duncan said.

So am I, friend, so am I, Jordan thought.

"For example, those brass chains. I always put exactly the same number of links in the chains for each truck. Never vary. You start varying, you get sloppy."

"So how many do you use?"

"Exactly sixty-four. Sixty-four on each chain. Always the same. And two chains on each truck."

"That's very interesting, Mr. Duncan. I have a small son, so I may be stopping by one of these days to buy one for him."

"Be my guest. Anytime at all. And thanks for calling."

Exactly sixty-four links. She counted the links on Lima Clemente's collector logging truck. There were exactly sixty-three links.

"Binte, I'm going to take this little truck along with me.

I'll sign a paper that I took it so you won't get in any trouble. Are you sure this belongs to Mr. Clemente?"

"Positive. One night when I was over here cooking dinner—the man doesn't eat until ten at night, if you can imagine that—anyway, he showed it to me. Proud as punch of it he was. A person would think he was a little boy himself."

The toy truck safely boxed, Jordan left and headed for Aberdeen and Hunter Kleoh. He could send it to the lab, see if the link she had found in a fir cone was originally a part of the small truck and trailer.

3　　It was four o'clock when Jordan arrived at the Enforcement Center.

Prefontaine saw her drive up and rushed out to meet her before she could even get out of her truck.

She reached across the seat and opened the door on the passenger side. "What's wrong, Paul?"

"We've just gotten a message from the Pacific Tsunami Warning Center."

"Where was the earthquake?" she asked, climbing out.

"Hokkaido, Japan. We've got to get the warnings out right away. We're running them off the copy machine right now."

Inside, she read the warning:

An 8.2 magnitude earthquake occurred this morning at Hokkaido, Japan. This quake did generate a tsunami wave of unknown height. A tsunami WARNING has been issued for the Pacific Coast by the Pacific Tsunami Warning Center. This may produce a series of waves that could cause damage to the Washington coast. We want to emphasize the word "MAY." These waves may continue for several hours after the initial wave. Arrival time is predicted at 8:30

tonight. The U.S. Coast Guard is pulling all boats off the Washington coastal waters, including the bays.

Persons living along coastal areas may wish to take precautions by moving to higher ground or a quarter mile from the shore. We will continue to monitor the situation and provide information as it becomes available.

Grays Harbor County Emergency Management and the Board of Commissioners will keep you updated.

Jordan flipped on a small television on Prefontaine's desk. All the channels except for those public service had newsreaders talking about the earthquake and the expected tsunami.

"Only several months ago there was a 7.2 earthquake in Kobe, Japan," the newsreader said. "The port city of Kobe, the sixth largest city in Japan, lay in ruins. The word Kobe means 'God's Door.' The city handled twelve percent of Japan's exports to the world. It began with a rumble that became a huge roar. There were five hundred aftershocks. Also, there were eighteen hundred dead, four thousand injured. The quake toppled hundreds of buildings, knocked trains off their tracks, lit thousands of fires. The fire trucks couldn't get through because the streets were blocked by toppling buildings. Japan's highly touted new building technology that promised damage-free buildings in the event of an earthquake did not work."

Jordan had heard enough.

"I'm going to find Old Man Ahcleet and Tleyuk and take them to the lodge," she told Prefontaine. "They'll be safe there."

"Aren't they are home?"

She shook her head. "Grandfather and Tleyuk are working on the training today."

"Get going, honey. Maybe when you get back you could help us pass out these warning notices."

"I'd be happy to."

Jordan was just stepping out of Prefontaine's office when

she saw Old Man Ahcleet coming in the front door. She hurried to meet him.

"Where's Sparky?" she asked.

"That's what I'd like to know," Ahcleet replied.

She rushed her great-grandfather into Prefontaine's office.

"Paul, Grandfather says Sparky has disappeared."

"What do you mean, disappeared?"

Old Man Ahcleet threw out his hands. "Disappeared. Gone. I can't find him anywhere."

"When did you see him last?"

"When we had finished the training in the river."

"Are you sure he didn't get swept away by the river?"

"He was already out of the water. We were through with that part."

Fear had Jordan in its taloned grip. She wanted to scream at the old man, to shake him. Maybe he didn't truly remember what had happened. After all, he *was* in his nineties.

Prefontaine took one look at her face, then said, "Well, we all know that nothing around here would hurt him."

Outside his office tribal policemen were rushing out with handbills to pass out, warning people about the possibility of a tsunami.

Willing herself to be calm, Jordan said quietly, "Grandfather, tell us step by step what happened from the time you and Tleyuk walked out of the house."

"Nothing much that doesn't happen every day we train. We walked down the road with that damn cat of Old Lady Scatt's at our heels."

"It's Tleyuk's cat now since the old woman died."

"Forget the cat," Prefontaine said. "Then what happened?"

"Not much. We kept on walking until we got as far as the cannery. That is where Tleyuk goes in the water. The cat didn't follow us all the way. It turned around and went back to our house, I guess."

"And?"

"After the training, when Tleyuk was out of the water and had changed his clothes, I suddenly had to do my body's business so I told Tleyuk to stay right there and I found a toilet and did what I had to do. When I got back, Tleyuk was gone."

"But he can't have disappeared like that," Jordan said.

"He did," her great-grandfather replied. "I've looked all over town for him. Nobody's even seen him. Of course, they're all rushing around like chickens with their heads cut off with this tsunami business. Those damn devils under the sea out there are causing trouble again."

Prefontaine and Jordan exchanged glances.

"Grandfather, I want you to stay here with me," the police chief said.

"Okay. Where's your candy machine?"

Prefontaine told him.

"You got change?"

Prefontaine handed over several quarters.

He looked at Jordan. "With everything that's going on I've got to stay in place here."

"That's okay, Paul. I'm gone," Jordan said as she rushed out the door.

Her first stop was Old Man Ahcleet's house. Maybe it was a simple mix-up and Tleyuk had gone home. She whispered a Calling-on-Guardians prayer as she anchored her power wagon outside the house and raced up the stairs.

She threw open the front door. As she did so, a small white envelope fell to the floor.

Hurriedly she picked it up and saw her name written on the outside. Tearing it open, she read, *Tleyuk and I are on your island. Please join us.* The hurriedly scrawled message was signed *LC.*

She ran inside the house and called Hunter Kleoh, whom she had seen just a couple of hours earlier.

"My son's been kidnapped," she said without preamble. "I know where he is but I have no way of getting there."

"Where is he?"

"On a small island about three miles off the coast."

"Have you received any ransom notes or calls?"

"No, Hunter, it isn't that kind of a thing."

"I won't waste time asking for the details right now. What can I do to help?"

"Do you have influence with anyone in the Coast Guard?"

"The FBI has influence with everyone. What do you need?"

"I want a helicopter with pilot to take me out to the island."

"You don't need the Coast Guard for that. We have a helicopter standing by. I'll fly you myself. You can tell me the details on the way."

They arranged to meet on the beach at Moclips in half an hour.

First, Jordan drove back to the Enforcement Center to tell Prefontaine and her great-grandfather what was happening.

Only then did she drive to Moclips to await the arrival of Hunter Kleoh. Within forty-five minutes they were in the air.

4   As they flew over the island Jordan saw Lima Clemente sitting on a log in front of a driftwood fire on their beach, where they had made love.

By his side, on the sand, Tleyuk lay on a blanket asleep, or drugged. On Lima Clemente's other side was something else. A machete.

In the distance sat the helicopter in which he'd first taken Jordan to the island, now *her* island.

"I should come in with you," Kleoh said.

"No, Hunter. That would be a mistake. I know this man and am beginning to suspect what he's capable of."

"All the more reason for a backup."

"I'm going in armed. I want you hidden, but nearby, in case I need help."

"Who is this guy, anyway?"

"A friend."

He slanted a glance her way. "Some friends you've got, if you don't mind my saying so."

"I don't mind."

Lima Clemente glanced up as they flew over but she knew he couldn't make out their features.

Hunter Kleoh landed on the northern end of the island, on the high plateau supported by steep basalt palisades rising directly from the sea.

They made their way down the cliffs and through the forest until, although hidden themselves, they were within visual distance of Lima Clemente.

She strode forward into the clearing while Kleoh stayed hidden by undergrowth. Since she wasn't exactly sure what she was dealing with, Jordan knew that for her son's sake she must remain as calm as possible and definitely not come screaming in like some hysterical woman.

Lima Clemente smiled and rose, beckoning her to come closer.

"Won't you sit down?" he asked, politely gesturing to a seat beside him on the log.

He did not ask where she had gotten the helicopter and pilot. It was as if his entire focus was simply on her being there with him.

"I'll stand, thank you."

"Then so will I. No gentleman remains seated while a woman stands."

"I know you're a gentleman, Lima, and because you are I'd like you to tell me what you're doing with my son."

"Isn't it obvious, my dear Jordan? We can all leave from here."

"Leave and go where?"

"Why, back to Chile, of course, where we can marry. Later we'll all return and make our permanent home here."

She studied the man. He didn't look or act crazy for what-ever that was worth.

"Haven't you heard about the big earthquake in Japan and the tsunami that's expected tonight?"

"Of course. We'll be long gone by then."

"Lima, I never agreed to marry you."

"Don't you love me?"

She studied him. "I did."

"You no longer love me?"

"I'm afraid."

"Afraid of what, Jordan?"

"Afraid that things aren't right."

"What kind of things?"

She decided to come right out and ask him. The time for dilly-dallying around was gone.

"Lima, did you have anything to do with the killing of that little boy we found in the forest?"

She held her breath waiting for his reply.

He lifted the cross that hung at his neck and kissed it before replying.

"Because I love you, Jordan, you must know the truth," he said. "Since you follow the old beliefs of your people, I know you will understand mine."

"How can I when I don't know what they are?"

"To ensure success in your country, I did not kill but I was present at the sacrificial offering of Antonio Salinas to our gods."

Jordan felt claws seize her heart.

"Antonio, the person I loved most," Lima Clemente went on, "now lives joyously as a young god in the company of the old gods. After his death he brought me you to replace the love I felt for him in a much more complete fashion. Does that not mean I did the right thing?"

Instead of answering his question, Jordan asked, "Was your business partner, Xavier Escoro, present at the sacrifice?"

"Yes, Jordan, he was."

"What did it have to do with him?"

"He was the boy's grandfather."

"Is he related to you, Lima?"

"He is my father."

"Then you are—"

"Antonio Salinas's uncle. His parents died of fever, which, of course, made Antonio an orphan. That was a sign from the gods that we must sacrifice him."

"Do you mean to tell me that little boy was murdered in a horrible fashion by his own grandfather and his own uncle?"

"Of course not, Jordan. The actual killing was done by Machi Juana, the sorceress from Antonio's village. She was aided by her assistant, a man named Maximo Coa. Grandfather sent for them as well as for Antonio when we heard that the boy's parents had died."

"Why didn't you do this terrible thing in your own village? Why do it here, in our forest?"

"Because Antonio did not become an orphan until after we had left our homeland." Lima Clemente paused, intently studying her. "You think we are savages, don't you?"

"It was a savage killing, Lima."

"It might seem so to you, Jordan, but the method of the killing was laid down long centuries ago. It has to be done in a precise fashion or not done at all."

"How about not at all? Did you ever think of that?"

"When we practice our religious beliefs in the prescribed way, we are calling upon the supernatural powers of an ancient civilization. This is the basis of our success and believe me, Jordan, we are *most* successful. The old gods shower us with gifts."

"Have there been other sacrifices?"

"Yes. But Antonio was the best of them all, the one the gods appreciated the most, because he was of our own blood and we both loved the boy dearly."

"Why do you wear that crucifix around your neck?"

"Because I am also a Catholic," he replied simply.

Lima Clemente reached down and picked up the machete, then stood before her, holding the lethal blade.

"I wonder what gifts would appear if together we make Tleyuk a young god? He could keep Antonio company."

Absolute terror filled Jordan's heart. She bit down hard on her tongue to keep from crying out. This man was insane! She knew she must show no fear. And she must not draw her gun. Not yet.

Then she saw something that was impossible.

Standing about thirty yards behind Lima Clemente, staring at him with huge golden eyes lighted by the westering sun, stood an apparition in orange and black.

It could not be what it seemed to be.

But it was. Jordan froze.

5   Lima Clemente saw the change in Jordan and was puzzled. Suddenly she looked scared to death. He was certain that what he had just told her did not have that effect on her.

Was it something behind him? Perhaps the pilot who had brought her here. But why should she fear him?

Then came a bone-chilling sound, that great sawing voice that he'd heard before.

But it couldn't be.

Just three days ago he and several of his men had confined the Siberian tiger in a pit that they covered with boulders so that, left unfed for several days more, its appetite would be whetted for the hunt soon to come.

Slowly Lima Clemente turned and met the only thing in the world he feared: the golden eyes of death.

In those instants before the attack, Lima Clemente knew that the big cat understood the human anatomy, knew how to go for the head and the vulnerable belly of primates.

He knew that its usual attack was to leap onto its victim

and hook into the shoulders with the front claws, while its back legs kicked like those of a domestic cat playing with a ball of wool.

He knew that the long talons, unsheathed, could disembowel a man with several swift kicks, stripping his guts out.

He knew that at the same time the tiger sank its teeth into the face or throat of its prey, it reached over with one front claw to hook the back of its victim's scalp and tear it off the skull.

He knew that frequently the dome of the skull came away with the scalp, like the top sheared off a soft-boiled egg, leaving the brain exposed.

The tiger sawed again, its savage cry even more vicious and eager.

One more thing Lima Clemente knew: You must never run from a big cat. You must never turn your back on a big cat. Their instinct is to pursue. If you run, they must charge, just as a domestic cat cannot resist the flight of the mouse.

Lima Clemente turned and ran.

Amba exploded in a silent rush behind him. Lima Clemente never even heard the tiger come.

It landed with all of its weight in the middle of his back and between his shoulder blades.

Lima Clemente was hurled forward, feeling the claws bite in and hold, hooked into his own flesh.

The tiger slammed him to the ground, driving the air from Lima Clemente's lungs. The man felt as though his ribs had collapsed.

He could feel the cat on his back gather itself, bring up its back legs, coil its body like a spring, then lash downward across his buttocks and the back of his thighs, opening his flesh to the bone, slicing through blood vessels and arteries.

Lima Clemente was a big, determined man. Somehow, he managed to turn and now the tiger was beneath him,. He looked down into fanged jaws opened wide.

The tiger snarled. A hot mist of spittle blew into Lima Clemente's face and he smelled the stink of carrion.

Lima Clemente knew he was a dead man even as the tiger cocked its back legs up in the instinctive disemboweling movement; he was beyond feeling when the tiger's head shot forward and sank its fangs into his face and throat.

Shock held Jordan in its grip.

She had her gun out, and was trying for a killing shot at the animal, but from the beginning of the encounter the tiger and Lima Clemente were in such a position that if her aim was off even by a whisker her bullet would hit Tleyuk.

Tleyuk had awakened during the battle between man and beast. Terrorized by the scene being enacted in front of him and frozen into silence, he backed into the driftwood log on which Lima Clemente had been seated as if he wanted to disappear into its depths.

He saw his mother in the distance signaling him frantically to be still, not make a sound, but when the tiger rolled over and got up, and the little boy saw what had happened to the nice man who had brought him to his mother's island, he began to shriek.

The tiger, who was starving, licked its prey all over and took a bite or two.

Disturbed by Tleyuk's screams, still consumed with vast hungers, the tiger got up and began pacing toward the boy, its hot orange stripes glowing in the sea air.

Now Jordan's fear was so great she could not even hold the gun, shaken as she was by an emotion that was a combination of terror and anger.

"You'll not get my son," she muttered. "If I have to tear you apart with my hands, you'll not get my boy."

She had forgotten about Hunter Kleoh somewhere in the background. She had forgotten she was human. She had forgotten she was a woman.

All she knew at these moments was that she was some

great female force—human? animal? who cared?—trying to protect its young.

In her eyes burned a fire perhaps fifteen thousand years old, an ancient bond formed between mankind and animals when each could understand the other simply by lifting the mask that separated them.

She shouted for her guardian spirit and for the Listening Ones. Whatever she was now, she could feel and recognize the adrenaline pouring into her system, seemingly in such vast quantities that it ran out of her eyes and fell on her paws.

She lifted her arm and saw the sheathed claws. She looked at the other arm and saw the apricot fur. She thought cougar thoughts or, more correctly, one cougar thought: *Rescue my young.*

Four-legged, she raced toward the tiger that was now sniffing Tleyuk. With a full-throated scream, using the power of surprise, claws unsheathed, she landed with all of her weight on the tiger's back.

Startled, the tiger snarled and stood up on its hind legs, front claws extended, looking like a British coat of arms, trying to shake the weight off its back.

Now two thunderous voices sounded in screams and snarls. The cougar dug its claws in deep, seeming to steer the tiger away from the little boy.

Up and down the beach they raged, tiger and cougar, in mortal conflict, one motivated by hunger, the other by mother love.

Or perhaps not love. Something deeper, stronger, something for which there exists no word in the English language.

The waves roared in, all unconscious of the life and death struggle going on within their grasping reach.

At last Amba managed to throw the cougar off, but at the cost of a shredded back. He stood at the water's edge, biting the rising sea in anger, before turning to face his attacker.

Suddenly there was a tremendous rush of noise and water greater than the roar of the surf.

Looking around, Amba saw that the creatures of the sea, the killer whales, were back, and were slithering up on their rubbing beach.

Amba stood motionless, gathering his strength. Angry, thwarted from his food, he glanced behind him. The cougar had retreated to the log where the small two-legged creature was huddled near the prey Amba had killed.

Was it going to eat his food?

He turned back to the creatures of the sea and waded in, not as surefooted as he was during the first encounter. This time he slipped off one of the whales' backs as it carried him into deeper water.

Waiting below was Orca, the queen of the sea. She opened her vast mouth and bit the great tiger in two, then spat out his hindquarters. For a time the upper half of Amba bobbed up and down with the tide, but soon it disappeared.

Orca's pod stayed close to their rubbing beach. Their instincts told them that something was wrong with the sea, some kind of danger was coming. They felt safer huddled together near their rubbing beach.

6   Tleyuk was sitting on his mother's lap. "Mom, what happened to the cougar?" he asked.

"What cougar, honey?"

"The one that fought with the tiger. The cougar with the blue eyes."

"I guess she went home."

"The tiger's gone, too."

"Don't worry, Tleyuk. I don't think either one of them will be back."

"Mom, who's that man?"

"What man?"

"That one over there, coming out of the forest."

By now it was almost dark. Still holding her son tightly, Jordan stood up and looked where Tleyuk was pointing.

The man moved toward them, looking around as he ran as if he expected something to leap on him.

"Hunter!" Jordan exclaimed. "What happened to you?"

"I fainted."

"What?"

"Honest to God, Jordan, I passed out. Where's the guy the tiger killed? Oh, over there. Where's the tiger?"

"He went into the sea, Hunter."

"Will he be back?"

"No, he won't."

Kleoh took off his jacket to cover the dead man but Jordan told him to put it back on. He was going to need its warmth.

Hunter Kleoh shook his head as if trying to get it to work again.

"I don't know what's wrong with me. I must be coming down with something. I see that your son is okay. We'd better get out of here, don't you think?"

"It's too late, Hunter."

She pointed toward the west where they could see in the far distance an enormous wave, one as tall as a five-story building, moving slowly toward them.

"Run!" Jordan exclaimed.

"Run where?"

"Up in the trees. Hurry up."

Still holding Tleyuk she sprinted across the sandy beach and into the forest, Kleoh right behind her. He stopped at a huge Douglas fir, but she yelled at him to get away from it.

Finally she came to an ancient cedar tree and began to climb up from limb to limb with Tleyuk on her back. When they were settled on the highest branch that was strong enough to support them, Kleoh came panting up and clung to the branch directly beneath them.

"What was wrong with that first tree?" he asked.

"Nothing was wrong with it, Hunter. But it's a Douglas fir and they're very shallow-rooted."

The tsunami came quietly and with stealth. It covered the island, except for the high palisades upon which the FBI helicopter was moored.

It also left untouched the high branches of the cedar tree where Jordan, Tleyuk, and Hunter Kleoh had sought refuge.

*The goal of
life is living
in agreement
with nature.*

—ZENO,
ancient philosopher (335–263 B.C.)

Chapter 27

1   It took Jordan a long time to recover from the emotional shock of learning that Lima Clemente had been a participant in human sacrifice and from witnessing the manner of her lover's death. Eventually she no longer cried in the night.

She sent the other half of the gold medal belonging to Antonio Salinas down to Father Lavate with a letter explaining what had happened. She also arranged for the pitiful remains to be shipped to the village, but she doubted the condors would accept them, preserved as they were.

In due time she dealt with Anson's library, deciding to keep his books, for were not books friends?

It took the community a long time to recover from th
devastation left in the wake of the tsunami. There were tho
who said the Quinault people would never be the same.

There were others who said, "What nonsense! Th
Quinault people have always been here and they always wi
be here. So what's a big wave?"

But the Quinault were lucky. Paul Prefontaine and h
staff had gotten everybody to higher ground. Even Ol
Woman Scatt's cat survived, to Tleyuk's delight.

There were fatalities, although none among the Quinault
The water was so cold and so rough that those taken by th
tsunami who were later found were stark naked, the sea hav
ing torn the clothes and shoes right off their bodies.

Soon, events were being referred to as Before th
Tsunami or After the Tsunami. BT or AT.

Like horrors from an old nightmare, Jordan received th
results of various testing requested by the FBI.

The forensic examination of Antonio Salinas's han
showed that the young boy had carried extra blood vesse
in his extremities.

The board certified vascular surgeon explained in hi
report that "a variety of different stresses in which there is
sustained reduction in blood flow promotes new blood ves
sel growth, a process called angiogenesis. This is under th
regulation of certain vascular growth factors, includin
Fibroblast Growth Factor and VEGF (Vascular Endothelia
Growth Factor) among others."

Contrary to what Anson had expected, his remains an
those of his son were discovered by energetic hikers wh
had gone into that particular deep remote canyon in th
Olympic National Park just for the hell of it and found mucl
more than they had bargained for.

When Jordan heard that one of the bodies bore an unusua
ring set with sunstones she knew exactly who the dead were

Edward Eagleton was seen no more, having forsaken hi
role of Bigfoot researcher and returned to being what h
was: an agent with the Special Operations Branch of th

U.S. Fish and Wildlife Service, Division of Law Enforcement.

Ruby Campbell, who'd been working as a "friend" of the same organization, was cheated out of his hoped-for seizure of the head men in the international poaching ring: Lima Clemente and Xavier Escoro. He kept the buried money.

The seven-hundred-pound black bear that Antonio Salinas's grandfather claimed to have evicted from the old log shack somewhere deep in the ancient forest moved back in.

When he found the ruffled lavender umbrella with one broken spine he picked it up, threw it out the door, then went outside, picked it up, and hugged it to himself with all of his considerable strength.

But it's difficult to hug an umbrella to death.

He threw it down and sat on it. When he got up the umbrella looked the same.

So, using teeth and claws, he ripped at it until all the lavender covering was in ragged pieces on the ground.

Now it was dead.

He threw its skeleton into the underbrush and went back into his house and readied himself for a long winter's nap.

Overhead, remote from the world of men, the great trees of the ancient forest whispered together.

Acknowledgments

Very special thanks to Robert Gleason, author and editor; to Tom Doherty, publisher; to Robert Gottlieb and Debra Goldstein of the William Morris Agency; to Miriam Clavir, conservator, The University of British Columbia, Vancouver, B.C.; to James. T. Willerson, M.D., Editor in Chief, *Circulation* magazine, St. Luke's Episcopal Hospital/Texas Heart Institute, Houston, Texas; to Kenneth W. Goddard, Director, National Fish & Wildlife Forensics Laboratory, Ashland, Oregon; to Larry Workman, Quinault Indian Nation Communications, and editor of *Quinault Natural Resources*, Taholah, Washington; and to the wonderfully helpful people at the Hillsboro, Oregon, public library.

And to Karen Stokes whose skilled hands always rescue me from the computer swamps into which I frequently wander; to David Stokes; Matt Stokes; Melinda Stokes Richards; Megan Stokes Enfield; to my sons-in-law, Jeff Richards and Ken Enfield; to my five granddaughters, Heather, Meagan, Sarah, Samantha, and Aleea Jewel.

And especially to Joe, who lives when he was supposed to have died, because he knows how much we all love and need him.

Additional Reading

recommend *Land of the Quinault* by Pauline K. Capoeman, Editor, Quinault Indian Nation, 1990; *How We Die* by Sherwin B. Nuland, M.D., Vintage Books, A Division of Random House, Inc., New York, 1995; *Spontaneous Human Combustion* by Jenny Randles and Peter Hough, Dorset Press, New York, 1992; *The Highest Altar: The Story of Human Sacrifice* by Patrick Tierney, Viking, New York, 1989; *Faces in the Smoke* by Douchan Gersi, Jeremy P. Tarcher, Inc., Los Angeles, California, 1991.